ANICET OR THE PANORAMA

Atlas Anti-Classics 22

First English edition of 2000 copies.

LOUIS ARAGON

ANICET

OR THE PANORAMA

Translated, introduced and with notes by Antony Melville

ATLAS PRESS LONDON

Published by Atlas Press
BCM ATLAS PRESS, LONDON WC1N 3XX
Translation ©2016 Antony Melville
©2016 Atlas Press
All rights reserved.
A CIP catalogue for this book is available from
The British Library
ISBN-13: 978-1-900565-69-1
Printed and bound by CPI, Chippenham.
UK distribution: Turnaround
www.turnaround-uk.com
USA distribution: Artbook/DAP
www.artbook.com

We are grateful to the Centre National du Livre
for their generous financial assistance with this publication.

The endpapers show photographs of the entry to the Passages des Panoramas on the Boulevard Montmartre, and the Passage de l'Opéra, which was destroyed soon afterwards. The Dadaists met in the Café Certa in this *passage*, which opened on to the Boulevard des Italiens, depicted on the cover. Musidora appears on both cover and endpapers, from a postcard of the period.

● CONTENTS ●

Louis Aragon photographed for *Dada* 7
(*Dadaphone*), March 1920.

INTRODUCTION

Louis Aragon completed his first novel, *Anicet, or the Panorama*, in March 1920, two months after the first public Dada event in Paris. He had begun writing it two years earlier as a 20-year-old medical orderly in a field hospital at Chemin des Dames on the Western Front, a few months after the beginning of his friendship with André Breton, the future director of the Surrealist movement. He and Breton had been medical students at the Val-de-Grâce military hospital in Paris, when they passed many hours together reading the works of Lautréamont. Breton failed his exams and spent the last months of the war as an intern in a hospital some miles from the front. Aragon passed his, however, and he experienced trench warfare at its most severe, since Chemin des Dames had seen one of the most catastrophic French attacks of the war. Aragon was stationed there during the Battle of the Observatories, a series of intense skirmishes shortly after this defeat, and was awarded the Croix de Guerre after being buried by shell explosions three times in one day.

Anicet can be seen as a formative text of Paris Dada, since its development occurred in parallel with the creation of the Paris branch of the movement during the course of 1919 by the "Three Musketeers" (as they were known): Breton, Aragon and Philippe Soupault. In March of that year they had founded the ironically named *Littérature* (after a dismissive phrase from Paul Verlaine: "All the rest is literature"), just a few weeks after Breton first read Tristan Tzara's *Dada Manifesto 1918*. The same month Aragon gave a reading of the first four chapters of *Anicet*, an event organised by Breton and which appears to have taken place at the home of Soupault. Aragon was on leave and the reading was well received, and when he returned to war duties with the French forces occupying the Saarland, he rapidly

7

wrote chapter 6 before his demobilisation in June. His return to Paris coincided with the moment *Littérature* began to be transformed from a fairly conventional literary journal, albeit with strong modernist tendencies, into a mouthpiece for the Dada movement: the July issue contained the first texts by Tzara to appear in France, along with the first of several selections from Jacques Vaché's letters to Breton and Théodore Fraenkel (and in the September issue, to Aragon).

The Dada movement had first exploded into life at the Cabaret Voltaire in Zurich in 1916, and the first two issues of Tzara's magazine, *Dada*, from that year quickly reached Paris and were read by Breton and Aragon. By January 1919, when the third issue appeared, both of them were in correspondence with Tzara and in *Littérature* they began laying the groundwork for Dada's appearance in Paris. When the long-awaited Tzara finally arrived there in January 1920, the Paris group were quick to surpass the scandals he had created in Zurich (somewhat to his chagrin). These events coincided with Aragon's completing the manuscript of *Anicet*.

A key figure during these events was Jacques Vaché, who makes his appearance in the novel in chapter 6 as "Harry James", and becomes a significant off-stage presence. This was the *nom de plume* Vaché had used to sign one of the two texts of his published before his death in January 1919 from an opium overdose, which Breton firmly treated as suicide. The latter's meetings with Vaché in Nantes in 1916 (when Breton was 18) had helped to free him from the literary heritage of Symbolism and the early "cubist" poets, Guillaume Apollinaire, Pierre Reverdy etc. Vaché, a sardonic dandy verging on the supercilious, took nihilism to new heights of aestheticism. For him "the gesture" — something throwaway and ephemeral and above all worthless — was more valuable than any work of art; Breton was liberated by this position, and refused to acknowledge that there was any need to regret that: "Jacques Vaché did not create anything. He pushed art to one side, the ball and chain that held the soul back even after death".[1]

When Vaché's *War Letters*[2] appeared in book form in September 1919, Breton introduced them with a "Disdainful Confession",[3] an elegant and succinct account of the ideas of at least some of the Paris Dadaists at this time. In it Breton quoted Maurice Barrès with approval: "The important thing, for preceding generations, was the passage from the absolute to the relative… the question now is to go from doubt to negation without losing all moral value". The stakes could not be higher, and what could follow this horrendous conflict? Breton saw Vaché's outlook, his "ubic" (as in Alfred Jarry's *Ubu Roi*) and nihilistic "'umour", with its emphasis on the gesture rather than literary creation, as prefiguring Dada: negation, a clean sweep, was necessary. Aragon, then engaged in the literary creation of *Anicet*, reviewed *War Letters* — or rather he evoked its author[4] — in these terms:

> It is unprecedented for a young man to doubt himself to the point of launching into an end-of-season sentimental poaching expedition. Towns on the water have no more than a mediocre effect on their aficionados. For a twenty-four-year-old boy one would be more inclined to expect misbehaviour on the turf or in the virtual domain of thought. That day, however, my hero bore in his buttonhole the flower of *things on his mind*. He strode up and down the over-ripe boulevards (stifling heat) whistling idiotically, and could offer only sophistry to passers-by. A cinema tout tried in vain to entice him into a cooler grotto, but the colonel's son walked past with his head held high, along a pavement more regular than his heartbeat. What emotion did he bear in his mind that we could not see? Nothing could have led one to expect it. And that is how the idea of suicide won the day. Jacques Vaché met his death in a moment of reflection.

Vaché could easily be taken here for the protagonist of *Anicet*, and his influence on the novel is unmistakable.

Anicet begins with an account of Arthur Rimbaud, here portrayed as Arthur, an old man recalling the life that had made him a legend to Aragon's generation. Shortly before writing this chapter Aragon had published a gushing eulogy of Rimbaud, in which he described him as "a one-man orchestra, the sole symphonist of his times".[5] Now he was writing its corrective, to release himself from the shadow of the "poet with wind at his heels". This first chapter, "Arthur", is followed by its counterpart, the story of Anicet, in which the protagonist rapidly overtakes the "Rimbaldian" ethos and speeds towards "modernity" and a "modern" idea of Beauty and of Woman. Here Anicet is close to Aragon himself, an identification that is not at all consistently maintained, especially in the later chapters.

Having thus confronted Rimbaud, Aragon proceeds to a critical review of certain contemporaries whose aesthetic or moral stance mattered to him. In this respect, *Anicet* is a sort of *roman à clef*, depicting the panorama of a social scene which includes specific and identifiable people, largely from the artistic circles to which Aragon was linked. This could be compared to the procedure the Dadaists later devised under the name of "Liquidation",[6] where each member of the group was required to rate writers, thinkers etc., both past and present, with a mark ranging from +20 (indicating approval) via 0 (indifference) to -25 (disapproval). The expectation was that most subjects would incur Dadaist contempt, but Vaché received a score of 20 from Breton (Lautréamont was the only other one to get this mark from him), and Aragon gave him 19; these scores were higher than those they awarded each other.

In the novel Breton appears as Baptiste Ajamais, and is as devastated by the death of his friend Harry James as Breton was by Vache's.[7] Ajamais dwells on James's incomprehensible suicide; he flirts with it himself, but in effect passes the challenge on to Anicet where it takes on an unexpected form. Vaché had predicted for himself a fate in provincial exile; that may be the fate awaiting Baptiste at the end of the book.[8]

Aragon himself wrote lengthy explanations of *Anicet* in two "keys". One, dated 1923, was inserted into the copy he gave to Jacques Doucet, whose rich collection of documents from the period is housed in the Bibliothèque Jacques Doucet, the second one was written for a book collector in 1930; it is conserved in the same library and was published in 1961 by Roger Garaudy.[9] The circle of Mirabelle's admirers is identified as follows: Blue was definitely intended to be Picasso, though this is no portrait, and the only real reference is to his wealth and fame. Jean Cocteau appears as the first "mask", his name, Ange Miracle, being taken from the frequent use in his writing of those two words. Omme, the physicist, originally represented Paul Valéry (in reference to his prose work *Monsieur Teste*), but in the course of writing came more to resemble Alfred Jarry (the theft of the ohm standard echoes the standard centimetre possessed by Jarry's Doctor Faustroll, and Valéry once described *Monsieur Teste* as a sort of biography of Faustroll). Omme, of course, is a homonym of *homme*, the French for man, so he represents Man in the cerebral definition of Valéry and Jarry. Chipre represents Max Jacob, the Jewish writer who was famously baptised into the Roman Catholic Church in 1915 with the name Cyprien. The Marquis della Robbia is not identified as a real person, but the diplomat-thief, a sort of Raffles, or upper-class criminal, was a standard character in silent films. Pol represents Charlie Chaplin (known as Charlot in France). The final "mask" represents André Breton, his name, Baptiste Ajamais as noted earlier, being taken from Breton's poem "Façon" (from his first collection, *Mont de Piété*, published in 1919):

… elles	… they
font de baptiste: A jamais!	act as baptist: For ever!
L'odeur anéantit	The scent annuls
Tout de même jaloux, ce printemps,	Yet jealous, this springtime,
Mesdemoiselles.	Young ladies.

Anicet, and Aragon, are seeking a new way to live, which is why this novel, written amid a conflict that far surpassed even the wars of medieval Europe, barely mentions the war. There are only three brief references — in chapter 3 which was written before the Armistice when, Aragon tells us: "the war was expected to go on for ever".[10]

> Omitting to mention the war for us was a system which, however misguided, was itself directed against the war. We thought that speaking about the war, even to curse it, was to give it publicity. Silence seemed to us a way of blocking it out, or jamming it.

Aragon was rejecting war literature by the likes of Henri Barbusse or Erich Maria Remarque, both in its content and its modes of representation. *Anicet* is an anti-novel, rigorously non-realist, its descriptions and conversations absurd (Arthur, for example, in chapter 1, speaks as Voltaire *wrote*, as Aragon later pointed out).[11] While parts of the book were written in the driest possible parody of literary prose, the trappings of such "high" culture are combined with the plotting mechanisms of cheap fiction, detective stories etc., and especially with the speedy edits of popular film. Cinema was brand new, the most modern of art forms, and was seen as a representation of the future. It was the heyday of the silent film, with Charlie Chaplin the most famous star of all, possibly even more popular in France than in England or America. Pol regularly executes a Charlie Chaplin turn, whether weeping and trying to run away, or getting caught in a revolving door; and his fat-man foil is represented by the café-owner and gangster Boulard. Cinema also features as the setting for one of the key scenes in the book in chapter 6, where Anicet, with his new friend Baptiste Ajamais, watches a film starring Pearl White. Aragon and Breton were above all devotees of the long-running series *Les Vampires*, directed by Louis Feuillade, which began in 1915 and featured a gang (the Vampires) led by the anagrammatically named Irma Vep, who was frequently to be seen in a cat suit breaking and entering, and escaping across roofs. She was played by the actress Musidora (depicted on the cover and endpapers of this edition of *Anicet*), who herself performed in the third Dada event at the Salle Berlioz in March 1920.[12] She was a figure of great importance to these young Dadaists searching for a model for "modern beauty", as Sanouillet explained:[13]

> Musidora… embodied Woman for a whole generation of youngsters, but modern woman, moving freely in her black tights, in a world that was both real and fictional, luxurious, refined, mysterious and amoral. She taught disregard of conventional mores, a spirit of adventure and disdain for death. Above all she was the great initiator into matters of love, Baudelaire's "black Venus with disturbing eyes", so "expert in voluptuousness" that Surrealism would borrow her notions of this new art of love which had not yet been named eroticism.

Aragon himself specifically discussed Musidora in an unpublished manuscript from 1922/23, and a lot of what she represented went into the figure of Mirabelle:[14]

> The received idea of the world for a whole generation was formed in the cinema, and one film summed it up, a serial. All the young men of the day fell in love with Musidora in *Les Vampires*… The impulse that swept up these precise, charming adventurers posed for the first time in a blatant and grandiose manner the intellectual problem of life, that of every human creature: the impossibility of avoiding final catastrophe.
>
> … There is an idea of sensual pleasure which we have made our own, which arrived via this beam of light, amid images of swindling and murders, while elsewhere people were being slaughtered, and we simply took no notice.

By 1930, when Aragon wrote the second "key", Dada had been transformed by Breton into Surrealism, and Aragon was drawing away from this group, on his way to becoming a committed Communist (he had joined the Party in 1927, with Breton and Paul Eluard). He later became the editor of the official Party newspaper *L'Humanité*, and distanced himself increasingly from the attitudes expressed in his first novel. When *Anicet* was republished in 1964 he wrote a new preface, used in all subsequent editions, which describes the "keys" as a "tissue of lies" (apart, that is, from his identification of the main characters).

According to this preface, Aragon originally intended the full French title of *Anicet* to be *Anicet, ou le Panorama, roman*. To use "*roman*" (novel) in the title of a novel was not so unusual in French, and Aragon wrote that he had wanted to include the word purely because the assonance of the sound "*Panorama, roman*" was irresistible — a suitably offhand Dadaist attitude. However, he went on to explain, he had omitted the last word of the title, and also falsified the date of its first composition, because, in 1930, certain attitudes were disapproved of by the Surrealists:[15]

> It would have been unpleasant to have to say I had started writing *Anicet*, as was the case, at Chemin des Dames, or at least before Chemin des Dames, in September 1918, since being a war veteran was frowned on by our group; and when I wrote "with no assumption this would be a novel", it was a similar statement, in that we considered the wish to write novels to be as tasteless as the Croix de Guerre I had to hide in shame.

In the 1930 document Aragon had also identified the person on whom Mirabelle was based: "I can on the other hand reveal the real name of Mirabelle who around that time was called Madame Marie Menardier and has since remarried a kind of diplomat who plays no part in this novel…" He cited these words again in his 1964 preface, with this explanation: "Since I had been asked for a key to *Anicet*, I was duty bound to say who Mirabelle was", and commented, "This ridiculous name, and the invented diplomat, could all pass for pure bravado on my part, for the benefit of certain women I wanted to impress (even if fate had supplied them with husbands)." In the end, however, he concludes that Mirabelle "Is no one, because she is essentially a concept… her features conceal an idea, that of 'modern beauty'."[16]

In the same preface he also wrote: "the rest of the key is composed in terms which suited the version of facts which fitted the atmosphere of the Surrealist group in 1930. Hence the disdainful attitude to Jean Cocteau, the bad joke about Max Jacob's looking like the chief of police at the time, etc."

The Aragon who returned to Paris after the Second World War was a different person from the young man who had emerged from the First. A justly decorated Resistance veteran, he was assuming his position as the primary literary representative of the French Communist Party, then loyal to Stalin. It was thus necessary for him to disapprove of his explosive first novel, with its mixture of idealism and nihilism, neither of which sat very comfortably with the "socialist realism" which was then the approved aesthetic for Communist authors. Not least perhaps because some readers might have found that its more discomfiting features made it far superior to the works written under the aegis of "the Party".

Notes

(Citations from Aragon's "Preface" of 1964 are from the current Gallimard edition of 2009.)

1. From "Pour Dada", *Nouvelle revue française*, 1 August 1920, reprinted in Breton's *Les Pas perdus*, Gallimard, 1924.
2. Given Vaché's attitude to the war the title was not only ironic but was perhaps also intended to deceive patriots into buying the book.
3. Included, with the full text of *War Letters*, in 4 *Dada Suicides*, Atlas Press, 1995 & 2005.
4. *Littérature* 8, p.29.
5. In "Rimbaud", *Le Carnet critique*, 15 April/15 May 1918, p.8, cited in Yvette Gindine, *Aragon prosateur surréaliste*, Geneva, 1958.
6. Published in *Littérature* 18, March 1921, pp.1-7.
7. See, for example, his letter to Tzara of 22 January 1919 in Michel Sanouillet, *Dada à Paris*, Jean-Jacques Pauvert Editeur, 1965, p.440: "What I loved most in the world has just disappeared: my friend Jacques Vaché is dead".
8. See "Disdainful Confession", *4 Dada Suicides*, p.248.
9. Roger Garaudy, *L'Itinéraire d'Aragon*, Gallimard, 1961, pp.97ff and 106ff.
10. "Preface" of 1964, p.20.
11. *Ibid.*, p.18.
12. *Dada à Paris*, p.164.
13. *Ibid.*, p.72.
14. Collection Doucet no. 7206-10, quoted in Garaudy, *op. cit.*, p.25.
15. "Preface" of 1964, p.12.
16. *Ibid.*, p.16.

ANICET
OR THE
PANORAMA

ARTHUR

All Anicet had retained from his years at secondary school was the rule of the three unities and the relativity of time and space; that was the limit of his knowledge of art and life. He clung to these concepts like a limpet and based his entire conduct on them. This resulted in some bizarre behaviour, but did not cause his family alarm, until the day he behaved in public with gross indecency. People then realised he was a poet, a revelation which caused him some initial surprise, but which he accepted good-naturedly, modestly assuming that he was no better judge than they were in these matters. His parents apparently went along with the general opinion, since they did what all parents of poets do: called him an ungrateful son and instructed him to travel. He could hardly refuse, since he knew that neither railways nor ocean liners would modify his *noumenon*.

One evening, while dining at an inn in some country or other (Anicet mistrusted geography, based as it is not on intangible realities, but on data supplied by the senses), he noticed that his companion at table was leaving every dish untouched, yet seemed to be experiencing all the intense gastronomic pleasures of a gourmet. Anicet immediately understood that this strange guest was a free spirit who refused to have recourse to the *a priori* forms of sensual perception, and who could clearly savour the qualities of his food without feeling the need to transfer it to his lips.

"Sir," he said, "I see you do not share the credulity of most human beings, and that out of scorn for their foolish representation of extension in space you refrain from those empty gestures by means of which they imagine they can change their relationship with the world. Just as certain peoples believe in the power of written signs, so does the common man superstitiously attribute to his actions the power to overturn nature. I find such a pretension as risible as you do; it shows how frivolous are the minds of our contemporaries (a word devoid of meaning, which I borrow, as you will appreciate, from their discourse) and the ease with which appearances can play games with them. People call me Anicet, I am a poet and in compliance with my family's wishes, I am pretending to travel. I am quite unable to conceal the fact that I am burning with curiosity to know who I am sitting next to. The distinction I see in your features and the excellence of the principles you have displayed on this occasion leave me with no keener desire."

Anicet fell silent, feeling exceedingly pleased with himself, with the touch of amiability he had managed to bring to his remarks, with his phrasing and the delicacy of the sentiments he had expressed, and indeed with the sprinkling of archaic expressions by means of which he had so subtly mocked the concept of time and the puerile, earnest chronology of those dullards who, at that very moment, were licking their lips under the illusion that their palate and a cream tart were about to come into mutual contact.

The stranger needed no encouragement and began his tale as follows:

"My name is Arthur and I was born in the Ardennes, or so I have been told, but I cannot be at all sure that the assertion is correct, particularly since, as you have divined, I do not in the least accept that the universe can be broken down into distinct and separate locations. I would say simply 'I was born,' if even this proposition did not mistakenly present the fact it expresses as an action completed in the past, instead of a state where time is boundless. The verb was created in such a way that all of its modes are a function of time, and I am convinced that syntax in itself anoints man as a slave to this concept, since he can only conceive thought through syntax, and his brain is essentially no more than a grammar. Perhaps the present participle *being born* would approximate to my thought, but you are well aware, sir," — at this point, he thumped the table — "that there will be no end to it if we adapt our speech to the reality of things, and that the keeper of this inn will eject us from the room before I reach the end of my story, unless along the way we make purely formal concessions to the categories we abhor like false gods, and which we will force to serve us, as it were, if we are not to serve them.

"My name is Arthur and I was born in the Ardennes. Very early in life I was given a tutor who was meant to teach me Latin but preferred to talk to me about philosophy. He had occasion to regret it, for I very quickly noticed that his conduct failed to live up to the principles he had laid down. He acted as though God, before creating the Earth, had calculated the ten-millionth part of the quarter of the Meridian. I was infuriated by such dishonesty. When I reproached him rather vehemently with the contradiction, this philosopher without integrity complained to my father who, being a simple man completely ignorant of the categorical imperative, gave me a good thrashing in the presence of my sisters. I decided to leave home, for I already had that acute sense of privacy which was to dominate my life later on. Initially I took to the road, begging for my daily bread, or preferably stealing it. It was during this period that I learnt to form an idea of water, woods, farms and all the other constituent elements of the landscape, independently of their links with the senses, to free myself from the lie of perspective, to imagine on a single plane what others, like children spelling out their letters, perceive as being on several, to shed the illusion of time segmented into hours and instead experience simultaneously the passing of centuries and minutes. One fine evening, being weary of these rustic vistas, I slipped on to a train and, to avoid buying a ticket, travelled from C— to Paris hidden under a seat. I did not mind travelling this way, aware as I was that it is no more than a foolish preconception that leads travellers to prefer a different position. I used the journey to make myself familiar with viewing the world from ground level, which gave me an idea of how it appears to small animals. Then I woke up to the fact that nothing is easier than to relocate on to several planes what we see on just one, which was the converse of what I normally did to pass the time. All that is required is that, instead of looking face on at the elements you wish to dissociate, you look at them sideways. I immediately applied this procedure to reposition further away from my face the boots of the passenger sitting directly above me. In my enthusiasm for these exercises, I recited poems in my head which scanned with the rhythm of the train over the ballast and debased the very principle of identity."

Anicet allowed himself to interrupt, "So are you *too*, sir, a poet?"

"In my idle moments," continued the narrator. "I reached my destination in a very happy frame of mind. Imagine what Paris means to a sixteen-year-old boy with a capacity for marvelling at everything in myriad ways! From the moment we reached the station I was overcome with delight; everything contributed to my joy, all the coming and going, the houses creating perspective, the oriental way of writing CAFÉ on the pediments of palaces, the evening festivals of light and the walls covered with hyperbole. There was little sign that I would ever grow tired of a spectacle which could be endlessly varied by the methods I had for admiring it, until an adventure came along which gave me the leisure and seclusion required for developing new ones.

"One morning, when I happened on a funeral procession, I imagined the dead person, as I had trained myself to do, outside the framework of time defined as a sequence of events. I saw him simultaneously in the most affected, the most banal and the most natural of poses, performing all the base and foolish acts of a life devoid of interest, with its petty vices and petty virtues, so lacking in seriousness that I sniggered with contempt and quite audibly at the sight of passers-by doffing their hats to this polished box containing the mortal remains. In those days, the unfortunate outcome of a recent war, political dissension and the ever oppressive yoke of romanticism could drive the inhabitants of the politest city in the world to uncharacteristic acts of violence. An individual I didn't know stopped me and told me to remove my hat in the presence of some sort of symbol of our humility. I honoured the importunate fellow with a few choice epithets and did no such thing. He sought to force me to oblige, so I gave him a practical lesson in philosophy. It ended up at the police station, where I was cast into a dark room and forgotten for three days. To enjoy greater freedom than my gaolers I only needed to abstract myself from time or space, but I preferred to take advantage of this solitary confinement to explore new forms of escape. Mathematicians have conceived spaces that are other than the ones we know, and they tell us these have n dimensions. However, they are unable to shed the habit of thinking in three dimensions and cannot visualise their own creations. Thanks to my previous mental gymnastics, it was mere child's play for me to perceive the world as I pleased, giving n the most diverse values; I was in the process of conceiving space in one-third of a dimension when the gaolers remembered I was there and hauled me before the police commissioner. My replies were somewhat affected by this recent exercise and, as a result, the public servant in question, who had a puerile notion of the relativity of concepts, could not understand anything I said. He was convinced he was speaking to a madman and had me released.

"Paris became for me a lovely game of buildings. I invented a kind of comical Thomas Cook's Agent who, with a guidebook in hand, sought vainly to navigate the maze of periods and places through which I moved with such ease. Asphalt began once again to melt under the feet of pedestrians; houses collapsed; some climbed on top of their neighbours. The inhabitants of the city wore several outfits, all simultaneously visible, like plates from an illustrated history of costume. The Obelisk recreated the Sahara in the Place de la Concorde, while galleys, the ones you see emblazoned on the city's coat of arms, floated across the roofs of the Admiralty. Machines operated around the rue de Grenelle; exhibitions were held where gold medals were distributed with a different date on each side; these exhibitions coincided with royal visits and visits from extraordinary delegations. People lived quite happily in apartment blocks which were on fire, or in giant aquariums. A forest suddenly sprouted near the Opera and gaudy, striped cotton cloth was sold beneath its iron branches. I moved the Abattoirs and the Canal Saint-Martin to other parts of town; nor did I spare the museums and art galleries, and one day all the books from the Bibliothèque Nationale suddenly buried a crowd of gawping onlookers.

"I could go on to describe the host of different trades I plied: newspaper vendor, reciting as though they were poems the titles of the newspapers I was selling; sandwich-board-man because I liked top hats; railway porter; meat porter at La Villette. My strange lifestyle made me an object of curiosity and won me friends and social contacts. In certain circles I was for a time all the rage, like a conjurer or a tightrope walker. And then a few denizens of the Left Bank with time on their hands decided I had genius. I was admitted to select circles, given board and lodging by members of the Academy, and was sought after by women from high society. Daily contact with my fellow beings had developed in me that strong sense of privacy which I have already referred to and which is part of my nature. To avoid baring my soul I began to decline invitations. It was at this time that I got to know Hortense, who was entirely ignorant of life but not of love. She was passivity itself, and indulged my fantasies without understanding them. She went along with all sorts of experiments, submitting to all my caprices and allowing me to penetrate *ad nauseam* the secrets of her femininity. In her presence, confident that she would understand nothing, I could shed every mask, think aloud and reveal my innermost self. She was a precious manual which I abandoned after three weeks; I had become familiar with the feminine vision of the world, as far removed from the male vision as that of Japanese waltzing mice which are able to perceive only two-dimensional space.

"Among the friends who found I had a few natural talents there was one who became particularly attached to me. Whenever L—* managed to read my thoughts, I would beat him till he bled. He followed me around like a dog. His perpetual presence upset my sense of privacy and my only escape was into a universe I constructed for myself. L—'s attempts to gain entry were so pathetic that I would sometimes mock him until I drove him to tears. Around this time, the shame I felt, whenever anyone sensed what I was really thinking, became so acute that a simple question like *what time is it?*, if I happened to be about to speak, would cause me to blush deeply and life would become unbearable. It made me aggressive, suspicious and arrogant. I would slap the face of any individuals who upset me. My behaviour caused scandals at meetings and formal dinners. When one such incident was reported in the press — in a sarcastic tone and referring to me directly by name — that was the final straw. I could not bear people looking at me in the street and so decided to go abroad.

"L— went with me to London, where for a time the fog was a novel source of distraction. Oh golden dream on the banks of the Thames, after a while one grows weary of comparing all your street-lamps to chords played on the organ. Fortunately, relief was at hand in the shape of a shop girl in one of those establishments which sell pickles and piccalilli, perfuming an entire neighbourhood with pink vinegar, the incense of some unknown form of worship. She resembled one of those English dolls, the heroines of Golliwog stories who are invariably called Peg, Meg or Sarah Jane; she had an egg-shaped head and very black dyed hair, rouge on her cheeks, eye make-up, no nose, cylindrical limbs and an angular body made of pieces of wood held together with dowels. As soon as she became my mistress, I realised just how mistaken I had been; her plump young curves were perfectly harmonious, her movements as supple as could be. Being used to Hortense, I let myself go and thought aloud in front of Gertrude, transposing life as I wished, and being entirely natural. I rapidly had to admit that she could see right into me;

nothing escaped her of what I let her glimpse, no little game was too complicated for her to understand its rules and how to play it. After momentarily rebelling against this perceptiveness beyond my control, I could not but admire this Gertie, so like me that I already thought I knew her perfectly enough that our two selves could merge. The lucidity and intelligence with which she followed me were disconcerting. In these adventures of the mind she guessed the direction I was going to take, got ahead of me, surprised me by the agility with which she leapt from one system to another, and in turn taught me a thousand new sources of amusement. In spaces of our own invention we pursued each other, ran away, hid and ended up meeting at the back end of some universe or other. Everything led to love-making. It became the supreme object of our lives; the least gesture or laugh took us down that path. I felt far beyond the emotion of those first days in Paris, now that I gazed with Gertie from the dome of St Paul's cathedral over this other metropolis which I adapted at will, using the same techniques, but attaining a more noble, more perfect joy, from within which I could view with pity the feeble astronomies of the past and the enthusiasms of a sixteen-year-old youth. When the act of love reached its height, our twin selves felt limitless, everything was easy, responsive, for love is the ultimate abolition of all categories. We did not seek to deny that love was our master, but in turn it served us well. It lent itself to our whims, for we knew how to prolong the act of love, to pause, begin again. We experienced love in all its forms, invented new variations, and applied to love our own methods of ecstasy. We surrendered to it, confusing time and space in all their dimensions. Everything took on an erotic meaning, became an altar at which love was worshipped. Pretend rivalry in imagining things took us to the wildest realms of fantasy. We made love in every land, under every roof, in all types of company, in all kinds of costume and under every name you can think of. It was a wonderful honeymoon. 'Gertie, shall we visit the "Italian" lakes?' We tried to disappoint each other, but our disappointment itself became pleasure. At the precise moment one of us lost control, the other fled to another world. Then the trick was to force that one to return. What more could I wish for? There were times when I felt the need to be alone and Gertie was in the way, pestering me until I got rid of her with some lie; times when I wearied of our equality, two combatants each a match for the other; times when I grew weary of forever saying *we* and never *I*. Sometimes there was a gulf between our lips though they were joined in a kiss. Sometimes, irritated by her perspicacity and cunning, I felt hostile, hard, with a male urge to strike her; her mocking wounded me, her teasing excited not just desire but hatred for what was an affront to my sense of privacy. In short, this dialogue became unbearable and an excuse to leave (L— wanted to return to France) came as a relief. One day I embarked on a ferry at Dover rather than on the Milky Way.

"A few arguments with L— which degenerated into quarrels, a journey during which at one point I thought I was going to die,★ the certain knowledge yielded by my recent affair that art is not the prime purpose of this life, a scandal at the time surrounding my name, the publicity it received and the resulting slanderous gossip, a thousand and one reasons, each more offensive than the others, made me decide to change my life. I determined to give it a different purpose and to devote my energies to trade and the acquisition of wealth. Having sold off what remained of my past I armed myself with a load of baubles and beads and set off for East Africa, intending to work in the slave trade.

"The ease with which I was able to adapt to other ways of perceiving reality, and the absence of any of those links which bind together Europeans in exile, quickly distinguished me in the eyes both of the natives, who were unused to a white man showing such perceptiveness in relation to them, and of the settlers, who were soon obliged to use me as an intermediary in their dealings with the local people. There was scarcely an exchange or a business deal I did not have an interest in, or was at least involved in. I grew shamelessly rich at everybody's expense and they all said how grateful they were. I was becoming a sort of economic potentate, as indispensable to life as the sun is to crops. This rapid success went to my head like wine and I thought of nothing else. Poetry for me lay only in my ledgers, in the columns of figures headed DEBIT and CREDIT. I was intoxicated with numbers, with all forms of measurement. Everything to do with the measurement of time, space or quantity suddenly appeared to me to be the most marvellous of human creations. My admiration for these unities, so meticulously and arbitrarily chosen by man to support his power over nature, was prompted by the conviction that there was no reality that gave them legitimacy. There is nothing purer, less sullied by foreign elements, than mathematical concepts. They are mental constructs requiring someone to imagine them in order for them to exist; they have no basis or existence outside the mind of the individual conceiving them. To my eyes the finest poems were as nothing compared to machinery and engineering drawings. A clock, that astonishing realisation of a hypothesis which, in the absence of its owner, continues quantifying something that is only a reality when he is present, was an even greater source of wonder to me than to the tribes I was showing one to for the first time. I put as much care into the study of the exact sciences as once I had into penetrating the secrets of lyric poetry. I began to feel with great pride that perhaps I was the only one who experienced their beauty. Sometimes I tried to communicate this sense of beauty to the tribal witch-doctors — eminent, wise men, more open to philo-sophical speculation than the high and mighty in Paris. They failed to understand me and shook their heads. One of them said to me, 'Here is a date, a second date, a third date. There are three of them. My eyes see them, therefore the number three is not just seen by the mind, but by the eyes as well.' Even the wisest of men pursue this false line of reasoning, failing to grasp that the dates exist, but not the relationship between them, which they alone can establish. I maintained very little contact with Europe. From the few letters I received I learnt that my disappearance and silence were much regretted and that fame awaited me, were I to return. The news left me unmoved, for to such vulgar laurels I preferred the position of despot and sage I had created for myself in these African countries. My intellectual superiority was universally acknowledged and materially I had everything I could possibly wish for. One or two displays of generosity crowned me as a god; my name entered the region's dialects, I became a legend. I was party to every religious discussion; I was asked to rule on all questions of conscience; I dealt with issues such as the dogma regarding the sun and the worship of idols. I was called on to explain natural phenomena, cataclysms, and to interpret signs in the heavens.

"And so one day in a village where I had business, a young girl was brought to me with great ceremony. She was said to be mad and was considered holy by the inhabitants. A European who had settled in the district and worked there as a doctor offered an explanation: 'This young negress, probably deaf but not dumb, was born with a quite complicated nervous disorder. She has never learnt to communicate either by voice or by miming. Her uncoordinated gestures seem to be without purpose. She cannot move even to perform natural functions, which servants therefore have to anticipate. Fortunately she never offers any resistance when anyone moves one of her limbs. It is as though she were new-born, and these simple people respect her as a supernatural being.' As soon as I saw the girl, I was struck by her great beauty. She clearly had that rarest form of virginity, one that was untouched by male desire, so great were the fear and reverence in which she was held. The first thing I noticed was that apparent lack of coordination referred to by the medical officer; when she tried to grasp an object, it was as though her gaze was under a separate command and came from a different being from the one that governed the movement of her hand. Nor was there any connection between this movement and the distance to be covered; sometimes an object passing before her would retain her attention several minutes after it had disappeared from view, and she seemed to be reaching out for it in the now empty space, or in a quite different direction. Any doubt in my mind as to the root of the problem vanished as soon as the term *synchronism* came to mind, since it perfectly described what was missing from her actions; she was isolated from her fellow beings purely because she had no sense of time and probably no sense of space either. When Gertrude used to abandon, temporarily, the normal modes of perception, her behaviour was similar; to anybody else it was quite inexplicable, but to me it was unmistakable. It occurred to me that, by using my old skills, I would be able to communicate with this girl who was 'mad by philosophy'. And so it turned out. After a few days' instruction I managed to communicate with her in monosyllables, with gestures which seemed uncoordinated to onlookers, and through touch. My growing reputation as a witch-doctor was immediately confirmed, since her ability to communicate with me was proof positive of my magical powers. The black virgin was given into my care. I took her to a dwelling where I strove to complete her instruction. At the very outset she led me to understand that, having reached puberty, it was her intention to take a lover, a necessary evil it seemed to her, and that it was quite normal it should be me, since I had won her as no one else had. I could hardly refuse her this service, and with the help of love it proved a simple task. I gave her many names later on, but now whenever she comes to mind, I think of my African girl as *Viagère,*★ a name you will not find in any list, but the one she preferred. Even now, many years after, at an age when desire has faded somewhat, I cannot pronounce it without a certain emotion. Her powerful intelligence had developed with unusual precocity, despite not yet having acquired from those responsible for her in early childhood the knowledge required to view the world in the ways that are normally adopted. And so she lived among her own people like a foreigner who does not understand the language spoken around her. But her mind, already formed when I began her education, yet free of any preconceived ideas, easily acquired the various systems I set out before her. She was quickly able to apply them, not in the way Gertrude did, for whom the normal way of viewing the world got in the way, but by adopting a broadly philosophical and general viewpoint which I had only managed to attain by dint of constant effort. She became able to communicate with men, but their words served only to reinforce her immense admiration for me and a clear sense of my superiority over others. Everything she knew she derived from me; I had fashioned her in my own image. Her only religion was her love for me. Our love was of a different order from what I had experienced in Paris or London. Calm was the constant, not the hunger to know which spurred me on in Hortense's arms, nor that discomfort with being known which prompted me to flee Gertrude's. I had no need to explore her soul, which was the creation of my genius, and, since she was a reflection of me, the word *privacy* was meaningless in her presence. Proudly I mused on the extent to which, in shaping her, I had exceeded the feeble imaginings of men. Falling in love with a statue with such intensity that it comes to life is nothing compared with banishing the darkness surrounding Viagère and summoning her from her larval state into life. Life with her did not have love as its object; it was love itself. Nothing about my mistress could shock me, as all that she was came from me. The instinct of self-preservation alone meant that not for a single instant could I stop loving her, nor she adoring me. It is only when I tell the story that I use the first person plural to refer to the two of us. We were one person, one will, one love. Sensual pleasure was inexhaustible for us and thanks to my skill in removing myself from the physical laws created by man, I constantly found within me the resources to prolong it. All the variations I had subjected my past lovers to became superfluous; the act itself was sufficient with no need to invent other scenarios.

"Nevertheless we included the outside world in our love-making; it was at the very heart of the endless embrace which bound us together. Instead of exploring each other's feelings when we witnessed a spectacle, as I had done in the course of my previous liaisons, our own emotional reactions were of not the slightest interest; we were concerned purely with the atmosphere surrounding us. We were curious only about others, and not about ourselves, since we were constantly exchanging the best of our energies and giving back to each other the gift we had just received. Without interrupting our physical intercourse, our minds strove to know the real substance of objects and what conception the universe might have of us. Thus it was that we learnt that the lion devours men solely because he takes them for plants on the run; that we understood from giant red ants that they believe in the immortality of the soul; that we discussed with mimosas theories that assimilate light to vibrations and emanations; that snakes taught us the real explanation for hypnotism, based on the great speed of light, the impossibility of man measuring the infinitesimal fractions of space and time, and the confusion of time and place that a look gives rise to by its suddenness, artificially wiping out the forms of his perception. Each fresh discovery gave our sensual pleasure a new form so that, by gently deceiving ourselves, we could pretend to believe our pleasure was purely intellectual, linked to the satisfaction deriving from the work we had accomplished. And so, without its source ever changing, our rapture took countless forms. It lasted truly an eternity.

"But France is where I died, more than twenty years ago now. Scornful as I am of the way the human race views life, I have no hesitation in ignoring that fact, and dining this evening anachronistically in your company. It is not in the least surprising, sir, that my behaviour should have prompted you to engage me in conversation, since it is the behaviour of someone who has abandoned poetry at which he excelled, it seems, like no other, whose experience of love surpasses that of anyone here on Earth, but who now knows how to be self-sufficient, who has spurned the offer of glory, who without the least twinge of regret has turned his back on public acclaim, has given up great wealth without even knowing its extent, has come back from life which he can quit at will, and from death which he is too familiar with to believe in, and who, for all those natural talents and accumulated knowledge, has retained only the garrulous affability of an old man, a retired provincial official, drinking his too-hot coffee with little sips after a meal in some inn, in conversation with a certain Monsieur Anicet, a poet who is pretending to travel to humour his family's wishes."

ANICET'S TALE

"Sir," said Anicet, "could I always be sure of enjoying such excellent company as yours, then I should dine in an inn every evening of the week. By a quite remarkable piece of good fortune your story was precisely what I was waiting for at this point in my life, and you saw clearly that it held me spellbound. You will forgive me if I make a few critical observations regarding the way you set about it. I noted an element of disorder, which is fairly typical of the period you are supposed to have lived through, an element of anarchy — a consequence of the romantic upheaval still affecting the finest minds at the turn of the century — and an element of complexity, which reason finds deplorable, and which someone as free from contemporary prejudices as you are could easily be rid of. You have portrayed yourself in childhood, adolescence and adulthood; you have taken me to far and diverse corners of the globe; you have recounted at least three love stories. It would have been very simple and far more effective to submit your narrative to the rule of the three unities, which offers the advantage of reducing to a minimum the importance of human concepts and enabling one to achieve an otherwise unattainable clarity of expression. By doing so, without pandering to exoticism, you would have been able to present within a single décor your love affair with just one woman who could have assumed, one after the other, the different attitudes of your successive mistresses within a unity of time of your choosing, for example, a single day. Do not object that, if you had done so, you would have distorted reality, since I know that is of no consequence to you, and I am sure you will agree, if you care to give it a moment's thought, that you would not have reduced the effectiveness of your story in any way at all, but rather conferred on it the composition and purity it lacks. Please do not take offence at comments which only go to prove the interest your tale arouses in me, and are simply the spontaneous thoughts of a young man of today, whose temperament and concern for style mean that, as a matter of habit, he always submits to a rule, not because he is convinced of its truth but because he believes that what matters is that we submit to a discipline, whatever form it takes. The era we live in is not inclined to revolt and happily treats breaches of the rules with indulgence, but it does not believe that it is in possession of the truth. This is why, as a true child of our times, I make my behaviour and my writings conform to a set of rules, which are probably without foundation, but which for me possess the great merit of having become outmoded, of being apparently unacceptable to others and — since I do not believe in time, place or action — no great burden to me. To illustrate what I have outlined in this preamble and reciprocate the trust you have shown by confiding in me, I shall endeavour in the tale that follows to apply both the principles peculiar to myself and those we have in common. Please note, sir, that strict adherence to them entails the constant use of the present indicative. It replaces the past historic which modern taste considers pompous, ill-suited to the expression of intimate feelings and all too often accompanied in relative clauses by the ungainly imperfect subjunctive. Forgive me if such lengthy prolegomena serve merely to introduce the brief *Tale of the Perfume Salesgirl, or, How to Behave in Public.*

"Let the tale begin, for I borrow from the theatre the rule to which I bend it, by describing the single scene in which it will unfold. This impersonal, neutral place where anything might happen, where the various characters may come and go at any time of day, where old friends can meet, lovers rendezvous, courtiers and townspeople rub shoulders is, I grant you, neither the colonnaded vestibule of a tragedy, nor the public square of a comedy, but it shares features of both, just as what follows shares features of both genres. The action takes place in present-day Paris, in one of those bustling arcades which lead from pleasure to commerce, from the boulevards to the business district. This is the path taken every day by Anicet, son of a good family, from his father's house to the pleasant domain of gallantry, and the one his father, a stockbroker, also takes to go from his office to the Stock Exchange, with his head full of figures, paying no attention to the temptations on his path. For a young man of twenty such as Anicet Junior, there are any number of objects arrayed in the shop windows to tempt his eye and arouse his curiosity: the display in a wallpaper shop, or in a grocer's selling exotic foods: mandarin oranges from Cambodia, nut-galls, jujubes and, in pride of place, a glass egg filled with cocoa beans; or a tailor's window, where striped trousers and jackets on hangers, draped down a sloping white backing-board, render sensitive souls speechless with the amazing discovery that an article of clothing can be sufficient in itself; another tailor's shop with a display of rolls of fabric — three or four shades of grey, ranging from iron to pearl, chiné cloth in beige, red and green, large and small checks, slanting or straight, with lines and dots of every size and shape; an orthopaedic supplier's with severed hands and barbaric corsets, Chinese footwear with horrible plaster casts of various types of false feet, crutches like witches' broomsticks and hideous bandages that disfigure gilded lead replicas of the Venus de Milo; the window of a sewing-machine maker, amongst whose savage beasts seamstresses venture like animal tamers (how I would love to see one eaten alive!); the vitrine of a hairdressing and perfume salon with wax dummies draped in pink silk, curling tongs, bottles of distilled essences bearing entirely imaginary names, and the bust of a gentleman with medals on his chest, whose beard and hair are white on the right side of his face and black on the left. Finally, there is the entrance to the Furnished Rooms, set with green potted plants either side, which opens straight on to the stairs with their grey carpet bordered in red and fixed with brass runners; beneath a blue and white gas-lit sign this threshold opens with professional discretion and no porter's face to discourage one from entering. Under the glass roof protecting the arcade from the weather, a sentimental man about town can feel far enough removed from the world to indulge his fantasies, yet close enough to draw from its industry the grounds for a quite singular enthusiasm.

"This man about town is Anicet Junior, who is talking to himself, not striking his tongue against the inside of his mouth or forcing air from his lungs over the vocal cords, while moving his lips in the puerile manner of an actor on stage:

"'Scenery where my senses can take their pleasure, I baptise you *Passage des Cosmoramas*.* Among my old toys I have a conjurer's box, containing shelves with metal mirrors where the goblets are kept, along with the vanishing balls, the black and yellow magic wand, the coloured handkerchiefs and the five-franc coins stamped with Napoleon the Third's effigy that can be multiplied at will — in fact all the paraphernalia for transfiguring worlds. This place is like that box, where everything is offered up for me to transpose into life as I wish. The signs in the shop windows are crying out to have their meaning changed; if I read *English Spoken Here*, the modest shop is transformed into a place of mystery and make-believe where people gather to pretend they are in England: a marvellous form of escape which I find riveting. The capital letters above the shop fronts are transformed into disturbing hieroglyphics. The names of manufacturers take on a threatening significance. The fake daylight produced by the contrast between the lamps in the shop windows and the pale light let in by the glass roof lends itself to many a mistake and all kinds of interpretation. In their false perfection the orthopaedic appliances, sinister imitations of nature, take on a strange appearance like demons lying in wait for an amputee, to take possession of him by coming between his will and his life. "Write, wooden hand!" cries the one-armed man, but it continues to describe a broad arc with mechanical precision, and takes no notice of observations. The unfortunate cripple suddenly becomes aware that the moving object attached to his mutilated arm is a grotesque and slowly rotating scorpion. To avoid being stung, I offer it the tropical fruits from the grocer's display. They range in colour from pink through red to purple, and take on the appearance of raw meat, while the burst figs bleed like pretty cancers. Yam roots increase and multiply; they crawl, they climb, until a whole virgin forest emerges from the glass egg, where the cocoa beans have been preserving the aromas of the Indies and the Americas. From the naturalist's shop, unnoticed by me till now, the wildlife — identical in every detail to the engravings in rare books — escapes to populate the branches, thickets and creepers, but though the musk rat, cassowary, otter, eider, Siberian squirrel and golden carabus beetle have been restored to life, they all retain the shabby, dusty look of stuffed animals. The vegetation becomes so dense and the animal life so abundant that nature takes possession of me; I feel constricted, suffocated, strangled: worm-like creatures brush against my face, while insects crawl under my clothing. The sheer strength of my imagination overwhelms me with terror despite all my efforts to persuade myself that I am not in danger, that it is all an illusion, that the singing birds are just wallpaper designs, that the scratching of the jackals' claws on the dead leaves, the howling of the white wolves, the hissing of the boa constrictors are all merely the whirring of sewing machines; that the man devoured by a tiger, leaving only his head and shoulders, is just an advertisement for hair dye. I seek a way out of the forest, but I do not know the magic words which would release me from its spell. Overcome with anxiety I look around me but to no avail. A sign suddenly catches my eye. I read it out loud: OFF THE PEG AND BESPOKE TAILORING. The spell is broken and I am saved. I thank God. I had never left the arcade where I can revel in sensual pleasure. But the world is now in darkness and the electric lights in the shops have won the battle against daylight. As I have returned from a long journey and the scene that meets my gaze looks strange and unfamiliar, I cannot really grasp its meaning and have no clear sense of what point in space or moment in the millennia

I am living in. Nor, in all likelihood, do the dummies in the two tailors' shops, which give life to the clothing they display. Their heads, arms and hands appear to have remained in another era. I transport myself there and by a curious inversion of values I can see around me only heads, hands, legs, hats, gloves and trousers that are out of fashion. But what style are these fragmentary creatures dressed in? I recognise the opera hats and court shoes as Second Empire. I am between two rows of dandies and stockbrokers; one individual in a cornflower-blue nankeen suit has just come back from a drive in his tilbury along the Allée de l'Impératrice; another, with a shagreen-leather portfolio under his arm, Habsburg-style side whiskers and a neck-high muffler, is whistling a quadrille and tapping his feet in anticipation of the dance; then comes an English lord; a fourth person is wearing a velvet waistcoat, with rings on every finger, and tight-fitting trousers, as pink as the thighs of a blushing nymph: this fine turkey-cock must be a couturier judging from the crowd surrounding him, while this dark-skinned rider is part of the entourage of the emperor of Brazil: a handsome young thing, a walking wardrobe… but now we must join the ladies! Those ready to share their favours join the fun. When you look at their faces, you cannot tell them apart, for they are all wearing their hair in *bandeaux* like that divine creature, the empress Eugénie; what distinguishes them is their dresses, which have names in keeping with contemporary taste: Lady Rowena, Stephanie, Bourgeois Rendezvous, Desdemona, Absence, Camille, Repentance, Sans Souci, Think of It For Ever, The Torrent. Now what is happening? All the ladies are hastening to greet a new arrival. I must find out who it is. The crowd murmurs his name: Palikao, Palikao,★ the most charming politician of the day, the future War Minister. He, it seems, is the puppet master everyone was waiting for. The whole crowd begins to dance. The men line up opposite their partners and there is much leaping, curtseying and whooping. When you see the gentlemen's legs skimming the heads of the ladies, it is suddenly clear why their trousers are moulded to their calves. And what is this music? Going like the devil. The *entrechats* follow faster and faster. I am the only one without a partner. Jostled at every turn I can find nowhere to stand; the dance tune whirls around in my head, I have no choice but to join in. I search desperately for a lady, but all of them are taken. I am at a loss what to do. Then, at that very moment, out of the perfumery comes the partner I have been waiting for; she is sixteen and wearing a Moorish costume. Given the innocence of her years I invite her to dance the mazurka. But we join in the can-can. She puts such energy into it. I would never have imagined anyone could kick so high. She flexes her leg, then it suddenly springs into the air. Her pointed toe kicks me unexpectedly in the chest and I recoil a few paces. When I have got over my surprise, we rejoin the dance, and our bodies move closer together. The little demon leads me into a dance the like of which I have never experienced, an indescribable series of amazing acrobatic leaps and caperings. Never having learnt to dance like this, I wonder how on Earth I can keep up with her. All the dancers form a circle around us. Driven on by some mysterious force, I perform the noisy bacchanal as if I have been dancing it all my life. I am intoxicated by these gymnastics and with every sequence I come to know more intimately another of my partner's physical charms: the firmness of her breasts against my chest as I lift her by the waist into the air, the allure of her arms clasped around my neck for the next move, contact more intimate even. Spurred on by the applause of the spectators and exulting in the beautiful figure surrendering to me, I sustain my athletic efforts. But she continues to be my guide and teacher, for whenever the dance brings our bodies together, she teaches me art and sensual delight, saying:

""""Although you cannot define it, the feeling you are inspired and borne along by, which has taken possession of you, is called *desire* in French, which translates into Latin as the name of love itself. By this ingenious connection the Ancients showed that this movement is what really counts when it comes to passion. For desire is no more than the anticipation of sensual pleasure coupled with our expectant representation of the object of our excitement. It is not the power of love that is infinite but the power of desire. It transforms at will imperfections into beauty and interprets the information fed to it by the senses according to the ideal our mind has created, so that we are always certain of realising that ideal. It banishes all concerns alien to that single, dominant idea and simplifies our too-complex psychology, which forms an obstacle to the achievement of greatness in our actions. So it is that desire, working on two levels, never fails to alter both the universe and ourselves and at the same time enhances the beauty of both. Our present situation makes it difficult for me to go into detail and show you exactly what I mean, but you cannot deny that by revealing one or two general principles I have placed in your hands a most powerful method for achieving ecstasy. Let me assure you that it is desire and desire alone which makes me so beautiful and transforms you to such a degree that you are able to perform a dance you had never even heard of, desire which makes men gather round and admire you, for in normal circumstances you are not considered particularly attractive. Are you not amazed to feel how gracefully we move in harmony with each other? The patterns of movement we created retain the nobility of the purest conceptions of Man even though it is sensuality alone which drives us towards a very predictable ending. No choreographer could improve the harmony of our movements, for Beauty is the natural and inevitable outcome of our desire. Our growing mutual attraction causes us little by little to have eyes only for each other.

""""In paintings of the Commedia dell'Arte two very big dancers, occupying almost the whole canvas, respond to each other's movements, while right at the bottom of the picture we can see a tiny, distant town square with colonnaded houses and people so small they are barely visible. Have you noticed, my handsome lover, how, as this eloquent discourse unfolds, our surroundings have taken on the form our words have been describing? The setting for the movements inspired by our mutual sensitivity feels obliged to conform to our vision of the world. We are partners lost on Robinson Crusoe's island. Other human beings, towns and palaces are so remote they never even enter our thoughts. At our feet there remains only a giant palm grove reduced by perspective to the appearance of a mere tuft of grass. We need only come closer together for the landscape to be simplified. But at this moment in the dance a new sense intervenes in the way we imagine each other. Divine touch disrupts our way of seeing. Let us prolong this extreme point of desire. Motionless, we slowly get to know each other, afraid to lose the power to extend our playing to infinity, to analyse our bodies and damn our souls. We tremble with feeling at this pause we have agreed, which wears us down but does not overcome us. The instant holds us suspended. But then you are drawn to me by a faint blue star tattooed on the curve of my arm, a mysterious sign in the bend of my elbow. You have moved, the spell is broken; I can wait no longer, nor can you. Press your lips to the star, red kissing blue, and hold me tight. Before you clasp me to you, whisper once more the name I long to hear during the act of love: *Lulu*. Why do you pause now that my head is thrown back, and my hair? Come, make yourself comfortable."

"'I do as my tender, beautiful teacher bids, her instructions resembling so closely the promptings of nature that for me she is its very personification. I feel parts of me coming alive as I would never have believed they could. Pleasure pervades and spreads, defines and prolongs itself with all the geographical whimsy of a winding river. I suddenly experience the beginnings of what I can call ecstasy, and, heeding my lesson, I announce the news to my partner with the word *Lulu*. Immediately she trembles. I chase her breath, and as she escapes from normal dimensions I do not realise I am lost in a whirl of sensation.

"'At the very moment of passing from desire to satisfaction, Anicet Junior falls silent. To begin with his imagination is so weak it drops him in the midst of matter. Next comes a fleeting paroxysm, in which he remains suspended like a machine out of gear, or a ship on the crest of a wave. Then everything suddenly collapses beneath him. He feels the slight giddiness one gets in a lift going down. It occurs to him, appropriately enough, that he is hungry, that fresh buttered rolls are really quite delicious and that he finds himself in a ridiculous situation from which he does not believe he has the energy to extricate himself. It irritates him somewhat to realise he is suffering from the proverbial sadness,★ so to redeem this banal vulgarity to which he has descended he turns his attention to the outside world, and looks. What meets his gaze is his worthy father, whose entrance had been long prepared and who, unable any longer to ignore his offspring's impudence, raises his hands to the heavens. It is a classic situation, with everybody on stage you would expect. There are the old spinsters, witnessing the young man's misconduct and bestowing on him sylvan and mythological names, as the press would do the next day. All the other characters from the Grand Guignol are in attendance and indignant at being there: the Commissioner with his official sash, representing Order, Law and Society; the *gendarme* with a very considerable sense of his own importance; the landlord who blames Tolstoy for the immorality of his contemporaries; the Calabrian brigand himself, punctuating with a customary "*Diavolo*" his declaration that acts offending public decency should be performed either behind closed doors or in the open countryside. No one, right down to the crocodile, fails to shed tears over the dissolute behaviour of young people. Anicet Junior manages to retain his sense of dignity amid general condemnation. He adjusts his clothing with a noble gesture which briefly draws his attention to the perfume girl, who is now asleep. If truth be told, he realises with some surprise, though without tastelessly making a face, that his seductress, in returning to the present day, has reverted to the age of fifty, which she had hitherto concealed. Her hair is dyed with henna, her make-up cannot disguise her wrinkles, and it wouldn't take an expert to notice that her teeth are too perfect and her charms kept rather too well in place. Anicet finds the sight nauseating, particularly since there is no doubt in his mind that he has been deliberately deceived. He feels somewhat resentful at having paid such close attention to these ruins, which, though they still look very nice, are nevertheless irritating to have mistaken for a well-appointed palace. So, she has been lying shamelessly, taking advantage of his disorientation in that setting, and with the excuse of teaching him to consider the universe she has taken his innocence by stealth. Deceit of this magnitude deserves immediate punishment. Anicet lifts the vile old woman's head and without ado neatly wrings her neck. The assembled onlookers are less upset by this latest action than they were by his previous outrageous conduct. One or two stuffed shirts are horrified to note the peculiar refinement of performing an act of indecency right outside an establishment offering furnished rooms, where a modest two francs would have hidden from the good people of Paris a debauchery which is acceptable only when there are fewer than three spectators. Prompted not only by the call of duty but also by professional conscience, the Commissioner and the *gendarme* come forward and proceed to arrest the young libertine who, as prudence dictates in all such circumstances, assures them he will offer absolutely no resistance. Enter the stagehands who, by adding a few benches here and several clerks and municipal employees there, transform the scene into a magistrate's court. The judges appear wearing their official hats and ermine-fringed robes, but indulging in no other eccentricity. The crowd take their seats in the shop windows, while Anicet is personally delighted he is to be tried at the very scene of the crime, amidst all the circumstances we may describe as attenuating. He finds the pomp and ceremony of the proceedings quite charming and is eternally grateful to the magistrates for the free entertainment they afford him. He finds the three-point speech pleading insanity, delivered by the lawyer representing him, deliciously funny. He is lost in admiration for the energy of the state prosecutor whose passionate rhetoric is worthy of Cicero. Finally, when with all due ceremony he is asked if he has anything to say in his own defence, he rises to his feet and, with all the urbanity we have learnt to expect of him, outlines to the court the true version of events: a highly regrettable incident in which he is the principal injured party, he was duped and is the first to recognise the fact. In a colourful speech of great spontaneity he explains to the court the sequence of events, summoning to his defence the surrounding window displays which must all share a small part of the responsibility in this affair. In the course of his brilliant exposé he even indulges in a few rhetorical flourishes and adds a touch of that slightly biting wit which so often earns him applause. But the court does not seem convinced. Rather it accepts the assurance of the learned Doctor that Anicet is mad but harmless and should take a course of hydrotherapy, and hands over our youthful orator to his family who seize the opportunity to order him to travel. In the finale, while the crowd gathered stage left launches into a song insulting the traveller, and his family hang their heads in shame, Anicet is seen gaily heading off into the distance with a stick over his shoulder, and a handkerchief tied to the end containing all his worldly possessions: a gold watch which was a present from his mother, an ivory ruler given to him by his father, universal scorn and a few philosophical principles. As there is no curtain to bring down on the spectacle, we will have to make do with a well-timed power cut as a convenient reminder to the worthy gathering that, no matter how frivolous the comedy or superficial the banter, light is given but briefly to Man and those pleasures we feel most sure of are in fact the most illusory and the most ephemeral.'"

"I did not enjoy as much as you did the rather over-theoretical structure of your narrative," said Arthur, "but although I may have occasionally yawned during the introduction and main body of the story, the final part, as you noticed, held my undivided attention. It particularly affected me for a reason you cannot know, so I must enlighten you. Both the blue star on her arm and the pet name she was fond of, but above all the way she spoke, left me in no doubt that your perfume girl was the self-same Gertrude I told you about just now. From the description at the end of your story, she had lost the striking beauty and freshness which set her apart from all other women and above all praise in the long-gone days of our love affair. I had been keeping up to date with her escapades and so it did not surprise me that such a lively girl could deceive you with so few cards to play. I am in fact grateful to you for having done away with her, as she was starting to cheapen my memory of her by going with any Tom, Dick or Harry, and in places that would never bring her the respect I would have liked. She had taken to courting cheap popularity among young people by debasing the methods she had learned from me and as you discovered, was indiscriminately passing them on to the locals. So it remains for me to thank you for the service you have unwittingly rendered me and for the description you gave me with all the artistry one might wish, despite the slight touch of pedantry you do not always keep in check; it will wear off only as you get older, but for the time being it is a very minor fault as I am sure you will forgive an old fogey for pointing out."

"Far be it from me to take offence," replied Anicet with a smile, "but what for the moment I find rather hard to stomach is the realisation that, in what has passed between us, there is a hidden meaning, a pretentiousness and ambition out of keeping with the triviality of the occasion, which is after all nothing more than mere dinner-table conversation. To put it clearly, briefly and in Greek: a symbol. If you don't mind, I shall bring it into the light so that it can be rebutted forthwith. We represent, as best we can, two different generations. Whereas yours, in order to achieve maturity, needed to be initiated in the arms of an Hortense, who would represent for you, depending on your mood, romantic poetry or whatever meaning of the universe was then in fashion, my generation began life in the arms of Gertrude, as we were already familiar, while still at school, with the Hortenses of this world. This lady, who was the most beautiful woman of her time and the ideal of your contemporaries when you left her to follow your own destiny, gradually made herself available to all men as her charms faded. She was able to capture my attention for a moment and delude me with the phantasmagoria of another era, as Hortense did you. That simply served to earn me the hatred of today's grocers and a fate rather like the one which befell you after the funeral episode. Once, however, I realised what old-fashioned love potions I was using, I did not persist in my error, but set off in search of the modern conception of life starting from the line which marked the

45

horizon for your contemporaries. We have compared the cycle of your days, which is now complete, and my own, which is just beginning, and so, sir, it only remains, I believe, for us to go our separate ways, taking from this meeting, for my part, as I learn from your example, the desire to find my Gertrude and my Viagère (which is the essence of this story), and for your part the memory of your particular loves and the total incomprehension of a younger generation of which you are not part."

THE EPISODE IN THE HOTEL ROOM

Just when they had nothing further to say to each other, the innkeeper, with the tact for which innkeepers are well known, approached the two conversationalists, who, given the late hour, were now all alone in the dining-room. With cap in hand, he much regretted having to disturb them, but was obliged to inform them that police regulations required all hotels, restaurants and other premises selling alcoholic beverages to close at nine o'clock in the evening, and since his own establishment fell into all three categories he was subject to this regulation three times over, so he requested the two gentlemen, as politely as possible but with appropriate firmness, while making clear this was a general rule and should not be taken personally, to retire to their rooms. Arthur immediately took leave of his companion and was shown to the room he had booked. Anicet, being less prudent, had omitted to reserve one, and asked the innkeeper for the best room he had left. At this the latter seemed to plunge into the depths of despair.

"Sir," he said, "I could have let you have the room occupied for several years before the war by the future king of the Hejaz, who at the time was just a student and did us the great honour of paying court to one of the kitchen girls we had taken on for menial work, but I'm afraid I had to give it to a very rich but rather overweight merchant from Halifax, whose snores can be heard even down here."

"No matter," said Anicet, "I shall make do with something more modest."

"There again I could have had the room made up for you which was slept in for some mysterious purpose by that Malay ballerina who has since been shot as a spy, but around six o'clock it was taken by a suspicious-looking fellow, whom I forced to pay cash in advance."

"Well then," said Anicet, "I shall make do with whatever you've got."

"But I don't have a single room left, I'm very sorry sir."

"An attic, or a store cupboard would do."

"The latest arrivals are sleeping in the hayloft, and though there is a certain distinction about your person which immediately caught my attention, I have to ask you to seek lodging for the night elsewhere."

Anicet was not prepared to let so small a matter get the better of him and did not doubt for a second that among the travellers staying at the inn there would be one who was kind enough to share his room, as is only right and proper in such circumstances. He made this known to the innkeeper, and politely asked him to identify the obliging stranger who would be good enough to take him in. This was duly done and the innkeeper invited our hero to follow him to the suite of rooms where he was expected. Though the flickering light of a candle tends to distort our impressions, while they were climbing stairs and walking down corridors Anicet thought he briefly glimpsed a rather secretive expression on his host's face, which he was tempted to ask him about. But suddenly he stepped to one side, opened a door for Anicet and disappeared.

The young man found himself in a room dimly lit by a paraffin lamp at its centre; an opaque lampshade directed all the light down on to an oval table on the edge of which, beside the lamp and its light, one further burden was lightly perched: a hand, transparent and apt to inspire love. When he had grown more accustomed to the darkness, Anicet discovered attached to this hand the most beautiful arm in the world and, attached to that arm, the only woman his heart had ever quickened for.

His first thought was to rejoice out loud at this unexpected encounter, this strange coincidence and stroke of good fortune, and even to be quite open about the vulgar train of thought my hero sometimes allowed himself to follow, about windfalls and talk of the Devil; but he rejected such notions as gross and out of place. His second thought, which they say is the right one, was to enumerate in a quiet but audible voice the charms offered to his gaze. He refrained, however, because he anticipated, though without any justification, that he would have ample opportunity to do so in full light. Instead, he merely noted that the lady was tall, beautiful and dark-haired and did not seem too shy. At this point in his thinking he remembered that he had not come here to try his luck, flirt, or whatever other euphemism you may prefer, but to sleep. He expressed his intention quite clearly as follows:

"Madame, do forgive me for disturbing you, but no doubt it was your husband or your brother who was so good as to…"

The lady was so good as to realise that he had no wish to prolong his sentence any further, so it would not be strictly true to say that she interrupted him when she replied:

"Sir, I have neither a brother nor a husband and it was I who asked for you to be offered a place to rest here."

So struck was the young man by the nicely judged tone of reproof with which she corrected him that for a few seconds her proposal seemed quite natural. But the unsettling beauty of that hand resting on the edge of the table quickly brought him back to a sense of what politeness required. He could no longer fail to realise that he was being propositioned and told himself so in rather crude terms. It may be difficult to believe but this lusty young bachelor, normally so eager to give proof of his vigour, was not so much flattered as irritated by the way he was being treated. He reminded himself he simply wanted to sleep, and clung to this thought, resenting the idea that he had been taken for a f…, a label he would not have dreamed of attaching to the person who had invited him to her room and whose bearing commanded both respect and admiration. He felt threatened, became defensive and surly, and his only thought now was to beat a retreat.

"Madame," he said, "I could not possibly accept a kindness which might compromise your reputation. By accepting it I fear I would be taking undue advantage of you."

"Shame on you sir! How dare you behave with such petty-mindedness now, after baring your fine soul in the freest of terms to that rather stout old man? You were talking so loudly that other people could not fail to hear you, which is hardly what decency called for. Yes, Anicet, we sent for you quite specifically, as we might have called in whoever happened to be there. Perhaps your youthful vanity is now satisfied and you will spare us having to beg you any further."

Anicet was not taken in by this childish stratagem and felt distinctly pleased with himself for seeing through it.

"Madame," he said, "you can easily understand, I am sure, that a young man, however well brought up he may be, could not guarantee to respect the virtue of a pretty woman for an entire night. Furthermore, he wishes to sleep, and thirdly, he seeks to avoid an adventure which has been set up for him by someone else."

The final relative clause was timed to coincide with our hero's exit and was delivered with a bow as he stood on the threshold. He was stopped in his tracks by a short, sharp, disdainful laugh.

"What can you be thinking, you conceited simpleton? You presumably imagined that a woman who is neither old nor ugly (although, from what you have described, it would be no particular impediment if she were both), cannot offer a night's lodging to a young man without you-know-what, that a plural *s* is all that separates her granting a favour from her granting favours. The boldness of the assertion is evidence of your innocence. But since you fear for my honour, as much, I hope, as you do for your own, go on your way sir, I shall detain you no longer."

In all the books that Anicet had read, virtuous ladies were of few words and displayed no wit; nothing inspires desire so much as rejection; and similarly, nothing signals the fall of a beautiful woman so well as a lady dismissing the suitor she has been leading on. And since one cannot be twenty with impunity, he could not help but notice that this scornful beauty had long legs much to his taste, which inevitably affected his complexion. When a man's thoughts have taken this turn, sense flies out of the window, to return only when he has either plunged his head into cold water, or satisfied the promptings of his nature. Anicet had thus no sooner gauged the distance between her supple hips and her feet hidden in darkness than he felt just as determined to stay as he had a moment before been determined to sleep under the stars and keep control of his faculties.

"You must not accuse me of being presumptuous, since I would in that case have expressed myself quite differently, but blame rather the excessive timidity of a young man fearful of making unwelcome advances. Allow me to show you what I mean." So saying, Anicet moved a step closer to her.

"Not so fast, sir! You have changed your tune pretty quickly for someone so desperate to sleep."

"That is because you have turned my head."

"Apart from the fact that your remark is platitudinous in the extreme, not to mention equally banal and thoroughly tasteless, the words you use are self-explanatory so there is no need to add to your comment with an indiscreet hand."

"Love alone, madame, leads me on towards this fearsome place."

"Then please stop," she said, moving quickly back, "you understand love in the crudest possible way."

"There is only one way."

"That is worthy of a market trader, it's quite revolting. I ask you again, spare me the spectacle of your self-indulgence."

"Close your eyes then, darling."

"Now then, mister, I might have put up with your uncouth behaviour, but I am not going to tolerate your bad language. Let's have a bit of order here."

She sprang backwards, leaving her would-be lover in some disarray at her feet, and clapped her hands three times.

Immediately a number of doors, completely hidden in the darkness, could be heard creaking open. Anicet reckoned there were seven, and as if to confirm his auditory arithmetic, the shapes of seven men stepped through them and advanced as an ensemble till they surrounded the characters from the previous scene. When they were close enough to the light for it to be clear they were all wearing masks, they appeared to find it unnecessary to take any further measures. All the same, Anicet, who was painfully aware of the ridiculous situation he now found himself in, could not fathom their intentions and searched his memory for a comparable situation which would give him the key to this theatrical scene. But the only parallels he could find were in historical novels, which would mean referring to Marguerite de Bourgogne or Lucrezia Borgia, whose respective life-styles suggested that any adventure such as this could only have a somewhat unpleasant outcome, so he dismissed the solution they might have provided to his problem as being romantic and out of the question.

"You have nothing to fear from these gentlemen," said the lady, "but please come to your senses. You must realise that it was presumptuous of you to believe that a woman as well guarded as I am had anything to fear from your thoughtless behaviour, and I would have to be very fond of you for you to succeed in making life difficult for me."

Anicet adjusted his clothing, taking all the time he needed to calm his ardour, which was now of no use, and gather his wits. Then, when he had recovered some sense of personal dignity and decorum, he made a low bow which expressed courteously and unequivocally both how much he regretted giving offence to such a beautiful person without having been able to offend her further, and his firm intention to leave the place, which had, it would appear, been witness to his failure, but also to the elegant manner of his departure, even though it pained him to leave without knowing the reason for this masquerade, which could not be wholly explained as a question of décor. But the singular beauty who was directing the scene guessed his intention and cut short his retreat:

"You would be wrong to think that I am the sort of woman who is angered by a compliment, at least a naïve one. To show you those friends I take pleasure in welcoming and so demonstrate the extent of your error, I should like you to stay for at least as long as it takes these gentlemen to pay me their individual respects."

Her physical charms, the graciousness with which she communicated her command and plain curiosity easily persuaded him that he could not escape such a clearly expressed wish. He compared himself instinctively with Michael Strogoff, when the Emir of Tartary, who was on the point of burning out his eyes, instead invited this intriguing character to a ballet choreographed by Madame Stichel — and prepared to enjoy himself as best he could. "Bring on the dancing girls from Lake Baikal," said the Emir, which is to say our anonymous beauty turned to the masks and with fashionable coquetry asked them whether they had brought a posy of violets or one of those little pots of mignonette, which smells so modestly of friendship.

One of the seven men stepped forward, bowed, presented to the lady a silver-covered glass ball, of the sort you see in gardens, and said: "Dear *Mirabelle*, here is the globe in which astronomers contemplate the universe so that they see everything as round, circular or spherical, which is most convenient for establishing a system or for making calculations. In it you will see the world in simplified form, easy to take in, nicely theoretical and enhanced by a few ornamental highlights. Your image will appear at the centre of everything, albeit subject to the distortions produced by spherical mirrors. And so, to console you on days when you are sad, you will always have to hand a convenient way of looking at life which will allow you to reduce everything to yourself, and have no difficulty bringing order and reason into your way of conceiving phenomena. When you are tired of searching it for general ideas, you can use this ball simply to play with the sun's rays. I picked it like a flower from a park on the outskirts of Paris."

Mirabelle took the globe and began throwing it up to the ceiling and catching it as it came down. Her pleasure in the game was clear to see, and was heightened by the delicious fear that the fragile object might shatter if she dropped it, and by everyone present imagining the dreadful noise the crash would make. Anicet watched the light inside the globe grow and dim as it rose and fell. He could make out his own face, at the lower pole, like the central knot of a spider's web. All the rest of the stage, with the seven men, the table, the lamp and Mirabelle, was more or less reflected depending on what height the globe was at. Some elements of the scene appeared disproportionately large while others were squeezed smaller and smaller. Anicet compared this vision of the world with his own, without knowing which to prefer: "We believe," he thought, "that what we see exists exactly as our eye tells us, but if the ball was our eye we would find it was just as hard. What is more, the only reason it would have a different viewpoint from our own is because the point of infinity in perspective would then be situated at the intersection of two of the ball's radii, whereas we locate it at the hypothetical point of intersection of two parallel lines." Watching Mirabelle play, he suddenly felt deeply humiliated by the futility of his thoughts, which he would once have been proud of, but which this serene beauty seemed very far from noticing, absorbed as she was in the pleasure of catching the ball then throwing it up again like a small satellite on its own trajectory.

The second mask moved into the circle of light; the only thing Anicet noted about him was the curl of his lip. He placed on the table a polygon made of shot silk, pink and grey in colour. Depending on whether it was viewed with or against the nap, the material took one colour or the other and made the person looking at it feel sad or gay. "I stole this from a large department store," said the bearer of this gift, "as a sample. The remnants of fabric, like a pile of pretty monsters in chains, were begging me so sweetly to set them free that I did not dare resist. A piece hanging loose tempted me to cut out the shape of pure beauty, so I grabbed a pair of scissors from the manager, a bearded Lucifer. What a magnificent sacrifice of wasted trimmings! I trembled as I massacred this flesh, which veers between rapture and melancholy, for fear the shop assistants might make me pay for the piece I had wantonly damaged. The moment of highest pathos came when the steel slipped and cruelly slashed the face of beauty. The rasping of the scissors as they cut the threads intoxicated me alarmingly, and when the end of this exquisite carnage was in sight, I prolonged my delight, remaining for a moment motionless, holding between my fingers the superhuman shred now almost completely detached from the roll, which seemed alive like an unfinished statue. I found it quite wonderful. Here it is, severed, dead, it holds no more charm for me and owes its clumsy shape to my excitement while I cut it, which I am now quite unable to understand." All eyes turned to the polygon the second masked individual had placed on the table, and the twin spell of the pink and grey possessed them so that their heads swayed back and forth to view the cloth from one angle then the other. As they followed with their eyes they experienced the same confusion that had taken hold of the impromptu tailor as he cut these shimmering edges; they were suddenly enraptured as they clearly perceived the shape of beauty itself, then, as they swayed back and saw the grey, they succumbed to the sadness that follows orgasm. It was at that moment that Mirabelle, moving her shapely arms in an all too perfect ellipse, placed the first gift on the shifting silk. On such a carpet the globe appeared dull, timid and naïve, and merely reflected the evenly matched duel of the two colours on which it lay.

The third mask obeyed Mirabelle's wish the moment they sensed she was about to voice it, and stepped forward. Everything about his movements was mechanical, as though several independent wills separately controlled the individual parts of his body, drawing particular attention to each, and one sensed that every one of those parts was alive with the desire to please their beautiful hostess. The acute awareness of seeming ridiculous, and the impossibility of avoiding it, made the slightest of his movements dramatic, and while Anicet's first reaction was to mock this marionette, he quickly realised he was in the grip of a strange and powerful emotion as he watched this character struggling against the material world in such agony that every least gesture had to be reinvented at the very moment he was repeating it. His mask left visible a short, thick, dark and bristly moustache. The puppet handed Mirabelle a mandarin wrapped in transparent paper marked with red inscriptions, but became carried away by emotion and so anxious that she should understand he was giving her the most delicious fruit she had ever known, to bite into directly, that he spontaneously held it up to her mouth. She gripped the twisted end of the tissue paper in her teeth and began to swing the fruit to and fro like a sort of heavy flower, which was bound to end up on the ground. This prospect appeared to cause the masked man violent anxiety and he followed the oscillations of his gift with great trepidation. Then he explained its value as follows: "I no longer remember the name of the theatre I was in when the salesgirl came past: 'Sweets, toffees, crystallised fruits, gum drops, mint pastilles,' she cried. So that she could be heard more clearly the actors had fallen silent. She showed me her basket and I was conscious that all eyes were on me. I had no money but I was afraid of appearing impolite and took this mandarin. The salesgirl gave me a smile and I thought it right to smile back, then she seemed to be waiting and I realised that for the sake of appearances I had no alternative but to take out my purse, though I knew it was empty. My flushed cheeks, my embarrassment, fear and the fact that everybody was staring at me prompted me to a sudden decision; I jostled the salesgirl and her basket went flying over the balcony into the stalls. I arched my back, tucked my elbows in and leapt over the seats as I made a run for the exit. The whole audience was yelling most unpleasantly, so I turned round and put my finger to my lips, as a sign for them to quieten down, but saw that I was being chased. I headed straight for the door, but a colossal ugly negro was blocking the way. I took off my bowler hat, so my hair could stand on end, and only after very careful thought did I put it back on. I made a smart about-turn and forced my way through the seated spectators to reach the balustrade at the front of the circle. I thought of jumping off, but the water looked too cold, so I climbed up on to the balustrade and ran as quickly as I could right round the theatre. The negro was hard on my heels, but, as there was only room for one person on the balustrade, he was using the knees of the audience as a running track and I was able to leave him behind. When I reached the end, I turned round and ran back the way I had come to the other end. I repeated this exercise several times and was thus several laps ahead of my pursuer. But suddenly I fell into the stalls. The din became even more intense and I only just made it to the door, stepping on the heads of the women and children and stamping on the elderly. The final obstacle was the usherette, but I knocked her down as I rushed past. Suddenly I was outside, free, and still clutching the precious mandarin which I now had no idea what to do with." Mirabelle plucked the fruit from her own lips and took it out of its paper wrapping. The moment it emerged from its covering the golden apple★ seemed to glow strangely. Everyone on stage breathed in its sweet smell and became convinced that this peculiar, tiny, fragrant sun was the heart of the person who had offered it. They understood the priceless value of the gift when Mirabelle had peeled it and devoured the segments with a smile. Her smile caused the third of her admirers to withdraw into the ranks and make way for the fourth. All Anicet noticed about him was his highly distinguished bearing and, when he spoke, that deliberate but slightly guttural accent which makes it impossible to tell the difference between a well-bred Italian and an ill-bred Slav.

"This piece of paper, beautiful *Mire*," he said, holding out to her a page covered with figures, "has the power to throw Europe into total disarray and, if you knew how to use it, could, in your hands, be the most dangerous of weapons. But you will never be able to decipher the cryptogram. It is a diplomatic document of the highest importance which I obtained by gaining entry to the second floor of the Ministry of Foreign Affairs by means of a flexible bamboo pole several metres long which I clung to while my accomplice on the pavement below was swinging it like a pendulum. Once I had been projected into the room containing the state secrets it was child's play for me to seize this document, which was locked in a safe whose combination had been given to me by the Minister's mistress, a most devoted person, and then return to the street by the same way I had entered. No sooner was I in my automobile than I swapped my black body-stocking for a suit of the same colour made by the very best tailor, secreted the precious document in my wallet, pinned two large rubies to my dicky, slipped a diamond of the first water on to the middle finger of my left hand and lit up a Corona in a handsome cigar-holder made of corundum. With the electric lamp I checked in the mirror to make sure there was not a hair out of place and that my whole person exuded charm, and when I had made that final little adjustment which guaranteed that my appearance was most distinguished, I smiled in the mirror and said in a loud, clear voice: 'And now, Gonzalve, take me to the Elysée Palace!' Gonzalve is my chauffeur. The Minister for Foreign Affairs would have been pretty surprised if someone had told him that this gentleman with perfect manners, this superficial man of the world who had been introduced to him by the Vice-President of the Council and Lord Chief Justice and who was discussing diplomatic thefts with him, had for the past fifteen minutes been holding in the left inside pocket of his jacket this document which could set the whole world ablaze, when he thought it was securely tucked away in his safe. But he was too caught up in recounting brilliant stories about robberies from the diplomatic bag, and once done with that his only thought was for the buffet, so I took the opportunity to give him the slip and here I am."

Slowly Mirabelle took the paper; the thought briefly crossed our minds that she might set fire to it with the lamp, or crumple it up into a ball, or throw it on the floor, but she carefully folded it and stowed it in her bosom, then addressed the fifth masked admirer in the following friendly terms: "And what have you brought me, my dear *Omme*?" The only impression Omme made on Anicet was that he left no impression at all. He stepped slowly forward and said in a blank voice: "Here is the ohm standard which I stole for you from the vaults of the Institut des Arts et Métiers where all the standard units for the world are held in safekeeping. Since there is no object known to man which has not been revealed to us by the resistance it offered, and since we can therefore conclude that the notion of resistance is the basis of the whole idea of knowledge, and since, thanks to physics, we can state with a fair degree of certainty that the idea of resistance presupposes those of length, section and resistivity, which is tantamount to claiming that to calculate the resistance of a conductor it is necessary to know its natural coefficient, in other words its resistivity, as well as its dimensions, and since, on the other hand, when the nature and dimensions of an object are known, we can be sure, without boasting, that we know the object itself, it is easy to see how a keeper of the Department of Weights and Measures was moved to declare that the ohm standard is the source of clear thinking in every philosophy. So this column of mercury, the length and section of which were precisely calculated for an electromotive force of a single volt to generate in it an electric current measuring one ampere, will appear to you, if you give it a moment's thought, as it really is: the gift which is the most useful, the most urgently needed and the one most befitting your character and mine."

Mirabelle continued looking at this fifth token of esteem for just as long as politeness required. Then her voice softened as she addressed the sixth dorophore: "And what play-thing have you managed to discover, my painter of paradise?"

"Here," said the painter, "is the big signal which used to stand at the fork where the railway line from P— to M— branches off from the Pontarlier to N— line. I made off with it, when the signalman was momentarily distracted, with the result that at this very instant, as I hand you this beautiful, round, white flower with its red centre, in the absence of the usual signal, the 24.30 slow train and the 0.29 express are colliding."

Anicet could not help but compare this latest gift to a whole sequence of objects: a blood stain, an eye, a sexual organ, a fairy-tale hat — but he had to admit that the painter's comparison of it to a flower was excellent, and he admired the geometric elegance of its iron stem. The seventh and final masked admirer had now stepped forward and the only thing Anicet noticed about him was his obvious poverty.

"This photograph," he said, handing Mirabelle a tiny oval picture, "portrays Isabelle R——,★ in the days of leg o' mutton sleeves. She used to play the *Blue Danube* waltz on the piano with great feeling and wept when she read *Pêcheurs d'Islande*. In the hope of finding a soul mate, she went to dances at the Hotel de Ville, wearing very low-cut dresses. Once, a nicely turned-out gentleman assured her in the street that he knew her from years ago. Since she was incapable of appreciating their beauty, the Big Wheel and the Galerie des Machines★ haunted her dreams. She wore a coral necklace from Naples and belonged to a lending library in the rue Saint-Placide. She had given her portrait to a young man who lost it on one of the boulevards (I do not know its name, but in summer its trees have dark, funereal foliage) and there it was found by a young poet of no talent with whom I used to have lunch every day in a small bistro where you could starve quite cheaply. He had found it on the tarmac and when he picked it up he fell head over heels in love with this insignificant girl, whom he would never meet, to the point where his passion for her took over his whole life and I had to kill him to get hold of this yellowing, faded, frameless, valueless photograph."

Anicet racked his brains in vain to make sense of this performance. He could not conceive that the ceremony did not have some symbolic significance, and ran through every detail in his search for a clue, quietly repeating to himself the number of masks — seven, which seemed to have a prophetic quality, but failed to yield the key to the mystery.

"You must be dying to know what that was all about." said Mirabelle. "You are trying to read too much into an occasion, which is no more than it appears to be, and holds no hidden meaning behind these enactments, which you would call sinister if you were asked about them. These gentlemen all feel some affection for me and so bring me little gifts, which they think will give me pleasure. But since I can see there are still one or two points that may be troubling you, I encourage you to question these gentlemen, who will be able to satisfy your curiosity far better than I can and reassure you completely." Turning to the fourth mask, she added, "Marchesino, do please tell our guest about the aims, rules and history of your association. We must put the young man at ease."

"Madame," said Anicet, when he had been given a seat, "I would not like you to think that this masquerade has unduly affected me. If in your eyes I appeared at first rather more disconcerted than is usual, your beauty alone is to blame. But just as a black face-mask does not make a devil, glass balls for garden decoration can be bought cheaply from stalls by the Seine, fabrics are sold off at the end of every month, one stolen mandarin is no different from any other, I know nothing whatsoever about secret diplomacy, this particular ohm standard looks very much like a barometer, a scrap-metal stall can supply any number of painters with a railway signal, and we all have a photograph album at home that goes back to our childhood. So there would not be much need to put me at my ease, if I weren't offended by the nakedness of my face when I look at your gentleman friends' masks. If you wish to dispel any embarrassment on my part, tell them to take off their masks or to give me one, so I can wear the right uniform."

"Madame," the document thief grumbled, "your young man does not exactly seem embarrassed; the insolent manner he sees fit to adopt hardly encourages me to share our secrets."

"That's enough, Marchesino," said Mirabelle, "his self-assurance is very superficial. As for you sir, who are so fond of irony, your Voltairean diction is out of season and I don't like it. The incredulity and mocking tone you use are quite out of place and betray a mind so petty that you must be blushing to have revealed it."

The effect these words had on Anicet was so great that he felt ashamed of his behaviour. So mortified was he that he had to admit he had fallen for the beautiful woman who was the cause of his vexation. This new idea took him by surprise and he warmed to the masked individuals afflicted by a similar weakness. "Gentlemen, I must apologise for my incorrect behaviour. But my curiosity overwhelms my bad manners and now my only wish is that you tell me some of what I do not know about you, in so far as you see fit to do so. Please do not be offended if I repeat my request that you take off your masks, which I swear do make me feel genuinely uneasy. Besides, it is a long-standing tradition that in such circumstances the one whose face is bare should exhort his masked companions to abandon their anonymity. Please recognise that not to heed my request would be to fly in the face of that tradition."

"Sir," said the Marchesino, "we wear masks primarily for fear of being judged by our faces rather than our minds. So to satisfy you each of us will tell his story, so that our features have no bearing on the way you think of us. Since I for one can see no reason to refuse you such a small satisfaction, I shall tell you my life story. I was born in the Abruzzi…"

"Dear sir, please say no more. If you recount your adventures, politeness will require that each of your companions does likewise and that I listen with equal attention. The exercise seems wearisome, and you will think the same if you pause to consider that I have just submitted to a story of substantial dimensions and indeed perpetrated one myself; then I have witnessed your parade of gifts, and there are seven of you if I count you correctly. Without presuming to prejudge the matter, I may be allowed to think that when it comes to the turn of the gentleman who gives photographs to provide us with his potted autobiography, both the reader and I will find ourselves gently nodding off, and you will be the first to take offence. To avoid such awkwardness, please keep your masks on, and I will make no further objection if you just tell me why there are seven of you offering such unusual gifts to a lady whom you call by such a very fine name."

"Depending on our mood, we call her *Mire* or *Mirabelle*, without attaching any meaning to these terms other than that both are as pleasing to the ear as she is to the eye. As for the fact that there are seven of us here paying court to her, it is purely a matter of chance and not premeditation. The number of her devotees has gone up and down over the years, varying between two and a hundred, and yet our form of worship has not changed at all."

"Forgive me if I interrupt you," said Anicet, noticing suddenly that the beautiful object of their attention had disappeared, "but I can no longer see our delightful friend, despite all my efforts to peer into the shadows around us, nor the gifts you offered her, which have mysteriously vanished from the table."

"Do not be too surprised by the suddenness of her departure. It is quite usual for Mirabelle. It's simply not possible for us to see her for long. When you least expect it, she slips away from the gaze of those who wish to take in the detail of her beauty, but were prevented from doing so by a mysterious spell as long as she was present. That way she retains the allure of a form which has only been glimpsed. Once she disappears, we never know when she will deign to allow us once more into her presence. Any new appearance generally seems to be a reward for particular actions or words. It is almost as though Mire follows her admirers around, spies on them, listens to them, and then, when their words or actions please her, she reveals her beauty to them as a reward for what they have done. We have not been unaware of the evocative power that particular words, phrases and attitudes have for her. Each of us has two or three stratagems we use to attract Mire, but we employ them without conviction, rather mechanically, and rarely with success. A former fellow admirer, who had a gift for moving his audience when he talked about suspension bridges, noticed that she came running up whenever he touched on the subject. Being just as besotted as all of us, he abused this knack to such an extent that Mire grew tired of hearing him speak and no longer showed herself except when he was away. He died in a fury of despair, which is to say he left us and became a commercial traveller. The only reward we receive for our loyalty, our devotion and our labours is to gaze upon Mirabelle as often as it pleases her. Perhaps one day one of us will arouse her admiration enough for her to give herself to him, but although each of us hopes to be the lucky individual, the possibility seems so remote there is only rivalry between us and no jealousy. Even if she happened to favour two or more of us, they would still get on well with each other, for she has such a generous nature that she could bestow her love on many men without anyone feeling frustrated. She is only known to have had two lovers, who died quickly enough to give pause for thought. The last one to have gained her favours did so by his ability to transfigure the horrors of war for her, and departed this life on the very day the war ended.★ In the hope of becoming his successor, we are all therefore striving to discover how life can be embellished; nothing can hold us back from that quest. We have set aside all preconceptions, but being good Cartesians, of course, we cannot live without rules of conduct, and have adopted our aesthetic as a moral principle, which is very convenient, and you will surely appreciate its ingenuity. This subterfuge means that we are now a civilised group wholly committed to bringing to light new ways of looking at the world. Among our number you will currently find only artists; there are two poets, a painter, a criminal, an actor, a dandy and a physicist; in fact, we are exactly what the Académie Française should never have ceased to be. But we are not the ones who choose our members from among those who aspire to join us. The beauty whom we serve takes on this task, and the reception ceremony, fantastical and variable as it is, always follows in broad outline the scene in which you have been participating this evening. Indeed, I can no longer conceal from you that Mire has designated you to become one of us and has asked me to propose that to you."

The mask fell silent and it was clear that he was pleased to have maintained the suspense for so long. Anicet, whose only clear recollection of this whole episode was the fugitive Mirabelle, was filled with gratitude to have been offered the opportunity to see her again. When she had reprimanded him, he had declared to himself his love for her and it did not occur to him to question it. For certain thoughts occur to us without our even realising it and then take on the appearance of established truths, which must then be fought for longer to drive them out than the obvious certainties which are always at the mercy of our imagination. A little too dramatically for my liking, the young man held out his hands to the masked admirers, not leaving the author time to demonstrate his powers of psychological penetration.

"I am delighted to accept," he exclaimed, "for, at the point when Mire invited me up to her room, I was seeking a purpose for my life. I shall not be surprised to have found one so quickly, for the speed with which it has happened is more than sufficient proof that I was destined to be one of you. Tell me what I have to do to pledge my vow, even give the pupils of my eyes, such is the ardour I bring to joining you in the most perilous ordeals. I solemnly renounce all that is not Mirabelle, though I only had to be willing to follow in my father's footsteps to have a bright future as a stockbroker. In my eyes there is no happier lot in life than the one I am now adopting. It was just the same when, walking in the streets late at night after the theatre with friends, the projects we conceived while intoxicated by the darkness and our talk seemed so fine and generous that we had no trouble equalling the loftiest geniuses mankind has ever known. In the inspiration of this moment I know I shall not be open to ridicule if I compare myself to Buffalo Bill abandoning his empire in the plains to sign up with Barnum and Bailey. And lastly, as I now am a member of your club, it remains for me to ask you what name you have given it, as is customary."

"Our association is anonymous," said a voice, "and therein lies its strength. The world has a vague feeling that it exists, but, as it has no name with which to categorise it, has no hold on it and can never feel settled about its existence. The history of recent literary movements has taught us to be suspicious of all labels. The classics had no name and we are the classics of tomorrow."

The moments that followed were given over to Anicet introducing himself to his new companions. He told them what we have already heard about him, and then by general request recited with his best expression the following poem, to give them an idea of his style:

> *I'm dressed to the nines for a gala*
> *Fine feelings that from chivalry*
> *I pose to play to the gallery*
> *In a glorious boa of chinchilla*
> *Which out of purest gallantry*
> *I compare to the arms of Mary.*

But he could clearly see that it was not to his companions' taste. And so it was with a certain brusqueness that they announced the group's intention to set out immediately on an expedition whose purpose was unimportant, but which would serve to test his youthful courage, and provide an opportunity for him to show what he thought of ordinary prejudice.

"Let nothing surprise you," said the fourth mask, "and act in accordance with the dictates of beauty. We shall be better able to judge your aesthetic creed by your actions than if we rely on the mediocre six-line stanza you have just churned out."

"Gentlemen, lead on," replied Anicet, "I shall strive to do nothing that might displease Mirabelle. In this instant, when I follow you out of this room, concealing my face behind the black velvet mask you have provided for me, I pause on the threshold, turn round to survey the room and see there, as I should, the whole of my past life flash before my eyes. It emerges from the surrounding darkness and gathers in the naked light of the lamp on the table. Farewell to my beautiful life in society,

I leave you and sacrifice you to the pure ideal of art and love; farewell to my joyful flame; farewell to the fire of my days."

As he spoke these words, the wind from outside, which had been filling his cloak, carried it off like a leaf, rushed into the room where the only thing living was the lamp, and blew it out. Anicet could see nothing any more but the dark.

4

ANICET AT THE POOR MAN'S HOUSE

In the six months that he had lived for her alone, Anicet had only managed to glimpse Mirabelle occasionally and by dint of the most perilous exploits. A few minutes in her presence was his payment for the remarkable machinations of the museum thefts: in the space of a single day, thanks to the complicity of security staff, every work by Greuze, Boucher, Meissonnier, Millet, Harpignies, Pissarro, Carolus-Duran, Antonin Mercié, Bartholomé and Dalou vanished from the museums of Paris. The exhausted museum directors called the police to search for the missing works but to no avail. The most subtle detectives got nowhere, and the case was about to be shelved when one evening, as the theatres were emptying, Paris was stupefied by the sight of an enormous bonfire on top of the Arc de Triomphe. The stolen items were burning, and burned so well that nothing was left except little pieces of broken statues. It was all over the papers for a fortnight. Not a day went past without a headline reading THE VANDALS. Ludicrous conjectures were rolled out, blaming the Freemasons, the Jesuits, or bandits in cars. Flattering articles about the painters and sculptors whose work had been destroyed popped up like grass between the paving stones. In order that sensitive and artistic souls could stand outside and lament the loss inflicted on France and on Art, every reproduction that could be found (there was no shortage) was wheeled out and displayed in shop windows — *The Broken Jug, The Gleaners,* the *Gloria Victis.* Fond references were made to an American millionaire who spent a fortune on an exact reconstruction from colour postcards of Detaille's *The Dream.* All of France and the world with her vied to weep over this massacre of Beauty. *Le Temps* announced one evening: "The legitimate indignation, universal outrage and unanimous cry of horror at the still unexplained hecatomb of masterpieces of French art is well known. Our readers will be happy to learn that the office of the Under-Secretary for Fine Arts, in the face of the police's bungling incompetence, has taken steps at considerable cost to bring to the continent the famous American detective Nick Carter, who has agreed to take on this mysterious and troubling case, and is expected at Le Havre very shortly. It is our fervent wish that this remarkable sleuth will unmask the culprits, track them down, and bring to justice these vicious evil-doers who did not baulk at attacking the noblest, most beautiful visions man has received from Nature." When Anicet had fully savoured the style of this news item, he folded his paper and broke the seal of the letter he had just received. He read:

My beloved son,
Since you left, the house has been so dead and life so dreary that I do not know what keeps me in either, other than the hope you will return. Alas, your father has told me of the fatal decision you claim to have made, never to come home. My child, my child, I cannot believe such a thing. You had the eyes of a boy who loves his mother, and I will never get used to doing without those eyes. I am told you are seen in public with horrid people, and are badly behaved, but I do not listen to such things. I know you well; you never act except on the basis of profound convictions. Your father is furious and has asked me to tell you that if you are not back here within one week he will cut you off and forbid you ever to come near him. It destroys my soul to write such brutal things, but he won't be dissuaded. My little lamb I pray you, don't tempt him, give in and come back to us. Remember that I love only you, and that I am reaching that irreparable age when nothing exists but the past. Perhaps if I still have you I

have another twenty years to live, but if you are gone everything is dust. Think of our life together, your childhood, all the things you owe to me, the love of beauty I instilled in you. Do you remember how on sunny days you would get me to sit in the window so the light played through my blonde hair? Remember the sunflowers you used to pick to put in my bedroom. Remember how we spent Sundays reading together, etcetera, and the evenings… Grrr…

My dearest, can all that peace and sweetness be ended? Anicet, don't leave me to die alone, don't leave me loveless. Old age is a horrible prospect for those who have no child… Oh… Oh… I was a young woman, and then one day I think it's time to dye my hair. How it flies by, it flies by. There is no sadness to match this. Tut… Tut… Do not abandon me to the night like this. My little one, if what they say is true and you want to leave us for a woman, marry her, whoever she is: I shall obtain a pardon for you. Or live with her, I will close my eyes; I will even be your accomplice. I will accept anything, but please come back. Do not leave your old mother grey and grieving for ever.

Hélène

"It's a nice bright day today," said the Marchesino when he saw that Anicet had finished reading. "This cold little January is frighteningly bright."

Anicet did not answer; he was turning the letter over between his fingers with infinite care, then rolled it up delicately, with careful concentration. When he had finished making it into a cone, when he had got it just so and shaped to perfection, he took a cigarette lighter out of his pocket. He lit the edge of the paper; the flame travelled round the top of the cone, flickered like a handkerchief waving farewell, flared all too brightly then died near the point, reducing slowly to a bluish circle which gradually diminished, briefly detached itself from the paper, floated in the air like a miraculous nimbus, then disappeared more hurriedly than expected. All that remained between Anicet's fingers were a few ashes, which he shook off, so that they danced briefly in the sun and scattered.

The Marchesino saw tears on Anicet's face.

"You are crying?" he asked.

"Have you never shed tears of pleasure? The moment of delight can touch such intimate parts that it commands this tribute from the eyes. I certainly felt the deepest joy at that bonfire the other day on the Arc de Triomphe. But then I was burning objects I abhorred, while I have just watched flames consume what once was all my love. A tender renunciation of something that no longer touches my heart, but when I look back, how could I not weep as I renounce myself? I am betraying the child I was, decisively, and I have no fear of admitting to myself the death of my old affections. The shackles have fallen away; I have ceased to be the slave of my past."

At this point it became apparent that the two speakers were in a Café Biard★ near St Philippe du Roule. The barmaid washing up looked at young Anicet with such round eyes that it could no longer be concealed that she was his mistress and he called her *Traînée*. The mandarin-thief mask, who instead of a black eye-mask was now wearing his clown-like naïve face, with a bowler hat, a wicker cane and a ready-made bow tie, leaned across the shining zinc bar-top to kiss Traînée as her work brought her alternately to one side and then the other of the pile of plates which precisely blocked the way between her and her unhappy pursuer. The café owner (old man Boulard), an overweight colossus in shirt sleeves, surfaced between the nickel-plated tanks, slid the skin of his bald forehead from the front to the back of his skull so that his eyes stood out of their sockets and his black moustache rose up towards his eyes; he swivelled his orbits from left to right then from right to left and mewed hoarsely, "A Kneipp malt, Monsieur Pol?"

Monsieur Pol drew back in fright to the swinging glass doors stamped with white letters, which gave way with this extra weight and spilled the astonished admirer out on to the street.

"It is easier," Anicet went on, "to sacrifice the uncertainties of the future than the security of memories. Man has a dread of risk. Myself, I am betting all that I currently possess on a vague possibility. Here is my last thousand-franc note; my family will not give me any more and I have no profession. If I hold it up to the light I can look again at the white of the watermarked medallion. Under Article 130 of the penal code anyone who forges or fakes legal tender, or who makes use of such forged or fake notes, shall be punished with forced labour."

In his right hand he held the precious paper in the air; his left struggled clumsily to light the lighter. A drinker they had not noticed, clean-shaven and sporting a black and white checked cap and an unmistakable American accent, dashed over to halt this inflammatory gesture. "Just a minute, sir, if you don't want that bank-note, I'll take it." He reached out to grab it. But at that moment Pol had come back into the café and seen from the way Traînée's eyes were fixed on the magic piece of paper that this lovely person, with her shapely biceps, springy blonde hair, her rosy cheeks and the lace scarf which cradled her chin, would belong to the man who gave her the disputed thousand francs. He gave the swing-door a violent push to make a sudden draught which tore the bank-note from Anicet's fingers, blew it out of reach of the American, lifted it over Pol's head and carried it fluttering down the street. Pol ran after it, the American behind him; Traînée followed crazily after them, holding up her skirt then lifting her arms in the air, then clapping her hands to her cheeks in fright, and behind her came the café owner, running to catch Traînée. The group could be seen through the windows twisting about like a swarm of flies. They wobbled, ran forward, then back, then away, so that in perspective you could believe they were zigzagging up the façade of the buildings.

"My mother presumably imagines, on the strength of what has been reported to her, that I want to marry that girl," said Anicet, pointing to Traînée, who her boss had caught by one foot. "But I shall also sacrifice carnal love to the goal I wish to achieve. I leave my mistress to Pol without the slightest regret. And may I, my dear Marquis, leave you to settle the bill?"

With these words Anicet left the café and walked away. Once he was out of sight, he took from his pocket another thousand-franc bill and placed it carefully in his wallet. But he did not see the American, who was following him from a distance, cloaked in a hasty disguise. "Poverty," thought Anicet, "is also called misery. *A priori* I have no idea if I can stand it. For me, what is a poor man besides a beggar or a street vendor? I suppose it is also, like my friend the painter M., a married man who lives in a small three-room flat on the sixth floor of a seven-floor block, furnished with garden benches and modern-style wallpaper. There are three doors on the landing, and the electricity only goes up to the fifth floor. But this discomfort still costs him six hours a day in an office, and three inspections on New Year's Day. One might as well be a stockbroker and earn a hundred thousand francs. The work I feel capable of requires more absolute poverty. Only the Poor Man can tell me about that."

This is what he called the seventh mask, whose name was Chipre, and who lived in a room so empty you had to use the bed to have three seats. The entire décor consisted of one chair, a plank fixed to the wall to make a table, that was loaded with pots of glue, paper and bottles of coloured ink, a second plank to serve as a bookshelf, which held the 14th volume of *Fantomas*, volume 3 of St Augustine's *Confessions* and the *Almanach Vermot*, a short man of indeterminate age and collarless, a window with no curtains through which could be seen the children of workmen from all three sections of the building trade, a wobbly stool on which Anicet was perched and a fan labelled "little North wind" on the table.

"You get used to this life as much as you do to being a broker," said Chipre, "when it can't be avoided. You can't really appreciate that joke because you've always had a family. 'Jean,' my mother used to say, 'give a sou to the poor man.' At your age that was all I knew about poverty. But once I left my people, I went through some hard times. The first time I really felt miserable I was in the street with a woman… oh yes. Youth. She was admiring the violets on a fruit and flower stall. When I tried to pay for the bunch I found I had just one sou in my pocket. It was only later that the hunger started. One day a friend and I started crying while we were reading

'The Fall of an Angel'. The thing being that that very morning we had looked out of the window of our attic at the pavement of the Boulevard de Bonne-Nouvelle and wondered if we should throw ourselves out and down on to it. But what freedom: to escape classification, not to be the fruit-seller on the corner or the deputy manager in the Department of Minor Roads." Overheard, a couple walking past:

"My duck, what does that gentleman do?"

"Well, nothing, my dear, he's a poet."

"What can't one get used to in the long run? Having no money prevents you from mixing with people who have it. So rich people only see their own sort and that's nothing to envy them for. People who come to see me, like you, come because it's me they want to see, and they are enough for me. I don't need all the luxuries people have, I have enough imagination to make up for them, and I can't abide works of art, or books. So my friends have stopped sending me theirs, they know I take them straight to a book-dealer. It doesn't bother me at all. You see, young man, the great benefit of being poor is it gives you the right to be alone." It was getting dark, and cold as well.

"There's no need for us to see each other to talk," Chipre went on, "it means you can lie as much as you like. A lamp that let you see people's thoughts would be such an intrusion! These short winter days bring drowsiness. In that state I can hear the sounds outside and the voices of prophets. I keep my eyes closed, as if I were at sea, and listen to the whole house, the concierge shouting, the gossip reported by the woman on the second floor who cleans for people who aren't married, just think, the children's eyes, the chatter about politics. All that slips from my mind without my noticing, and I only have to change position slightly and let the ideas bubble up, suddenly floating above the floor, for another poem to populate the Earth. Hang on, let me turn the light on, you're not used to being in the dark."

As soon as the paraffin lamp was lit, with its paper lampshade cut round without

ANICET OR THE PANORAMA

using compasses, it got darker in the room. Anicet could no longer make out Jean Chipre as he said: "Poverty, poverty. Richness in art is called bad taste. A poem is not a jeweller's shop window; creators are those who make beauty from materials of no value. I would be full of admiration for a sculptor who worked in cardboard. Blue, who is the genius of our time, uses wallpaper, newspapers, sand and labels in his pictures. I find even more objectionable the richness of people who always use three words where one will do. Let us be poorer."

He flicked mechanically through the notebook Anicet carried around to keep his spirits up, which contained his poems. Scanning them as he spoke, he picked out the sixain Anicet had recited the first time he met Mire:

"It's fine as a sixain," he said charmingly, "but it might work better done as a quatrain — see what you think, let me transpose it roughly as it comes to me, from your well-made version to my clumsy version:

> I'm dressed to the nines for a gala
> Fine feelings that from chivalry
> I pose to play to the gallery
> In a glorious boa of chinchilla
> Which out of purest gallantry
> I compare to the arms of Mary.
>> Fine feelings: I am all dressed up
>> Playing to the gallery
>> Glory: chinchilla collar up
>> More gallantly: the arms of Mary.

"You see how much redundancy that cuts out. But then, you're the one that's right; here I am blathering away and your poem is delightful:

In a glorious boa of chinchilla

"It's well put, it's elegant, it's distinguished. There's no one like you for distinction: the flower of modern poetry. Is that how you like it? The flower of modern poetry, the poet's buttonhole and the painter's despair? But believe me and take a vow of poverty. You need to be able to hold back from facile development, limit yourself to expressing an image without pursuing it. Abundance is damaging. Above all avoid description; it is fussy and too comfortable, unhealthy richness. We have known for some time that all trees are green. Kill description. You must not be led by the wish to shine. You must be animated by a real spirit of sacrifice; you must risk not being heard, rather than exploit an image or situation. Keep the spirit of poverty in everything you do. Christianity understood most admirably how important this spirit is, by making it a requirement for priests, who only remain chaste because of it. Blessed are the poor in spirit."★

Anicet was cold. What gave Chipre authority in his eyes was that his aesthetic was so perfectly aligned with his lifestyle that he didn't notice when he went from considerations about existence to considerations about art. It could genuinely be stated that his aesthetic was his moral code. But Anicet was more sensitive to cold than to words, and was shivering so much he could not commit himself to poverty. The simple fact of having a different aesthetic approach would allow him to live without being penniless. Anyway, do you believe your aesthetic is an organ as essential as your heart or your lungs? He had come in search of resignation, but Chipre's example was giving him the strength to make up his mind to stand firm. He thought of it not as a romantic rebellion, but a clandestine operation with no preliminary declaration, for fear of the police and public opinion. Theft and plagiarism are discredited for perceptibly analogous and perceptibly flimsy reasons.

"… this holy person," Chipre was saying, "had started out like all our blessed saints by being the lover of a woman of loose morals."

He was interrupted by the door crashing open to reveal a grimy, argumentative-looking character, Blue the painter, who could easily be recognised as the mask who had presented the red disc, if one had never set eyes on his uncovered face before, which was quite simply celestial. Blue turned his purple mouth towards Chipre, who watched it open like a star. "I have come," he said, "to gaze on you, life of our sufferings, dear Poor Man, with the sweet pity of our shared history from which I am the only one that escaped. In my astrakhan-collar top coat I approach you, Penniless Jean, gentle companion of my chilblained youth, coal-less winter in a studio bare of furniture, at the hour when the gas lamps, guardians of the streets, forget the sadness of daytime which leaves them on the pavements like emaciated harlequins, and dance in the joyful dark. How sweet it is to share for a moment the cold you still live in! Look at me: I am glory. I have realised our dream, and exchanged my coloured papers for bank-notes from heaven. Now the Man Who Made It is moved to see the aged image of his years of struggle and worn clothing, and is intoxicated by the thought of the fabulous price he paid for the cap of finest cloth which he now wears every day. It is as if you had appeared to me in a mirror, a model friend who has not betrayed the first idea I had of myself. But your eyes do not just reflect the faithful gaze of the mirror; they are amazed by my wealth and status. As the creator of the new fantasy fauna of mermaids and hippogriffs, I have painted myself a magnificent destiny in the form of a gilded, circular, modern chimera. Please admire the expensive cigar I am about to light: only three people in the world smoke these — a millionaire, a convict and me." The red glow at the painter's lips grew brighter, and from the first puffs of smoke a gentle warmth flowed around the room, the very odour of wealth; it seeped into the four of them, transforming them, transporting them till, when the light from the cigar lit the scene with the power of an electric arc-light, Anicet was off in a plush English-style smoking-room — sitting in a leather armchair, surrounded by the aforementioned characters, who like him were wearing nicely cut dinner jackets. The lighting seemed to come from all sides, and presumably from an adjoining room the muffled sounds of a gypsy band could be heard, punctuated from time to time by the laughter of a woman in a low-cut dress. On a dark rosewood table, polished, clean and uncovered, carefully positioned, an excessively long-necked bottle and four excessively thin-stemmed crystal glasses awaited Blue, Chipre, Anicet and the Unknown Guest. For the first time they paid attention to him; Blue went on: "Now that we are here in this drab décor, I'd like to introduce you to Bolognese,★ the art critic and representative of American magazines."

"So you're an art critic are you, sir?" Jean Chipre asked. "Let me have a good look at you, Mister Critic. I've never seen an Art Critic close up. What a piece of luck! I am walking all round an art critic and he's not bitten me. But if you don't have coloured feathers like a parrot, how can you be an art critic? Is it by vocation that you become an art critic? Or do you need a protector in the government? Is there a career path for art critics? Does it keep you fed and watered? What exactly does the art critic's trade consist of? Do they take a vow of chastity? Never procreating must be very hard. Not forbidden to drink, are you? Art critic, oh! Really an art critic?" The tone in which Chipre uttered the last few words showed he was wearing a monocle. He filled the glasses and jostled them slightly in the process, so the crystal could be heard to suffer aloud, and the vibrations made the four guests acutely aware of the volume of air in the room.

"In seventy-three papers," said Bolognese with an undisguised Yankee accent, "I've prepared the judgements of posterity. In ninety-seven papers I have passed the judgements of posterity. But even if I'm a member of a temperance society, I'd love another shot of this liqueur." He poured himself another glass, drank it down like the first one, and went on: "My trade is easy to work in if you know how to make use of little gadgets, a kind of gauge called criteria, from the American word criterion. In addition, an art critic possesses a number of clichés, and the pointer on the criterion shows the number of the cliché to be used. Nothing could be simpler.

The art critic's mission is in fact to seek out artists whose theories and works might disturb the peace, and lay them open to the vindictiveness of people of good taste. At the slightest threat of disorder the critic must set things right by exposing fraud and anarchy. He does not recoil from scandal, but only stirs it up to condemn it. When all is said and done, he is a kind of art detective, an art policeman." He downed a third glass with this fine comparison; there was a fourth, and then Bolognese smiled congenially.

"Mister Bolognese," said Anicet, "since this is your field, would you tell me whether a true lover of beauty should be poor or rich (if you understand my meaning)?"

Bolognese answered: "Young man, which of the two critics are you asking here? The contemporary critic, or the one who represents posterity? For the latter, true artists are the ones dying of hunger, but the former holds that they are the ones who can afford new furniture."

A slow waltz could be heard in the adjoining room. Bolognese downed a fifth glass and the world started to turn in time to the music, the little bookshelf on its pivot, the hands on the clock, the ideas in their heads. The four of them had ceased to look at the landscape from the same viewpoint, so an impartial spectator who could not choose which of their four visions to follow would have got nothing from the scene but a blurred photograph with multiple exposures. This dislocation was matched exactly by the muffling of the conversation caused by the music. The characters' thoughts pulled in all directions following the whims of their auditory sensations; they no longer ran together; indeed, they no longer even intersected at any point; they went off on to different mental planes. For a while longer, Chipre and Blue kept in touch by simultaneously recalling shared memories, then merely parallel ones, till they lost sight of each other and drew further and further apart. Stuff and nonsense reigned unchallenged.

Blue, with his eyes full of tears, said, "Man is a meagre being who looks after the children while his wife is doing her hair."

ANICET: Love cannot do without furs or lap dogs.

JEAN CHIPRE: A girl had spent the whole day intently threading wonderful-coloured beads, but she had no idea what they were called. "They are opalines," said her mother. The child stopped playing straight away.

BOLOGNESE: Time is money as you say in France.

ANICET: Love is the only goal in life.

SOMEONE: You change goal as often as you change your shirt. What's the big thing about art and goals?

JEAN CHIPRE: The shop only had odd stockings left, a yellow one and a black one. His wife went out with bare legs, and as they were pretty the fashion caught on. But the other women were all knock-kneed.

BLUE: I'll never be able to paint hair.

BOLOGNESE: Fame…

BLUE: Oh flowing hair, Oh Shipwreck.

The music stopped. Clapping gave way to silence. Once silence was re-established, things came back into balance, like the pieces of a kaleidoscope when you stop turning it. Light and shade separated out, and bluish trails floated again across the smoking-room. The incoherent talk ceased when Anicet managed to make himself heard asking Bolognese a question, as he put down on the table a glass he had just drained.

"How does one know that art is present in a work?" he asked. As if echoing his words the fireback shook with laughter.

"Because you can only find ready-made expressions to talk about it," the critic answered.

"No," said Chipre, "it is because when you look at it you feel persuaded you could have made it yourself."

"Though your cheeks might be troubled under the make-up," countered Blue.

Anicet summed up: "If I've understood the three of you correctly, a work of art is one which leads you to lose your critical senses. Which means the critic is either inept or sacrilegious."

"Well indeed!" exclaimed Bolognese.

"The value of a work," Anicet went on, "therefore depends on the emotion it arouses."

"And what does that matter to you?" asked Blue.

"I can see where you are coming from," the critic interrupted. "You want to demonstrate the relativity of aesthetic value. But what is emotion to start with?"

"Emotion," said Blue, "is love which does not know itself, when a woman spontaneously opens her eyes or her heart, or the moment a head is turned."

Anicet asked him respectfully, "So for you, is the feeling of Beauty[1] the same in art as it is in love?"★

"Art is just one form of love. That is obvious in dance, from which the plastic arts are derived, and in song, from which music and literature are derived. I have only ever painted to seduce."

Anicet thought tenderly of Mire. What work would he create to deserve her love? He thought how alluring the pheasant's dress was, and feared the painter, as master of colours, might win the prize he sought before he could. Bolognese gave credence to this concern by saying to Blue:

"Dear Master, sir: it is said you are working on a picture which will, so to speak,

---

1. As Anicet was speaking, the telephone beside him asked, "So, do you have a feeling of Beauty, sir?"

crown all your previous work. Should one believe what is put about and have any faith in allegations which for myself…"

"In spite of the stupid style of your question, hornet, I shall deign to answer. I am tired of always describing familiar objects, and wish to express myself definitively, so have applied myself to the real object of art and love: the human body. I have been working on my canvas for a year. It is about representing the body with all its capacities. I do not want, like other artists, to paint a man walking or a woman bathing, I want to paint the human body. It is a vast, tragic subject, a document to witness man's presence on the Earth. The sight of my picture should enable people to conceive of all our species' faculties, and at the same time grasp the particular splendour with which I think it is adorned. I have submitted to this yoke to achieve the undivided possession of Madame Mirabelle. My painting will be for her the decisive caress that shows her without a doubt that I am superior to the universe, for it will show that I can see as none has done before the sweet lies told by appearances. All the means I have summoned for this will prove with blinding clarity that I am master of the games of love. None of the known procedures will appear in it. To achieve my purpose, I have brutally suppressed my easy charm, and all my seductive qualities. I have sacrificed the best of myself, the part of which I was proudest, most confident, to reach for purity. I have bound myself to the most rigid discipline; but my work will be so fine that Mire will open her gown for me alone."

Anicet listened with mounting amazement. So Blue thought, unlike Chipre, that one can attain purity without a vow of poverty.[1]

The Man Who Made It was once again performing before the Penniless Man. And if art is a form of love, should it not live in luxury? "You little idiot, this is just an enormous joke," said a voice in Anicet's ear. He looked round but saw no one

1. At this point the telephone rang. Anicet picked it up impatiently, and went on with his train of thought.

there. Everything was pushing him to get away from poverty by any means, including the indolence of the time of day, the thick pile of the carpets and the yielding softness of the low, leather armchairs. He stood up to shake off the atmosphere and make his decision solely according to his own convictions. Once on his feet he was face to face with Jean Chipre. The Penniless Man was fixing him with eyes like electric light-bulbs. His whole being radiated the strange magic of poverty. He already seemed to be dressed in nothing but his miserable everyday suit with elbows worn till they shone like suns. Anicet was disturbed to feel the mirage of poverty rising to his head. It dawned on him that Chipre was becoming the protagonist of this scene. The inanimate objects around them seemed to be aware of this and arranged themselves following the rules of composition around this central figure as if a label were attached saying: "Portrait of Monsieur Jean Chipre, Poet." Everything was subordinate to him, and Anicet feared he might succumb to temptation and deny the principles he had just acquired. Blue's cigar was already waning, the spell of his smoke was wearing off, and the smell of the concierge's frying chips came back amid the scent of tobacco. Anicet feared that the whole luxurious décor would collapse around him. He was afraid he would find himself back in the cold smoke of Jean Chipre's room and to avoid that danger he rushed to the door of the smoking-room and opened it.

This produced the effect that occurs in the theatre when an actor opens the door backstage on to a room full of people. The extras who had been mumbling the sound of conversation yelled the lines written in the script: "You are the prettiest woman in Paris — Only tramps have any luck — Punctuality is the politeness of kings — My husband — The crimson silk stole." Flirtatious voices rose above the murmuring smiles. Anicet paused in the doorway into the world, took a step forward and then looked back. He saw Jean Chipre as a ghost with a lolling head, which grinned at him. He let the door close behind him and stood in the reception-room.

As soon as he stepped out, Bolognese's face lost its look of inanity; the critic's eyes were aflame, and the reader will easily guess that he was the American from the Café Biard, and with a stroke of genius realise that he is in fact Nick Carter the great detective, even though his arrival in this story has only been occasionally hinted at. And the void left by his absence made it clear that the central character of the preceding adventure had really been Anicet himself.

That young man, pale with his sudden resolve, stood in the adjoining room, beside the closed door, listening with some anxiety to the heady ragtime being played for the smart crowd.

THE MAP OF SOCIETY

From the doorway, Anicet watched the comings and goings of the world's elect in the electric light; he could not stop himself thinking of words that had charmed him as a child:

Fabulously elegant animals were out and about.

Before mixing with humanity, he leaned against the door jamb to collect his thoughts. If we suddenly come to a stop, our life passes before our eyes and we hanker after the joys of the past. But Anicet brought to this activity the cold resolve which was his contemporary, and his eyes reflected only the wish to make life systematic. "This ideal our elders were so keen on," he thought, "I have looked at it too closely not to feel its ineptitude, and it is because I am confident of finding the same stuffing inside that I have lined up against it this other conception of the universe, without checking it beforehand. Consenting to the idiocy that awaits us does not mean being duped, if we are careful to take no notice of it. We are probably just replacing one mediocrity with another, but what does that matter? This is the only one that is clearly visible. So, now I have broken all my ties with the baggage I was dragging behind me. From now on, my shadow will walk in front. Whether this or that is my goal, I will only attach myself to the risk involved, and it may be I will go nowhere. I have sacrificed the old enchantments to devote myself to the conquest of Mirabelle, though I've never even seen her face. And now I have resisted the romantic seduction of poverty, one of the most fearsome serpents for the young, who are easily bewitched by these animals that are so sleek one would swear they are pure. The road to success is the only one open to me; I shall repeat, but mockingly, the phrase used by a man from an earlier age, thinking he could stigmatise ours: 'In my day one did not "Make it"'. I, for one, will do all I can to 'Make it'. To achieve that while using only such low tricks as do not leave one stained or deformed, is the challenge (a simple concern for comfort and physical cleanliness). The programme: to apply my principles by committing deeds forbidden to other men because they, being weak in spirit, do not know how to construct them into a system. The world is laid out before me, the times (for I am merely a good apostle) I must be fused into, for only they will give me the triumph I desire. Here is the age at my feet, the moment I wish to cast myself into it. Its floors are polished and sloping, its chandeliers sparkling, dizzying to look at; one could take them for so many suns, if one did not know what the light is like outside! Like a diver who gauges his spring, stretching out his arms and then holding them up with his hands together, I puff out my chest and adjust the grey silk waistcoat which is all they know about me, check the moral carnation is in place in my buttonhole, and one, two, head first into the rushing stream!"

He took the shock on the back of his neck, was borne away by the crowd, tacked across two currents, then opened his eyes at last: the most desirable of all the women who follow art, Princess Marina Merov, was there before him in her night-coloured dress painted with symbolic constellations. Her shoulders were bare because Marina knew they looked good, but her neck, which was not perfect, was swathed in a dishevelled blue fox. Her eyes were so dark and deep one did not notice she was blonde.

"Well, *adamantine* poet," she said, "have you gone rogue that we never see you? Come on, let's have a poem right away."

Princess Merov, who carried a certain amount of authority in three or four salons, was becoming agreeably plump. In spite of her rather peremptory tone, Anicet felt sure that if the ethics of symbolism required him to lay himself bare, his cosying up to this influential personage would not harm his pose of dignity, and might make Marina inclined to talk up his talents with the very people whose votes he was chasing. So he hastened to satisfy this woman, about whom he had the precise thought that she was merely a good likeness of herself. This effort of imagination deprived him of the resources required to choose a poem to suit the occasion (for example, a love poem), and since he had been talking about it earlier with Chipre, Anicet recited Sixain 31, to which he did not attach much importance in spite of inflicting it on anyone and everyone. He recited it with unintended lyricism; that is, one could easily have believed from the intensity of his feeling that Anicet was composing it as he spoke. As he pronounced the title he stuttered, turned pale, then blushed. Once he was scarlet all over, her eyes did not leave the poet's face till well beyond the sixth line. After the title, he paused for some time as if he could no longer find the first word, then started too fast, got muddled, declaimed the second line in a single breath without any expression, spoke the third line inanely, got tangled in the chinchilla collar, left far too long a pause before the final couplet, which he spilled out like a child reciting its lessons, thumping out the rhythm and not raising his voice on the last syllable, so it hung like a raised finger; his audience was left waiting in vain for a seventh line, and Anicet looking stunned as if he had forgotten how it ended.

There was a rather prolonged moment between the last sound he made and the precise point at which it became certain this was indeed the last sound. A second, a noticeably painful second, passed between that instant and the moment the princess dropped the expression of rapt attention and polite comprehension she had carefully maintained since the first "Hm!"

At this point one could see that she had ceased to listen, then that she was starting to think, was thinking, and a frown showed she was searching one by one for the words to express her reflection, she had found them, she was going to speak, she was speaking: "Lapidary, my friend," she said, "lapidary. Really a pendant. An emerald. But allow me to invent some faults in this perfection, a defective vein, a spot that is so easy to gloss over."

Though he was feeling increasingly irritated, Anicet acquiesced, and even asked her not to hold back.

"To start with," said Marina, "the title, delightful as it is, comes from a trivial expression, and the image it contains is expressed in the first two lines in the shape of a comparison. That comparison, which is already elliptical, is not established clearly enough because of the arbitrary omission of the conjunction *as*. To be complete and comprehensible, you should have written: *I put on ballroom finery as I might dress in fine feelings*. Or *vice versa*, perhaps? The second half of line two: *that from chivalry*, is false naïveté, which does not introduce a new idea, forms a pleonasm with the first half of the line, and frankly only seems to be there for the rhyme. The third line I find quite vulgar. I won't quibble with the way you make octosyllables rhyme with decasyllables, and decasyllables with eight-foot lines, though I would point out that nothing is as fresh as rhymes between two lines of the same ilk. I do, however, draw the line at the chinchilla collar, called for by *gala*, and only brought in by a complicated form of expression where the final *s* of *glorious* collides with the *b* of *boa*. My preference is for the end of the piece, where the fortunate return of the rhyme with *ry* gives the whole thing a little Mallarméan appeal. I still might point out a suspect adjective in the fifth line, and the misuse of a proper noun in the sixth, not justified by the context, which entails neither a famous woman nor a goddess. So to keep their charm the last two lines should have been happy to say: *Which I gallantly compare to my mistress's arms or my lover's* — or even *the Virgin Mary's*. Overall you really do show exquisite feeling."

Anicet gave the princess a long look, then said, "Madame, a poem which does not please you completely is not worthy to see the light of day. This sixain will not be published; you have condemned it to death."

Emotion, pleasure and fear are the same colour. Marina could not believe her ears. She switched to madly loving what she had just killed off, this sacred caterpillar of a written word. Anicet's sacrifice gave her so much importance. She declared the young man a genius and felt an immediate itch to leave him and go to sing his praises elsewhere. "He adores me," she thought, and ran off, taking advantage of the arrival at that moment of Ange Miracle, the dandy who could be recognised as the first mask, the man with the glass ball, by the sincerity of his tone of voice alone.

"What are you doing, my friend," he asked, "among these silly stuttering socialites?"

"And what about you?"

"I'm not at risk any more. It's an old story and rather a long one. To put it simply, I've done all that. But you should take care."

"Other people can take care, that will be more reliable. I have come here to succeed."

"Succeed here? Your successes won't last more than twenty-four hours, after which people will have to look up their dance cards to remember the name of the very thin poet who was not as much fun as H— the conjurer or the lovely Melinda. In this world, only the snobs who dress up every morning as people with taste are occasionally bearable; but on no account catch them before breakfast. Not to mention the ones with breeding: their psychology is clear and simple, run on the very principle for which the word prejudice was invented. It would be impossible to tell them apart if they did not take the helpful precaution, as families do by giving Christian names, of equipping themselves with a single occupation, to give them a specific flavour which is not the same as all the others'. So, when they meet they only display the one characteristic, always the same one, and that is what is called being your own man. This means one subject of conversation per head, and so that everyone has their turn to shine, they invented politeness. A man can spend his whole life being someone who went off to the back of beyond; another one, who takes the shape of a lawyer, is really just an oyster shovel; a third once shook the hand of, who was it? Life's charm boils down to a handful of elements. Besides politeness, which provides inner policing, society people have dreamed up an institution to defend themselves against non-society people, it's called taste. Then there is etiquette, and the proprieties, which can be breached, infringed or flouted. And then, since feelings tend to create exceptional situations, loving and hating are forbidden, and they invented gallantry to manage relations between men and women — a kind of mock dinner; but, as you can imagine, as soon as they are back in their cupboards these mannequins take their clothes off and make love. But they do it in a hurry for fear of people finding out, and there being a scandal. There is a scandal any time the proprieties are not upheld. Ridicule never killed anyone in this world, but scandal is a death sentence. Anyone who causes a scandal is unceremoniously flung out of society's gates."

"But," said Anicet, "I cannot do without scandal. As soon as I appear I cause a scandal — if I stretch my arms, or sneeze, or think. It is a mistake to believe men invented the three-piece suit the day they came up with the notion of nudity, as that idea presupposes the notion of clothing, and the latter assumes sickness and cold. It was only later that the habit of covering oneself with animal skins and dry leaves started to be explained by morality and public decency. Once that idea had taken root, the idea of scandal was born the first time a man or a woman exhibited themselves in public, because he or she were unashamed, since they did not know they were shocking people. Our mental nakedness also disgusts spectators, and when we write, we write ourselves. Poetry is as much a scandal as anything."

"How could it live in here?" asked Ange. "So much the better if it dies."

As he was leaning his head to one side and narrowing his eyes like a man on the point of quoting Virgil, a large form bumped into him, parted the two interlocutors with no attempt at an apology, broke the thread of their thoughts, blurred their attention and promptly resolved itself into a stout man standing beside the buffet who was too dark, in a jacket that was too pale, with a tie round his neck fit for a dentist. It was extraordinary; the servants would never allow a character in a get-up like that into a reception. "You realise," said Miracle, "this fellow is dressed exactly like you and me, but he is so vulgar that even in evening dress pure poetic artifice means that we see him as if he was wearing an ordinary jacket, and he does not seem credible in these social circles in spite of his efforts to fit in. Since you wish to know, his name, as you might have guessed, is Pedro Gonzales.★ He is a multimillionaire, may well be Mexican, and there is scarcely a door that is closed to him, or a hand that refuses to shake his, though no one knows his origins, or has any idea where he is going. Besides, if this 'society' which believes it is the whole universe was made up entirely of Gonzaleses incapable of taking off their jackets, it would be worth a thousand times more than the current reality. Beneath all the possible disguises, these rag dolls usually wear a less casual and more repulsive costume; they are forbidden to remove the covering of mindlessness and ugliness that clings to them like a poisoned shirt."

Miracle was carried away by his eloquence and soon Anicet lost sight of him. He found himself in a crowd of mature gentlemen and ladies of uncertain age who were wholly concerned with talking:

"Whatever you say, for me, it's…"

"You don't say."

"Never seen anything like it. What are things coming to? If it had been me, well now."

"Oh dear, not brilliant. I have my ups and downs. Bad circulation, you see."

"You can't move in Paris these days."

"Oh do you think so? What is the government doing?"

"I'd like to see you in their shoes."

"Servants are getting so uppity. My chambermaid said…"

"It's revolution, the end of the world."

"Funny people you find at Madame Six's! It is a bit of a mixed bag, don't you think?"

"I gave two sous to St Anthony of Padua and I still haven't found my Aberdeen."

"Superstitions."

"I don't believe in all that, but I have a friend who reads cards and gave me some very impressive predictions."

"Monsieur Bahut, the little man with fair hair, and Wertheimer, the journalist, have exchanged cards."

"Tell me about it."

"Frankly, I wash my hands of it; what happens will happen. He stands warned."

"I'm not saying every day. It's not the same thing, but once, by chance."

"Admit it, it's nothing."

"Old Monsieur de Poutre, who I knew very well, completely agreed with you. He had married a Janina, you know, the banker Janinas? They were caught up in the Union crash. These people turned up everywhere. So Madame Janina, Eugénie Janina, was a lady-in-waiting to Conteau de Léry, the Conteau de Lérys who organised the Fête des Tuileries for ten years. They added the name Léry to theirs when old Blaise de Léry died after quite a tumultuous life — they say he was the lover of that little actress… Thérèse was it? I forget her name, who went on to marry Baron Brizot, the parliamentary deputy, whose grandson is our old friend Damour. And just a few days ago when I ran into the young Poutre, the youngest one, the eighteen-year-old, at the —s', but their name makes no difference, and I was reminding him about all this history, which alas makes us no younger, he told me his cousin Poutre, Antoine's daughter, had married an American Brizot, one of the ones whose speculative activities almost wrecked the old Baron's election. The young man told me the Janinas haven't a penny to live on, and their daughter believe it or not is playing in an orchestra."

"Were you at the dinner the other day at the Marquis della Robbia's? They say, but what do people not say?"

"The more I think about it."

"Strictly speaking."

"Truth be told, we will never know. But what you can be sure of…"

"These people are really the lowest of the low. I cannot begin to think how one could stoop to look at them."

"Gambling debts are debts of honour."

"No trifling with principles."

"As they say."

"One would have to be forsaken by God and man to…"

"How much?"

"Maybe."

"More… More…"

"That…"

ANICET (thinking):
Oh, Mirabelle, Mirabelle, Mirabelle.

Then Anicet stopped thinking about Mirabelle and desired her. A metallic, strident and prolonged laugh rang out behind him and he turned round to see Mire surrounded by a ring of admirers. Anicet was so agitated that he failed to see Pedro Gonzales standing close to the apparition. Surely it was Mirabelle; how could he mistake her?

"Who is that woman?" he asked the person beside him.

"Oh that's Madame de B., don't you know her? I was just talking about the Conteau de Lérys. Well they are distantly related by marriage to the de Monthéraults. I couldn't tell you the exact relationship. One of the de Monthéraults, I think Guy, killed himself three or four years ago, there's no mystery about it, because of this charming Madame de B., who is the most untameable tigress in Paris society. The de B. family coat of arms is worth looking at. There you are."

Anicet could not believe it. So, the mysterious beauty he served was called Madame de B. So, she was in 'society', had a house, and servants, and a car, her name was in the phone book, she lived like other women, and rather than waiting for her to appear, one could visit her on her weekly afternoon, at tea-time. Did her divinity fall away, or was it born from this unexpected existence which was so touching? Anicet[1] no longer knew where he was or what this luminous musical atmosphere was around him. He was losing his footing. In the little room adjoining, Mirabelle was speaking very loudly, with pretty bursts of laughter. Was this the woman for whom he had renounced his past, broken all connections with his family and given up an easy life? For whom he had put himself on the margins of society? For her, or because of her? He suddenly grasped that Mire had only appeared this time once again because the intensity of his desire had called her to life. But she had made herself able to appear in this décor, and it was around his ideal — there is no other word for it — that Anicet could see the crowd of guests thronging now. Right now he could see quite clearly that in any condition of existence, in any social *milieu*, he would be able to conjure up the beauty he desired. A thrilling discovery. Now he could, with full confidence, look the people around her in the eye. To dominate them it is useless to follow their rhythm, and there is no more need to submit to the rules of a social class than to the slavery of poverty. He felt his life advancing through the drawing-rooms and spilling out into the universe, and he understood that it was

1. Pathetic.

far bigger than this squalid box — it contained it. But before he left he wanted at last to see the unknown face of Mirabelle. He strode across the parquet, as shining and empty as the ocean, and reached the doorway to the room where Mire's voice was preciously dedicated to nothing but frivolity.

The competitive jostling of her gallant admirers prevented him from getting any closer; beside the dark mass of men in dinner jackets, the Man in a Pale Jacket stood like a fabled dragon, a guardian beside the blurred outline of the object of so much yearning. In spite of all his efforts Anicet could not break through the wall of snobs. Their dark frolics hid from him irrevocably the face of beauty. A small symbol for simple minds. Driven by an unconscious force, the young man whose nostrils seemed to be straining for the free air outside wove a path towards the exit.

On the pavement he was dazzled by the glare of the street-lamps. A beggar asked him for a light. "Thank you so much," Anicet answered absent-mindedly, "but I don't smoke."

MOVEMENTS

For a long time Baptiste Ajamais had been able to pass as the man who makes you think, "I've seen that face somewhere before." People on the Boulevard St Michel who saw him come down every day around noon with a book or a friend, would never have imagined he was a member of a secret society.

All the same, his steely eyes and the haughty set of his mouth belied a more complex character than was revealed by his easy-going manner and slightly clumsy hands that were peasant enough not to disappoint the girls. Once you could see him as more than a faceless passer-by, his mimicry would catch your attention: the way he pursed his lips, his long eyelids when he blinked; the way he brought his fists together when he was paying attention; a wandering smile with his lower teeth touching the upper ones; a rather piercing laugh, much higher-pitched than his speaking voice, which was usually deep and slightly croaky; one intonation to say "cretin" and another for "my dear friend"; his habit of rubbing his hands together, and various unexpected emphases. It was easy to make the mistake of thinking of Baptiste as the kind of hero inevitably named Raoul who is in love with a great lady in stories by Ponson du Terrail.★ But one didn't need to spend much time in his company to dispel that illusion and realise how much respect he had for love and how big a part that passion played in his life. Anicet had set out to paint his new friend's portrait, and composed a bad sonnet, which he tore up; but he kept the title and the first line:

MONSIEUR BAPTISTE ON HIS HIGH HORSE

For a woman you wait for but don't believe she'll come

The model thought his portrait a good likeness.

He must have been born at the mouth of some great river, in some ocean port, to have that grey shine to his eyes and for his voice to have that seashell sound when he said: "the sea". Somewhere in his childhood there were docks dozing in the heavy air of a summer evening, with three-masters standing on the dead-flat water of the quays, which will not set sail until the wind is fair. A picture of streets sloping gently in suburban sunshine, edged with little houses kept by retired sailors who tend their tiny gardens with four exotic plants, as if they were buffing up the bridge. But when chance brought him back to the place where he was born, at an age when women are as beautiful as a promised land, all Baptiste looked for was a reflection of Paris, the elegance of the ladies out walking, the turbulent joys of the secretaries leaving the Ecole Pigier. Life took on the dampish tinge of fresh laundry, and Baptiste little by little came to taste the delicate pleasure of spending precious hours in the cool of squares. In the evenings he had the brightly lit magic of cinemas in the busy part of town, surrounded by girls with velvet chokers, and sailors, tender as passing visitors so often are, with their eye already on distant lands.

Occasionally a letter arrived which linked Baptiste to one or two men who would now be around fifty. He thought they would be able to reveal the universe to him, when in fact they could only teach him their history. He was unaware that he carried within himself a hidden world richer than imaginations. No one had told him, seeing him wander around Nantes in July 1916, like a miser with his shadow, how stupidly scared the children were in the back streets when he walked past them like an automaton. To give himself a purpose, he wrote flirtatious poems and was hugely pleased with himself for the first use in poetry of the word "chignon". But then he met Harry James, the modern man compared with whom the heroes of popular fiction, American serials and adventure films were mere fragmentary reflections. Who can tell what passed between these two? It is a mystery — but when Baptiste Ajamais returned to Paris a few months later like a man who has looked at himself in a mirror and would now recognise himself if he met himself in the street, a profound change could be seen in him: he bore the mark of major decisions, and an air about him which should have given pause to quite a few people. In fact, Harry James had given him a glimpse of Mirabelle and he had theoretically fallen in love with her.

This shared attachment to such a difficult beauty brought Baptiste and Anicet together around this time. It was not the cause, but the occasion of their friendship. It never crossed their minds to call what linked them rivalry: the word *emulation* came up, but neither of the two friends ever thought to question it. So their relationship began where run-of-the-mill friendships end, and because of the woman who would later be the death of it. The myriad details which distinguish one generation from its forebears gave them a feeling of kinship. Their outlook, sensibilities and tastes were contemporary. Their elders lived in cafés and relied on various potions to bring embellishment to their lives. They, on the other hand, only felt at ease in the streets, and if they happened to stop at a café terrace they only drank grenadine syrup — because it was such a lovely colour. And since along the boulevards they found fresh air in the heart of Paris, they felt no need ever to go to the country.

Naturally, since they lived outside, they were at the mercy of the seasons. The weather weighed heavily on them. The name of the month in which it was written could be found in almost everything they wrote. It is something of a miracle that when I picture Baptiste, I can only imagine him in summer, either so early in the morning that the bakers are not yet open, and you have to walk the streets with your hunger in hand, or at that moment of calm around 5p.m., when manners are relaxed a little and the air seems made of the sand you use for drying ink. In the Avenue de l'Observatoire there is a very ordinary bench which is most welcome when one has been running around all afternoon in spite of the heat, following one's nose aimlessly, but looking like a man in a hurry who knows very well where he is going. Baptiste only exists in full sun.

In summer the coolest place is in cinemas on weekday afternoons, and the two friends had taken refuge in the shady asylum of the Electric Palace. They were taking no notice of the people next to them, talking at full volume, among other things about their opinion of the films. So, you watch life go by, you engage your sensitivity, you turn away to explore your mind and your eyes return to day-to-day goings-on.

"What makes theatre so dead for us," Anicet was saying, "is probably the fact that its subject matter is morality, which governs all the action; our age is barely interested in morality. In the cinema, life is filled with speed and Pearl White's actions are not about following her conscience; they are about sport and hygiene — she acts for the sake of action.

"When all is said and done, the heroine of this adventure has no need to get dragged in when there are so many dangers lying in wait. She can't really tell which of the parties has right on his side. But that doesn't stop her launching herself into the *mêlée* with body and soul. A traitor has stolen the diamond for the nth time. Pearl strips him of the jewel at revolver-point. She jumps into a cab. The car is a trap. They throw Pearl into a cellar. Meanwhile the robbed robber is trying to break into her place; a journalist surprises him and he runs off over the roofs; the advertising man gives chase, loses the trail, and then by chance in Chinatown runs into the one-eyed man who had a sleazy role in an earlier scene. He follows him and comes to the cellar where Pearl is languishing and is about to rescue her. But he in turn is being followed by the hoodlum who ran away from him, so has unwittingly put him on the right track, and when, having blown up the building with a newly invented explosive, he finds the girl fainting, she is tied up and relieved of the diamond by her diligent adversary.

"In all that there was room only for gestures. It was only the *tour de force* that made it gripping. Who could think of questioning it? There was no time for that. That's the kind of entertainment that suits our times."

Baptiste must have deeply disliked this piece of rhetoric; he said, "That's enough of that, it's always the same thing. You know full well that I know what it amounts to. I can see what you're getting at — in fact it's surprising how well I can see it. One of these days I shall lose my temper. You talk and never do anything; in the street you read all the posters, you get excited by shop signs, you *do* lyrical, and what does it amount to? Fake, facile, conventional; you get worked up, you get worn out, and it never goes any further. Well, I am getting to know you a bit, and I can see exactly what you're after at the cinema. You're looking for elements of the lyricism of chance, the spectacle of intense action which you delude yourself you are engaged in. On the pretext of satisfying your modern urge for action, you get passive satisfaction from taking yourself to the most baleful school of inaction there could be — the screen young people now come to sit in front of every day for a tiny sum to use up their energy watching other people live. Don't talk to me about cinema any more; it has nothing to offer us; impurity rules there, and the day well-meaning people bring artistic standards to it, the few things about it that attract us will fade away. The harm this mechanism does to you by taking away your zest for life has no counterweight. I've had enough of it!"

"Now then," said Anicet, who was seriously annoyed, "I see no reason for this outburst. I don't believe you have any right to think me incapable of action."

"Can you tell me what your line of action is? You just let yourself live; you are frighteningly docile. Take Harry James, he and I can't be together for more than three days without our quarrelling. The mark of vigorous spirits is that they are forever clashing. Yours, as soon as a new path is on offer, it takes it up, rushes along it, and is content. You never stand up against anything put in front of you. What makes me admire Harry James is that you can't tell whether he might kill himself tomorrow for no reason, or commit some beautiful crime. He is recognisably an undisciplined force, a real modern man, who would never be reduced to being a mere spectator. He is nothing like an artist or a speculator; first and foremost, he lives. He ardently seeks out the most violent pleasures and bends everything to his imagination. Far from getting the circumstances to fit some poetic system, he dominates the situation and acts with such intensity and speed he seems not to think or to follow any kind of plan. An audience would think he was a puppet. By a curious irony he appears to be at the mercy of the events around him; but this is precisely because he eludes them, he is detached from the ordinary laws of action, allows no exterior visible reality to influence him and gives no one time to see the real interior motives of his actions and his words. With him one can't help but feel constantly anxious. But with you one feels completely calm — you are someone who will never kill himself. Your slightest movement is preceded by a psychological explanation. One would have to wait a long time to be surprised by you."

At this point Anicet started to protest.

"Can you tell me," Baptiste went on, "what you are doing to win Mirabelle? What you have in mind to prevent Blue deserving her more than you? Can you tell me? It's pointless to ask."

"Come on," Anicet replied, "how do you know I don't have something in mind? Would I tell you in advance?"

Anicet could feel himself lying; he had nothing in mind, but felt deeply humiliated by the comparison with Harry James. He realised all he would do was go on following the directions he was given, and that he was under the influence of

Baptiste. However much he was aware of it, he gave in to the shame of inaction and submitted, of his own accord, to being a mere instrument. So what power did this authoritarian character have over him? In the half-darkness, you imagined you could make out his fascinating eyes and knitted eyebrows. There was no denying it, Baptiste held sway over Anicet, but what for?

Suddenly, these words appeared on the screen as part of the weekly newsreel:

PARIS: A SOCIETY WEDDING

The canvas of the screen was painted with the image of the church of St Philippe du Roule. The bridal procession was about to emerge from the church. In one bound the spectators were transported in front of the newly-wed couple. Against the black frame of the doors they were shown down to their knees. Anicet was dumbfounded to recognise Mirabelle on the arm of Pedro Gonzales, who was waving to people right and left, puffing out his chest and glancing casually towards the camera. Anicet scarcely noticed him; he stared in desperation at Mirabelle, who stood up straight with a distant, unmoving, impenetrable look in her eyes. He would probably not have seen anyone else; but Baptiste, who was more in control of himself, pointed out in a blank voice that Princess Merov was standing in the foreground. Marina was dressed in black, and trying to express through her composure the complex feelings of the heroine of a novel at the wedding of the man she is in love with. Behind her, Bolognese, the art critic all of Paris knew was the Princess's lover, wore the polite, tender expression he thought fitted the occasion.

The band, which up to now had been content with a Montmartre café number, broke into a hearty rendition of Mendelssohn's "Wedding March". Anicet suddenly understood what the scene he was watching meant.

So, he had sacrificed everything — social position, his mother, his mistress, and worse: his peace of mind, for Mirabelle to give him the slip with the first millionaire-type jackdaw she found lying around. To have no more purpose in life, to know no hope is allowed, no mistake possible, and looking back to see only the smoking ruin of a past wrecked by oneself — could there be a worse situation for a twenty-year-old who had chosen one path, one love? The triumph of one of the seven masks would have hurt him a thousand times less; he could have fought the winner, rivalled him in seduction, and the struggle itself would have been a new interest. But it was pointless to engage in battle with Pedro Gonzales.

The Mendelssohn march seemed to be hammering on Anicet's skull when a stupefying development occurred: Mirabelle turned her head, gave Anicet a long look, without lowering her eyes, and smiled. Her smile contained all the pity in the world, the weakness of women and of males, the sadness of poverty and resignation, such resignation! Her lips sketched a slightly downward arc around a sun, a shape more unnerving than the pout of a kiss. How could one give up the temptation of such a beauty? A voice in his ear murmured: "The perfect time to act!" Anicet shuddered as he realised he was a slave to some external will. Then he had exactly this thought: "This has lasted no longer than a flash of lightning."

On the screen someone to whom he had paid no attention seemed to be following with passionate interest the movements of Mire's lips. It was a figure in the foreground, on the steps of the church, so one could only see his head and shoulders. Suddenly he turned round, having taken Mirabelle's smile as being for him. Anicet recognised Omme, looking paler than the linen on which his face was painted. "He looks like you," said Baptiste. When he saw it on someone else's face Anicet understood better the drama playing out inside him, which must have been betrayed by his own features. For a moment he identified with the distraught character looking out towards him from the canvas, and no longer knew if he was looking at a screen or in a mirror. The image caused him unspeakable confusion, at the singularly disturbing idea that a mirror could present another person's ghost as his reflection. He wanted to call out to Omme, "*My pain*" at the precise moment that slow, heavy tears could be seen rolling down the physicist's cheeks. "You're crying," Baptiste confirmed. Anicet was about to protest, "It's not me, it's him!" But he felt slow, heavy tears rolling down his own cheeks, to collect somewhere on the edge of his jaw, pause and then plunge into the darkness.

Omme and Anicet stared into each other's souls, and the one no longer knew if the other was not himself acting under some magic spell. His personality dissolved with a strange sound like a ten-piece band. Omme, in spite of his emotion, remained firmer and seemed to be taking no notice of Anicet. He was the one who broke the illusion by walking down the steps of the church. He went through the gate and turned into the alleyway that runs up the right side of St Philippe.

Grief strikes men of science as hard as anyone else, but they are less prepared for it, since grief is a particular case and they are in the habit of considering only the general. Omme was trying without much success to be methodical in analysing his feelings. He was sure of one point: he was subject to a range of painful sensations. He tried to pinpoint them and listed them as follows: involuntary trembling of the lips, laboured breathing, and a sort of constricted feeling near the waist. He thought of trying to align these sensations with prior ones that were comparable, but not painful. The only equivalents he found were associated with desire. In which case, was it not the same image that had aroused in him both movements, desire and despair? Finding himself outside the same Café Biard where earlier we saw Anicet burning a letter, Omme went in and sat down at a table.

Two solutions presented themselves to relieve Omme of his sadness: to forget Mire, or to kidnap her. Men who have only lived in laboratories tend to imagine extreme approaches. First, Omme forced himself to forget the traitor. He attacked her image and tried to disfigure it; he exaggerated the imperfections of her body and her face, invented tics which he added to her features, and called on ridicule to help him. His efforts were wasted; the more defects he found for Mire, the more Omme loved her for her faults. Next he tried replacing a violent feeling with its opposite, by changing his passion for Mire into hatred of her new spouse. But he was quite unable to think of Pedro Gonzales without seeing his enigmatic bride standing at his side, and she soon absorbed his attention and reawakened his pain. He tried a thousand ways of transferring his affection to an object close to Mire, but it never worked; inevitably the image returned of Mirabelle, standing straight and silent on the steps of St Philippe, looking at Omme and slowly smiling at him. How could Omme have kept any self-control? He could not find his mind, he was losing himself; his inner world seemed as blurred and trembling as the outside world when seen through a wall of tears. Omme sighed, unworldly as he was; in that case the only thing to do was to kidnap Mirabelle. But how? At that moment a whirling genie took pity on the physicist, dropped from the sky and laid both hands on the table.

"What will you have, sir?"

"Mirabelle," Omme was about to answer, but raised his eyes and saw Pol waiting for him to order a drink.

Since he had become Traînée's lover, Pol spent what little spare time was left him by his job as an actor, in the café. That meant he could keep an eye on Traînée, and act the part; behave like a jealous tyrant, pinch her hard when everyone was looking, in fact, satisfy the wish for pity that every man holds in his heart, and all the while helping Traînée serve at table — not that the sturdy young woman seemed at all overwhelmed by the work. "Pol," said Omme, "are you still in love with Mirabelle?" Pol looked seriously worried and glanced five or six times at his mistress to check she hadn't heard. But she was busy polishing the counter and gaily singing a sad love song, so he composed himself, opened his mouth, paused for a moment and pronounced "Maybe". Omme described the spectacle he had just watched. Pol dropped his guard completely in his surprise, and cried out sharply, "Mirabelle married!" His shout cut short Traînée's singing. Rightly indignant, the girl came striding over, taking no notice of the pile of plates she knocked down as she went, seized Pol's head in both hands and shook it hard until the patient's eyes were rolling in their sockets. "That wretched woman," she cried, "who have you given yourself to? Look at the result of being so stupidly indulgent. He still thinks about this Mirabelle in spite of all his denials. I know I have offended divine majesty with my weakness and lustfulness, but is my crime so great that I should be so horribly punished? You coward, taking advantage of my sex's inferiority to make me suffer a thousand deaths — see, if I go to my grave, you can say it was you who put me there." Pol had started to see everything spinning at mind-boggling speed. His bow tie had fallen off, and his face was drained of blood. It would be hard to tell which hurt Pol more, the despair into which the bad news had thrown him, his fear of being hit, or remorse at hurting Traînée. He spluttered, "It's not me, I don't care about Mirabelle, Omme is the one in love with her, I don't like, I don't like being hurt." His face was so full of pain that Traînée thought she had strangled him. She let go, and he slumped to the floor looking dazed. "My God, I've killed him!" Traînée shouted, and in her mourning was already starting to smash the crockery when the café owner, that balding giant, Boulard I think he's called, rushed over to rescue his possessions, slapped Traînée, kicked Pol up off the floor, grabbed two teaspoons and turned to Omme to address him: "If I have understood correctly sir, a lady to whom you are rather attached has got married without your agreement. Since your sweet looks have failed to dissuade her, you will, with a heavy heart, have to force her into better feelings towards you. Only you are not in the habit of operating in this way. If you're prepared to trust me, I have something to propose to you."

"Speak," said Omme, "whoever you are, sent from heaven or hell. I can't refuse any help now, wherever it comes from."

Boulard signed to two men leaning on the bar. They came over and sat at Omme's table and the four of them put their heads together and started talking in low voices, so mysteriously that Traînée felt drawn in and reckoned she should look casual to put people off the scent, so she took up her fantasy exactly where she had left off. Pol, without being asked, took on the important role of lookout, and fearing that someone might surprise the conference, nervously checked all round the café. Suddenly he jumped and gestured to the conspirators to be quiet. And indeed, there was a couple coming down the street.

It was Princess Merov with Bolognese, walking with their arms linked like rustic lovers; Marina still wore the expression of outrage she had put on to go to the wedding. "So, my dear friend," Bolognese was saying, "I can imagine you are miserable to see one of your admirers, to whom, if I am not mistaken, you had not refused all hope, casting off your chains so quickly and accepting others which, one has to admit, are lawful. But I am sure you see I am having to be rather gracious not to take offence at the gloom you are displaying in response."

"Now Nicholas, you speak French like a foreigner, your vocabulary is devoid of rare words and your turn of phrase has a hint of German about it, loaded with euphemisms and *longueurs* which are simply not acceptable in conversation. I hope you have no illusions about the nature of the relationship that got me this pearl necklace from Pedro Gonzales, which is the envy of Paris. As for this gentleman's charm, it is the inevitable effect of having an income of four hundred thousand, and it should make you blush to be forcing a woman to explain. But what really leaves my soul in desolation…"

"Pardon?"

"You understand French even less well than you speak it. I was saying that what really upsets me is to see him prefer that insignificant B— who is unable to keep to a rank appropriate to her fortune. Don't they say that she has compromised herself in the lowest sort of hotel with that boy Anicet, you know, the one who composes mottled verses? She must have been running after him, since it's public knowledge that he lived only for me (though I always held him off) and has wit enough, in spite of his youth, not to get fixated on someone so uncerebral. She has not even read

Verlaine."

Bolognese suddenly seemed much more interested. "Do tell me, Rina mia, what you know about this adventure. I have a weakness for these stories which are so extraordinary for us virtuous Americans. You say that Anicet…"

Deep in talk they had reached the rue de la Baume. Marina stopped in front of a small town house and exclaimed, "This is the place where my rival believes she can enjoy with impunity hours of happiness with the man she took from me by I cannot think what wiles. But even if the stones of these walls tell her what I said, I swear before them that I will take back my Pedro, for the expressionless eyes of that mindless slut will not make him forget my nitid looks for long."

The walls heard nothing more of Marina's revenge until the following Sunday at the hour of evening mass. While the bells of Roule were ringing, Pedro Gonzales's chauffeur came in to announce that the car was damaged and would not be working that afternoon. He then went down to find the three servants not off duty that day, exchanged a few words with them in a low voice and looked out of the window to see what was happening on the street. Two men were pacing up and down the pavement; they looked up and gave the chauffeur a prearranged signal. Just outside the Gonzales mansion, a tall woman with her features concealed behind a thick veil seemed to be waiting for someone. The two men tried to upset her by staring at her, and were irritated by her appearing with such bad timing. A telegram delivery-boy came by, walked straight up to the Gonzales mansion, rang the bell, waited, then disappeared inside. He had barely left when Pedro Gonzales appeared on the doorstep with a telegram in his hand, looking vexed, and stepped into the street as if to hail a taxi. One of the two men made to block his way, but to the man's complete amazement the veiled woman reached out and touched Pedro's arm. He turned round, said hello, and enquired what the lady wanted. She lifted the veil and the man heard Gonzales exclaim, "Marina! What are you doing here?" The couple fell into deep discussion; the woman was asking the man to grant her something

ANICET OR THE PANORAMA

which he was refusing with some trepidation. However, Pedro was visibly softening his resistance. Suddenly Marina took his arm and the two of them went off towards St Philippe. The man following behind was left in a pretty awkward position. He signed to his companion to stay put. The couple led him to the small street that runs up the side of the Roule church. There Marina pointed out to her companion a cheap, scruffy hotel, the ground floor of which was occupied by the Café Biard. Pedro protested, "You are mad." But she insisted and the two of them went into the hotel. The scout went into the Biard. Omme and Boulard were waiting for him. "Well," said the café owner, "have we got him?"

"I wasn't able to catch him," the unknown man answered. He then told them what had happened.

"Aha!" cried Boulard, overjoyed. "If he is in the sack he won't be out too soon. Let's get to work." Omme, whose pale, earnest face bore the marks of love-lorn disarray, threw a large cape with a black silk collar around his shoulders and placed a top hat on his head. The three of them set off towards the Gonzales mansion.

Just then, two young men were walking down a side street which leads from the Boulevard Haussmann and comes out close to this mansion, one of them with his head inclined in thought, the other with his finger raised to make a point. "Anicet," Baptiste was saying, "now is the moment to present yourself to Mire. When inaction weighs you down, shake it up a bit. Make clear you have not given up on your path of action. Don't forget that winning Mirabelle is just one episode and when it comes to it, whatever airs she gives herself, it is the first step in your life towards a mysterious purpose whose shape I can begin to glimpse." Anicet felt like an actor about to go on stage to play a part he has just been given but has never read. His head was spinning on the brink of catastrophe; if in a moment he could not find what to say to Mirabelle, how could he continue on the boards? He feared he would look ridiculous and was trembling with real love for the woman who would witness it. Above all he was frightened he would find her too beautiful; and he was tortured by another thought: what was Baptiste's motive in casting him into the midst of the action like this? But he had no time to think about that; Baptiste said, "On you go now," and pointed to the Gonzales mansion.

All of these movements converged so that just as the man posted to watch the house was walking up from the left towards Omme, and Boulard and their accomplice were arriving from the right, Anicet in the middle was stepping into the mansion which was the centre of all this interest. "Hell and damnation," shouted Boulard when he saw him. In the top corner of the canvas, with his arms crossed and with an enigmatic smile, Baptiste looked like the presiding genius of the whole adventure.

But Anicet had no idea he was the centre of all this attention and looked ahead of him into the cool shadows leading to the goddess's rooms.

MIRABELLE, OR DIALOGUE INTERRUPTED

A fresh smell, like aniseed, was the first sign for Anicet, as he stood undecided at the threshold of a room with lowered blinds, of the woman's presence, and of the nonchalance with which this lovely creature prepared to receive him. He caught sight of Mire sitting at her dressing-table, on the far side of the Pacific Ocean, a fearful space of foaming wool, a pentagonal carpet which climbed the room obliquely from the young man's feet to those of the faithless woman. She did not turn to face him; she went on unfastening her black hair, and eyed the intruder in the mirror on her table. The thought that she was seeing him in that little oval, the opposite of his real situation, as a minuscule puppet broken by reverence for her, while he could see in it only Mire's face and her silver eyes, troubled Anicet as if he felt himself being wafted away by some magician's wand and taken to a virtual world out there beyond walls and seas. It made him feel light, light as if he were tipsy. The face in the mirror looked intently at Anicet; a dialogue began between the disembodied head and the distant image. "Please excuse," said the mirror, "my state of dress. But your face suggests the awkwardness of someone who does not know what to say, and yet has much on his mind."

"Madame Mirabelle…" said a character who was speaking with no orders from Anicet.

"I find your agitation quite amusing, and I am not fool enough to attribute it, as you might wish, to the intimacy of this encounter. The truth does not escape me; you come here like a provincial arriving in the capital, with a pile of complaints brewed up in the solitude of St Flour or some such place. Another woman might have been content to flirt a bit, to embarrass you with her coy looks and send you home with your load of inarticulate recriminations. Well, my friend, I'm one to take the bull by the horns. The Anicet who has presented himself to me does not dare to say aloud what he thinks of a marriage which I know full well puts the cat among the pigeons."

The reflection replied, "Mire, you have no idea how much you have hurt me. What can you know about the wretchedness of a life which has lost its bearings?"

"Ha! did I ever ask for your commitment? Some people just have no self-doubt. Until someone has forced me to love them, do I have to have a bias towards love? You glory in all this honour and patriotism and sentiment and affection you have rid yourself of; can't I be allowed to have freed myself of a few of the scruples that you still suffer from? You didn't think of that. Anyway, what has changed, I ask you? I got married because I needed money, and none of you, not even Blue, was capable of satisfying my requirements and providing the luxury I cannot live without. But I have no intention of depriving myself of the courtiers I so enjoy. I shall gather you together again, right here, in front of MY HUSBAND. Or are you going to protest in the name of virtue, or marital fidelity? One never knows with people like you."

"Mirabelle, to please you I was ready for anything."

"Ready for anything, Anicet, but not to do anything. Did you not realise that I am a supernatural being who can hear you speaking and thinking wherever you are? I remember your dumb astonishment when you discovered I have a life like anyone else's. I was lowered in your sight for having a flat, and servants, a place, a position, and not living in the metaphysical space into which you dispersed me when I vanished from your field of vision. How many times have I shrugged my shoulders when you talk of your decisiveness, or of action, or energy? You're not even aware of your idleness; there is nothing that can be done for you. You orate: 'Action. Action,' — what are you waiting for? I listen to you mumbling, 'I shall repeat, but mockingly, the phrase used by a man from an earlier age, thinking he could stigmatise ours: "In my day one did not 'Make it'". I, for one, will do all I can to "Make it"'. A fine resolution, but one you will never get further with than putting into words. You are singularly ill suited to 'making it'. As I have said, I can only live amid wealth, and I would have to wait much too long to find that with you. My spouse is a canny old ruffian; he has made his fortune seven times over in some crazy countries, and six times so far he has lost every penny. 'You shall be my seventh ruin,' he said to me on our wedding night. I mean to be."

"Mirabelle, you only needed to tell me…"

"I needed to tell you nothing. It was enough that I wanted money. I know what it's like to starve. It has happened to me several times, in several different attics. I have stood there, shivering, with chilblains and no coal. I have had enough of studios where you pose for some madman who works without any food, of hours spent in rooms with peeling walls, of small consolations, torture for some people, cobbled-together aesthetics, pictures sold for a crust of bread, I've had enough of all that. Look at my nails, painted in cornelian, my fingers soft with cream. I tell you I am a goddess or something close to that. Just please don't imagine you are going to set up Beauty with a nice little apartment. Beauty? You really did believe I was that mildly demented girl represented all through mythology with white, statue's eyes, didn't you? You will never unravel this mystery, or fathom where I get this magic power to spy on everything, and still be Madame Gonzales in this little mansion in Roule. Who knows? So many strange things have happened. You shouldn't put your hand in the fire and swear that Mirabelle is not the ideal of all young men your age, that she is not this higher quality which resides in thousands and thousands of objects and makes them shine with the spirit of the splendour of life and of blood. And you should not put your head on the block if she is not the first adventuress to come along whom your youth, and the problems of men who are high on enthusiasm, or the disruption of their senses, wrap in borrowed prestige and dress up as a divine being — as they might any *café concert* star. But whatever personality you fancy attributing to me, I have the right to be myself; I have not promised you anything, I am as free as the air, and it really makes me laugh to see you moralising at me. After all, you have had plenty of time to win me."

"Mirabelle, oh Mire! Don't you realise it was for you, without thinking, at the first sign from you, that one fine morning I ruined my life? What is left for me if you cheat me? Suddenly, in the fullness of my joy, the bough breaks; there is no reason I should ever recover the lost meaning of the interrupted sentence. Whichever way I turn I find only desert. If I look for something better, I find a few oases. In the end you get tired of limp enthusiasms, a bit for this and a bit for that, between one bout of depression and the next. The simplest thing if I could find the courage would be to kill myself."

Mirabelle opened the right-hand drawer of the dressing-table, took out a revolver and placed it on the marble tabletop.

"You can but try," she said.

"Mire, now I have come right up and I am standing beside you, a life-size man, not the shrunken, hesitant image you could see a short while ago. I am close to you, standing straight, a man who hasn't much longer to live. That gun can sleep on the table without my blushing for shame. It would have been pretty theatrical to kill myself in response to your challenge. But I am strong enough to resist provocation, and prepared to run the risk of being lost in your eyes for that very reason. I came here to win you, and I have not given up all hope and will not fail in the task I have set myself.

"What name should I give to the pleasure you take in presenting yourself to me alternately as a woman and as an abstraction? Oh! I can assure you, you are wasting

118

your time; I will swear with my eyes closed that Mirabelle is the goddess to whom my days are dedicated. What does it matter to me, I ask you, what the source is of the power given to you? Your eyes are enough for me to explain miracles, conjuring tricks, spells and deaths. Your words do not trouble me any more than your dilemmas. I know very well I have a hold over you, however much you deny it. It is not for nothing that I have given you my life, my place in the sun, everything I could apply to lifting worlds up high, which now is only good for submitting to you. You claim not to have promised me anything; but it is not my fault if you are alive, if you have shown yourself to me, if you have imposed yourself on my heart. You, the Beauty of the Day, the Wonder of Time, revealed yourself to me in order to possess me, consciously, and if you wanted me not to be so feverish at the sight of you, if you wanted to escape me afterwards, you only needed to run away from me, or not to exist. Thank God, before I knew you I knew a different beauty, less fresh, perhaps less seductive, but one which let me come close. Since you have the gift of reading my soul every second, and for months none of the most secret movements of my being have been hidden from your eyes, how can you make out that I have done nothing to win you? You would not bother to call for the worthless homage of a man who performs for a woman an action he deems insignificant; no, you require an act which engages the heart of a bold man in danger, don't you? When you met me, I had my own conception of the world but it would have been easy for me to guess what sort of homage you liked and what moves I had to make to win you. I would have been like an actor who always gets applause and becomes the husband of every petit-bourgeois housewife. You expected more from me, didn't you? The passion with which I have thrown myself into seeking you has recast everything in me, even my sensibility. The path to get from where I was to you was quite a journey, and deserves at least a retrospective glance from you. Remember that I come, as if walking out of deep woods, from a time when to look into oneself required a system of mirrors. Back then, one attached no importance to the goal one was aiming for. It was just a matter of taking pleasure in the method used to achieve it. The world was governed by minds which reasoned about themselves. It was the age of intelligent solutions, even the phrase *art for art's sake* was not controversial, it was inscribed like any other motto on public buildings. To become a great man all one needed was the recipe; poets were a kind of Brillat-Savarin. Sensations were separated, compared, confounded. Just blame physiology. If you had lived in those days, you would have fallen in love with me if I discovered a spice or a way of using it. I knew only that world, with its pontiffs, its laws and its *modus vivendi*. Suddenly, in the midst of this familiar landscape, I met a marvellous being who took no notice of these refinements, and whose beauty seemed so new to me that at first I could not manage to fix her features in my memory. How you would have laughed at me, Mirabelle, if I had addressed you with the words of praise I used then. You should realise that my elders, being attached to different images, would probably have found you ugly, and would not have understood the charm of a beacon which intoxicates me beyond reason. To come within your orbit, what an effort I had to make at every moment. For weeks I had to watch the slightest movement of my heart. I threw away my eyes and put in new ones. I learned to be moved by charms and favours which I found repugnant. I was stronger than the man who remade the world — I reconstructed myself. And now it really is art for art's sake, it really is a case of being enraptured by a method. Now that you have plunged into my heart without asking permission, you have seen there, written in my substance, the phrase which encapsulates your ideal: the end justifies the means. Means, those old discarded divinities.

"Nothing could be seen from the outside of the work being done within me. I appeared to be a lifeless character, but in spite of your magical science, you were wrong. Just wait till the walls crack and the bricks come showering down, then you will know what lay behind this deceptive immobility. This is a fine change in the world Mirabelle: no more problems to solve, they aren't being set any more. I'm not bothered any longer by the difficulties, which up till now have been food and drink to mankind. I just want to be a machine for reaching goals. All that old psychology, regret, conscience, prejudice and lack of prejudice can go on the scrap heap in one block. In the new world where I walk in my naïveté, no one has heard of all that. I gather that in Japan[1] there are priests who venerate morals and feelings. They must be sheep. But now let us get on with talking about life. I am like the lift-boy in a hotel; what do you think he cares what is in the cellar, or what's going on in this shaft that holds the lift, or all those cables which are too complicated to make common sense? What matters is the UP button, and all I know is this: I am going to the 4th floor, to room number 413, and in room 413 is Madame Mire, more beautiful than the catastrophes that lay waste my body when it stands before her."

"Anicet, you are forgetting your part and mine. Did you not come here with despair in your heart?"

"I do not know what you mean by that word, which I have never heard except in dreams. I can no longer disentangle what is tragic from your unfastened hair. That is now the only reality besides the white splash of your dress and the table at which you are sitting, and which extends you as if it were more flesh, weakly lit with strips of light falling through the blinds. The senseless movement which carries me towards you I can no longer call desire, or any other human name. A few fine roars could still be found in my throat to enrich the vocabulary of gallantry, a few uniform yelps that cannot be described on paper. The time is past for refining the language of love. They say it is a winged child with mirrors on its feathers, and lakes, and alpine scenes and songs for rainy days. I know nothing about that; I don't believe I can say the name of that god any more. Besides, what do I believe? Yet another word like a discarded goatskin, with no more meaning than a right hook. Don't you understand that I'm dragging words out of myself like teeth, till I lose all intelligence, feeling, reason, judgement and am reduced to nothing but will, madame?"

1. Every country is in Nature. [Original publisher's note]

To tell the truth, it must be dizzying to be right at the top of the room, in the triangle of light, close to the dressing-table; Anicet looks as if he's teetering on the edge of a precipice. Mire's hair coiled round and round like an electric siren, and Mire's eyes were now just flat, dark, metallic discs from which the sun's rays were reflected in random directions, and then suddenly criss-crossed in a lattice of incomprehensible letters and numbers which might hold the key to the Universe, but failed to intrigue Anicet.

Not knowing what concern made her hesitate, the young man heard the voice of a gramophone reaching him: "Anicet, look out for yourself, I have already told you, nothing has changed. My marriage has not broken anything. There is still time to win me. You have as much chance as the others, yes, my friend, as any of the others. But look out for yourself, and for me — I don't know how this room got so warm, or why I feel this sporadic need for air."

A loud click as the door opened interrupted Mirabelle, and suddenly the tables were turned — the protagonists became the audience; the meaning of the room was changed. The top of the page was now the doorway. From below, Anicet and Mirabelle could see a tall figure with its left hand on the open door, wearing a velvet mask, a top hat and a cape with a collar. His right hand clasped a dagger and he spoke with the needling tone of a traitor, to say:

"Good afternoon, madame."

"My God, what is this pantomime? Dear Omme, you are not too clever with your entrances; you must be sweltering in that outfit on a summer afternoon."

"Temperature," Omme replied — he had dropped the mocking tone — "only affects the mind in inverse proportion to its preoccupations. Over my heart I wear the Andes, as a pendant on a chain. An extra coat makes very little difference."

"Please explain more clearly," asked Mire; "in addition to the weight of your sorrows, are you not also carrying a fearsome dagger?"

"Its blade is no more cruel or cold than you. It will help me to avenge your treachery."

"Presumably you mean to sacrifice me, as your style of performance would have it, to your just wrath and resentment. Please do."

"Be silent, perjurer, I come to seize you from the unclean hands to which you have abandoned yourself. Beauty in the hands of Commerce! I left my laboratory, my regular routines, my petty everyday feelings, my test tubes; there was not a moment to spare, no margin for hesitation. The job called for this costume and explains it. Here I am, in the wrong skin, dressed for the part. Don't be frightened; any setbacks, surprises or hitches have all been planned for. My accomplices are ready to rush in as soon as I give the signal, and are waiting outside in a taxi. All your servants have been paid off. Your husband is in our hands and will not be back in a hurry. All you have to do is follow me without resisting. Please forgive me, Monsieur Anicet, for so rudely interrupting your *tête à tête*."

"No," said Anicet, "I do not forgive you, and I warn you that Madame Mire will not go with you except of her own free will, or…"

"Ha! so you're getting worked up, are you? My experience in solving problems has given me the capacity to foresee every eventuality. Your resistance, therefore, does not in this case either surprise me or disconcert me. I have the solution to hand: it is this dagger, whose purpose was not at first clear to Madame Mirabelle. It will invite you to prudence and patience."

"Your threats will not prevent me…"

"Enough!" said Omme, and he advanced towards Anicet with his dagger raised. The young man saw in his opponent's eyes the intention to strike; his hand gripped the edge of the dressing-table (his hand was naturally fearful) and as luck had it his palm felt a metal object on the tabletop. The instinct to defend himself made him grasp it, and by the time the idea of *revolver* had reached his consciousness, he had already fired. Omme lay there at his feet like a poor scientist who once changed his habits with all the ingenuity of a forty-year-old in love. Anicet's thinking was a few steps behind events; as a result, he was floating in a kind of stupor like the puff of smoke from the revolver. A human life does not really amount to much. You don't really expect to destroy one. Omme's death did not trouble Anicet, just its being so sudden and with no psychological preparation. The consequences of his action escaped him; or rather, he could not yet imagine them. Mirabelle had already removed from the body the dagger, the cape and the hat. She quickly handed them to Anicet. "Come on, put on the disguise, and the eye-mask I am sure you have in your pocket." While he did what she said without thinking, she had locked the door, opened a wardrobe, pulled out the big cloth that covered the clothes inside, thrown it over Omme and wrapped the corpse in this winding sheet. She took one look at the living man and said, "He was about the same height as you," and just as Anicet grasped the strangeness of her using the past tense, someone rattled the door with threats and curses. "Open the door," Mirabelle whispered to the young man. He did so automatically. Boulard and his two henchmen rushed in, while one of the servants kept watch in the waiting-room. Boulard gave a sigh of relief when he saw Anicet. "I thought something had happened to you; I heard a shot." Anicet found it hard to understand that he was being taken for Omme, and was even about to correct him, but the newcomer gave him no time. "Ah," he said, "you have already bound up the fellow. Nice work, that can't have been your first time. Now boys, pick up the trinket, and there's only the princess to deal with. Now lady, best just to smile and follow us."

"If you don't mind, sir," said Mirabelle, "following our conversation there have been one or two changes to the gentleman's original intentions." She pointed to Anicet. "We have both agreed that I shall stay here." Boulard was perplexed and gave the fake Omme a questioning look. Anicet realised that he should answer; he nodded his agreement. "In that case," said Boulard, "we just need to head off with the parcel. My respects to you, madame, and sorry pardon. Gently now boys, gently does it. After you, your worship." And he stepped aside to let Anicet lead the way.

Mirabelle was left alone before the mirror. She could hear their footsteps going down the corridor. Then the creak of the stairs. Then the front door opening and closing. Outside, she heard a car start. Then Mirabelle burst out laughing and started pinning up her hair. "These people," she said, "really aren't too smart. I wouldn't give little Anicet much of a chance once they uncover the trick. What a fool of a youngster! Twice I was at his mercy; once when we were alone, but he didn't dare; and again just now, when he could have ordered those men to carry me off, but he didn't have the presence of mind. Nothing will come of this child."

A lively discussion followed between Mire and her mirror. She rang the bell, and the movement she made to reach for the button showed her arm, the most beautiful serpent on Earth. "Anne," said Mirabelle to the maid, "from today I am doubling your wages. Let me know immediately when Monsieur Gonzales gets back."

THE DOORS OF THE HEART

It is easy enough to fit five people in a taxi, but when the fifth is a corpse it does not obligingly squeeze its legs under the seat. Boulard's efforts to get the cadaver to behave caused the late gentleman Omme the physicist's mask to slip, so that above the black eye-mask his face could be seen, afflicted for the moment, and probably for all eternity, with such a stupid expression that Anicet burst out laughing, as if he had just got the punch-line of a rather subtle joke. The café owner tore off the young man's mask with his left hand, and grabbed his wrists with his right, saying, "It seems we've got someone different here. No matter, my pretty fellow (not that anyone would exactly call you pretty), you'll pay just like anyone else. This little expedition will cost you the mere bagatelle of ten thousand francs; admire my honesty, I am asking only for the sum your victim promised. It's not expensive to buy our silence." The two sidekicks had drawn their guns; the taxi was under way. In the rear-view mirror Pol could be seen sitting next to the driver with a shocked expression on his face (he had been keeping watch outside) trying to indicate to Anicet that he was innocent of all this. "I am very sorry," said Anicet, "not to be able to reward your valour better, but I haven't a sou left; besides, I am very pleased to have met you, as you will save me the trouble of committing suicide, which is always romantic but very wearying to stage. Gentlemen, I am in your hands." The three accomplices looked perplexed. "We would be happy to oblige, sir," said Boulard, "but that's not the thing, we need our payment. We didn't take this job on for peanuts. What can we get you to work on? Boys, time to search our client."

One of the accomplices felt Omme's pockets and extracted a wallet, which yielded a ten-thousand-franc note, plus a thousand francs in hundreds. Boulard split the ten thousand francs with his two mates, then with the ten hundreds still in front of him he said: "May I ask you now, do you know anything about painting?"

"My God," said Anicet, "you really are nosy; but I won't pretend I haven't been friends with the very best painters, which has given me a thin coating of artistic education."

"Perfect, perfect. You are the man I have been looking for. Just take these thousand francs so you can show an interest in our little operation and relieve your black thoughts; and now that we have arrived, get out with me, so we can talk business somewhere quiet. If you don't behave, I'll blast you. Out we get, my friend."

Anicet got out of the car and found he was outside a certain Café Biard which he recognised; Monsieur Pol was already holding the door open. Boulard came up, turned to the two men who had stayed in the taxi, and bade them take the toff to his destination.

When Traînée saw Anicet walk in, she screamed and fainted behind the counter. Pol ran to her, tearing at his hair, but halfway across he changed his mind, did a quick about-turn and nipped back outside. No one gave a further thought to the poor girl.

"Young man," said Boulard once they were seated, "you need money; you are in our power, and you have too much to fear from the police to tip them off about us. We have a little association, headed by a high-ranking diplomat who we'll introduce you to one of these days, which exists to exploit the wealth of the Roule neighbourhood. Unfortunately none of us knows about painting, and our touts have set up some nice opportunities with some of the gallery owners. We don't want to be getting our hands on rubbish, do we? You see how you can be of use to us? As you'll have spotted, we get a pretty nice return, and the risk is always kept right down because we have so much business experience. Are you going to accept my proposal?"

Anicet thought about Mirabelle's requirements. "I have no choice," he said; "I will join you."

"Very good. We shall test your mettle this very evening. We have a little excursion in mind to a local painter. This is on behalf of a rich American who sells pictures in the United States. Our boss doesn't know about it. This time we're working around him; it's quite a nice little pot. Always pays well, export work."

"I'm your man," said Anicet, "get me a beer."

Pol was trying to come back in, but he was stuck in the revolving door as it spun round and round, carrying him back out each time he got into the café. The boss grabbed him by the scruff of the neck and yelled, "A beer, you imbecile!" Pol's face was a picture of misery as he served Anicet his beer. Now that he was alone at his table Anicet began to feel the effect of the day's efforts. He gradually slumped back on to the bench and you couldn't be sure his eyes weren't closed.

All the same, he could see two drinkers at the next table who were talking. They were Masons or maybe transvestites. One had a false beard, the other looked fake; no, actually he looked very young.

The first one said: "Now then, youngster, you overstepped the mark with my wife. I shall kill you when we are alone in no man's land. But first tell me what you felt. I have never been able to remember my first time, because I was drunk that night, and maybe I was not paying attention either." The other one turned round on his seat like an animal in labour and said: "To tell the truth, I expected more from desire. There is no excuse for it lasting such a short time; you can make love before you're done counting the windows — there are only three in the kind of hotel you and I can go to with our modest means. All the time you can hear footsteps in the next room. The neighbour can't rest, it's as if he's being gnawed at by regret. I get sensitive to everything at the very moment I shouldn't be able to see anything. Wind? was that the wind? I hear great marvels of the imagination sailing past the shutters, coming and going like serving-maids. There is a list of things to remember on the wall: pay the milkman, the shopping list, the doctor's; the woman's eyes get drawn to these clumsily chalked-up words. She talks about it — oh! I was far away and these worries would make me smile, if at all, on an after-work quickie. She explains jealousy to me, because I have never known that, have I? I am as new as a shiny new coin. 'The hardest thing for a woman of the world is being unable to resist the craving to eat the chairs and curtains when her lover, the sun, enters her rival's room,' she says. It is really worth being the ardent young man when your partner blocks her ears to stop the sound of the whirlwind her lover is blowing between up and down. So you leave the bed, and have to start all over again. Love is just a great big yawn, believe me. We wouldn't be here wearing out our livers if it weren't for this woman, like a sewing machine nodding its head in such a delicate and unreal way."

"Did you notice? Then there's the awful moment when you wake up and the woman is asleep in spite of the heat. What is the remedy then for sadness, when you turn your head left and right and all you can see in the distance is an island as deserted as a coconut in the branches of a tree?"

"Don't talk like that to me; if love comes with such horrors, how can I, who planned to devote myself to love, remain on this Earth?"

"That is simple: I shall kill you in a couple of hours. But don't pretend you know about love because of this bit of play-acting, which will cost you your time in the light. You need to have lived side by side with a woman. You have no idea what a crazy animal you caressed out of curiosity. When you can't hold out any longer and you absolutely have to go to her, she ups the ante, she still knows nothing, men scare her, and she wants to be courted. You have never seen yourself in front of her, drunk and clumsy, with your eyes rolled up like shirt sleeves, her breast crawling with strange creatures and with such heavy hands — yes, hands, the worst thing is the hands! She, of course, walks about in the room as if she were off to the Bois de Boulogne. When I see that sort of thing, I become unrecognisable, I leap at her and grab her by the hair; that's why she tells everyone I beat her and treat her like a poodle. Other times she grabs hold of me in the middle of a nightmare; if I wake up, with my lips still thick with sleep, she weaves me around with caresses and everything starts spinning. Impossible to say what time it is, or what bad dream of a flat I am in at the mercy of a relentless lover, unable to find the four-leaf clover of sleep. Later, cherished intimacies become familiar duties. The woman accepts, and her joys wear down hypocritically into grudging moans. As soon as her task is done, she pushes you away with a limp movement of her hand. The first time you are subjected to the soft pressure it drives you crazy; you want to bash your head against the wall. Then habit, oh yes, habit! brings you to all sorts of compromises. And one day those intrusive demons, domestic troubles, invade your bed, like little saw-toothed shadows, and you start talking about the gas bill between clinches. The woman you saw go mad like a flame just now while she was licking your feet and hands and dancing on the bed, is at the same time, and it is nothing to be proud of, the joyless wife who disgusts you as bitterly as absinthe."

When he looked at the speakers more closely Anicet noticed they were wearing rather choice fabrics. The younger one bent his head down on the table and went on. "Please stop grinding my heart with your thoughts. What will become of me if love does not make life worth living, now that I have broken all my precious vases? Maybe you are right about this woman, the most deceitful housewife in the capital. But I have often seen in palaces great tigresses baring their teeth and flexing their retractable claws, their flesh browner than desire. They breathed luxury, as they say. Like as not, once you have made love with them, you can never shake them off. There are smells you only smell in the hallways of hotels with rooms by the hour."

"Who did you take Mirabelle for then, if not one of these foreign beauties? Did you think she was just a free-living bourgeois? To have a misunderstanding like that she must have kept her hair hidden while your bodies were entwined like souls in a cage."

"No, it was neatly tied up and she was careful not to mess up her hairstyle. Oh, if you had seen her with her hair down! When she unfurls that darkness, then you feel her power. All the forces of Hell grow in that forest. All you can do is repeat: 'Mirabelle, Mirabelle.' Such weakness! And then you suddenly realise she has come from far away across the ages and the oceans with great jewels in her ears, of rock salt, the terrible grin of flesh cut to the bone, and the pendulum motion of her walking like the breathing of the tides. There is nothing you can do to escape. Steamers are useless; she catches the same one as you. When you think you are free, a sound makes you turn round and it's this big rocking-chair gently moving as it calls you to its arms and reclaims you to poison you. If only one could cut off all of Mirabelle's hair and throw it into the sea!"

Anicet would never have believed Pedro Gonzales was so melancholic. He was sitting opposite this fat man, toying with a straw in his half-drunk over-sweet drink. The young man whose place he had taken, well, he was not there and no one minded.

"Love," said Anicet, "yet another sun slapping my fingers; it is incomprehensible, but still other people find life bearable. Did you think I was going to throw myself into a fantastical adventure to bring your lady wife pearls to eat? It was supposed to start with an article on modern painting, then the programme featured a black body-stocking like you see in films, and comfortable pistols and knotted ropes hanging suspended in the dark. And yet, what a useless disturbance all that would be, if love only had the bitter face you wear, to top it all. I had dreamed (one does say dreamed, doesn't one?) of singular satisfactions in summer in a new apartment block. What a magnificent role the woman would have had, if she had wanted it.

How much more subtle my lines would have been than hers. The neighbours would have blushed when they met us in the staircase because our titanic games made so much noise. The sourness of our kisses would have made tap water from the Seine taste like a divine liquor, a minty freshness to die for. We would have been fabulous customers to the point where we would have given up this delicious lie and recovered our real natures in the vapours spewed out by lilies over the Southern seas, among bleeding atolls which force us to interrupt our love-making to watch them go by, like parcels of red wrack, in the wake of our hearts."

This image seemed to be deeply moving for the people listening. Everyone thought Pedro Gonzales was about to speak; but a thin woman with poor clothes, clasping to her tuberculous chest with her left hand a shawl which was slipping off, started speaking:

"Monsieur Anicet, you will find me very bold, and probably after I have tried you will say bad things about me and load me with insults. I don't know how to explain my approach; you would have to imagine an unlikely story. Only I have heard they were trying to persuade you not to love, so lying on my mattress I remembered all the tenderness, all the declarations and light-headedness, and I got up to come and tell you what a sweet ulcer it is that they call *love*. It is a wasting sickness, a fire that runs from your head to your feet, and you can't say which moment is better, the one when you calm the fever behind the curtains, or when it is running at full spate; you are alone, standing by the open window, with the sheets still hanging up blue on the line, and your eyes look far out till they bump against house-fronts and sweep along pavements but do not find your lover, that delightful liar who smiles so nicely in his pearl-grey waistcoats! Dear love does not know how to deceive, sir; it has strange cruelties, bitter as exotic fruit from the special trays."

"Stop that rot," said another woman with a dramatically made-up face. "Love is not that kind of unhealthy resignation. I have known it in the most torrid of climates; it sought out the only fresh air in the country, and between the walls of shade combat was joined, more like dying than anything else. Sometimes, outside the squares on the board, the couple's very life was at stake. They certainly thought so; there was a feverish rush to reach each other, clasp each other, to overwhelm eyes that were too wide, and lips that were too ripe. I have been through these dark, dry passions in the Southern winds. We trembled with fear of being discovered; we were bound to each other by complicity beyond reason, and sometimes stampedes were unleashed against our love. And then, man, horse and I felt so united that I had to speak, speak in spite of the voracious sun and the sandbanks of air constantly glued to my gums."

Pedro Gonzales twitched limply, just long enough to put one in mind of a slug, then with some effort produced these words: "Don't listen to women like that, little one, they will give you wrong ideas. I know one who was hardly twenty but who had already gone mad." He stopped, then started again in a wavering, fatuous vein: "She was mad about me. So we went to the Acacias on great brown bays. I've forgotten what happened after that, except what she said at the moment she was dying: *So did they have nothing else to do when they invented love?*"

Suddenly Anicet heard a voice calling softly behind him. He made to turn round, but steely hands on his shoulders prevented him, and a stranger with a foreign accent whispered in his ear. "Love is your last chance. There really is nothing else left to keep you on this Earth. Who knows? No one else could test this potion for you, and other people's experience is no use to you. You have probably already tried the imperfect fantasies which fused you to other bodies like a bunch of grapes. Silly young girls who bored you sooner or later, you listened to them naming all the objects in the bedroom, and giving a succinct account of their primeval activities; the clock stands on the mantelpiece, the blinds are down, but day has not yet broken. I wish I had satin slippers; they say there are women who own three thousand diamonds! That kind of love is a less innocent game than used to be believed, because it consumes ardour itself. That is not the love you need. Give up these empty-eyed girls for ever; once, you had no trouble abandoning Traînée. She does not even occupy your idle thoughts. If you heard her again speaking about life, or asking you for the sensitivity that hangs in your heart like a dead leaf, you could kill her without feeling any the worse."

"Isn't she already dead?" asked Anicet, "or did I take my wish for reality?"

A scream rang out from behind the bar, and they saw Traînée get up with her face distorted; she was rolling her eyes like billiard balls, flailing her arms ridiculously, then put both hands to her neck and shook herself violently. When she fell down Anicet laughed quietly; he knew it wasn't possible to strangle oneself. The voice behind him went on:

"Did you ever ask yourself what Mirabelle would mean to you? With her, you would not need to fear gossiping, tempers or being misunderstood. When you are in her arms you won't find she is a demanding partner. Just be careful not to draw the wrong conclusion from her virtues and only admire her as an ill-defined ideal, which is what her courtiers do. She would escape you as she escapes that whole gallery of artists. Artists produce remarkable petitions full of principles… but enough of that, you will find out later. But you should at least take note that in an age when one can deny God, Country and Family without unleashing a tempest, you could still get your eyes put out for declaring that art does not exist. Art and Beauty are mankind's last divinities. That is how come your rivals, who seem free of prejudice, are lumbered with the dead weight of Art, a deified abstraction, a preserve that is good at best for feeding fossils. They make the remarkable mistake of taking Mirabelle for the *Beautiful*, when she looks ugly to a lot of people and in fact is *Woman*. When it comes down to it, Anicet, *Woman* is the last lifebelt left to you. To win her you'll have to fight, to keep her you'll have to fight; even to love her you'll have to fight — that is what can make you interested in living. If that is not enough, my friend, you might as well pack your stuff."

The word *stuff* made it all quite clear; it explained the enigmas. *Stuff*, yes of course, *stuff*. It hung on the air like smoke, seeped in everywhere, changed the scenery. One can't pretend the meaning of the word *stuff* was very clear to Anicet, but it's a word that flaps so nicely in the wind it probably refers to some kind of fabric, a silky fabric with white stripes on white. This summer everyone will be wearing *stuff*, it's so silky, so light, the best for leaving shapes vaguely moulded; the catalogue is searching in vain for the adjective *flosh*. Unless I'm wrong, what I had taken for a white scarf is in fact the beam from the spotlight. It's falling on the stage of a music-hall, where no one is dancing yet, so its halo seems innocent of intention and is projected indiscriminately on the boards as if it had its own life. Suddenly it is being moved, and jumps around searching for the missing actor. It lingers over the detail on a fancy decorated pillar hidden in the shadows, but which the spotlight brings partly into view before our curious eyes. A gong announces a dancer, but no one can see him. We know his name and nationality by the big number 8 on the side of the stage. Man and light-beam run around looking for each other. There is a lot of toing and froing while the spotlight picks out bits and pieces of the dancer, an arm coming past, a leg, a torso, then following the music his body embraces the beam and here is a fine cowboy, with open-necked shirt, sleeves rolled up, there on the boards that are basking in the light, miming some kind of dramatic monologue. What is clear is that his life is at stake. What has happened to push this actor from the Western prairies to the brink of despair? The pistol in his hands is frightening. How long can this go on? We are too entranced by his leaps, bends and movements to have any way of telling them apart. The sudden bang of a pistol shot, and both dancer and spotlight disappear. Nothing remains but darkness and the smell of gunpowder. The lights come back on in the auditorium, but the stage is bare, with dull scenery. When the performer comes back to take a bow, he is overly made-up and vulgar in the light, and bows too low for someone who has just killed himself. Anicet shifts uneasily on his folding seat; he has just read in the programme the title of dance 8: *Hymn to the Human Body*. The stagehand puts up 13 in place of the 8.

Anicet is firmly unsuperstitious and quickly checks the programme:

13   WOMAN

The lights went down too fast for him to read more.

Delicate music modulates the tunes men are quietly humming in the audience, upping the tempo a little. The song and dance routines float up from the stalls and catch the heartstrings of a spectator standing up at the back of a box. There is not a single music-hall tune which does not carry a delightful, touching memory for one of the people out in the darkness in the gilded seats of the circle with their plush-covered arms.

The bluish footlights are enough to see the curtain split open like a heart. Behind it is another curtain, unbroken, heavy, with regular folds. A light spot appears high up to the left, and in the spot a woman's head. With no surprise Anicet recognises Mirabelle — he had been expecting her. She looks like a pretty advertisement for toothpaste. She is singing in English and he can't understand because she is not singing slowly enough. But he manages to catch the word *Darling* like a silver bell. Suddenly the head goes out; but the light comes up again low on the right; the song goes on and Anicet is moved to hear the word *lip*. After another eclipse the head reappears further down again stage left, and the words must be really moving — you can feel the breeze out there of eyelids being fluttered by people who have understood. The word *arm* surprises Anicet like a caress.

Now the head is in the centre of the stage at floor level as if Mirabelle were lying flat on her front. There must be some magic in the song for Anicet to get that thrill. But he only picked up the word *love*, which uncoils across the hall, a cold serpent that brings a shiver to the women's bare shoulders and the men's dark clothes. Darkness returns along with silence.

Then the second curtain is drawn apart, while from ten points on the upper circle there bursts forth the cold, fast sound of an electric arc-light sparking up. Ten stage-lights spew out white fire.

And now the spotlight is on a high stool at the centre of the stage on which Mirabelle, with her chin in her hands and her elbows on her knees, sits looking at the void with eyes gentler than death. Mire is wrapped in a great black coat, which hangs down well below her bare feet, flowering on these falls of darkness. Mirabelle is singing again as if that is what she came into the world to do. Suddenly she throws up her head and stretches out two ring-laden hands, separated by two bracelets, manacles of slavery, from two arms whiter than daylight. The coat falls from her shoulders and then Mirabelle is truly made visible to everyone as WOMAN. Anicet thinks she is naked, she is so beautiful; but in fact she is clothed in the most costly fabrics and the rarest jewels. Occasionally one of the cut stones shines like a railway signal. Mirabelle's song is over, but she holds the clear, high challenge of the last note.

Now how do you think the images won't get mixed up?

Anicet could feel all around him the presence of other spectators. He had his eyes closed; he knew he was asleep in Boulard's café. He would have liked to wake up, but he could not. Someone took pity on him and punched him on the head. There was a great flash of light in his skull, and he awoke.

They had just turned the lights on; it was getting dark. "Have I been asleep that long?" asked Anicet. "It's already dark."

"You were out like a dormouse, mate," said Boulard, "so you'll be all the more ready for our little job."

"Oh I thought I was far away, you cannot imagine everything that went through my mind. So when did I start dreaming? The street-lamps are on."

Outside by the lamp-post a man and a woman were parting; Anicet was astounded to recognise Pedro Gonzales.

"So at what point did I start dreaming?" he repeated.

"What? No idea, mate," said Boulard, holding out two revolvers, "just take these lovelies."

The moment Anicet felt the cold metal a scream was heard, and then Monsieur Pol moaning behind the bar. "Oh my God," he said, "she is dead, my turtle dove, my pigeon, my viper-bodied baby, my sweet Traînée, my mistress."

He had picked up her body by the armpits and all sweating and tearful he dragged her out to the middle of the room. Anicet leapt over to look for signs of strangulation, but he found nothing. A small empty bottle marked Poison, which Boulard found behind a pile of plates, explained the mystery. Pol was quietly groaning beside the body. Anicet did not miss Traînée, but he was shattered by her dying. "It's OK," said the boss, "there's no need for a doctor since she's dead, and given that we don't want the police poking their noses into our business, we'll just have to make this pretty child disappear. It's a pity though, she could have been quite useful." He hefted the body on to his shoulder and disappeared into the back of the shop.

Pol was still groaning and rocking back and forth and left and right. He seemed to have the germ of an idea, stopped for a moment, then got up and went off into the back of the shop as well.

The two extras who had gone with Omme's corpse now arrived at the door. "Boss there?" one of them asked Anicet; "it's time to go."

"All yours, my boys," said Boulard coming back without his burden. "Come on my friend, off we go. We will explain everything."

As they went out Anicet saw Pol come back with a stepladder, a hammer, nail and rope. "He's going to hang himself," he thought and went out laughing at the idea of the burlesque scene about to unfold, when the rope would break and Pol would reattempt his miserable business and fail once again.

"It is good," he said, "to be alive in the evening."

DECEASE

A plait drops loose out of the unbound night. It hangs heavy and dark in the void and plunges into a crack between the houses. The man at the end of the rope sees the walls tip to a dangerous angle. The hulking buildings look to him as if they have been tossed about all round the courtyard. As the rope slips gently down from the roof, the man's field of vision swings up to the sky and he groups the stars, as he fancies, into constellations unknown to astronomers. These vertiginous patterns remind him of the figures on a tapestry long ago, in a room where love, for the first time, smelling of Madeira, opened for him a cream-coloured gown decked out with ribbons. They spin around his head as those mural flowers did then. The man is annoyed by this comparison, which dogs him and bothers him. Now he has reached a window; he tugs on the rope as a signal; it stops. The man climbs on to the window ledge; he takes something out of his pocket, squats and makes a few rapid hand movements — you cannot hear the creaking noise they make because you're too far away. Suddenly a large pane of glass comes loose and noiselessly follows the hand moving back. The moonlight which whitens the house is unexpectedly bright in this mirror; the man's arm is through the hole in the glass and searching for the handle.

Anicet is not surprised by such dexterity, though he is not used to this approach to opening windows. He lets go of the rope and jumps into the room like an elf.

You know the wonderful allure that makes love-making secret and mysterious. Crime has a similar charm. Prudence requires us to operate at speed; but the greatest enjoyment is slowly savoured, and a sensitive murderer, or a delicate burglar lingers at the very spot they should have fled. I remember reading, maybe ten years ago, the story of a thief who had broken into a bank vault, opened the safe and removed its contents, but could not bring himself to leave, and sat pressing his beating heart against the door of the safe. He said sadly to the police who had been called as soon as the break-in was spotted: "Is it already dawn? Oh, give me another hour." The moment his foot hit the floor Anicet felt dizziness run up his outstretched leg and through his body, turning his skull like a winding key. Danger and loneliness, those sleek greyhounds of the night, licked his hands, his face and his eyelids. He wanted so much to say out loud, calmly: "Here I am in the house." The danger of making the slightest sound only made this fantasy more tempting. Like wanting to speak when you're asleep, Anicet resigned himself to having to voice this problematic thought, but the words were wrapped in little scrunched-up bits of sticky paper and scraped the walls of his throat, getting stuck and not wanting to come out. When he made a big effort so the words could escape like breaths, they had lost their meaning along the way, and were no longer recognisable. Or other phrases came out, crazy exhalations of the mind, betrayals disguised as intimate secrets: "The fuchsias have been propositioning me again," or, "I would like to eat coloured women."

Anicet felt he was no longer master of his thoughts, and fixed his attention on a memory, to pull him up. At first it was just a point of light with shadows of associated ideas dancing around it like branches in front of the sun. Then the boughs drew back, and came together round the edges of the sunlight, a delicate web held constantly tight, which simply formed a dark halo, a black band, a line, a thin line, the outline of a memory; then Anicet was looking straight into the sun. It was, with no premeditation, lovely childhood sunshine, one Thursday when they were off to the Pole aboard the *Ingenious*; everything was ready to go, their rations for the winter, furs, oil to keep the sea calm, forks for pronging whales. But at the corner of the rue des Martyrs they realised, Oh dear! That they had left behind the ball bearings for the dynamos. The memory was getting specific, as precise as the laughing face of the girl, whose name I can tell you, wait a moment: she was called Arabella or Marie, she was surely a princess in disguise. I thought she bore herself like a queen. Immediately I saw the sea and the ships of the Compagnie des Indes.

Anicet knew from this detail that he was back on track and, like a fish in an aquarium, set off, following the floor plan he had just checked, towards the salon where the painter had set up his studio. The thin beam of his torch sliced the night, showing the door and the door handle. Anicet was now revelling in the darkness; he had so often dreamed of bold men who break into the dark interior of houses while outside the silent, complicit moonlight (will that do for *luna amica*?) passes for Kodachrome? Those lovely American film posters! And what if, in a moment, the torch were to shine on someone's face? The intruder pulled out one of his pistols and cocked it with a click that was sweeter than human music. Then he gently opened the door and slipped into the adjoining room. He walked straight across it into the salon-studio.

If we had only one fact at a time about the world, and we lacked our faculty for bringing together a thousand perceptions and concentrating them on a single object, we would be constantly in the state our hero was in at this point in the story. In this unfamiliar room where everything seemed to be precisely where it was not expected to be, each time he bumped into an object our young villain sketched out one aspect of this paradoxical world using his torch as a paintbrush, and had no idea how to link this new phenomenon to his previous discoveries. So his eyes were confused to find on the floor, between a series of canvases leaning against the wall, a jumble of brightly coloured rags, sequinned velvet, strings of wooden beads, empty boxes and tins of food as dangerously noisy as the unbelievable musical instruments suddenly encountered by his foot with an appalling crash (you get over it, a few deep breaths steady your heart). Another time, Anicet's foot found a soft lump and the torch revealed the bloated body of a red-cheeked mannequin. A little further on, something slipped so suddenly that Anicet jumped as if in the dark he had touched a fast-moving naked snake. Horrible fear made his lips tremble, his eyes go wide, his mind feverishly lucid.

While he was waving the dim light of the torch in the air, the novice burglar picked out, though his senses had not yet registered it, a loaded easel which was about to tip over beside him. He was just in time to throw out his arms and clasp them round the neck of the beast on the point of falling; having avoided catastrophe, Anicet stood in the dark with his hands attached to a pistol and a torch, and his arms round an object which would escape him at the slightest movement. He felt like a cart-driver bracketed to his horse and sliding with it over the ice. He would need luck to get his burden back into a stable position. It is commonly thought that a man who sees a bear first runs away, and then is frightened; I don't believe that, but rather that the man is frightened (that sudden loss of blood from his limbs, and life from his body, like falling), then runs away (the reaction which turns into running when the machine rushes to catch up on the time lost to fear), because he is frightened of the bear, I mean, he pays proper respect to the real cause of his trouble, and mentally gives it a name. Thus Anicet died for a moment in the dark, then avoided the imminent disaster with robotic precision and now, when the danger had passed, could imagine the horrible crash which would have woken the household, Paris, Europe and the police. A creaking cupboard gave him as much of a fright as if the easel had really collapsed and the painter appeared in the doorway. "So, whose house have I ended up in?" To begin with, the paintings told him nothing; first there was a light, dancing landscape with small ancient figures, which did not stop it being set somewhere near Paris; then there was a lakeside with a richly dressed woman holding an open letter and looking up at the smiling apparition of a young tradesman on his day off in the top corner. Anicet, who had thought he was looking at a disciple of Corot, felt disconcerted and looked for more clues; he saw a simply drawn house which faithfully represented *the House*, the one that cannot be dignified with this tender name without adding a possessive, the House which has been described with its roof, its windows, its door (only strangers see anything remarkable about it), this warm place somewhere in the world, you surprise me traveller when you find it has CLASS — this friendly corner where outside there are just stars and a garden fence.

At this point Anicet lost himself in early childhood memories of when dogs opened huge jaws, and the Earth was peopled with very gentle giants. The next canvas touched another level of his being; it showed a tall, thin adolescent whose hands were suffering from being empty, a boy who has not yet learned that bodies are beautiful, or the secret hidden in this vest a size too big — too pure to be harmonious. Finally, to remove all doubt from Anicet's mind, a still-life showing, besides the ambiguous interplay of a guitar and some bottles standing on a pedestal table, the entwined shapes of a pair of lovers whom neither the world nor the charm of ordinary objects could trouble any longer. He was so profoundly stupefied that by the time the word *blue* had arisen in his thoughts Anicet was far beyond being surprised at the amazing thought "I am in Blue's studio." Everyone had known this for an age. His first thought was to get away; he would tell the people up there an intruder had disturbed the theft and anyway... his second thought was pure curiosity, and then immediately came the third: the decision to make an even better job of stealing from Blue than from any other painter. Deep in his heart, the third thought had probably come before the others; it had such a strong pull, such a burning fire in his lungs, like oxygen after a long run in cold air. But the force outside our minds which disciplines our instincts had presented it as an Antiphrasis, then, since it carried no conviction, let the excuse of curiosity pass, and finally gave in to the basic desire which was destroying his resistance. It is easy to do damage to people who don't matter, but how sweetly one violates oneself by knowingly harming a friend! And Anicet felt for Blue the kind of love people take for admiration. The seductive power Blue exerted on him made Anicet aware what a rival he had in this painter for the conquest of Mirabelle. And yet, one could not deduce, from the feelings aroused by looking at Blue's miracles, what Mirabelle would feel; if only genius alone had worked with that elusive beauty! But who could be sure of finding the path to all hearts? Are there not paths towards the love of a woman which are opened by neither beauty nor valour?

To guess what effect Blue could have on Mire, one would need to apply one's full powers to knowing what effect they might have on a person. When Anicet tried to grasp how this approach would work on himself, his investigation was limited by his emotions. By analogy, he equated the feeling with that of waking as a child when you no longer know the names of familiar objects; you can recognise them, but part of them has faded into infinity. Or you find again the syllables which designate the accessories of everyday life, but it is the first time you have seen a table or a chair; everything looks new, surprising and eloquent to our hearts, and we must be on the point of discovering a fundamental truth. The most banal reality suddenly speaks directly to me with such a muffled tone that it brings tears to my eyes. The feeling that arises is the love of life suddenly provoked by the sight of a still-life. What human issue is at play behind these inert images? Nothing could be less expected to make one think of life, but here it is palpitating (how lovely that crude word is). What pain or joy lies at the heart of the artist that reveals it to us? You would think he was about to reach a dangerous crisis in his life. It is alive with a wonderful secret which communicates deep anxiety, transforming it for us so that we will never know what drama these tobacco tins mask, or what ecstasy these mandolins recall. Here there is only pure emotion, and it is so akin to the feeling lying dormant within us that it will rouse it, as the harmonic pitch rouses a mute vase at the far end of a room. This spell is inescapable, for we no longer know where it comes from.

What comes to us rings true — we cannot refute it. How we tremble suddenly at the sight of a pipe; what weakness puts us at the mercy... at the mercy of what?

Anicet burst out laughing unashamedly. "I have just been taking myself seriously," he said aloud, and his imprudence did not bring on a catastrophe. This piece of bravado gave him proof of his existence. Blue's seductiveness had for a moment distracted him from his own personality, but the sound of his voice was enough to give him back his sense of individuality.

Initially he had thought of destroying these works, which he found intimidating, but he also realised that to nullify them was nothing; he needed to find more powerful spells. The painter's fascinating power could be quite clearly explained: was he not making himself a substitute for our senses in interpreting the world? And who are we for ever in love with, if not these intermediaries? How could we not be charmed by someone who constantly offers a human equivalent for external things? Poor poets, trying to compete with your wretched verbal images! And yet there are cries that come from deeper in men's hearts than the easily reached zone where the love of coloured shapes holds sway. If only we knew how to give our instincts their true voice rather than the monotonous chanting of vocal cords, what power we could have over all our fellow men, whether or not their hair is the same length as ours! To test the idea, Anicet closed his eyes, felt the pang of jealousy and his insuperable fear of Blue's triumph, then desperately cast aside the form his mind offered to express these feelings, pushed down into his suffering till all he could feel in the universe was his inner burning, and let out the cry that automatically came to his lips; he intoned, very softly, as if someone else was speaking, watched intently by Anicet: "MY GOD". It came from his inner depths, and no one wished to laugh at it, but nothing, nothing could excuse these words, this fruit borne of habit. Mechanically Anicet added: "IT IS VERY STRANGE". But what was he talking about with the muffled voice of people we thought were dead who half wake up to reveal the secrets of the tomb? The other Anicet now understood that man's deepest voice carries none of the spells that are the stuff of poets. Words really matter very little to him. In Blue's canvases what most troubled Anicet was the sureness of his forms; chance never seemed to have taken charge of this or that. It was as frightening as an expert chemist who could consistently reproduce any natural entity. And is even that really intimidating? Could this confidence in one's science or art, which was implied by the creation of these forms, be compatible with seduction? When it comes to it, this level of skill is a bit of a blind alley. To move someone to the point of subjugation, one is better off relying on the clumsiness which invents a caress or a look as the moment dictates, some nervousness in speaking and hesitant gestures.

On one easel there was a big picture with a veil so carefully placed over it that this detail was enough to show how greatly the painter cared for this work. Anicet laid it bare with a quick movement of his hand, for he was keen to find proof right here of his conviction. With one glance he realised he had in front of him *Hymn to the Human Body*, the painting everyone was talking about without having seen it, in which Blue believed he had given the best he had. The young man sighed with relief; what came before his eyes was just a perfectly executed Academy piece, a figure of proportions with its ratios in well-known numbers. Anicet suddenly saw that Blue, in reaching perfection, had passed from the realm of love to that of death and glory. He pronounced the names of several great men, and smiled.

"You must tell me what you think of this picture… Hello, Anicet! What are you doing here, my friend, with a torch and a revolver? You see, I was bringing our dear Marquis to see my studio. I wanted to show him my *Hymn to the Human Body* which I see you have been looking at. What do you think of it? No, don't force it!"

Anicet mumbled some muddled compliment. Blue's appearing with the Marquis in tow scared him stiff. What would he say? He was blushing at the need to lie with no chance of being believed.

"Do not try to explain your presence here," said Blue, "we all have our little secrets and life would be impossible if the neighbours made a fuss about it. Won't you have a drink?"

Steps could be heard crossing the next room. Someone heavy was picking their way forward. Suddenly, like an owl in daylight, Boulard stepped into the light, flabbergasted to find himself before the tenants. But his fear changed to terror when he saw the Marquis's face.

"I'm so sorry boss," he said, "I did not know the painter was one of your friends. Otherwise you can be sure I would never have dared! I only got involved in this business with my mates when a tout put us on to it at the last minute. Nice job, you see. Never pass up an opportunity. You're frightened you'll put your foot in it, and then you make a blunder with something else. Oh dear. Then, we have a new recruit to get going on the job, this young man and… But you know him too? Well then I've had it! He'll have told you everything; that we weren't planning to cut you in, we were working for an American. Oh blimey! Pretty smart, all the same. Well, you get a bit tired of always giving the biggest share to gentlemen in smart suits who are scared of getting their hands dirty. You see, boss, it's always us that do the heavy lifting. Well then. You shouldn't hold it against us. You're a clever man."

"Just start by clearing off," said the Marquis, "this time I'll let it pass. But don't let me catch you again. Off you go. The gentleman (he pointed to Anicet) will stay with us."

Boulard backed out. Once they were quite sure he had gone, the Marquis turned to Blue and said:

"Let me explain."

"Not at all, not at all, my friend, that is your business. Have a drink."

"So," said the Marquis, "you have got yourself attached to my little team, Anicet, have you? That is most amusing."

Anicet did not deny it. The Marquis repeated, with a thoroughly vexed look, "that is most amusing," and added to himself, "now how can I get rid of this indiscreet youngster who knows too much about me?"

BLUE (*he has meanwhile gone back to stand in front of* Hymn to the Human Body): It really amounts to nothing, doesn't it?

MIRABELLE'S "AT-HOME"

The dress code is fixed; the servants are to wear masks, like the guests. This is how an unknown newcomer slipped into the house to replace Eugène who had taken the opportunity to go to the cinema. Unknown? Not really; it was Nick Carter, the detective, so cleverly made up it is a pity no one could admire the fine handiwork. He hung up Anicet's cape beside the other five, and politely pointed out to the young man under his breath that he should adjust his eye-mask before going in, as it was riding up on his forehead.

Let's see: Blue, Chipre, Pol, Miracle, the Marquis; and Baptiste?

"Are you alone?" asked Blue; "how come Baptiste is not on time? It is most unlike him." Anicet could feel that his words relieved a lengthy silence; the assembled company were too impatient for Mire to appear to be able to engage in small talk.

"Which way will she come in?" asked Pol.

The Marquis pointed out the room's three doors.

"That's not possible," said Pol, "she always arrives via some mysterious route. She arises. Remember."

"We are at rue de la Baume now," Della Robbia replied, "and Madame Gonzales is married."

"I never believed that story," said Chipre, "Mirabelle is no ordinary woman, after all."

"That is what we thought before we knew her real identity."

"I tell you she is a solar myth."

"A mental conception."

"A fixed idea."

"An image."

"A symbol."

"Oh, be quiet," said Anicet, "she is a woman of flesh and blood, or we would not find her so beautiful."

"I'm sure," said Pol, "she is going to come out of the piano. Pianos are so lovely; if I was rich I would have a piano."

He lifted the lid and ran his fingers along the keyboard. A note that was stuck sounded hollow. Pol recoiled in terror.

"What shall we call her?" asked Miracle.

"Madame."

"And her husband," Pol added, "we will call Pedro."

Baptiste was ushered in. They scarcely had time to notice the look of deep affliction on his face before the big door at the end split apart and slid back to either side. The size of the salon was doubled, and in the new half Mirabelle could be seen beside her prince consort. She was wearing a black muslin skirt with a high, wide belt, and her only upper garments were two lawyer's door-plaques held in place by a chain wound round her several times. Her legs were bare, and her feet shod in small mother-of-pearl slippers like the ink-pots they sell at the seaside. She was adorned with a single piece of jewellery: a long, heavy necklace of shells as uneven as the mood of the sky, and less sonorous than the sea. She had her hair in the latest fashion and carried a big copper fireguard as a fan. Her appearance was accompanied by a polka emanating from the white and gold belly of one of those sideboards equipped with little dolled-up statues which beat time with their arms. Suddenly a Roman candle lit up in a Meissen vase and cast green gloom over the seven masks, while in the adjoining room a yellow flame sprang from a stone carved head, and wrapped itself around the couple. A naked cherub on a column holding a garland of flowers threw it down, jumped to the ground, knelt before the fireplace where the flap was open and shouted: "Oh ho up there!" The distant voice of a chimney-sweep replied: "Ah ha down there!" and the child disappeared. A white goat came past between the couple and the assembled company, bowed, and went out again using its horns to open the door. This was followed by cyclists dressed as shepherds, a Neapolitan rope-dancer, and a pantomime performed by seals in full costume; then all the lights went out.

At that moment the Gonzaleses were projected on to a screen, which had till then been invisible, standing on the steps of the Roule church on their wedding day. The titles announced to the esteemed audience a presentation of the couple's life, offering an example for young people in the future. First came Pedro Gonzales, son of poor workers from Córdoba. This was an excuse to show a few views of Córdoba, its resources and sights, and the guests were told the number of inhabitants of the town. The day-to-day life of the Gonzales parents was shown, a model couple in their miserable hovel. Madame Gonzales was seen doing the washing, wiping the noses of her seven children, making an eighth one and praying to the Holy Spirit whose image hung from the head of the bed. Monsieur Gonzales was shown working himself to the bone on various building sites, then one evening when he came home, listening to the emigration agent promising marvels and mountains. Then came the family's journey and their domestic virtue during the crossing: the youngest Gonzales, namely Pedro, sharing his bread with sick old men. Then California, the Gold Rush, the father's tragic death, crushed by I forget what, Pedro's difficult childhood, and the hard work and ingenuity with which from the age of twelve he dragged his mother, sisters and brothers free from their upright, hard-working poverty. This paragon of a son was seen nursing his sick mother, protecting his sisters from vice and getting them married, reclaiming his older brother from drink and having him take holy orders. It went on for a full half-hour of good deed after good deed, till he ended up in prison. There he was shown learning mathematics. Then he escaped thanks to his talent for playing dead.

Next he was seen building up a nice wad of cash robbing coaches, moving into speculation and amassing quite a fortune, of which a sketchy idea was given via a few views of his properties; then coming to live in France, seeing Mire and falling in love with her, going into a decline, calling the doctor, declaring his love, being accepted with great sadness by Mirabelle with words something like this:

"I am of unknown origin; my past is lost in the depths of time. Never try to find out anything about my childhood, or it will be over between us."

Now she told him about her young life. The story began in Marseille, in a hotel beside the port. The girl was shown sitting on an unmade bed, her face expressing despair at some unknown cause. She got up and walked around the room. Sometimes she tore off great strips of wallpaper with her fingers. With much emotion she stroked a little child-sized satin skirt. From time to time she lifted her eyes and stared reproachfully at the sky — the scene she is alluding to is shown: in a sumptuous palace in Italy an old man surprises a young man reading Aretino. He gets very angry, throws the banned book into the lagoon, and drives the adolescent away with appalling curses. The girl in Marseille sighed, and wrote on a sheet of exercise-book paper:

"Farewell. In death as in life, I am yours, Mirabelle."

The scene then changed to the back room of a café. A black-eyed fisherman entered with the body of a drowned girl over his shoulder. He laid her down on the table, nodded and took from his pocket the photo of his dead fiancée. The sailor was very upset and in a moment of confusion said vile things about the girl he had rescued. She opened her eyes and we saw it was Mirabelle.

From now on she wore black. A mysterious protector ensured her life was comfortable. But everywhere she went men caught fire and were consumed. Stone-throwing mothers drove the innocent girl out of a village in Asturias where she had gone to bury her painful secret.

A little later, she was watching the sun sink into the sea and thinking of her mysterious destiny, and of two lovers she had not managed to be cruel to, who had paid for her weakness with their lives. Just then, a man with hair as red as the sunset caught her attention with his remarkable bearing. He lit a cigarette with the last rays of the sun. Then he stretched out his arms, unhooked a few clouds, narrowed his eyes, and dropped all of them except one which he fixed in his buttonhole. Suddenly he leaned over to Mirabelle, pulled her to him and made her a mother.

The next scene showed the young mother nursing her baby, while its father, Harry James, was guzzling the christening sweets. Next came Harry James with a pedlar, trading his son for a fine meerschaum pipe, Mirabelle's despair, and the anger of her lover who went out, stole a car, and disappeared. At this point in the story Pedro Gonzales reappeared in tears, kissing his fiancée's hands, and the show ended with a portrait of the couple who, with the lights back on, advanced towards their guests as if nothing out of the ordinary had accompanied their entrance.

This was the cue for a meandering conversation, long, unfocused, vain and annoying, in which Mirabelle never missed an opportunity to mention her husband, to put him forward and show him an embarrassing amount of affection. She was playing with her guests like a cat with a mouse. She repeated, "My husband this, my husband that…" with an exasperating laugh. Sometimes when she noticed a furious scowl, or someone's lips moving, she closed her eyes voluptuously and held out the fingers of a hand with no ring, a naked hand. If she had talked a little longer to one of the masks, she corrected the favour with a *we*, which united her with Pedro Gonzales as she nonchalantly leaned against him. She was particularly sweet with Anicet; it surprised Mire that he could have come through an adventure as dangerous as their last encounter.

"Who was it told me, Monsieur Anicet, that you were injured in an accident? There's no truth in that, is there?"

"Absolutely none, madame, life is horribly dull and I haven't a chance of even the slightest accident."

Curiosity may be as hard to manage as a cat, but there are times when you have to keep quiet. However composed Mire may have seemed, she could not stay still, and her movements criss-crossed in figures of eight which looped around the point where Anicet stood in silence.

A servant kept coming in on the flimsiest pretext. He was thinking: "I must be able to uncover some kind of secret here. It is all too remarkable to be natural: this is a plenary meeting, so what do these entertainments mean? I am quite lost. But I am not wasting my time; it will be worth having been this crazy Marina's lover since she has been getting Monsieur Gonzales to confess about what goes on here. All the same, I do not really understand the relationship between all these people. It is a pity I can't see their faces. The only one who let himself be recognised is young Anicet, who I certainly keep running into. If I knew Madame Gonzales was his mistress it would make things a lot clearer."

Patience has its limits, and the guests were starting to look askance at the too-happy husband. Jealousy lay dormant in them with the exception of the Marquis della Robbia, whose concerns were divided between Mirabelle and Anicet. It was pretty bad that the youngster had such detailed knowledge of the gang the Marquis was running. We are just too unsure of ourselves to have confidence in someone else. Anicet could turn the brilliant diplomat's life upside down any time. He wanted to be free of this threat, and the attention Mire was giving to this dangerous holder of his secrets did nothing to dissuade Della Robbia that he should get rid of Anicet. But how to find an opportunity? It was as slippery as a live fish between his fingers.

Wishing to avoid or delay the storm, Mirabelle remarked that Baptiste was looking pale. "What has happened to you, my friend?" she enquired, "you look exhausted. You are not ill, are you?"

"Yes," Blue added, "Baptiste arrived late; he cannot be his usual self."

"It wasn't me," said Baptiste, "it was my train that was late. I have come in from the country and I hope you will excuse my lack of conversational brilliance; today I was at the funeral of my best friend; it seems you knew him, madame, he was called Harry James."

Mire cried out softly and fainted into her husband's arms. They rallied round, but she came to quite quickly. Her eyes first sought the man who was holding her. "Oh, it's you Pierre. What a fool I am! What terrible news! No one has ever done me both so much good and so much harm as the man whose name you just spoke, Monsieur Ajamais, and I no longer know if I should hate him or weep for him. I would be in despair at this moment were it not for the support I find in this model husband. But what did the poor man die of? I assure you I feel strong enough to hear about it."

"Madame, Harry James preferred death to the slow, grinding procession of days. He chose the hotel room, where so many crime-page stories end, as the most appropriate weapon for shutting off the light from those who no longer know what to do with it. I will spare you the details, they are all as searing as the sound of a saw."

"Harry killed himself? I can't believe it. What had happened to him?"

"The journalists are wondering about that, but they reassure themselves that it was an accident. A young man James had seen recently told me he had been acting strangely. 'Believe me if you will,' he said, 'well, he was as lively as a lark at party after party. We were living it up; completely natural. Joking around. There were women. And in the middle of the night he would start staring at nothing and you couldn't get another word out of him. Quite a character!' That is all we know for now."

There was a long silence; then Anicet whistled through his teeth and said: "Do you think suicide makes any difference to our cruel indecision? What we find satisfying in his thinking is this aspect of its being a solution, this definitiveness, which none of our actions has in such an obvious way. But maybe we are wrong; why should this be the *only* deed which allows us to act on ourselves when everything else is ineffective? If killing oneself really gets us anywhere, there must be other ways to resolve the problem of life."

"If you are right," Baptiste went on, "Harry James knew those other solutions. He had examined them, and you know which one he chose. A line in one of his letters troubles me. He speaks of a mysterious thing he tried out. Then it ended, black hole. A big silence, and then the three lines in the paper announcing his death."

Gonzales said: "I just can't understand suicide. I have several times found myself broke, dishonoured, buried. I never thought of skipping it. And you can see I am still here, with a beautiful wife, money, a Paris mansion, property in California, and thirsty, yes devilishly thirsty!"

Drinks were handed round.

Mirabelle drew Baptiste aside. "He was your friend," she said, "did he ever talk about me?"

"I couldn't swear to it. He didn't often talk about women. But I think I remember a story that could have something to do with you."

"Tell me."

"Harry James had a mistress at the time who was a sad girl he never touched because, he said, she was pregnant. The poor thing, who was crazy about him, punched herself in the belly to prove it wasn't true. But she really was expecting a child, and she died as a result. I asked my friend if he had always been so repelled by pregnancy. He said no, it went back to an earlier affair. 'That woman,' he said, 'was pregnant by me, and what I found repellent was that she endlessly talked about our future. Disgust at that merged in my mind with the idea of a pregnant woman.'"

"Monsieur Ajamais, do you know how cruel your stories are? That was most deeply hurtful."

Mire left. Everyone present was put out by the tone of her voice when she spoke to her husband. The only subject of conversation now was conjugal contentment, and examples were discussed till two in the morning.

When the masks gathered outside on the street they brought with them incoherent anger. The Marquis, who thought he could see the opportunity he was after, said it was essential they should talk. No one thought to disagree. Boulard's café seemed too noisy a place to gather in judgement. Miracle suggested a place he knew with a room they could be sure was secure. They set off behind him without spotting a shadow which left the Gonzales mansion and followed in the tracks of the little group, having checked his pistol was in order.

PRELUDE, CHORALE AND FUGUE

The whole gang walked back up the boulevards in the wake of Ange Miracle, then along rue du 4 Septembre, rue Réaumur and Boulevard de Sébastopol. "Oh, I'm so sleepy," Pol sighed, ill at ease in his hired suit, "where are we going like this? To Les Halles?" He did not get an answer. The seven men in top hats did not even surprise the rare people they passed, or the last street girls who were now without hope. "Come on," said one of them teasingly, "what kind of way is that to party?" They turned into the rue aux Ours. The pneumatic clock said three o'clock. A steam whistle made Anicet turn round; like a bad omen a real goods train with a real steam engine was slowly crossing the rue Etienne Marcel. The wagons were bursting at the seams with cabbages and carrots. "Here we are," said Miracle. On the door was a sign:

INSTITUTION FOR YOUNG PEOPLE

Ange gave a special whistle. There was a short wait. Then the door groaned gently on its hinges and they saw a half-dressed girl who was taking out her last hair-curler with her left hand. She drew back; "You are not alone, my Angel?"

"Forgive me, Elodie, I need to have a serious conversation with these gentlemen,

and nowhere seemed private enough for our discussion. Take us into the studio —
there is no one there, is there?"

"What an idea! Luckily it's the holidays and papa is away. I'm a bit scared though.
Come in gentlemen. This is certainly mysterious. This way. It won't take too long
will it? Have the torch. You will stay afterwards, won't you? On the right."

Through the darkness they had come to a huge room. A carbon filament lamp
gave out a feeble light which revealed just a few school benches, a block of drawing
paper and some window rails. The seven companions could only gradually make
anything out in the surrounding gloom. They were in the drawing area, a studio
with big windows, with plaster casts they could hardly see, models of arms, Greek
faces, the Discobolus, some carved stone flowers, Michelangelo's slaves and, on the
ground, several busts, torsos, reject heads, gouged out, decapitated or scalped,
demonstrating through their black wounds the emptiness of human conception.
Everything was covered with charcoal or chalk dust. Elodie withdrew; they sat
down; they formed groups. One leaned against the window bar. Anicet perched on
the professor's table.

"Friends," said the Marquis della Robbia, "what has always brought us together
is a feeling, a taste, for putting ourselves on the line, a theatrical cast of mind. Here
we are, seven of us, like something out of place in a room. It is not for want of
anything better to do that we have set ourselves a goal in life, but from the desire
not to achieve any other. We were seeking to constrain ourselves, and we have
gathered here to reduce our hopes yet further. We invented this ridiculous rivalry. I
imagine we attach some importance to our respect for each other and wanted a field
in which we would test each other simultaneously with matched weapons. I shall
say nothing about Mirabelle and what she may have become for us. But in the
course of one round, the game's purpose changed; it turned on its heels and a quite
different adventure has been offered to our desires. The narrowest of horizons is
always broadened by a turn in the road. In fact, what does it matter that a woman's

eyes are merely a mirror-lure for skylarks? There are emotions which make it worth existing, and the fact that they seem despicable to the men we were before we felt them does not make them any less indispensable. A new player has appeared who had not been predicted by the rules of the game, and he promises to make our pastime impossible. We had anticipated everything, except a husband. The husband. It is your task to decide how we react to the husband."

There was quite a commotion. Chipre suggested kidnapping. Pol talked of a seven-man suicide, using gas. Ange requested there be no violence; one can do so much harm with a more subtle approach. Blue yelled "Dagger!" Anicet played with his watch-chain and swung his legs back and forth under the table. It was Baptiste who imposed silence and then spoke:

"I know two ways of separating a woman from a man, which are to kill the man, or to bankrupt him. The latter is rather cruel. It reminds me of a flycatcher. Besides which, it is not very easy to accomplish. Shall I reveal that I had already been trying something along those lines? But I could not take action directly. I had to set up ten or twenty intermediaries who were unaware of what was going on. Financial deals are more convoluted than the Bois de Vincennes. The machine I set in motion has gone beyond my control. I have no idea what the outcome will be. If you are a man of resolve, you cannot make do with waiting for a problematic outcome. We must kill. It is simple: kill him."

There was a very long discussion. A confused discussion, in which the anguished voice of Ange Miracle stood out most of all, calling for gentleness, gentleness. Chipre was up for poison, the Marquis for a paid assassin. Blue went on crying "Dagger!" Pol was frightened and chopped and changed. Anicet said nothing. Since they kept asking him, he answered with various contradictory proverbs. Baptiste repeated: "We must kill him," so insistently that in the end everyone agreed they must kill him but could not agree on the method. The Marquis observed that the choice of weapon should be left to the killer. A rising discomfort troubled their hearts. The plasterwork on the walls took on a more sinister aspect. Someone suggested drawing lots. Eagerly they all seized on the idea — one in seven is a very low chance. "I'll draw the lots," said Baptiste. He had picked a sheet of drawing paper out of a box and was folding it in eight. He pressed the folds down with the back of his hand, then slowly tore along the lines. It made a rasping sound. Everyone watched him carefully. He mimed the actions of a fountain pen: removing the cap, the thread that unscrews, the pen coming out like sunrise, testing the nib on the eighth piece of paper, shaking it to get the ink flowing. Then Baptiste wrote out the seven names on the seven pieces of paper in copperplate. Pol held out the chalk for him to dry the ink. "No need," said Baptiste, "my writing dries by itself." Delicately he folded each paper in four, and put them all in a plaster urn which Blue had just found. Unanimously except for one, his own vote, Pol was chosen to do the draw. He came forward trembling, then suddenly moved to run away. The Marquis had to catch him and hold him in place. In silence he pulled out one lot, unfolded it, and read, with obvious delight: ANICET.

The relief was such that they all started talking very fast, while Anicet swung his legs back and forth at high speed. Apparently composed, Baptiste thrust his hand into the urn and pulled out the handful of pieces of paper. He unfolded them and put them in his pocket one by one without anyone noticing; on five of the lots could be read the word ANICET; only the last one bore the word BAPTISTE.

They all had something to say on the theme of "If it had been me". They gave advice to their proxy. They slapped him on the shoulder. They were all very friendly to him. The Marquis della Robbia, whose Italian accent surfaced from time to time, was particularly affectionate. He offered Anicet all the resources at his disposal to carry out this difficult task. "Thank you," said Anicet, "I will only ask for one thing: since I would find it unpleasant to go home today out of pure sentimentality, and I have to get this nasty job out of the way this evening, I would be grateful if you would offer me hospitality for the day. I shall not be in your way for long, as I shall rest and then leave on the stroke of eight." It was clear this proposal suited the Marquis. He rubbed his hands, laughed to himself a few times, and shook Anicet by the hand. "My friend," he said, "my friend." They decided to leave in small groups. Anicet and the Marquis were the first to go downstairs. Elodie opened the door for them. She asked Anicet if his name was not Jacques, as he looked like a young soldier she had known during the war. Anicet answered that he was called Jacques and left, leaving the girl standing on the porch thoroughly confused.

On the pavement opposite, a man was walking up and down and stopping to yawn from time to time. Anicet hardly noticed him, but the Marquis glanced over at him and was pleased to recognise Nick Carter, the detective. He hastened his steps and noted that Carter had decided to trail them after a brief hesitation. The morning smelt of fresh milk. "Rosy-fingered dawn," said Anicet, "is just a rag-seller with a tangle of hair and a face smudged with blue ashes." Being close to the market of Les Halles made him hungry. The high-pitched ring of the metal-clad wheels on the cobbles of the boulevard gave him the illusion of great clarity of mind. "I have slept well," he assured himself, and felt he was looking fresh. They walked through Les Halles.

"If you will excuse me," said the Marquis, "may I leave you for a moment by this vegetable stall?"

"Fine."

Anicet looked around. The Marquis saw their pursuer, after a moment's confusion, opt for Anicet, and keep an eye on him from the neighbouring aisle. Out of sight against a pillar, he scrawled some words on a scrap of paper. It was quickly done, and he read:

"This evening, at 9 p.m., Gonzales the banker will be assassinated by an anarchist. You have been warned!"

He folded the message and slipped it into a little business-card envelope. The Marquis addressed it:

MONSIEUR CARTER

In town

He whistled to a passing boy, and handed him the envelope with a few instructions. Then he went back to Anicet and they walked on together.

The detective following them was coming up to the rue de Rivoli when he felt a hand in his pocket. He grabbed a child's wrist. "Oh sir, I didn't take anything," the young messenger cried, "I just handed you a message. You can check, there's no record against my name, oh Lord, my poor blind mother!" Nick could see the child was telling the truth and let go of him. "Who gave you this?" he asked. "A lady, and she said you would give me twenty sous." The detective read the message and was completely astonished. A lady? "What was she like?" he asked again. "In mourning with a big veil hiding her face. My twenty sous?" He got the sous. But the man Nick was following had disappeared.

The Marquis della Robbia's house on Avenue d'Antin is familiar to everyone in Paris. It had been transported from Italy stone by stone, and is the house where Romeo saw Juliet for the first time; two marble plaques are let into the floor of the grand salon to mark the position of these characters' feet at the moment they first exchanged looks. The Marquis's wonderful collections fill much of the house. He settled Anicet in a small drawing-room on the first floor. "You have everything to hand here for sleeping, writing, or doing nothing. If you wish to eat or to see me, you only need to ring. I shall put Othello at your service; he is a negro, mute, and faithful. Farewell."

Once he was alone, Anicet looked around the room he was in. He was pleased to observe that everything in it was vile; every chair, every little pen-holder was an *objet d'art*. He found that so ridiculous that he was quite cheered up. He tore off some blotting-paper, soaked it in ink, and drew a German moustache on the

Roman Antinous perched on the porphyry mantelpiece. Then he lay down on the sofa and fell asleep.

He woke at around three in the afternoon, rang for Othello, had himself served a princely meal and talked to the mute valet in this vein: "To know, in the common meaning of the word, Othello, is merely to know how to name things or to learn how to do so. However, we can know the object without any word being linked in our mind to its representation. That fact leads back to the earlier case. Pass me the pâté, dear man: representation is only the word of the mind, and can we think outside words? So to know is simply to recognise. Truffles really are quite divine.

"Philosophical knowledge posits a series of mental operations that can be reduced to generalisations. I know an object if I have defined its generic properties, and if I have categorised it in relation to a higher order of knowledge (I know it and unknow it by a process of elimination).

"Does it bother you being mute, Othello? Another piece of that chicken. The operation of knowing therefore seems to come earlier than is commonly perceived. I'm not saying that to offend you. But a philosopher does not grasp the fact directly either; he observes only its shadow and does not say *this is this*, but *this is not that, not that* etc. After which, being pleased with himself, he makes the same mistake as his neighbour, the ordinary man, and says: I know AB because I recognise A and B which are already known to me.

"Wonderful this Nuits, my friend, what a Nuits!★ Your master is a happy fool. To analyse knowledge without visualising its object comes up against an obstacle: this notion of purposefulness which we struggle in vain to defend ourselves against.

"I am sure, Othello, that if you fell in love, love would give you a tongue, or your heart would speak if your lips were closed. If we consider a phenomenon for the first time, it cannot be so new that we do not find in ourselves all the elements it is made up of, and those are what we recognise before we think of what is new to us, which is the arrangement of those elements. When we fix our thinking on this point, our unconscious has already delineated from sensory data (comprehensible, already known) the inner object which is the correlative image of the external object. So our consciousness only acquires recognition and not knowledge.

"An era's degree of civilisation can be measured by the success of its sorbets. What wonderful times we are living in!

"So there is an abuse of language in the use of the verb *to know*. It is only recognition that we can study. That consists of stating the correlation (not the identity) which exists between the inner object and the external object, and comprises a judgement which can be formulated as follows: *The object which shows a correlation with my memory A' is the same as gave birth to A', which is to say A.*

"A dash of champagne. Here we find a new difficulty: if, to know or recognise A, we must compare it with A', it is evident that A' must previously be known to us — *a priori* there is no more reason for inner realities (developed in our unconscious) to be known to us than external realities — the problem has merely been displaced."

"You are not taking the consequences of your premises very far," said the mute, "and your language is neither clear nor orderly."

Anicet kicked him out of the room. Then he wrote a letter.

My dearest, if you do not see me within three days, get back together with Georges and burn our letters. With regard to our little theatre project etc., best give up on that. With much tenderness, MARCEL.

The envelope was addressed to:

Mademoiselle MARIE MANTE
7 rue Lepic, PARIS.

THINGS HAVE THEIR TURN

"Marina, do you love diamonds? The ones the size of your fingernail, you know? You're not saying anything; you're just looking at the floor. Marina, do you love me as much as you love diamonds?"

"Be quiet, you sentimental thing."

"Don't call me sentimental when you have your hair down like that. We can't always be talking about parties, first nights or stock prices."

"What makes you need to talk all the time?"

"Well I thought I was being nice to you. I force myself to talk to you, literally force myself. But in fact I have nothing to say. I never have anything to say to you. Does one ever have anything to say? It's all because of your hair."

In the classic adulterer's halfway house Pedro Gonzales is silent. He notices that the light is changing. He is lying: he does have something to say, something very curious. What if everything was about to crash? His confession teeters like a tear on the tip of an eyelash. His fingers are playing with Marina Merov's curls. A great silence brings peace to his soul. Such cowardice, and the sun going down.

"My love."

"It must be very late, isn't it?"

"How would I know? When I'm with you time flies by so fast."

"You would never spend your life with me."

"Oh Piotr, did you ever offer me that? My friend, why were you talking to me about diamonds?"

"Because, Marina… I don't know. Just an idea."

Silence reclaims its place. There is a bronze of Vercingetorix on a stand. Over the mantelpiece, a plaster Cupid and Psyche after Canova gives a flattering idea of humanity. A big sigh comes before the storm.

"Marina, in my country men live like brutes. They live off what they can lay their hands on. The women have very white hands. There are liqueurs which are deeper than wells. It lasts as long as it lasts. One day there is nothing left except your riding pistols, a saddle, a fast horse and the desert. You set off for somewhere else and start all over again."

"What a wonderful life!"

"More or less what mine has been. Right now, I have just enough left to get to the New World. With the various presents I have given you, we'll have enough to live on for a few months. Do you accept?"

"I don't understand. Don't joke about things like that, it's not funny."

"I am not joking. I am broke. Bankrupt. It's as simple as that. But at least I have you and I'm keeping you."

Silence. I recognise it, it's him, it's silence. The woman is looking at nothing. What is she thinking about? Very slowly her right hand (how beautiful her right hand is) lifts the strands of her hair. She is putting her hair back up. The shoulders of a woman doing her hair are more moving than… the hairpins on the stucco mantelpiece. Marina's fingers are struggling with the hairpins. Her clumsiness and nervousness make the gathering darkness more noticeable.

"Could you put the light on, my dear? I can't see anything in this light."

The wall lamp goes on, to the left of the mirror. The bulb is set in a glass orchid. Marina's reflection looks annoyed. What is happening? Pedro does not understand.

He stays sitting on the sofa with his hands unoccupied.

A touch of rice powder, a bit of lipstick, more hair-fixing. Her hand smooths a rogue eyebrow. It is quicker to put a hat on than to take it off. Why do violets make one think of break-ups? One more look in the mirror. Her umbrella. At the door, the lady turns round. She already has her right glove on; she looks down at her left hand where a sparkling ring catches the light. "My friend," she says, "I shall always remember you." It is over.

One-two-three, one-two-three (waltz). It is a mistake to think it is difficult to get up from a very low, soft sofa. We tidy up out of habit. Put on our overcoat; I was about to leave my stick behind. And my key? Pah, I'll just have to knock on the door now. With that sort of woman it's no good being surprised. Don't give it any thought. The stairs *were* a bit steep there. It really didn't bother me, really not. It's just that I would have thought she was a bit *wilder*. Luckily I have several strings to my bow. I still have my wife, Mirabelle, my thing. With her, I have guarantees. God willing, we shall still have a fine life over there.

L'intransigeant! Thank you.

Nothing new. Come on, I've got till tomorrow morning. The world is wide. It's a lovely night. Taxi! Not free. Too bad. Really, these soft collars *are* comfortable in summer.

> *Fine time of night,*
> *Makes our heads light.*

Toot, toot! Taxi! Rue de la Baume? No? Oh well, it is nice walking. I have plenty of time. Mirabelle. These delivery tricycles look good. Mirabelle, Mirabelle. It's a name that makes one close one's eyes.

In Paris, in the summer, nightfall is as sweet as a peach. A man can walk around town with great calm in his heart.

"Is Madame in?"

"Madame is waiting for you, sir, in the little blue drawing-room."

All the splendour of the world has taken refuge in the crystal pendants of the chandelier, in the silver of the mirrors, Mirabelle's jewellery and her eyes. Madame Gonzales sits half-turned towards him; her naked shoulders toy with the great fan of orange feathers stroking them. "You're pretty late back. You see, I dressed up for you."

"Mirabelle, you have a name that makes one close one's eyes."

"You do say lovely things. Here, take my hand."

The fan counts the seconds: happy people — have no story, happy people — have no story, happy people — happy people. "Mirabelle, we're going away. For ever. Just the two of us."

"What has got into you, my friend? You have been reading the wrong sort of books."

"Mire, I am broke. Tomorrow my bank will stop paying."

"Do you mean that? Is there nothing you can do about it?"

"The only thing is to get away. But you know I have not been stupid. All my money, millions, has been put into your name. Our marriage contract is for separate funds. We shall go and live in America and be rich and happy."

"Do you believe that?"

"What does this world matter that we're leaving behind? Over there we shall have property the size of kingdoms."

"You are out of your mind, my dear friend. Would you put my fan on the side table?"

"There you are. Mire, I am not joking."

"Do I look as if I find it funny? Don't think I am going to put up with the results of your bad investments. I have obligations, relationships, my own life. What do you think I would do out there in your colonies?"

"But Mire, I have to go."

"Well then, goodbye. You have generously made me rich. Everything is nicely arranged."

"Mire."

"Let's have supper; it is high time we ate. Don't look so sheepish, my dear, think of the servants."

"Mire."

"Let go of my wrist. You look ugly when you are flushed."

"Mire, the money, my money."

"Oh my, what a mean spirit you are, my dear! All the same, I won't hold you back. You have all your limbs; you are strong. It won't be the first time you've remade your fortune."

"Mire, life, my life! Is everything over, everything? So this one too escapes me. It is too much to bear."

"Don't shout. You are getting worked up…"

"Oh Mire, do you know how much you've hurt me?"

"Please don't make a scene! My word, I believe you're crying. I am surprised, I would have thought you were the last man to be capable of getting hysterical. How wrong one can be about people!"

The man has his head in his hands. He looks as if he is about to burst. He walks over and opens the door to his study; when he has gone through, he can be heard sobbing. The door closes.

Mire picks up her fan. She holds it and looks at herself for a long time in the mirror. A servant brings in a card on a tray. "Show him in." She waves her fan back and forth; then she shuts it, looks in the mirror and reopens her fan. Anicet is shown in. He is wearing a suit.

"We haven't had dinner yet, my friend, but you're not interrupting us. Would you like to join us? No? You have already eaten?"

"Thank you so much, but I'm not hungry."

"My dear, everyone knows you are in love with me; and a man in love who does not eat cannot keep going. I won't be able to boast of you any more."

"Madame."

"Do call me Mirabelle. My husband has no problem with that. Oh dear, don't look at me like that; it is ugly. What is happening to men this evening?"

"Mire."

"Call me Mire with the silver eyes. I like that. It is a long time since anyone called me that, and just now I am crazy for compliments. Quite crazy."

"Mire with the silver eyes."

"It is the name my friend Guillaume★ used to call me. But he went and died. He was very dear to me. What were you saying?"

"It cannot go on like this. It has been going on for a long time. We must…"

"Oh dear, please don't say the same thing again. My husband is nicer than you. Just now he said to me: 'You have a name that makes one close one's eyes.' Isn't that pretty? You too once wrote me a lovely little madrigal. Yes, it was lovely; I'm not exaggerating. I don't remember the words very well but… quite lovely."

"Mire, please stop; I swear I cannot go on."

"Sit down."

"This is going to turn out badly Mire. You must come with me."

"Oh no, not you as well? But we haven't got to that stage."

"Life is at stake, do you realise?"

"A child, you really are a child. Dear boy, before using words like that, you are supposed to make a speech with three proper arguments. Where did you go to school?"

"Listen, the sea has broken the dykes. I am bringing you this news. Give me your mouth."

"Oh you are seductive! Careful with my dress. Hey now, just lips. That's enough.

I almost thought something bad might happen. You need to realise, Anicet, my husband is in the next room."

"He is in the study?"

"He is in the study."

"I am going to kill him."

"Go right ahead. But not too much noise, will you?"

"Kiss me again."

"No, leave me alone, you're crumpling my dress! You clumsy thing, it will show."

Madame Gonzales escaped, opened the study door a crack and said: "My dear, Monsieur Anicet wants to speak with you. I'll show him in. See if you can calm him down; he seems rather agitated." There was the sound of a chair being moved, a few words, and then silence. Mirabelle took Anicet by the shoulders and pushed him into the other room. Then, having shut the door, she leaned against the wall to get her breath back. "Ah," she sighed, "that gave me a fright! You are so weak, girl. All these men churn you up." She quickly adjusted her clothes, picked up her fan and smiled to herself. She looked at the door and muttered wryly: "What's going to happen in there?"

In there were two men. Two men a bit like those toys with lead ballast which always come back to a vertical position. The fatter one was very pale, the thinner one was very red. Anicet noticed that the top of the inkstand on the desk was a bust of Napoleon wearing a laurel wreath. Gonzales noticed that Anicet's hand was moving towards his pistol pocket. "I gather you want to speak with me? I can tell you this is a very bad moment. But then, there's nothing you can do about that. I'm going to ask you something indiscreet. Please don't take it badly — you cannot understand. Please give me a straight answer. It doesn't matter any longer; only, if you say yes, I can give you one or two bits of advice, and tell you a story. A story, well, that is a bit of a crude word. So: are you my wife's lover? I swear it doesn't bother me. Tell me."

"Well no, sir, Mirabelle is not my mistress. But she will be, don't you doubt it, once I have killed you."

"Oh, did you come to kill me? That is useless. Lend me your revolver a minute."

"What?"

"Just lend me your revolver a minute. Don't you dare? I can perfectly well kill myself myself, you know. Give me the pistol. What is the risk to you?"

"Simply that you would prefer my death to yours. But then, you are right; what am I risking? Go on, kill one of us."

Pedro Gonzales took the pistol and tossed it in his hand. It was a woman's weapon, with a mother-of-pearl butt, quite a jewel. The banker cocked it, then turned it very slowly between his fingers and pointed it at Anicet. There was time to count to thirty without rushing. Then Gonzales made a quick semi-circular move and put the barrel in his mouth. It was like a bouquet. Anicet stepped back, but got slightly splashed. The body's fall had been quite dignified. The young man picked up his pistol and wiped it on the table covering.

Footsteps and words could be heard in the next room. Several people seemed to be discussing what to do; men. Anicet opened the door; he saw Mirabelle, who had conveniently fainted, on the sofa; a chambermaid was fussing over her. In the middle of the room was a group of policemen led by the detective Carter. He looked at the blood on Anicet's collar, the pistol in Anicet's hand, then at Anicet himself. He glanced into the study, saw a shape on the floor, and said with some satisfaction: "Please come with me, sir."

13

THE BODY CAGED

Whichever way you turn there are only walls. Image of life. Anicet did not feel very bothered by his new situation. If there had not been these walks down the corridor, the confrontations, the detective sometimes being so exhausting, the whole stupid business, Anicet would have felt fine in his prison. In one go all his worries had evaporated; his head was free, if his body wasn't; he could watch time passing very slowly along the walls. He relished the slowness itself; if time is long, my life gets longer. Between me and death, there is ample room for thousands of nothings more precious than fresh air; I can watch myself growing older, I let myself go the way a rower stretches out on his boat and gets down to the surface of the water, trailing his right hand and dragging it in the weeds. Whenever I am physically more alone than usual, I surprise myself, I discover myself. I had never seen myself except at those moments with a woman, a cab-driver, or a house. I compare myself with these specific images; I am so superior to them! The satisfaction of pride prompts me to go back over myself by heart. I always tend to restart myself, but if I catch myself doing so I tend to turn round straight away. That means retaking a path which I already know. This second mistake is not sensitive enough to alert me to avoid a third one. Then I go right or left, and having made the move I realise a circular permutation has pushed me into some new pattern. This could go on for a long

177

time if my mind was not so good at generalising.

The best thing about certain recorded catastrophes, mankind's calamities, is that they alter the scale of values overnight. What previously meant everything to me now counts for nothing, and so forth. After a cataclysm the dazed feeling gives way to greater lucidity and wonderful indifference. One of the advantages of this state of mind is being able to look at what had been most painful from a completely new point of view. The pleasure of being freed from a source of pain *without moving away* can only be compared to physical ecstasy. If some sickness meant that the slightest movement of my wrist hurt terribly, I would take delight in bending my hand down towards my forearm and then stretching it back right to the limit, when the pain would suddenly vanish. If I cry out when I knock into something, I say to people who show concern: "It's nothing," and accompany my smile with a gesture to show that my leg is not broken at all, or my heart. The only place perfect happiness can be found is in that smile.

What is there that can still move me to tears? Little by little my emotions are falling like leaves. All my past, linen drying in my memory, or in a herbarium, seems more distant than my birth. Every day we are born a little. So banal. Mirabelle! The name resonates like the names of queens down through the history of France. There are people who swear that only possession can dispossess one's mind of the memory of a woman. What a joke! There are no powerful memories once we have passed a certain moment in ourselves. If I want to, I can detach my thoughts from anyone or anything. It does not surprise you that I know how to open and close my eyelids. Well, then. And yet, when the reasons for living become these ridiculous toys, what is there left to keep us living? Dramatic tone again. Will that never go? Here's an exercise: look inside yourself, assess yourself, work out the relationship between your desires. Damn it, the game is not worth the candle. When I took an interest in someone else, I was only being interested in myself. The first puff of wind made that clear. These days I really believe I am not excited by my individuality. No question of the human race. That's a nice achievement: I have killed off the question-mark. Questions don't occur any more, it's quite simple. Here begins a life that is unified and pleasant. Beyond this point I am free of all suffering and all joy; what hurt was the capacity to be surprised.

This excursion, which was nothing special, brings us back to ordinary life. Bravo! The secret of serenity. I limit myself consciously but without thinking about the Why, which I would have hobbled myself with in the past. What a machine I am! Obedient, supple. If I quickly raise my right hand to my ear while snipping with my thumb and forefinger, I instantly become a barber's boy playing with scissors. One kind of walk makes me think of trains, another of a steamer. A particular effort sums up several feelings. I once knew a man who wished he had a muscular image for everything. That is not clever. One can easily express everything as a function of oneself. It is only a small step from there to taking oneself to be the world. I really have no need for the element of illusion men go looking for. It's not bad being in prison. Avoid: being too friendly with oneself; having too good an opinion of one's mind. If I avoid going down that route, I shall probably say one of these days: it's not bad being in my tomb. From that point on, nothing regrettable can happen to me; an admirably secure position. They can do what they like to me. "I am in the hands of justice" is no more unpleasant a statement than "I am in the world". Life is pretty reminiscent of military service.

The loud clank of bolts being drawn announced his lawyer's arrival. "Do me the honour of taking a seat, worthy Member of the Bar," said Anicet. "What happy wind brings you here? First, please tell me what's in today's paper."

"As facetious as ever, aren't you, my client? At least in your case morale is good."

"Tell me the news, Mr Lawyer: I am impatient to know if the beard on the Zouave at the Pont de l'Alma is under water. Is the Seine rising?"

"In summer? You surely don't think that. This isn't the flooding season."

"Do you think so? Maybe you are right. But I do remember a woman drinking a glass of vermouth in the Univers (you know, on the Place du Théâtre Français) who was saying to the barman: 'The Seine is getting dangerous. It has been above 5 metres, and at the same time in 1911, the year of the big floods, it went up to 6 metres 10. That's only a difference of 1 metre 10.' Well, I am hounded by the notion, Mr Defender, it hounds me."

"Indeed, most entertaining. However, in your own interests, which are also those of your Case, it would be preferable if you would tell me everything."

"Oh I would never dare. To such a polite, well-mannered man. I would be frightened of boring you."

"But that is what I am here for. And, you know what they say, mute as the tomb, or as a carp."

"Oh well then you must be a bad lawyer."

"Very witty, very witty. You are wrong not to trust me. So, listen to this: in the Pont-Descharmes case, where the banker was murdered, I got the servant acquitted though he had confessed to me that he was guilty. No one will ever know anything about it."

"I understand; you are bound by professional discretion. Well, do you know what I think? Professional discretion is a wonderful invention; much better than the cheese-wire. I would never have thought that up by myself. I really wouldn't."

"Here you have complete confidentiality. Total; you need not fear, no one can hear us. You can speak as in a confessional, um… I mean of course I am a free thinker. Come now, tell me everything without shilly-shallying."

"Right then, I shall tell you everything without shilly-shallying. I had been a week without eating when on the Boulevard de la Chapelle I met a friend I hadn't seen since we were at school. But I don't think I will ever be prosecuted for that. So I can wipe that clean, can't I? That would give you yet more details and be enough to get you talking."

"Professional silence."

"Where should I start? At the beginning, that trickster. I was born in the year it was so windy, of an unknown father and a salesgirl."

"Excuse me, I'm not going to listen to any more of this. Your father is a stockbroker, and your esteemed mother Hélène, *née* Guillequin, is the daughter of Monsieur Guillequin, the…"

"Nothing can be hidden from you. Since you have made your little enquiries I won't beat about the bush: I am accused of having killed Monsieur P. Gonzales, banker, at rue Laffitte. Are we agreed on that?"

"At last you are seeing reason."

"They say I was the lover of his wife, which explains everything. I am not going to lie; Madame Gonzales, the widow, has never been my mistress, and poor Pedro killed himself."

"Come on now, you can't mean that seriously."

"Clearly one can't hide anything from you. Mirabelle Gonzales was cheating on her husband with me. I used to call her Chochotte and we would meet secretly at Rosny-sous-Bois."

"That sounds more plausible."

"I had rented a *pied à terre* near the station. I am ashamed to talk about things like this."

"Nothing wrong about it."

"Not everyone is as thick-skinned as you. I may be a murderer, but I struggled hard with myself before I became an adulterer. Well, we used to meet on Thursdays and Saturdays at Rosny-sous-Bois. I can see it; you're longing to know what we did at Rosny-sous-Bois. You dirty pig. Well, I shall tell you since a lawyer is like one's mother, one can tell him everything. Well, we did crazy things."

"Clear as daylight."

"No, but…"

"I mean to say, it's as clear as daylight: a crime of passion; no one was ever hanged for that."

"Mine is no crime of passion; it was about stealing. Stealing P. Gonzales's money. A big sum of money."

"But Gonzales was bankrupt."

"I had no idea."

"So if the police had not stepped in, you are the one that would have been robbed."

"At least there is someone up there who, etc.... It is a great consolation for me to think of that from time to time. I sympathise sincerely with those unfortunates who wilfully deprive themselves of this succour in their misfortune, this light in our night. Poor Atheists! What do you think?"

"I am a free thinker."

"Oh really; I think you had already told me. You will go to Hell. I shall pray for you."

"You think (*sarcastically*) your prayer to the Supreme Being..."

"Remember the good thief, Mr Member of the Order of Barristers, remember the good thief. But what were we talking about? I was going to tell you how I roasted three lovely little children on spits."

"I see, you're back to the joking."

"I was the one who did the museum thefts too."

"This is a mania."

"You're the one who said it. Do take off your coat, I have a whole lot of crimes on my conscience."

On the white wall behind the lawyer's head a particular halo was floating, which had been trying for some minutes to take on the form of a large beast with a familiar appearance. Anicet remembered the effect once produced on a famous criminal by the word *guillotine*. It was three syllables he could not hear without an impulse of joy. He called the machine his pretty fiancée, his love, his consolation. "I do not know exactly how she is made," he would say, "but I promise to rectify that in the not too distant future." *Scaffold* on the other hand was a word that disgusted him. This distinction seemed more pleasant to Anicet than conversing with a lawyer, and while he was coughing up confessions in a thin voice, which were unbelievable if they answered to reality, or very believable when they were pure invention, Anicet fixed his mind on the image of the blade. He drifted into free association and the blade became the moon, the curve of a naked arm, the arch of a bridge, a coach door, a rainbow, the midnight sun, a scarf, a game of leapfrog, the hog's back of a mountain, the sordid beggarly demon which Socrates called Eros, the lamp that used to stand on the drawing-room mantelpiece at La Hêtraie, any old clock, or the eyes of certain women. The eyes of certain women really do cut off your head. If I had a pencil or a pen I could draw you the shape of eyes with that look. To explain, I always say the lower eyelid is longer than the upper one, but usually no one understands. When a head is cut off, what happens? As a child, I imagined cut-off heads, or limbs, as being like felled trees, a series of concentric circles with drops of blood pearling on the surface. Which side does the soul go, and a lot of other subtle questions. Does the woman exist who could resist the pleasure of folding her arms around a neck destined to become a necklace of blood and air? To tell a woman: "I have killed, now it is just you and me." There are probably still some erotic effects that are not widely known. But everything really comes back to the same pleasure. Is it very difficult to die? Silly question. All questions are silly. I expect any kind of thing from myself. With great fluency I feel capable of the most vulgar ideas. Giving oneself up to them is not a sign of weakness. There are dark corners in ourselves where we do not dust, for fear of the stars caught there which might fall down and cut us with their uneven points. People take them for any old idea and despise them as little stars of tiny importance. Among the many lights we hide from ourselves, the ones we most despise are certainly the memories we never get lost in for long, for fear we will not find the way back. And maybe the opposition is too violent between our present and our past; and the latter would hardly bear comparison with the present, which neither fades away nor deceives us. I do not know what happens in my breast if I look hard at my schooldays. The teachers promised me Normale or Polytechnique. What a paradise! No one imagined Santé.★ If I look back at life, I find my old companions; they are the same age as me, they have not aged any faster, but their place in the world is so clearly marked out! They are going from here to there and their actions are measured on the scale of the Universe. Two or three of them are already familiar names to ten thousand people. Some are married. Some are living it up. Some are doing nothing at all. Have they forgotten school rivalries? The green or gold laurels which were prizes for the year were so beautiful we sank under their weight. So much pride, so much pride. What epic poem held men spellbound like those endless prize-givings punctuated with applause? They read the papers now, Varèse, Loriston and Vandal. What do they think of me? They are confused and shake their heads: "Such a promising boy! I always thought he was a bit strange." They are lying; it is not true, they thought of me as good at literature. They did not find my looks worrying. The hall of memory, where all these naïve images are jumbled together, is reminiscent of the engravings on the frontispiece of a certain kind of novel; all the episodes are mixed together with no respect for dates or values, and pride of place is given to the little plant which grew on a window ledge I passed every morning.

"If there is one thing," said the lawyer, "my profession is passionate about, it is the psychology of our clients. We deduce it from the smallest detail. There is not one of your words, my friend, which does not allow me to discover something of you. But now that I know your case, and have it in my mind, I should like to ask you some questions out of personal interest." He took a small notebook and a pencil from his pocket. "Now, can you tell me what was the most emotional moment of your life?"

"Wait. I can't see clearly any more. We shut our memories away in a cupboard where we put clouds as well. They all quickly turn grey and the most insignificant facts take on as much importance as the thing that turned us upside down. However, when I look carefully behind me, I can see a big avenue in the sunshine, dead with tarred trees, and big leaves on the ground as dry as old tears. A child in a sailor suit riding on the back of a bench is singing to himself a tune that cannot be written down, in which spoken syllables break through from time to time for lack of voice. He can see in the clouds a battle between leopards and pumas, and Charlemagne holding his iron crown on his head to stop it falling off. Very occasionally a laundry van passes on the road; or a delivery van for the Grands Magasins du Louvre (think of those pretty balloons decorated with cocks they give out for free at the entrance if it's not too late in the afternoon). On the pavement, the fruit-seller's daughter is skipping remarkably well, but my parents forbid me to talk to her. Suddenly we hear a great shout and at the end of the avenue a rapidly gathering crowd is coming out of the block on the Avenue des Ternes, yelling and pointing to something wobbling along in the air. It is the fixed Printania balloon which has broken its mooring to fly off with the birds. My heart, my heart flies up. Dizzyingly high! Around that time there was an operetta playing in Paris called *Le Carnet du Diable*, which had a very sad and touching tune:

"I have lost my cockatoo,

It's flown away over the roof."

"Look, Monsieur Anicet," said the lawyer, "you are not being very nice. Please tell me which day gave you the most powerful emotion in your life."

"The day I was baptised."

DUEL

"Show him in," said Mirabelle, and she quickly let her hair down. When Baptiste Ajamais had bowed low before her, she said deceitfully, "Do forgive this darkness falling down my shoulders. I have hardly started the day, so you find me still getting my eyes open." His silence made clear that this was not the purpose of his early-morning call. For a few moments the air was as heavy as snowfall between the two of them. Mirabelle looked up at the dust dancing in the light coming through the Venetian blinds. "In summer," she explained, "I like the dark interior of houses, and the intimate darkness of my heart. My soul is very black, my friend. All that probably comes from my country; I am sure you would never guess where I am from and that you'd like to know."

"Me?" said Baptiste, "but I know nothing about geography and I don't really understand how people differentiate between places. There is the sea, and there are mountains."

"Well, in my country there is sea."

Baptiste said nothing.

"There is sea," Mire repeated, "there is the sea."

"Pity," said Baptiste, "it's such a boring note."

"The women in my country are very beautiful."

"Women are only beautiful in so far as men grant them that."

"In my country the men are very bold."

"You are bold yourself."

"In my country the men, the men…"

Mire stretched out her hand and touched Baptiste on his waistcoat pocket. He took out his watch.

"A quarter past ten, my dear," he said; "you were saying that in your country the men…"

"The men, the men… Oh, the bastards! What a bastard!"

Now the sobs welled up like a rising tide, and her lovely face was buried in a chaos of fingers and hair; her body shook, prostrated over the dressing-table. There was a bathrobe that fell away. There was the most beautiful woman in the world, stark naked and pretending to be embarrassed. There was her anguish at not knowing (for she could not see the man). There was a very long wait, like Purgatory. There was Baptiste who sat down, crossed his legs and remarked:

"You should realise, madame, that I have not touched you."

Mire sat up, furious, without saying a word, and with a trembling hand felt around for the missing garment.

"Oh," said Baptiste, "if you're too hot do stay as you are. It doesn't bother me. You have a most shapely bosom."

The humiliated woman's anger was so great it swirled around her like wisps of smoke. She had to shout:

"You idiot, you idiot, oh, if only I had some acid or my umbrella!"

The rice powder was within reach. The pot was in her hand; but the man, mainly concerned he would be showered with powder, grabbed the woman's wrist. The object flew up, span around and broke like a rose on the carpet. Mire cried out again because Baptiste was hurting her.

"You fool, let me go."

"On your knees, beg for pardon on your knees, beg the sun for mercy."

"Idiot, you are breaking my bones."

"Come on now."

"You… but what is all this about?"

"I have had enough of this, girl. Say sorry."

She looked at him. "Sorry, sorry. But I don't want to any more, you know you horrify me, I don't want to."

"I'm not going to insist," said Baptiste, "I want to talk to you."

She sat down, put her hair up, and closed the big blue dressing-gown like a nervous child. She hunched her shoulders.

"Tell me."

"Would you like a cigarette? No, too bad."

The business with the lighter took on a kind of enigmatic meaningfulness. Baptiste looked as if he was conversing with the flame. Finally, puffs formed curls. He leaned on the arm of his chair, with his left thumb pressing against his chin, so that the rest of his hand pressed against his lower lip and pushed it to the right. It was not very clear what was happening with his eyes. He surveyed Mire as if she were a tree, from the roots to the canopy, and gazed into the clouds beyond. She turned the tables.

"Speak, then."

"The horizon is not as far off as you think, Mire; this is proved by mysterious signs that come to us from there, and women's hearts are never as impenetrable as you would have us believe. Step by step things become quite clear, and I can see into you as if I had a verityscope. What a weakness it is you have. That is probably the secret charm which in spite of everything attracts me to you like a snake fascinated by a bird's dull eye. But let me blow smoke rings in peace for a moment." He fell silent and smoked, very slightly nodding his head. It was hard to tell if he was about to be very gentle or very rough. His voice picked up his monologue where it had broken off. "… unless we are never as sure of our past as of our future. I can decide to go somewhere, if I feel like it, but nothing can change things so that I was there. When it comes to it, what do Anicet, and everything from yesterday which is fading now, matter to me? If something really matters, that is the only thing which is in my power. I belong to myself after all! In a certain kind of story, we sometimes find machines that nothing can stop (preferably in factories, or ships). Once you step in, nothing in the world can save you. Nothing and no one. It has to be easy to put a spanner in the works. But it is a prerequisite that we must never turn a blind eye to fate, or what we are sacrificing to it. I am giving myself up, I am losing myself, I am escaping from myself: a whole litany of reflexive verbs with pronouns. Reflexive verbs, *men* call them. Men have never had vertigo." Baptiste's eyes played on the canopy of distant forests, and dropped imperceptibly to the silent woman. She felt the need to speak:

"What is going on?" she asked. "All I know is that I chose a tragic moment to distract you, a black point in your life. Do not hold it against me. How could I know?"

"All moments in life are tragic. Especially those that pass by with indifference. What a mask! Slowly using the wonderful power we possess to wreck ourselves. We would do a strange job as plasterers. It is all so logical. The satisfying nature of everything is a music that cannot be surpassed. I am increased by it all, and diminished by it all. I am limited. All in good time."

"Look," said Mire, desperately, "I didn't know, I didn't know. Oh, I was so clumsy!"

"How presumptuous, to dispose of oneself. The meaning of our actions escapes us, and we seek reasons as far as the eye can see. We can get out of any situation, but everything is irreparable. Why should we deplore that?"

"Can't you just tell me what was the abyss you stood before? Baptiste, I am trying to look deep into your eyes and find the cause of this drama. I offer you my hair, my friend, my hair; I cannot do more than that."

She spoke for a moment with a frightened look on her face, in a foreign language.

"Madness, dear lady, is not an acceptable solution, because madmen are never locked up as long as they remain in possession of themselves. Suicide would be a seductive honeymoon if we could be sure there was enslavement afterwards. Man's most beautiful poetic invention is Hell."

"Has it really come to that? Once again, tell me what has happened."

"What has happened is that nothing has happened since the world was world. The horrors that men have imagined to take their minds off the immense ennui that gnaws away at them are mere child's play. It is easier to bear humiliation, poverty, hunger, cold, every kind of physical ailment and the chimerical monsters of mental disturbance, than even the smallest of the *whys* our minds ask endlessly. Though it may seem universal, Newton's law is incapable of explaining even a single one of my eye's blinks. I am contradicting myself; that was to be expected. Don't talk to me about contradiction; it assumes the possibility of stacking thoughts on top of each other, in a puerile, honest geometry. But what was I saying?"

"You needed to speak to me."

"I needed to speak to you and I am speaking to you. To start with, it was not about me, but about someone else. But if you walk in the woods, whatever oak I take bark from I always make the same dryad bleed, which is me, myself. Mythology is very handy for expressing myself in conversation just now. After all, everything is just mythology. I am Greek, we are Greek; you are Helen."

"My name is Mirabelle."

"It is no good pouting because I looked at you. What do you think I would seek in your embrace? The end of the world proclaimed by the pupils of your eyes? I know it will never come. I do not believe in omens; they have nothing to tell me about tomorrow. Desire, it is true, desire. I do not even need to seduce you, just think. Even if, like some bird, I had to imitate the blue of the sky with all my plumage. But love-making has become too easy."

"So did you have to refuse me?"

"What do your refusals matter to *you*? Only mine matter. Do you feel sufficiently at my mercy? *They* talk about seduction like hairdressers. If I have seduced you, you will do what I order you to do."

"Baptiste."

"Let's see; this is something quite different. I was thinking about the remarkable power of men who make their women work. But that is still nothing; one can place infinite demands on a woman. We abuse ourselves if we believe we can merely abuse her. Let us see, would you throw yourself into the river if I asked you to? That is still too easy, just killing time. The favourite of one monarch chose death rather than dance naked in front of his guests. That monarch must have been really stupid!"

"Listen, if you will let me, I will carry out all your wishes, whether they are easy or vile. Just tell me…"

"I'm not promising anything; you can't get insurance for love."

"Listen; sometimes in the evening I find I am so alone, so strong, so full of the sea sound of the universe, that I could kill the first man, you hear me, the first man who comes by, if he so much as wishes to resist me. You have no idea what a woman's madness can be like. The abyss you people carry around with you is not worth talking about. Nothing equals our bewilderment. There are falls so abrupt that death would give a weak idea of them. You can bring that on if you like. Then you will see what sort of woman I am; isn't that wonderful? If I had a mirror at moments like that I would die. What is the wind, the tempest, or the great sun? You have never seen me stand erect with my hands outstretched, preyed on by the sickness of Earth; you do not know the words or the cries that come to me, or the disruption that can wreck your mind if I take the trouble."

"Trouble? Is it really trouble for you? Mire, you are lying."

"I am not lying. I cannot lie, because everything I say, I immediately think. What is God compared to woman? I am the one who created it all. Everything comes from me, and comes back to me. You are wrong if you think you can escape me."

"The only one I am trying to escape is myself."

"You egotist; how could you achieve that?"

"Egotist! What do you mean by that? Some words seem harder to catch than clouds. I came here to talk to you."

"I am going to have to get dressed."

"People will probably think I am acting out of friendship or some other silly notion. Too bad. In fact, for me it's neither here nor there whether Anicet lives or dies. But you must obey me. Anicet must walk free."

"What can I do about that?"

'You can go and see the Foreign Minister, you can promise to give him, if he gets the Attorney General to dismiss our friend's case, the secret document our dear Marquis gave you, on which the peace of Europe depends. You are a pretty woman; who could resist you?"

"Is that all I have to do to please you? I was expecting something much worse. Madwoman I am."

"That is all you need do for the moment. I want to test my power. It will bring you no reward. Do not underestimate the danger; you could fail, and be caught in a trap. The machines I referred to earlier include the law, the courts, the police and all the rest. Be warned: I shall look at your body broken on the rack, and then I shall come up with something else. Do you hesitate?"

"I don't know… I cannot see the danger."

"You should do. Have you ever thought what prison is like? There are women there who were once the most beautiful and most loved. Their wild, matted hair is frightening. Their hearts, in that dark night, are prey to anyone who might appear. And their thoughts? They envy the slaves who stitch away, mending life like stockings. They dream of the prison of men's arms which is gentler than the dance at the base of the globe on the furthest reaches of the Pacific. They think about not thinking."

"*Man's most beautiful invention is Hell.*"

"Go on, then."

Mirabelle's arm reached out and rang the bell. There was an extraordinary silence.

"Anne," said Madame Gonzales, "I shall get dressed right away."

"The blue dress, madame?"

"The black one, the deep-mourning one. And the crêpe Georgette hat."

The toing and froing of the chambermaids made no impression on Baptiste.

At this point Mirabelle started dressing; Baptiste started thinking. Only the maid wondered how it came to be that Mirabelle was dressing in his presence. I have other fish to fry.

BAPTISTE (*thinking*):

"The marvel of our lives is precisely that nothing is as important as we deem it to be. There is no event that I think of with terror. Here I am once again coming to the end of a meditation as pointless as the previous ones. This has been going on for six months. Nothing seems possible any longer, but there will inevitably be something else because there always has been something else. The thing is to push your limits in every direction before you die. Everything is an opportunity for me to extend my reach; I look for no other purpose in the world, or in people. They are the episode, the anecdote, and have value only in so far as they concur with the main thrust of the book. Anicet, Mire, others such as V—, for example, that is already receding behind me. The one thing that still really affects me is the time of year — penetrating, burning hot like coffee. Highest of all is the joy of no longer finding anything within me when I close my eyes. Nothing. I am empty. Outside, nothing catches my eye any longer. All the sights that in the past I found so breathtaking I had to stop and lean against a wall now leave me unmoved. If I see a shop-front or a viaduct, I say: That is a shop, or: That is a viaduct. Or maybe I am happy just to think: Shop, viaduct. Or rather, I go by without seeing them, and I look, and only see a viaduct or a shop. There is nothing unusual about that. I am in charge, quite simply. I think of the man who said: '*What does it matter, since it is always me who is me?*' We need to have the same outlook. The notion of identity is the best ball-game I know of. One of these days my head will miss the catcher. We shall see. What is conducive to suicide (I am reconstructing here my fine friend Harry James) is the wish or desire to get out of the game. I don't want anything myself. We shall see. Despair does not prove anything, it presupposes hope and that's it. I do not deny suffering, I take note of it; but I find myself taking to it like a duck to water. If, rather than any other hobby, I prefer women's breasts, it is because that horizontal hour-glass is the most dangerous of pillows. To be sure, I still have marriage left to do. One can complicate life according to taste, with the ball and chain to which a prisoner tells his endless lies. I am sometimes tempted by the most absurd commitments, in the certainty I can feel that they will never weigh on me as much as atmospheric pressure. And for that, the healthiest thing would be to go off to the country, disappear somewhere and hang around the Café du Commerce. Grow a new skin, like those lucky reptiles. I have just as much luck as they do."

Baptiste walked into the little Biard round the corner from St Philippe: "Bring me a brandy and something to write with!"

Monsieur Pol glided over. On the black waxed canvas of the blotter was a golden globe and an inkwell. Baptiste Ajamais took out a sheet of paper and a yellow envelope, then, leaning on the blotter, he carefully wrote out with his left hand:

TO HIS HONOUR THE PUBLIC PROSECUTOR

15

THE CAFÉ DU COMMERCE IN COMMERCY*

"In one way," said the waiter, "it could have turned out better, but in another way, what a relief for the town. A good-for-nothing drunkard. And didn't even respect himself, sir. He said things about himself which I felt a bit ashamed for him, and I used to say to him: Come now, Monsieur Malitorne, you're exaggerating, you're really exaggerating. So rather than end up in a hospice, to think he died like that. In one way…"

"Have you got the Paris newspapers, Ernest?" the old solicitor asked.

"Upon my word, sir, it's the gentleman over there has them."

The customer referred to was a young man of about twenty-five, wearing a stiff, threadbare, tight-fitting jacket over a very high-cut waistcoat with dirty white piping. His ready-made bow tie was held in place by a too-small tiepin bearing an effigy of the Virgin and Child, but not high enough to hide the stud of his starched collar. There was nothing remarkable about this young man besides a protuberant lower lip and hair that was a little on the long side. His eyes were completely hidden by a pair of blue-framed spectacles.

"Were you wanting *Le Parisien*, sir?"

"Very kind of you, sir," said the other, "but may I introduce myself? Maître Dorange, Arthur Dorange, retired solicitor. Have you recently moved to the town,

Monsieur…?

"My name is Baptiste Tisaneau,★ and I am the new clerk at the Crédit National Bank."

"Oh, so you have taken the place of Monsieur Malitorne? Poor man! But we haven't lost out with the change. He was a pretty awful partner at Manille the last few months. Do you play Manille?"

"I have my little talents."

"Excellent. You can make up our four. That's how life is — one player dies, another one comes along. Things are none the worse for that. What will you have?"

"That's very kind of you, sir; well I shan't say no. A vermouth with cassis."

"A vermouth cassis, Ernest, and a cointreau. Cointreau is very good for one's health. It tones you up."

"It seems to work for you. You look in good shape."

"I'm sixty-seven. You wouldn't think it."

"Sixty-seven! I would never have guessed."

"You see! But since you are one of us, a real commercial from Commercy (hee, hee), if I may confess a little weakness, my eyes are not so strong, and reading makes me tired. So, since you have been reading the Paris paper, might you be good enough to tell me the news?"

"Hm, not much to report. The Seine is getting very high, but that is news for Parisians. A widow, Madame Lazare, at 60, rue Ordener, has been murdered by a milkman's boy. The session in the Chamber was tense; the Prime Minister rightly denounced the activities of the anarchists, who, I'm afraid to say, have been trying to depreciate our paper money… Aha! A fine speech by the Marquis de Molènes about our ruined provinces. One can never say enough on that subject."

"Tell me, isn't there anything on the Anicet affair and all that?"

"About… ah yes, there is an account of the trial."

"Could you read it for me? If you don't mind? I'm rather interested in the case because I used to have business dealings with the defendant's father. A stockbroker, very decent fellow."

"Not at all, not at all. But we can hardly see. Ernest! (It is Ernest, isn't it?) Next time a little bit less cassis, would you? Just a thought. Could you light the lamp please? It is better a bit less sweet. The light's going fast, isn't it? Shall I read it all? When it comes down to it, light is life."

"You are quite right. If it is too long you can skip some."

Monsieur Tisaneau settled himself, glanced at the old man, and the young red-haired fellow playing dominoes at a nearby table, then turned to his new friend, cleared his throat, took a deep breath and started reading:

"'The public gallery was packed for the second day of the Anicet trial. Plenty of society ladies were in attendance, the sort who flock to the races, to balls and famous trials. Their presence was explained by the personality of several witnesses due to give evidence, for whom there had not been time on day one of the hearings. First was the famous painter Blue. He came dressed for travel — he was leaving two hours later for America where the millionaire Carnegie has commissioned him to decorate his summer palace. His testimony was brief: his relationship with the defendant had always been very distant; the latter had given the impression of being a rather shy young man and lacking in depth. The painter had seen him several times at Mme Gonzales's even before her marriage. He knew nothing about this lady's relationship with the young man, but the banker Gonzales had once said to him, "I really do not take to this young Anicet." The painter answered several questions from the prosecution, and then when the judge had apologised for troubling him for so little and wished him a good journey, M. Blue departed.

"'The next witness was M. Jean Chipre, whose election to the Académie Goncourt we recently reported. This lively writer delivered a paradox on the state of intellectual life, charmed the gallery and tried the jury's patience. He stated that he had met the defendant several times in one of the dives well known to the wilder crowd, where he himself went sometimes for psychological background. The defendant would spend money like water, and drain bottles of champagne at two louis a go, to impress the hotel residents. The prosecution at this point reminded the jury of Detective Carter's statement in the charge sheet that he had seen Anicet in a drunken moment set fire to the last thousand-franc note he had received from his family. That was six months before the events the witness was referring to. It was clear this argument affected the jury...' I shall skip a few of the witness statements...

"'Devastating evidence came from Mme Floche, the concierge of the flats in rue Cujas where the defendant lived. She said this tenant lived a very irregular life, and often came home with women, never the same one. He made a terrible mess on the staircase, did not keep proper hours, did not read the papers and generally did nothing the way normal people do. He received a lot of letters from abroad, principally from Germany. He received them under several different names. Often the text of the letters was incomprehensible. One of the correspondents always added suggestions for the postman in the corner of the envelope. Some things the defendant's visitors said on the stairs made even M. Floche blush, and thank the Lord! he had been in the artillery. One day he even knocked over on the landing little Marcelle Baju, a lovely child, the six-year-old daughter of a respectable tenant, Mme Baju, who took the stand to confirm this fact. M. Floche repeated his wife's points and insisted on one detail: the defendant slept elsewhere every Friday. He reported having heard him say: "I'm going to have to do in this idiot who bores us to tears with his stuff about the war wounded." What all that was about is a mystery; but M. Floche trembled to remember the cruel expression on the tenant's face.'

"So... Mme Gonzales's servants... a coachman who ate at the Café Biard where the bandits had their headquarters... Mme Belou, lodger at the rue des Petits-Carreaux... a butcher's boy who was Mme Gonzales's lover (these people!) when she was called Elmire Masson, known as Mamelle... A horse trader, M. Brugeon, who had been swindled by the co-defendant Pol... several street-walkers... The

Under-Secretary of the Foreign Ministry who entertained Mme Gonzales at the time of her unwise approach to him which brought her to the Saint Lazare police station… the café-owner Boulard's mistress… Police constable Lelard, who found the body of Professor Omme… A museum attendant called Jovial who had been gagged at the Musée du Luxembourg by masked robbers and recognised with certainty Anicet and Boulard… 'The Marquis della Robbia, the Italian attaché, also took the stand, and admitted having bought several Egyptian statuettes from Anicet, whose provenance he did not know, but which he would be happy to return to the Louvre, he said, as he had already bequeathed his world-class art collection to that museum. The judge reassured him that the word of such a perfect gentleman as the Marquis della Robbia would never be questioned, and said he was pleased to declare in public the French nation's gratitude for the magnificent gift the Marquis was offering… "This has taken a long time, don't you agree? So, the hearing is now adjourned." '

"When the hearing recommenced, more witnesses… Witnesses accusing the co-defendant Perroneau, known as Ange Miracle… It seems he was doing forgeries.

"'In the course of this parade, the individual defendants' behaviour was very varied. The widow of Gonzales' — or should we say the Masson girl — 'continually looked up and down the courtroom as if she was searching for someone who was missing. As time went by she showed increasing signs of impatience and tapped her feet two or three times. When her former lover took the stand and said she liked being beaten, she gave him such a stare he started stammering and talking about a day out in Chatou.

"'The waiter, Pol, never stopped crying throughout the proceedings. He gave the impression of being physically shattered. When it was put to him that he bet on the races he tried to protest, but then started sneezing. The café-owner Boulard's attitude was completely traditional; he was the sort who thinks that when the wine has been opened, you have to drink it. He made two or three mocking comments which earned him, rightly, reprimands from the judge, whose impartiality and clarity were admirable throughout. As for the other defendants, Jolicœur, Donzon, Barcelet and Perdrillon, who were on much lighter charges, we can comment on their shifty looks and faces ravaged with vice. But the most instructive one to watch throughout the trial has been the one who is obviously the ringleader, the man burdened with charges each more crushing than the last, who is accused of pillaging national treasures, burgling the jewellers Van Rees and Haarlem, stealing documents from the Quai d'Orsay and murdering the lady in the rue Cassette,★ Professor Omme, the actress Céline d'Harcourt, the banker Gonzales and many others who unfortunately will never be known — the principal defendant, this mysterious Anicet, wealthy son of a good family, who had the offer of an easy bourgeois life, but to satisfy his vicious urges preferred the path of crime and baseness to the one laid out before him. In line with his behaviour under interrogation we had expected him to be cynical, provocative, or indeed, if the solemnity of the setting and the proceedings brought about a reversal, to find him shattered, humiliated, hanging his head and dreading the sentence which would send him to the scaffold or to prison. Nothing of the sort; the defendant seemed completely uninterested in the case being argued before his eyes, in which it was his head that was at stake; he seemed profoundly bored and paid minimal attention only to the women who appeared as witnesses. At one point he seemed to be very concerned about a stain he had spotted on his clothes. Just once he looked over to Gonzales's widow, and had to suppress a giggle as if it would have been indecent. When the hearing broke off, he asked for a glass of water.

"'After the witnesses had been called came the prosecutor's speech.'"

Monsieur Baptiste stopped reading. "I shall skip the prosecution charges; we know the details. I will go straight to Anicet's lawyer, Maître Dessarts's speech for the defence."

"'Maître Dessarts, who could not deny the evidence, pleaded unsound mind, in spite of the medical opinion. He supported his case by quoting the text of several papers found on his client when he was arrested. The words he read were so lacking in logic that we have not been able to reproduce them for our readers.'

"There was general laughter and some booing. The judge had to call for order."

"'The prosecutor remarked that if criminals only needed to carry around Futurist poems to be declared insane, it would be all too convenient for them. The defendant at that point shed his indifference to approve the prosecutor's words. He was silenced. Maître Dessarts tried hard to cast doubt on the proof of various charges, and declared his client to be innocent of two or three secondary ones. He was brilliant, persuasive, incisive, ironic, bitter and moving. He delivered jewels of eloquence. He gave everything possible to a bad case. But he failed to shake the jury's conviction, impressed though they might be by so formidable a talent and such distinguished abilities...' The gas keeps jumping around."

"There must be water in the pipe."

"'When the judge asked the defendant: "Have you anything to add?" Anicet stood up and answered: "I have to add that it is not a group of men and a woman who are on trial here. Nor is it justice that is on trial. It is life that is on trial. I know it is a wasted effort; I know no one is watching the show that is really playing here. So, I have decided to put an end to it, and I confess that I am guilty of everything I am accused of. I add that all my co-defendants took part in my... call them delinquencies, or they at least knew about them."

"'These last words caused indignation from the other defendants and their lawyers. Violent disputes broke out. Jolicœur, Perdrillon and Donzon tried to attack Anicet. The guards had to restrain them, and insults were flung around the dock, so the judge halted proceedings. "The hearing will recommence tomorrow at 3 o'clock sharp."'"

"Thank you, sir," said the solicitor, "you are a very diligent young man. But I thought you read with some feeling. Surely you are not like me, you have not set eyes on this scoundrel?"

"Never seen him."

"You've not missed anything. He's not nice to look at. And not the sort of person a boy as serious as you seem to be should get to know. You are looking at our domino-players."

"Yes, I believe I have met the red-haired young man before."

"Monsieur Prudence?"

"Is his name Prudence? Do you believe that?"

"Of course. You are a funny one. Let me introduce you."

Monsieur Tisaneau followed behind the solicitor, looking unconvinced that Prudence was this man's name. Before being introduced he addressed him rapidly in English:

"*Harry James, I could not believe you were dead, but now I can no longer believe you were alive.*"

"I'm sorry, sir, I don't speak any other languages," said Monsieur Prudence, looking astonished.

"He must be a lookalike," said Arthur Dorange, "a lookalike. May I introduce you? Monsieur Tisaneau, who will make up our four for Manille. Monsieur Prudence, engineer for minor roads." Then turning to the old man, "And Monsieur Isidore Ducasse,★ the former Land Registrar and a fine upstanding gentleman."

Translator's notes to main text

Page 25. *L—* here stands for "Lelian", the name by which Paul Verlaine was affectionately known during his final alcohol-soaked years. From the anagram of his name *"pauvre Lelian"* (poor Lelian).

27. *I was going to die.* In Brussels in 1873 Verlaine fired two shots at Rimbaud, wounding him in the wrist. Aragon's account of Rimbaud and Verlaine ignores the fact that it was a homosexual relationship. It is now considered most unlikely that Rimbaud was involved in the slave trade (end of paragraph).

30. *Viagère* in French is a legal term meaning "for life" as in "a life interest".

36. *Passages des Cosmoramas.* Aragon in the "keys" confirmed that this was based upon the Passage Jouffroy and its extension on the other side of the Boulevard Montmartre, the Passage des Panoramas.

38. *Palikao.* The Comte de Palikao, General Cousin-Montauban, was Minister of War in 1870 when France lost the Franco-Prussian war. He was the victor of Palikao, when the Chinese were defeated in the Second Opium War.

42. *Proverbial sadness.* A reference to the Latin proverb *Post coitum omne animal triste est* (After sex all animals are sad), originally attributed to Galen.

57. *Golden apple.* A reference, presumably, to the golden apple presented by Paris to Helen: the Judgement of Paris.

60. *Isabelle R—.* Perhaps Isabelle Rimbaud, Arthur's sister, who with her husband Paterne Berrichon portrayed her brother as a model citizen and virtuous Catholic.

60. *Galerie des Machines.* This was a massive steel and glass pavilion built for the Exposition Universelle of 1889 (of which the Eiffel Tower was the focus), which remained in place until 1909. The *Big Wheel* (Grande Roue) was set up beside it for the 1900 Exposition.

64. *Day the war ended.* This is Guillaume Apollinaire. In his "key" Aragon admitted that though this chapter was written before November 1918, the reference was not prophetic, but was added later in homage to the great poet.

72. *A Café Biard*. A chain of cafés at this time. *Traînée* (a few lines down) translates as "slut", but the word has other meanings and to put that would be cruder than the text. In the following line the reader will recognise a description of Charlie Chaplin in that of the *"mandarin-thief mask"*.

77. *It's well put… Blessed are the poor in spirit*. Aragon in his "Preface" (p.18) underlined that the spoken words of the various characters in the novel bore no relation to how the persons they were modelled upon actually spoke. The single exception was this paragraph, a remembered exchange with Max Jacob, inserted for satirical purposes presumably.

79. *Bolognese*. Aragon wrote in the 1930 "key" that "Bolognese merely represents the police; take note that you should recognise in him merely my aversion for that institution…"

82. *Feeling of Beauty*. In this sentence, Aragon writes "of" rather than the usual "for" meaning presumably, "what feelings do you associate with Beauty?"

93. *Pedro Gonzales*. Aragon comments in his "Preface" that novelists get their ideas from somewhere and that Diego Rivera gave him the idea for Gonzales's physique, whilst the art-dealer Léonce Rosenberg's residence was a starting point for the Gonzales mansion.

99. *Ponson du Terrail* (1829-1871), author of the Rocambole series of adventure novels, whence the common French adjective *rocambolesque*.

167. *Nuits*, i.e. Nuits St George, a fine Burgundy wine.

174. *Guillaume*. I.e. Apollinaire, see note to p.64.

184. The *Santé* is the prison in the 14th *arrondissement* — on the rue de la Santé, which with a curious irony means "Health".

197. *Commercy*. A small village in Lorraine where Aragon's uncle lived. He went to stay there from time to time for writing sessions.

198. *Baptiste Tisaneau* is presumably Baptiste Ajamais, under a new, rather 'wet' surname. *Tisaneau* means "herbal tea water".

202. *Rue Cassette*. This is where Alfred Jarry's famous residence the Grand Chasublery was situated, an apartment divided in two horizontally.

204. *Isidore Ducasse*. The real name of the Comte de Lautréamont, author of *Les Chants de Maldoror*. He would have been 74 in 1920 had he not died aged 24.

4 DADA SUICIDES

Selected writings by
Arthur Cravan, Jacques Rigaut, Julien Torma & Jacques Vaché

With essays by Gabrielle Buffet-Picabia (on Cravan), Jacques-Emile Blanche (on Rigaut), Philippe Merlen (on Torma) and André Breton's "Disdainful Confession" on Jacques Vaché.

Translations by Terry Hale, Paul Lenti, Iain White, &c.
Introductions by Roger Conover, Terry Hale & Paul Lenti

These four took the nihilism of the movement to its ultimate conclusion, their works are the remnants of lives lived to the limit and then cast aside with nonchalance and disdain: Vaché died of a drug overdose, Rigaut shot himself, Cravan and Torma simply vanished, their fates still a mystery. Yet their fragmentary works — to which they attached so little importance — still exert a powerful allure and were a vital inspiration for the literary movements that followed them. Vaché's bitter humour, Cravan's energetic invective, Rigaut's dandyfied introspection and Torma's imperturbable asperity: all had their influence.

240pp., ISBN 0 947757 74 0

For a complete listing of all titles available from Atlas Press
and the London Institute of 'Pataphysics see our online catalogue at:
www.atlaspress.co.uk
To receive automatic notification of new publications
sign on to the emailing list at this website.
Atlas Press, 27 Old Gloucester st., London WC1N 3XX
Trade distribution UK: www.turnaround-uk.com; USA: www.artbook.com

MUSIDORA

C000056622

Cover photo ©Ebet Roberts

ISBN 978-1-4803-0520-5

HAL•LEONARD® CORPORATION

7777 W. BLUEMOUND RD. P.O. BOX 13819 MILWAUKEE, WI 53213

Contents

How to Use This Book

Piano Chord Songbooks include the lyrics and chords for each song. The melody of the first phrase of each song is also shown.

First, play the melody excerpt to get you started in the correct key. Then, sing the song, playing the chords that are shown above the lyrics.

Chords can be voiced in many different ways. For any chords that are unfamiliar, refer to the diagram that is provided for each chord. It shows the notes that you should play with your right hand. With your left hand, simply play the note that matches the name of the chord. For example, to play a C chord, play C-E-G in your right hand, and play a C in your left hand.

You will notice that some chords are *slash chords*; for example, C/G. With your right hand, play the chord indicated on the left side of the slash. With your left hand, play the note on the right side of the slash. So, to play a C/G chord, play a C chord (C-E-G) in your right hand, and play a G in your left hand.

Allentown

Words and Music by
Billy Joel

Melody: Well, we're liv-ing here in Al-len - town...

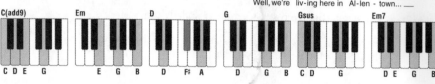

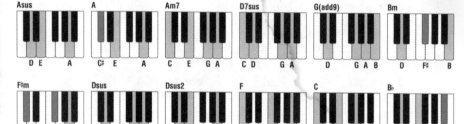

Intro
```
| C(add9)  Em  D  G/B |        C(add9) |
|          Em  D  G/B |        C(add9) |
|          Em  D      | G  Gsus  G     |
```

Verse 1

            Em7   Asus   D A/D D
Well, we're living here in Allentown

           Am7   D7sus   G G(add9) G
And they're closing all the factories down.

        Em7   Asus A   Bm
Out in Bethlehem they're kill - ing time,

F#m/A   Em D/F#   Asus A
Filling out forms,   standing in line.

          Em7   Asus   D A/D D
Well, our fathers fought the Second World War,

          Am7   D7sus   G G(add9) G
Spent their weekends on the Jersey shore.

        Em7   Asus A   Bm
Met our mothers in the U.   S. O.;

F#m/A   Em D/F#   Asus A
Asked them to dance,   danced with them slow.

        Em7   Asus   D Dsus Dsus2 D
And we're living here in Allentown.

Bridge 1

      F/A   G/B   C C(add9) C
But the restlessness was handed down,

      Am7   D7sus   Em G/B C D
And it's getting very hard to stay.

Interlude 1

C(add9) Em D G/B	C(add9)
Em D G/B	C(add9)
Em D	G Gsus G

Verse 2

      Em7   Asus   D A/D D
Well, we're waiting here in Allentown

      Am7   D7sus   G G(add9) G
For the Pennsylvania we never found.

      Em7   Asus A   Bm
For the promises our teach - ers gave

F♯m/A   Em D/F♯   Asus A
If we worked hard,   if we behaved.

      Em7   Asus   D A/D D
So the graduations hang on the wall,

      Am7   D7sus   G G(add9) G
But they never really helped us at all.

      Em7   Asus A   Bm
No, they never taught us what   was real:

F♯m/A   Em   D/F♯   Asus A
Iron and coke,   chromium steel.

      Em7   Asus   D Dsus Dsus2 D
And we're waiting here in Allentown.

Bridge 2

      F/A   G/B   C C(add9) C
But they've taken all the coal from the ground.

      Am7   D7sus   Em G/B C D
And the union people crawled away.

| C(add9) Em D G/B | C(add9) |
| Em D F |

Bridge 3

```
F          G/F        F
Ev'ry child had a pret-ty good shot
                G/F          Bb/F
To get at least as far as their old man got.
F                           G/F        F
   But something happened on the way to that place…
                G            C
They threw an A-merican flag in our
```

Interlude 2

```
|C(add9) Em D  G/B |              C(add9)|
 Face.
|         Em D  G/B |              C(add9)|
|         Em D      |G  Gsus  G          |
```

Verse 3

```
          Em7          Asus      D  A/D  D
Well, I'm living here in Allentown,
          F/A          G/B         C  C(add9)  C
And it's hard to keep a good man down.
       Am7           D7sus   Em  G/B  C   D
But I won't be getting up today.
|C(add9) Em D  G/B |              C(add9)|
|         Em D  F   |
```

Piano Solo

```
|F     G/F | F        |        G/F | Bb/F        |
|F     G/F | F        |        G   | C           |
```

Outro

```
|C(add9) Em D  G/B |              C(add9)|
|         Em D  G/B |
          C(add9)    Em  D     Em  G/B  C   D
And it's getting very hard ___ to stay.
          Am7          D7sus   G  Gsus  G(add9)  G
And we're living here in Allentown.
```

All About Soul

Words and Music by
Billy Joel

Melody:

She waits for me __ at night, __

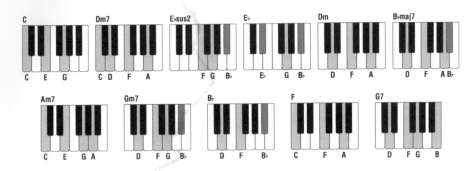

Intro

‖: C/D   Dm7 | C/D   Dm7 |

| E♭sus2   E♭ | E♭sus2   E♭   :‖

Verse 1

      Dm   **C**
She waits for me at night,

      B♭maj7   **C**
She waits for me in si - lence.

      Dm   **Am7**
She gives me all her tenderness

Gm7   **Am7 B♭**
   And takes away my   pain.

C   **Dm**   **C**
   And so ___ far she hasn't run,

      B♭maj7   **C**
Though I swear she's had her moments.

      Dm   **Am7**
She still believes in miracles

Gm7   **Am7 B♭ N.C.**
   While others cry   in   vain.

Chorus 1

        F   **C/E** **Bb/D**
It's all about soul.

        F/C   **C/Bb**
It's all about faith and a deeper de-votion.

       F/A   **Am7** **Bb**
It's all about soul,

             F/C   **C**
'Cause under the love ___ is a stronger emo-tion.

         Dm
She's gotta be strong,

G7/B   **C/Bb**   **F/A**
  'Cause so many things ___ getting out of control.

          Bb
Should drive her away,

         F/A
So, why does she stay?

       C/D **Dm7** **C/D** **Dm7**
It's all about soul.

| **Ebsus2**   **Eb** |**Ebsus2**   **Eb** |

Interlude 1

Gm7   C   Am7
Na, na, na, na,___ na, na, na, na.

Dm7
It's all about soul.

Gm7   C   Am7
Na, na, na, na,___ na, na, na, na.

Yes, it is.

B♭maj7   C   Am7
Na, na, na, na,___ na, na, na, na.

Dm7   Gm7   C Am7
It's all about soul.

Verse 2

            Dm   C
There are people who have lost

    B♭maj7   C
Ev'ry trace of human kind - ness.

         Dm   Am7
There are ___ many who have fall - en,

      Gm7   Am7   B♭   C
There are some who still ___ sur-vive.

       Dm   C
And she comes to me at night,

    B♭maj7   C
And she tells me her desires.

       Dm   Am7
And she gives me all the love ___ I need

  Gm7   Am7 B♭
To keep my faith ___ a-live.

Chorus 2

               F   **C/E Bb/D**
It's all about soul.

                 F/C   **C/Bb**
It's all about joy that comes out of sor-row.

                F/A   **Am7 Bb**
It's all about soul.

                  F/C   **C**
Who's standin' now, ___ who's standin' tomor-row?

          Dm
This life isn't fair.

G7/B   **C/Bb**   **F/A**
  It's gonna get dark, ___ it's gonna get cold.

          Bb
You gotta get tough,

                F/A
But that ain't enough.

              C/D **Dm7** **C/D** **Dm7**
It's all about soul.

| **Ebsus2**   **Eb** | **Ebsus2**   **Eb** |

Interlude 2

| **C/D** **Dm7** | **C/D** **Dm7** | **Ebsus2 Eb** | **Ebsus2 Eb** |

Outro

         Gm7   **C**   **Am7**
‖:   Na, na, na, na, ___ na, na, na, na.

         Dm7
It's all about soul.

Gm7   **C**   **Am7**
  Na, na, na, na, ___ na, na, na, na.

Yes, it is. :‖ *Repeat and fade*

And So It Goes

Words and Music by
Billy Joel

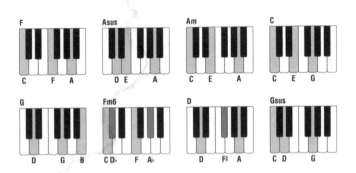

Intro

F		Asus Am	C F	G C
F		Asus Am	C F F/G	C

Verse 1

        F   Asus Am
In ev'ry heart there is a room,

    C   F   G
A sanctuary safe and strong

    C   F   Asus Am
To heal the wounds from lovers past,

    C F   F/G   C
Un-til a new one comes a-long.

Verse 2

        F   Asus Am
I spoke to you in cautious tones,

    C   F   G
You answered me with no pre-tense.

    C F   Asus Am
And still I feel I said too much.

    C   F   F/G   C
My silence is my self de-fense.

Chorus 1

         C/Bb   F/A Fm6/Ab
And ev'ry time I've held a rose

    C/G   Am   D/F#   Gsus G
It seems I ___ only felt the thorns.

     C C/Bb   F/A Fm6/Ab
And so it goes, and so it goes,

      C/E   Am   D/F# Gsus G
And so will you ___ soon I sup-pose.

Verse 3

     C   F C/E F   Asus Am
But if my si - lence   made you leave,

       C   F   G
Then that would be my worst mis-take.

    C   F   Asus Am
So I will share this room with you,

    C   F   F/G   C
And you can have this heart to break.

Interlude

| F | Asus Am | C F F/G | C |

Chorus 2

        C/Bb F/A   Fm6/Ab
And this is why my eyes are closed,

    C/G   Am   D/F#   Gsus G
It's just as well ___ for all I've seen.

     C   C/Bb   F/A Fm6/Ab
And so it goes, ___ and so it goes,

    C/G   Am D/F#   Gsus G
And you're the only one who knows.

Verse 4

    C   F   Asus Am
So I would choose to be with you.

      C   F   G
That's if the choice were mine to make.

    C   F   Asus Am
But you can make decisions, too,

    C   F   F/G   C
And you can have this heart to break.

Outro

| F | Asus Am | C   F |

G   C/Bb   F/A Fm6/Ab
And so it goes, ___ and so it goes,

    C/G   F   F/G   C
And you're the only one who knows.

Angry Young Man

Words and Music by
Billy Joel

Melody:

There's a place in the world _ for the an - gry young man,

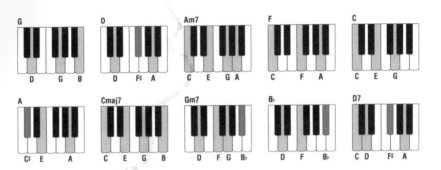

Verse 1

      G   **D**
There's a place in the world for the an - gry young man,

    Am7   **D**
With his working class ties and his radical plans.

    G   **D**
He re-fuses to bend, he refus - es to crawl,

    Am7   **D**
And he's always at home with his back ___ to the wall.

    F/A   **G/B**   **C**
And he's proud of his scars ___ and the bat - tles he's lost.

    G/B   **A/C♯**   **D**
And he struggles and bleeds ___ as he hangs ___ on his cross.

    G   **D**
And he likes to be known as the an-gry young

Cmaj7 D G/B C Am7 G/B C F/C C
Man.

| **Cmaj7 D** | **G/B C** | **Am7 G/B C** | **F/C C** | |

Verse 2

    G   D
Give a moment or two to the an - gry young man,

       Am7   D
With his foot in his mouth and his heart ___ in his hand.

          G   D
He's been stabbed in the back; he's been mis - understood.

      Am7   D
It's a comfort to know his inten - tions are good.

        F/A   G/B   C
And he sits in a room ___with a lock __ on the door,

         G/B   A/C♯   D
With his maps and his med - als laid out __ on the floor.

         G   D
And he likes to be known as the angry young

Cmaj7 D G/B C Am7 G/B C
Man.

Bridge

F   Gm7
  I believe I've passed the age

  B♭   C
Of consciousness and righteous rage.

 F/A   B♭
I found that just surviv - ing

        C   D
Was a no - ble fight.

G   Am7
  I once believed in causes, too;

C   D
I had my pointless point of view.

    G/B   C   A
And life went on no matter who was wrong __ or right.

D
Oh.

Verse 3

                G   **D**
And there's al - ways a place for the an - gry young man,

          Am7   **D**
With his fist in the air and his head ____ in the sand.

            G   **D**
And he's never been able to learn ____ from mistakes,

           Am7   **D**
So he can't understand why his heart ____ always breaks.

           F/A   **G/B**   **C**
And his honor is pure ____ and his cour - age is well.

           G/B   **A/C♯**   **D**
And he's fair and he's true ____ and he's bor - ing as hell.

           G   **D**
And he'll go to the grave as an angry old

Cmaj7 D G/B C Am7 G/B C
Man.

Instrumental

F	Gm7	B♭	C	
F/A	B♭	C		D
G	Am7	C	D	
G/B	C	A		
D	D7			

            G   **D**

Yes, there's always a place for the an - gry young man,

            Am7   **D**

With his working class ties and his radical plans.

       G   **D**

He refuses __ to bend; he refus - es to crawl.

        Am7   **D**

And he's always at home with his back ____ to the wall.

        F/A   **G/B**   **C**

And he's proud of his scars ____ and the bat - tles he's lost.

        G/B   **A/C♯**   **D**

And he struggles and bleeds ____ as he hangs ____ on his cross.

        G   **D**

And he likes to be known as the angry young

Cmaj7 D G/B C Am7 G/B C F/C C

Man.

Outro   ‖:**Cmaj7 D** │**G/B C** │**Am7 G/B C** │**F/C C** :‖

               │ **Cmaj7 D** │**G/B C** │**Am7 G/B C**

Baby Grand

Words and Music by
Billy Joel

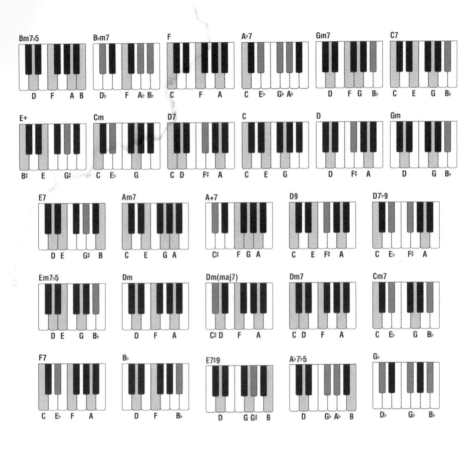

Intro

| | Bm7♭5 | B♭m7 | | F/A | A♭7 | |
| Gm7 | | | C7 | | |

Verse 1

F
Late at night,
E+
When it's dark and cold,
Cm/E♭
I reach out
D7 C/E   D/F♯
    For some-one to hold.
Gm
When I'm blue,
D/F♯
When I'm lonely,
Gm/F
She comes through.
E7   Am7
  She's the only one who can.
D7   Gm7
My baby grand
C7   A+7   D9   Gm7   C7
Is all I need.

Verse 2

F
In my time,
E+
I've wandered ev'rywhere
Cm/E♭
Around this world.
D7 C/E   D/F♯
    She would always
Gm
Be there.
       D/F♯
Any day,   any hour,
Gm/F
All it takes is the,
E7   Am7
  Is the power in my hands.
D7   Gm7   C7
And this ___ baby grand's
        F   D7♭9 Gm7 C7
Been good to __ me.

Verse 3

F
　I've had friends,

E+
　But they slipped away.

Cm/E♭
　And I've had fame,

D7　C/E　　　D/F♯
　　　　But it doesn't stay.

Gm
　I've made fortunes;

D/F♯
　Spent them fast enough.

Gm/F
　As for women,

E7
　They don't last

　　　　Am7
With just ___ one man.

D7　　　Gm7　　　C7
　But my baby grand

　　　　　　F　　B♭m7　F　Em7♭5　A+7
Is gonna stand by me.

Bridge

　　　　Dm
They say

Dm(maj7) Dm7
　No one's gonna play this

Em7♭5　　　A+7
　On the radio.

Dm　　　　　Dm(maj7)　Dm7
　They said　　melan　-　choly blues

　　　　　　Cm7　F7
Were dead and gone.

B♭
　But only songs like these,

Bm7♭5　　E7♯9
　Played in minor keys,

Am7　　　　　　　　A♭7♭5　Gm7　　　C7
　Keep those memo-ries hold　-　ing on.

Verse 4

F
   I've come far

E+
   From the life I strayed in,

Cm/E♭
   And I've got the scars

D7   **C/E**   **D/F♯**
   From those dives I played in.

Gm
   Now I'm home

D/F♯
   And I'm weary,

Gm/F
   And in my bones,

E7   **Am7**
   Ev'ry dreary one ___ night stand.

D7 **Gm7**   **C 7**
  My ___ baby grand

        A+7
Is coming home with me,

      D7
With me.

    C/E   **D/F♯**   **Gm7**
Ever since this ___ gig ___ began,

    C7
My ba - by grand's

         Bm7♭5 **B♭m7** **F/A** **A♭7** **Gm7** **G♭** **F**
Been good to me.

Big Man on Mulberry Street

Words and Music by
Billy Joel

Why can't __ I __ lay __ low? __

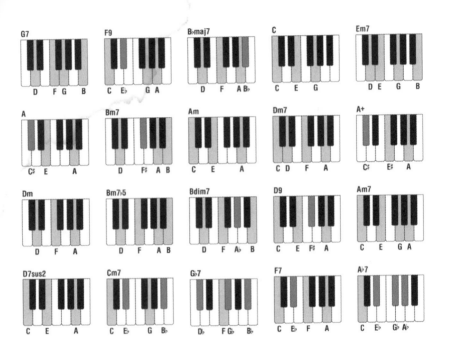

Intro

| G7 | F9 | | G7 | F9 | | |
| G7 | F9 | | G7 | F9 | | |

PIANO CHORD SONGBOOK

Verse 1

```
G7            Bbmaj7  C/F
Why can't I lay       low?
```

```
G7            Bbmaj7  C/F
Why can't I say what I ___ mean?
```

```
G7              Bbmaj7  C/F
Why don't I stay        home
```

```
G7                Bbmaj7  C/F        Em7
And get myself into some boring rou-tine?
```

```
              A    Bm7
Why can't I calm down?
```

```
Em7       A        Bm7
Why is it always a ___ fight?
```

```
Em7         A   Bm7
I can't get un - wound.
```

```
Em7         Am         C/D
Why do I throw myself into the
```

Interlude 1

```
│ G7    F9 │          │ G7    F9 │              │
  Night?
```

```
│ G7    F9 │          │ G7    F9 │              │
```

Verse 2

```
G7            Bbmaj7  C/F
I'm on the out    -   side.
```

```
G7          Bbmaj7  C/F
I don't fit into a     groove.
```

```
G7              Bbmaj7  C/F
Now, I ain't a bad      guy.
```

```
G7                Bbmaj7  C/F        Em7
So, tell me, what am I trying to prove?
```

```
              A    Bm7
Why can't I cool out?
```

```
Em7           A        Bm7
Why don't I button my lip?
```

```
Em7         A   Bm7
Why do I lash out?
```

```
Em7       A N.C.                    Dm7
Why is it I  always shoot from the hip?
```

Bridge

Dm7   A+/C$\sharp$
I cruise from Houston to Ca-nal Street,

    Dm/C   Bm7$\flat$5
A mis-fit and a rebel.

Dm7   A+/C$\sharp$
I see the winos talking to themselves,

    Dm/C   Bdim7
And I ___ can understand.

Am   Am/G$\sharp$
Why is it ev'rytime I go out

            Am/G   D9/F$\sharp$
I always seem to get in trouble?

Am7 N.C.
I guess I made an impression

   D7sus2 N.C.
On somebody north of Hester and south of Grand.

Interlude 2   *Repeat Interlude 1*

Verse 3

G7   B$\flat$maj7 C/F
And so, in my small   way

G7   B$\flat$maj7 C/F
I'm a big man on Mulberry Street.

G7   B$\flat$maj7 C/F
I don't mean al   -   ways,

G7   B$\flat$maj7   C/F   Em7
Only at night when I'm light on my feet.

            A Bm7
What else have I   got

Em7   A   Bm7
That I'd be trying to hide?

Em7   A   Bm7
Maybe a blind spot;

Em7   A N.C.
I haven't seen from the sensitive

Interlude 3	Dm7	A+/C#	Cm7	B7	

Side.

	Dm7	A+/C#	Cm7	B7	
	Am7	Am/G#	Am/G	D9/F#	
	Am7 N.C.		D7sus2		

Interlude 4   *Repeat Interlude 1*

Verse 4

G7   Bbmaj7 C/F
But you know, in my own   heart,

G7   Bbmaj7 C/F
I'm a big man on Mulberry Street.

G7   Bbmaj7 C/F
I play the whole   part;

G7   Bbmaj7   C/F   Em7
I leave a big tip with ev'ry re-ceipt.

        A   Bm7
I'm so ro-man-tic,

Em7   A   Bm7
I'm such a passionate man.

Em7   A Bm7
Sometimes I pan-ic,

Em7   Am   C/D
What if no-body finds out who I

Interlude 5	G7	F9		G7	F9		

Am?

	G7	F9		G7	F9		

Outro	G7	Gb7 F7		
	G7 Gb7 G7 Ab7		
	G7	Gb7 F7	
	G7 Gb7 G7· Ab7		

‖:G7   F9| | G7   F9| :‖ ***Repeat and fade***

Big Shot

Words and Music by
Billy Joel

Melody:

Well, _ you went up-town rid-ing in your lim-ou-sine, _

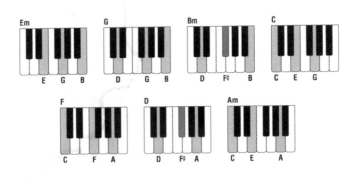

Em   E G B

G   D G B

Bm   D F♯ B

C   C E G

F   C F A

D   D F♯ A

Am   C E A

Intro

| Em | G | Em | G | |
| Em | Bm/D | C F/C | C | |

Verse 1

        Em   **G**
Well, you went uptown riding in your limousine,

     Em   **G**
With your fine Park Avenue clothes.

      Em   **D**
You had the Dom Perignon in your hand

         C F/C C
And the spoon up your nose.

        Em   **G**
Oo, and when you wake up in the morning with your head on fire

     Em   **G**
And your eyes too bloody to see,

       Em
Go on and cry in your coffee

     Bm/D   **C F/C C N.C.**
But don't ____ come bitchin' to me.

Chorus 1

 G/F F/C G/C   F
Because you had to be a big   shot, didn't you.

    G/C F/C G/F   F
You had to   open up your mouth.

G/C   G F/D G/D   F/G
You had to be a big shot, didn't you.

G/D Am/D G   C
All   your   friends were so knocked out.

G/E   G/F F/C G/C F
You had to have the last word, last night.

    G/C Am G/F   F
You know what ev'rything's about.

              F/C C F/C   C
You had to have a white hot spot - light,

         G/D D   G/D D
You had to be a big shot last night, whoa.

Interlude   *Repeat Intro*

Verse 2

              Em   G
And they were all impressed with your Halston dress,

      Em   G
And the people that you knew at Elaine's,

      Em   D
And the story of your latest success

              C   F/C   C
Kept 'em so entertained.

              Em   G
Ah, but now you just don't remember all the things you said,

              Em   G
And you're not __ sure that you wanna know.

          Em
I'll give you one hint, honey,

      Bm/D   C F/C   C N.C.
You sure ____ did put on a show.

Chorus 2

                 G/F F/C G/C F
Yes, yes, you had to be a big shot, didn't you.

    G/C F/C G/F   **F**
You had to   prove it to the crowd.

G/C   **G F/D G/D F/G**
You had to be a big shot, didn't you.

G/D Am/D G   **C**
All   your   friends were so knocked out.

G/E   **G/F F/C G/C F**
You had to have the last word, last night,

G/C Am G/F   **F**
So   much fun to be around.

              F/C C   F/C C
You had to have the front page, bold type,

            G/D D   G/D D
You had to be a big shot last   night, whoa.

Bridge 1

F   **C**
  Oh, oh, oh, whoa.

G   **D**
  Oh, oh, whoa.

F   **C**
  Oh, oh, oh, whoa.

G   **D**
  Oh, oh, whoa.

Verse 3

        Em   **G**
Well, it's no ___ big sin to stick your two ___ cents in

        Em   **G**
If you know ___ when to leave it alone.

        Em
But you went over the line,

        Bm/D   **C F/C C N.C.**
You couldn't see it was time to go home.

No, no, no, no, no, no, you had to be a

Chorus 3

    G/F F/C G/C F
Big shot, didn't you.

       G/C F/C G/F   F
You had to   open up your mouth.

    G/C   G F/D G/D F/G
You had to be a big shot, didn't you.

    G/D Am/D G   C
All   your   friends were so knocked out.

    G/E   G/F F/C G/C F
You had to have the last word, last night.

       G/C Am G/F   F
You know what ev'rything's about.

           F/C C F/C C
You had to have a white hot spot - light,

          G/D D   G/D D
You had to be a big shot last night, whoa.

Bridge 2   *Repeat Bridge 1*

Outro

```
||: G/F  F/C    G/C  | F      G/C   Am  |
 |  G/F            F  |   G/C              |
 |  G      F/D   G/D  | F/G    G/D  Am/D |
 |  G             C   |         G/E       |
 |  G/F  F/C    G/C  | F      G/C   Am  |
 |  G/F           F  |                   |
 |  F/C  C   F/C     | C              :|| Repeat and fade
```

Captain Jack

Words and Music by
Billy Joel

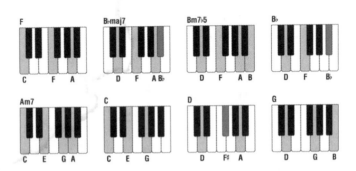

Intro | F | B♭maj7 | F | B♭maj7 |

Verse 1

F   B♭maj7
Saturday night and you're still ____ hangin' around.

F   B♭maj7
You're tired of livin' in your ____ one-horse town.

F   Bm7♭5 B♭
You'd like to find a little hole in the ground

    Am7 C
For a while, mm.

F   B♭maj7
So you go to the village in your ____ tie-dye jeans

F   B♭maj7
And you stare at the junkies ____ and the closet queens.

F   B♭maj7
It's like some pornographic magazine,

    Am7 D
And you smile. Mm.

Chorus 1

```
G              D        G/B          C          D
But Captain Jack will get you high ____ tonight
G              D        G/B      C
And take you to your special is - land.
G          D        G/B      C          D
Captain Jack will get you by ____ tonight.
G              D        G/B      C
Just a little push and you'll be smilin'.
```

Interlude 1 | F | B♭maj7 | F | B♭maj7 |

Verse 2

```
F                              B♭maj7
Your sister's gone out, ____ she's on a date,
F                              B♭maj7
And you just sit at home ____ and masturbate.
F                                      B♭maj7
Your phone is gonna ring soon, but you just ____ can't wait
        Am7        C
For that call.    Mm.
F                                      B♭maj7
So you stand on the corner in your new English clothes,
F                                      B♭maj7
And you look so polished from your hair ____ down to your toes.
F                              B♭maj7
Oh, but still your finger's gonna pick ____ your nose
        Am7          D
After all.      Mm, ____ yeah.
```

Chorus 2

```
G              D        G/B          C          D
But Captain Jack will get you high ____ tonight
G              D        G/B      C
And take you to your special is - land.
G      D        G/B      C          D
Captain Jack will get you by ____ tonight.
G          D        G/B      C
Just a little push and you'll be smilin'.
```

| *Interlude 2* | | F | | B♭maj7 | F | | B♭maj7 | |

Verse 3

F   B♭maj7
So you decide to take a ___ holiday.

F   B♭maj7
You got your tape deck and your brand ___ new Chevrolet.

F   B♭maj7
Aw, there ain't no place to go ___anyway,

              Am7   C
And what for.   Mm.

F   B♭maj7
So you've got ev'rything, aw, ___ but nothin's cool.

F   B♭maj7
They just found your father   in the swimmin' pool.

F   B♭maj7
And you guess you won't be goin' back to school

              Am7   D
Anymore.

Chorus 3

G   D   G/B   C   D
But Captain Jack will get you high ___ tonight

G   D   G/B   C
And take you to your special is - land.

G   D   G/B   C   D
Oh, Captain Jack will get you by ___ tonight.

G   D   G/B   C
Just a little push and you'll be smilin'.

| *Interlude 3* | | F | | B♭maj7 | F | | B♭maj7 | |

Verse 4

F   B♭maj7
So you play your albums ____ and you smoke your pot.

F
And you meet your girlfriend in the park - in' lot.
              B♭maj7

F
Oh, but still you're aching for the things you have-n't got.
               B♭maj7

      Am7   C
What went wrong? Mm.

F
And if you can't understand why your world is so dead
            B♭maj7

F
And why you've got to keep in style ____ and feed your head,
           B♭maj7

F
Well, you're twenty-one and still your mother makes your bed.
                B♭maj7

      Am7 D
And that's too long.

Chorus 4

G   D   G/B   C   D
But Captain Jack will get you high ____ tonight

G   D G/B C
And take you to your special is - land.

  G   D   G/B   C   D
Well, ____ now, Captain Jack will get you by ____ tonight.

G   D   G/B C
Just a little push and you'll be smilin'.

Outro

  G   D   G/B   C   D
‖: Oh, Captain Jack will get you high ____ tonight

G   D   G/B C
And take you to your special is - land.

  G   D   G/B C   D
Well, ____ now, Captain Jack could make ____ you die ____ tonight.

G   D   G/B C
Just a little push and you'll be smilin'. :‖ *Repeat and fade*

Don't Ask Me Why

Words and Music by
Billy Joel

Melody:

All the __ wait - ers in your grand ca - fé... __

Intro ‖: G   C/G | G   C/G :‖ *Play 3 times*

Verse 1

G Am7 G/B G   Am7 G/B A   Bm7 A/C#
All the   wait-ers in   your grand ca - fé

D   Em D/F# D   Em D/F# G   C/G
Leave their ta - bles when you   blink. Oh.

G   Am7 G/B G   Am7 G/B A   Bm7 A/C#
Ev - 'ry   dog must have   his ev - 'ry - day;

D Em D/F# D   Em D/F# G
Ev-'ry drunk must have his   drink.

      B7   Em
Don't wait for an - swers;

    G7/D   C#m7♭5
Just take your chanc - es.

            D7sus
Don't ask ___ me

| G   C/G | G   C/G | G   C/G | G   C/G |
Why.

Verse 2

G Am7 G/B G Am7 G/B A   Bm7 A/C#
All your life you had to stand in   line,

D Em   D/F# D Em D/F# G
Still you're stand-ing on your feet.

C/G G Am7 G/B G Am7 G/B A   Bm7 A/C#
Oh, all your choic-es made you change your mind,

D   Em D/F# D Em D/F# G
Now your cal - en-dar's com - plete.

B7   Em
Don't wait for an - swers;

   G7/D   C#m7♭5
Just take your chanc - es.

            D7sus
Don't ask ____ me

|G C/G |G C/G |G C/G |G C/G |
 Why.

Bridge

   D   C
Mm, you can say the human heart is only make-believe,

   D   G   C/G G
And I am only fighting fire with fire.

   E   A
But you are still a victim of the ac - cidents you leave,

   E7   A7   D7
As sure as I'm a victim of desi - yi - yi - re.

Verse 3

G Am7 G/B G   Am7 G/B A   Bm7 A/C#
All the   ser - vants in your new ho - tel

D   Em D/F# D Em D/F# G
Throw their ros - es at your feet.

C/G G   Am7 G/B G   Am7 G/B A Bm7 A/C#
Oh, fool them all but, ba - by, I can   tell

D   Em D/F# D Em D/F# G
You're no strang-er to   the   street.

    B7   Em
Don't ask for fa - vors.

    G7/D   C#m7♭5
Don't talk to strang - ers.

        D7sus
Don't ask ___ me

| G C/G | G C/G | G C/G | G C/G |
Why.

Piano Solo

D		C		
D		G		
E		A		
E		A7	D	

Verse 4

G   Am7 G/B G Am7 G/B A   Bm7 A/C#
Yes - ter - day you were an on - ly   child,

D Em D/F# D   Em D/F# G
Now your ghosts have gone a - way.

C/G G   Am7 G/B G   Am7 G/B A   Bm7 A/C#
Oh, you can kill them in   the clas - sic style.

D Em D/F# D Em D/F# G
Now you "par - lez vous Fran - çais."

    B7   Em
Don't look for an - swers;

    G7/D   C#m7♭5
You took your chanc - es.

        D7sus
Don't ask ___ me

| G C/G | G C/G | G C/G | G   C/G | |
Why.   Don't   ask me why.

| G C/G | G C/G | G C/G | G |

The Downeaster "Alexa"

Words and Music by
Billy Joel

Well, I'm   on   the Down-east - er   A - lex -   a,

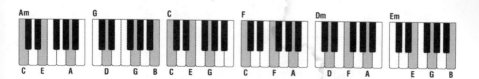

Intro |Am   G|Am | G|Am   N.C.|

                   C   G   Am

Verse 1   Well, I'm on the Down-easter Alex - a,

           C   G   F

And I'm cruising through Block Island Sound.

                    C   Dm

I have charted a course ___ to the vine - yard,

             C   G   F

But tonight ___ I am Nantucket bound.

            G   C/E   F

We took on diesel back in Mon - tauk yesterday;

            G   Am   G/B

Left this morn - ing from the bell ___ in Gardiners Bay.

   F   G   C/E   F

    Like all the lo - cals here, I've had to sell my home.

            G   Am   G/B

Too proud to leave, I worked my fingers to the bone.

Verse 2

                   C   G   Am
So I could own __ my Down-easter Alex - a,

      C   G   F
And I go where the o - cean is deep.

                    C   Dm
There are giants out there in the can - yons

           C   G   F
And a good ____ captain can't fall asleep.

      G   C/E   F
I got bills to pay and children who need clothes.

           G   Am   G/B
I know there's fish out there, but where, God only knows.

F   G   C/E   F
  They say these waters aren't what ____ they used to be,

          G   Am   G/B
But I've got people back on land who count on me.

           C   G   Am
So if you see __ my Down-easter Alex - a,

            C   G   F
And if you work with the rod __ and the reel,

              C   Dm
Tell my wife I am trolling Atlan - tis,

        C   G   F
And I still have my hands on the wheel.

Interlude

Am	G	Am			G	Am	
Em							
Am	G	Am			G	Am	N.C.

Verse 3

```
        C              G        Am
Now I drive my Down-easter Alex - a
            C               G         F
More and more miles from shore ev'ry year,
                C              Dm
Since they told me I can't sell no strip - ers
            C          G         F
And there's no luck in sword fishing here.
        G               C/E        F
I was a bay man like my father was before.
            G         Am          G/B
Can't make a living as a bay man anymore.
F               G           C/E                F
  There ain't much future for a man ___ who works the sea,
                G         Am        G/B
But there ain't no island left for islanders like me.
```

Outro

```
          C  G   Am
Ya, ya, ya,    yo.
          C  G   Am
Ya, ya, ya,    yo.
          C  G   Am
Ya, ya, ya,    yo.
         C  G Am
Ya, ya, ya,   oh.
```

The Entertainer

Words and Music by
Billy Joel

Melody:

I   am the en - ter-tain - er...

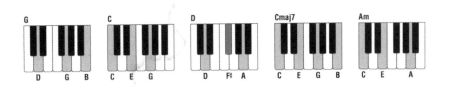

Intro

‖: G | :‖ *Play 3 times*
| G

Verse 1

> G   C
> I am the entertainer and I know just where I stand:
>
>   G   C   D
> Another sere-nader and another long-haired band.
>
>   G   C
> To-day I am your champion; I may have won your hearts.
>
>   Cmaj7   D
> But I know the game, you'll for-get my name,
>
>   Am   Cmaj7
> And I won't be here in another year
>
>   D   G
> If I don't stay on the charts.

Verse 2

      G   C

I am the entertainer, and I've had to pay my price.

                 G/B   C   D

The things I did not know at first I learned by doin' twice.

        G   C

Ah, but still they come to haunt me; still they want their say.

       Cmaj7   D

So I've learned to dance with a hand in my pants,

         Am   Cmaj7

Let 'em rub my neck and I write 'em a check

       D   G

And they go their merry way.

Verse 3

      G   C

I am the entertainer, been all around the world.

                 G/B   C   D

I've played all kinds of pal - aces and laid all kinds of girls.

      G   C

I can't remember faces;   I don't remember names.

       Cmaj7   D

Ah, but what the hell, you know it's __ just as well.

        Am   Cmaj7

'Cause after a while and a thou - sand miles

D   G

  It all becomes the same.

Verse 4

      G   C

I am the entertainer, I bring to you my songs.

                 G/B   C   D

I'd like to spend a day ____ or two, but I can't stay that long.

       G   C

No, I got to meet expenses, I got to stay in line,

       Cmaj7   D

Gotta get those fees to the agencies.

        Am   C

And I'd love to stay, but there's bills to pay,

       D   G

So I just don't have the time.

Verse 5

G   C
I am the entertainer, I come to do my show.

                    G/B   C   D
You've heard my latest rec - ord, it's been on the radi-o.

     G   C
Ah, it took me years to write it; they were the best years of my life.

                    D
It was a beautiful song, but it ran too long.

       Am   C
If you're gonna have a hit you got - ta make it fit,

      D   G
So they cut it down to 3:05.

Verse 6

G   C
I am the entertainer, the idol of my age.

                  G/B   C   D
I make all kinds of money when I go on the stage.

     G   C
Ah, you seen me in the papers, I've been in the magazines.

     Cmaj7   D
But if I go cold, I won't __ get sold,

     Am   C
I'll get put in the back, in the discount rack

     D   G
Like an-other can of beans.

Verse 7

G   C
I am the entertainer and I know just where I stand:

                  G/B   C   D
Another serenad-er and another long - haired band.

     G   C
To-day I am your champion; I may have won your hearts.

     Cmaj7   D
But I know the game, you'll for-get my name.

   Am   Cmaj7
I won't be here in an-other year

     D   G
If I don't stay on the charts.

Everybody Has a Dream

Words and Music by
Billy Joel

Melody:

While in these days   of qui-et des-per - a-tion, __

Intro

| D/F♯ Em/G G♯dim7 | D/A | Bm   G | |
| D/A | Asus | | |

Verse 1

                 D   G/B   F♯m
While in these days   of quiet desper-ation,

        Bm   Bm/A   E/G♯   E
As I wander through the world in which I live,

          G   A   Bm   Bm/A
I search ev'rywhere for some new inspi-ration,

          E/G♯   E   Em7 A
But it's more than cold re-ality can give.

       D   G/B   F♯m
If I need   a cause for cele-bration

      Bm   Bm/A   E/G♯ E
Or a comfort I can use ____ to ease my mind,

      G   A   Bm   Bm/A
I re-ly on my imagi-nation,

      E/G♯   E   Asus
And I dream of an i-maginary time.

     A
Oh,   'n' I know that

D   F#m7 G
Ev'rybody has a   dream.

D   F#m7 G
Ev'rybody has a   dream.

D   F#m7 G
Ev'rybody has a   dream.

F#m N.C. Bm   G   F#m
This is my dream, my own,

F#7   Bm G F#m
 Just to be   at home,

F#7   Bm   G   F#m   D7   Em7   Asus N.C.
 And to be   all a-lone   with you.

      D   G/B   F#m
If I be-lieve   in all the words I'm saying,

    Bm   Bm/A   E/G#   E
And if a word from you   can bring a better day,

    G   A   Bm   Bm/A
Then all I have are these games that I've ___ been playing

   E/G#   E   Asus   A
To keep my hope from crumbling away.

      D   G/B   F#m
So let me lie,   and let me go on sleeping,

   Bm   Bm/A   E/G#   E
And I will lose myself in palaces of sand.

       G   A   Bm   Bm/A
And all the fantasies that I will be keeping

      E/G#   E   Asus   A
Will make the empty hours easier, easier to stand.

And I know that

Chorus 2

D   F#m7 G
Ev'rybody has a   dream.

D   F#m7 G
Ev'rybody has a   dream.

D   F#m7 G
Ev'rybody has a   dream.

    F#m N.C. Bm   G   F#m
And this is my dream,   my own,

F#7 Bm   G F#m
 Just ____ to be at home,

F#7 Bm   G   F#m   D7
 And ____ to be all ___ a-lone,

      Em7
All alone ____ with you.

       Asus
Oh, ho, with you.   I know that

Outro

   D   F#m7 G
‖: Ev'rybody has a   dream.

D   F#m7 G
Ev'rybody has a   dream.   :‖ *Repeat and fade (w/ Voc. ad lib.)*

52nd Street

Words and Music by
Billy Joel

Melody:

They say it takes a lot to keep a love a-live.

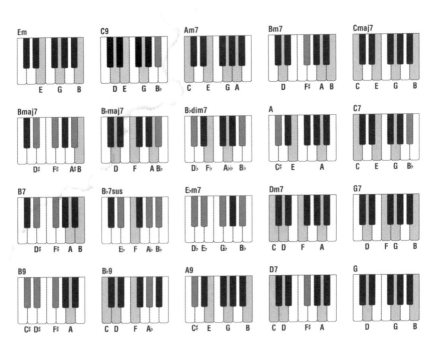

Intro   ‖: Em | | C9 | :‖

Verse

    Am7   **Bm7**   **Em**
    They say it takes a lot to keep a love alive.

    Am7   **Bm7**   **Cmaj7** **Bmaj7** **B♭maj7**
    In ev'ry heart there pumps a diff'rent beat.

    Am7   **B♭dim7**   **Bm7**   **A/C♯**
    But if we shift the rhythm into overdrive,

    C7 **N.C.**   **B7 B♭7sus B7 B♭7sus B7**
    Well, we could generate a lot of heat.

                          Em
Chorus   On Fifty-Second Street.

                 C9   **Em**   **C9**
                 Oh, oh, on Fifty-Second Street

                                          Em   **E♭m7 Dm7**
                 We're gonna have a little show parade

                          G7   **Cmaj7**   **B9**
                 Before they know the second bar was played.

                 B♭9   **A9**   **Am7**
                   We're gonna slip it to 'em short and sweet

                   D7 N.C.   **G**   **B7**
                 On   Fifty-Second Street.

Piano Solo | **Em** | | **C9** | |
                  | **Em** | | **C9** | |
                  | **Em E♭m7 Dm7**| **G7** | **Cmaj7 B9** |
                  | **B♭9**   **A9** | **Am7** | **D7   N.C.** |

Outro   ‖: **Em** | | **C9** | :‖ *Repeat and fade*
                                                                          (w/Voc. ad lib.)

BILLY JOEL   **47**

Goodnight Saigon

Words and Music by
Billy Joel

Melody:

We met as soul mates on Par-ris Is-land.

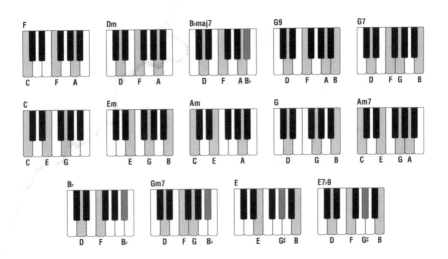

Intro | F | Dm | B♭maj7 | G9 |

Verse 1

              Dm/F   **G7   C**
We met as soul mates on Parris Island.

            Dm/F   **G7   C**
We left as inmates from an a-sylum.

             Em   Am   **Em   Am**
And we were sharp,   as sharp as knives.

           Dm   **Dm/C**   **G/B Am7 G**
And we were so gung ho to lay down our lives.

Verse 2

```
G          Dm/F     G7      C
We came in spastic, like tameless horses.

      Dm/F    G7        C
We left in plastic, as numbered corpses.

           Em  Am          Em   Am
And we learned fast      to travel light.

           Dm              Dm/C          Bb   G9   Dm   G9
Our arms were heavy, but our bellies were tight.
```

Verse 3

```
      Dm/F          G7    C
We had no home front, we had no soft soap.

      Dm/F          G7     C
They sent us Playboy, they gave us Bob Hope.

      Em  Am              Em     Am
We dug in deep      and shot on sight,

           Dm              Dm/C        G/B Am7 G
And prayed to Jesus Christ with all of our might.
```

Verse 4

```
      Dm/F     G7      C
We had no cam'ras to shoot the landscape.

           Dm/F          G7       C
We passed the hash pipe and played our Doors tapes.

      Em  Am          Em     Am
And it was dark,     so dark at night.

           Dm                  Dm/C
And we held on to each other like brother to brother;

      Bb                 F/A          Gm7
We promised our moth - ers we'd write.
```

Chorus 1

```
C/Bb        F/A  Bb     C    C/Bb
And we would all go down to-gether.

           F/A  Bb  G/B    C    C/Bb
We said we'd all go down ___ to-gether.

           F/A  Bb  Dm/A   G9     F    Dm   G9
Yes, we would all go down ___ to - gether.
```

Verse 5

        Dm/F   G7   C
Remember Charlie? Re-member Baker?

        Dm/F   G7 C
They left their childhood on ev'ry acre.

        Em   Am   Em Am
And who was wrong?   And who was right?

        Dm   Dm/C   B♭   G9
It didn't matter in the thick of the fight.

Verse 6

Am G/B   C Dm E   Dm/F E7♭9
We held the day in the palm of our hand.

Am G/B   C
They ruled the night,

Dm   E Dm/F   G9
And the night seemed to last as long as

Dm/F   G7   C
Six weeks on Parris Island.

        Dm/F   G7   C
We held the coastline; they held the highlands.

        Em Am   Em   Am
And they were sharp,   as sharp as knives.

        Dm   Dm/C
They heard the hum of our motors, they counted the rotors

    B♭   F/A   Gm7
And waited for us ___ to arrive.

Chorus 2

C/B♭   F/A B♭   C   C/B♭
And we would all go down to-gether.

        F/A B♭ G/B C   C/B♭
We said we'd all go down ___ to-gether.

        F/A B♭ Dm/A G9   F   Dm G9
Yes, we would all go down ___ to - gether.

Outro

‖: Dm | B♭maj7 | G9 | F   :‖ *Repeat and fade*

Honesty

Words and Music by
Billy Joel

Intro |Bb Bbm/Ab |Gbmaj7 F7 |

Verse 1

Bb   Eb
If you search for tenderness,

F   F/Eb Dm7
It isn't hard to find.

Eb   Gm   Am Cm7 F7
You can have the love____ you need to live.

Bb   Csus C
And if you look for truth - fulness,

    F   A/C#   Dm
You might just as well____ be blind.

 Eb   A7   Dsus D
It always seems to be____ so hard to give.

Chorus 1

Ebmaj7 F7 D/F#   Gm7 F
Honesty____ is such a lonely word.

Eb   F   Bb D
Everyone is so untrue.

Ebmaj7 F7 D/F#   Gm7 F
Honesty____ is hardly ever heard,

 Eb   F   Bb F7sus
But mostly what I need from you.

Verse 2

Bb   Eb
I can always find someone

F   F/Eb   Dm7
To say they sympathize

Eb   Gm   Am Cm7 F7
If I wear my heart out on my sleeve.

Bb   Csus   C
But I don't want some____ pretty face

F   A/C# Dm
To tell me pretty lies.

Eb   A7   Dsus D
All I want is someone to believe.

Chorus 2

Ebmaj7 F7 D/F#   Gm7 F
Honesty____ is such a lonely word.

Eb   F   Bb D
Everyone is so untrue.

Ebmaj7 F7 D/F#   Gm7 F
Honesty____ is hardly ever heard,

 Eb   F   Bb Bbm/Ab Gbmaj7 F7
But mostly what I need from you.

Bridge

Gm
    I can find a lover,

D/G
    I can find a friend,

Fm6
    I can have security

  C7
Un-til the bitter end.

E♭   F
    Anyone can comfort me

  E♭   B♭
With promises again

     C7sus C7
I know,

  F D/F♯ E♭ F7sus
I know.

Verse 3

B♭   E♭
    When I'm deep in-side of me,

F   F/E♭   Dm
    Don't be too con-cerned.

E♭   Gm   Am Cm7 F7
    I won't ask for nothin' while I'm gone.

B♭   Csus   C
    When I want sin - cerity,

        F   A/C♯ Dm
Tell me, where___ else can I turn?

   E♭   A7   D7sus D7
'Cause you're the one that I___ depend upon.

Chorus 3

E♭maj7 F7   D/F♯   Gm7 F
Honesty___ is such a lonely word.

E♭   F   B♭ D
Everyone is so untrue.

E♭maj7 F7   D/F♯   Gm7 F
Honesty___ is hardly ever heard,

  E♭   F   B♭ B♭m/A♭
But mostly what I need from you.

|G♭maj7   F7 |E♭m(maj7) F6 F7 |B♭ |

Hey, Girl

Words and Music by Carole King
and Gerry Goffin

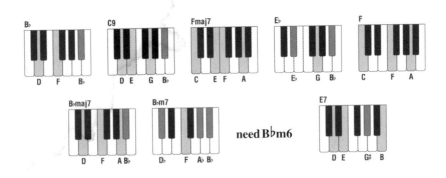

need B♭m6

Intro | B♭/C | C9 | B♭/C | C9 |

Verse 1

B♭/C C9   B♭/C   C9
Hey, girl, I want you to know

B♭/C C9   B♭/C   C9   Fmaj7
I'm gonna miss you so much if you go.

E♭/F   F   E♭/F   F
And hey, girl, I tell you no lie,

E♭/F   F   E♭/F   F   B♭maj7
Something deep in-side of me's ___ going ___ to die

        B♭m7
If you say so long,

B♭m6   Fmaj7   E7/G♯
If you say ___ goodbye.

Verse 2

Bb/C C9 Bb/C   C9
Hey, girl, this can't be true.

Bb/C   C9 Bb/C   C9 Fmaj7
How am I sup-posed to ex-ist   without you?

Eb/F   F   Eb/F   F
And, hey, girl, now don't put me on.

Eb/F   F   Eb/F   F   Bbmaj7
What's gonna happen to me when you're ___ gone?

         Bbm7
How will I live?

Bbm6   Fmaj7   E7/G#
How can I ___ go on?   Hey,

Sax Solo

| Bb/C C9 | Bb/C C9 | Bb/C C9 | Bb/C C9 |
Girl.

| Fmaj7 | |

Verse 3

Eb/F F   Eb/F   F
Hey, girl, now sit yourself down.

Eb/F F Eb/F   F   Bbmaj7
I'm not a-shamed to get down on the ___ ground

   Bbm7   Bbm6   Fmaj7
And ___ then   beg you to stay.

          Bb/C
Don't, don't ___ go away.

Outro

      Fmaj7
‖: Hey, _____ girl. No, no,

Bb/C
Don't go away.

     Fmaj7
Hey, ___ girl. Oh, no, please

     Bb/C
Don't ___ go away.   :‖ *Repeat and fade (w/Voc. ad lib.)*

I Go to Extremes

Words and Music by
Billy Joel

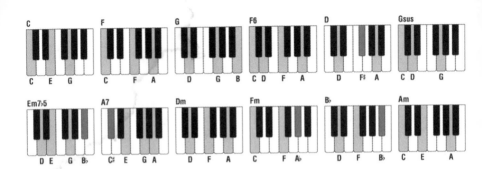

Intro

‖: C/B♭ |F/A G |C | :‖

Verse 1

C   **F/C**
Call me a joker, call me a fool.

F6/C   **C**
Right at this moment, I'm totally cool.

             F
Clear as a crystal, sharp as a knife,

           C
I feel like I'm in the prime of my life.

C/B♭   **F/A**
Sometimes it feels like I'm going too fast.

C/G   **D/F♯**
I don't know how long this feeling will last.

Gsus   **G**   **C**   **N.C.**
Maybe it's only to-night.

        C/Bb   F/A   G C
Darling, I don't know why I go to ex-tremes.

            C/Bb   F/A   G C
Too high or too low, there ain't no in-be-tweens.

        Em7b5   A7
And if I stand or I fall,

Dm   Fm
It's all or nothing at all.

        C/Bb   F/A G C
Darling, I don't know why I go to ex-tremes.

C   F/C
Sometimes I'm tired, sometimes I'm shot.

F6/C   C
Sometimes I don't know how much more I got.

           F
Maybe I'm headed over the hill,

           C
Maybe I've set myself up for the kill.

C/Bb   F/A
Tell me, how much do you think you can take

C/G   D/F#
Until the heart in you's starting to break?

Gsus   G   C N.C.
Sometimes it feels like it will.

        C/Bb   F/A G C
Darling, I don't know why I go to ex-tremes.

        C/Bb   F/A   G C
Too high or too low, there ain't no in-be-tweens.

        Em7b5   A7
You can be sure when I'm gone,

Dm   Fm
I won't be out there too long.

        C/Bb   F/A G C
Darling, I don't know why I go to ex-tremes.

Bridge

D   Bb
Out of the darkness, into the light,

F   C
Leaving the scene of the crime.

D   Bb   F
Either I'm wrong or I'm perfectly right ev'ry time.

Am   F
Sometimes I lie awake, night after night,

C   G
Coming apart at the seams,

D   Bb
Eager to please, ready to fight.

F   C   N.C.
Why do I go to ex-tremes?

Piano Solo

‖: C/Bb | F/A   G | C | :‖

Chorus 3

C   Em7b5   A7
And if I stand or I fall,

Dm   Fm
It's all or nothing at all.

      C/Bb   F/A   G C
Darling, I don't know why I go to ex-tremes.

      C/Bb   F/A   G C
No, I don't know why I go to ex-tremes.

        C/Bb   F/A   G C
Too high or too low, there ain't no in-be-tweens.

      Em7b5   A7
You can be sure when I'm gone,

Dm   Fm
I won't be out there too long.

      C/Bb   F/A   G C   N.C.
Darling, I don't know why I go to ex-tremes.

Outro

‖: C/Bb | F/A   G |

C
I don't know why. I don't know why. :‖ *Repeat and fade*

Just the Way You Are

Words and Music by
Billy Joel

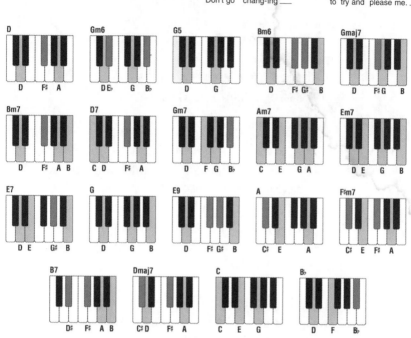

Intro	‖: D Gm6/D D G5/D │ D Gm6/D D G5/D :‖

Verse 1

    D   Bm6   Gmaj7   Bm7 D7
Don't go changing   to try and please ___ me.

Gmaj7   Gm7   D/F♯ Am7 D7
You never let me down before.   Mm.

Gmaj7   Gm7 D/F♯   Bm7
I don't imag - ine   you're too famil - iar

Em7   E7   G/A
And I don't see you anymore.

Verse 2

D   Bm6 Gmaj7 Bm7 D7
I ___ would not leave you in times of trouble.

Gmaj7 Gm7   D/F# Am7 D7
We never could have come this far. Mm.

Gmaj7 Gm7 D/F#   Bm7
I took the good times; I'll take the bad times.

Em7   G/A
I'll take you just the way you are.

|D Gm6/D D G5/D |D Gm6/D D G5/D |

Verse 3

D   Bm6 Gmaj7   Bm7 D7
Don't go trying some new fash - ion,

Gmaj7   Gm7   D/F# Am7 D7
Don't change the color of your hair. Mm.

Gmaj7 Gm7 D/F#   Bm7
You always have my unspoken pas - sion,

Bm7/E   E9   G/A
Although I might ___ not seem to care.

   D   Bm6 Gmaj7 Bm7 D7
I ___ don't want clever conversa - tion;

Gmaj7 Gm7   D/F# Am7 D7
I never want to work that hard. Mm.

Gmaj7 Gm7 D/F#   Bm7
I just want someone that I can talk to.

Em7   G/A
I want you just ___ the way you are.

|D Gm6/D D G5/D |D Gm6/D D D7 |

Bridge

Gmaj7   A   F#m7 B7
I need to know ___ that you will al - ways be

Em7   G/A   Dmaj7
The same old someone that I ___ knew.

   C B♭   C   Am7 D7
Oh, _____what will it take till you believe ___ in me

Gm7   G/A
The way that I believe in you?

Verse 4

D   Bm6   Gmaj7   Bm7 D7
I __ said I love you   and that's for-ever,

Gmaj7   Gm7   D/F♯ Am7 D7
And this I promise from the heart.   Mm.

Gmaj7   Gm7   D/F♯   Bm7
I couldn't love you   any bet - ter.

Em7   G/A
I love you just ____ the way you are.

| D Gm6/D D G5/D | D Gm6/D D G5/D |

Piano Solo

| D   Bm6 | Gmaj7 Bm7 D7 | Gmaj7 Gm7 | D/F♯   Am7 D7 |
| Gmaj7 Gm7 | D/F♯   Bm7 | Bm7/E E9 | G/A |

Verse 5

D   Bm6 Gmaj7   Bm7   D7
I ____ don't want clever   conver-sation;

Gmaj7   Gm7   D/F♯ Am7 D7
I never want to work that hard.   Mm.

Gmaj7   Gm7   D/F♯   Bm7
I just want someone   that I can talk ____ to.

Em7   G/A
I want you just ____ the way you are.

| B♭   C | Am7 D7 | Gm7 G/A |

Outro

‖: D   Bm6 | Gmaj7 Bm7 D7 | Gmaj7 Gm7 |
| D/F♯ Am7 D7 | Gmaj7 Gm7 | D/F♯   Bm7 |
| Bm7/E E7 | G/A   :‖ *Repeat and fade*

An Innocent Man

Words and Music by
Billy Joel

Melody:

Some peo-ple stay far a-way from the door... __

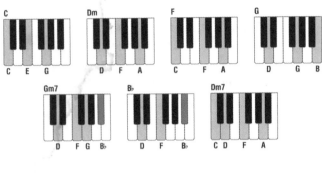

Intro | C | | | | |

Verse 1

    C
Some people stay far away from the door
        Dm
If there's a chance of it opening up.
F   **G**
They hear a voice in the hall ____ outside
                    C
And hope that it just passes by.

Some people live with the fear of a touch
        Dm
And the an - ger of having been a fool.
F   **G**
They will not listen to an - yone,
               C
So nobody tells them a lie.

Bridge 1

  Gm7   **C**
I know you're only protect - ing yourself,
B♭/F   **F**
I know you're thinking of some - body else.
G N.C.
Someone who hurt you, but

Verse 2

C
I'm not above making up for the love
                Dm
You've been de-nying you could ever feel.
F   G
   I'm not above doing an - ything
                     C
To restore your faith, if I can.

Some people see through the eyes of the old
             Dm
Before they ever get a look at the young.
F   G
   I'm only willing to hear ___ you cry,

Because I am an innocent

Chorus 1

C F/C C F/A G/B
Man.
| C   F/C   C | Dm7   C/E |
  F   B♭/F F
I am an innocent man.
G   C
   Oh, yes, I am.

Verse 3

C
   Some people say they will never believe
         Dm
Another promise they hear in the dark,
F   G
   Because they only remem - ber too well
                      C
They heard somebody tell them be-fore.

Some people sleep all alone ev'ry night
         Dm
Instead of taking a lover to bed.
F   G
   Some people find that it's eas - ier
                  C
To hate than to wait anymore.

Bridge 2

Gm7   C
I know you don't want to hear __ what I say.

B♭/F   F
I know you're gonna keep turning away.

G N.C.
But I've been there and if

Verse 4

    C
I __ can survive, I can keep you alive.

     Dm
I'm not a-bove going through it again.

F   G
I'm not above being cool __ for a while.

         C
If you're cruel to me I'll understand.

Some people run from a possible fight;

     Dm
Some people figure they can never win.

F   G
And although this is a fight ____ I can lose,

The accused is an innocent

Chorus 2

C F/C C F/A G/B
Man.

| C   F/C   C | Dm7   C/E |
 F   B♭/F F
I am an innocent man.

G   C F/C C
 Oh, yes, I am

F/A G/B   C F/C C Dm7 C/E
 An in-nocent man.

	Gm7 C
Bridge 3	You know you only hurt your-self out of spite.

Bridge 3

Gm7   C
You know you only hurt your-self out of spite.
B♭/F   F
I guess you'd rather be a martyr tonight.
G N.C.
    That's your decision,

Verse 5

           C
But I'm __ not below anybody I know
         Dm
If there's a chance of resurrecting a love.
F   G
I'm not above going back ____ to the start
                          C
To find out where the heartache be-gan.

Some people hope for a miracle cure,
         Dm
Some people just accept the world as it is.
F   G
But I'm not willing to lay __ down and die,

Because I am an innocent

Chorus 3

C F/C C F/A G/B
Man.
| C   F/C   C | Dm7   C/E |
 F   B♭/F F
I am an innocent man.
G   C F/C C
  Oh, yes, I am
F/A   G/B   C F/C C
  An in-nocent man.
Dm7 C/E G C
  Oh.

It's Still Rock and Roll to Me

Words and Music by
Billy Joel

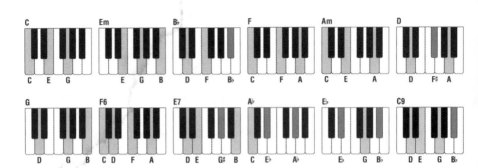

C	**Em**	**B♭**	**F**	**Am**	**D**
C E G	E G B	D F B♭	C F A	C E A	D F♯ A

G	**F6**	**E7**	**A♭**	**E♭**	**C9**
D G B	C D F A	D E G♯ B	C E♭ A♭	E♭ G B♭	D E G B♭

Intro | C | | | |

Verse 1

    C   **Em**
What's the matter with the clothes I'm wearing?

        B♭   **F**
Can't you tell that your tie's too wide?

C   **Em**
  Maybe I should buy some old tab collars.

       B♭   **F**
Welcome back to the age of jive.

Em   **Am**
  Where have you been hidin' out lately, honey?

   Em   **D**   **G**
You can't dress trashy till you spend a lot of money.

C   **Em**   **B♭**
Ev'rybody's talkin' 'bout the new sound.

F   **Am**   **G**   **C**
Funny, but it's still rock and roll to me.

Verse 2

|C| |Em|
What's the matter with the car I'm driving?

     Bb   **F**
Can't you tell that it's out of style?

C   **Em**
    Should I get a set of whitewall tires?

     Bb   **F**
Are you gonna cruise the Miracle Mile?

Em   **Am**
    Nowadays you can't be too sentimental.

    Em   **D**   **G**
Your best bet's a true baby blue Conti-nental.

C   **Em**   **Bb**   **F**
Hot funk, cool punk, even if it's old junk,

   Am   **G**   **C**
It's still rock and roll to me.

Bridge

   G   **F6**
Oh, __ it doesn't matter what they say in the papers,

     E7   **Am**
'Cause it's always been the same old scene.

     G   **F6**
There's a new band in town, but you can't get the sound

     E7   **Ab**
From a story in a magazine,

    Eb   **F6**   **G** N.C.
Aimed ____ at your average teen.

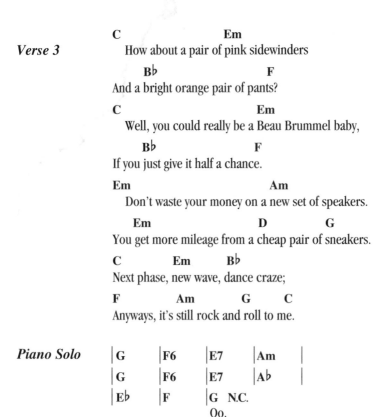

	C Em
Verse 3	How about a pair of pink sidewinders

     C   **Em**
How about a pair of pink sidewinders

       B♭   **F**
And a bright orange pair of pants?

     C   **Em**
Well, you could really be a Beau Brummel baby,

       B♭   **F**
If you just give it half a chance.

   Em   **Am**
Don't waste your money on a new set of speakers.

     Em   **D**   **G**
You get more mileage from a cheap pair of sneakers.

   C   **Em**   **B**♭
Next phase, new wave, dance craze;

   F   **Am**   **G**   **C**
Anyways, it's still rock and roll to me.

Piano Solo

G	F6	E7	Am	
G	F6	E7	A♭	
E♭	F	G N.C.		

Oo.

Verse 4

   C   Em
What's the matter with the crowd I'm seeing?
      B♭   F
Don't you know that they're out of touch?
C   Em
Well, should I try to be a straight-A student?
      B♭   F
If you are, then you think too much.
Em   Am
Don't you know about the new fashion, honey?
Em   D   G
All you need are looks and a whole lotta money.
     C   Em   B♭
It's the next phase, new wave, dance craze;
F   Am   G   C
Anyways, it's still rock and roll to me.

Outro

C N.C.   Em N.C.   B♭ N.C.
Ev'rybody's talkin' 'bout the new sound.
F N.C.   G N.C.   C9
Funny, but it's still rock and roll to me.

Keeping the Faith

Words and Music by
Billy Joel

If it seems like I've been lost in let's re-mem - ber,

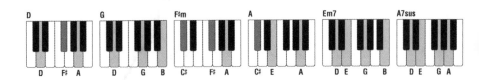

D   G   F#m   A   Em7   A7sus

Intro | D | | | |

Verse 1

          D
If it seems like I've been lost in let's remember,

If you think I'm feeling older, and missing my younger days,

          G
Oh, then you should have known me much better,

                        D
'Cause my past is something that never got in my way. Oh, no.

Still I would not be here now if I never had the hunger,

And I'm not ashamed to say the wild boys were my friends.

          G
Oh, 'cause I never felt the desire till their music set me on fire,

          D/A   G/B
Then I was saved, yeah.

                 F#m/A
That's why I'm keeping the faith.

G   **N.C.**   **D**
Yeah, yeah, yeah, yeah, keeping the faith.

Verse 2
         D
We wore matador boots, only Flagg Brothers had 'em with a Cuban heel.

Iridescent socks with the same color shirt and a tight pair of chino's.
    G
Oh, I put on my sharkskin jacket, you know the kind with the velvet collar
        D
And ditty-bop shades. Oh, yeah.

I took a fresh pack of Luckies and a mint called Sen Sen.

My old man's Trojans and his Old Spice after-shave.
        G
Oh, combed my hair in a pompadour
                 D/A
Like the rest of the Romeos wore, a permanent wave.
G/B   **F♯m/A**
Yeah, we were keeping the faith.
G   **N.C.**   **D**
Yeah, yeah, yeah, yeah, keeping the faith.

Bridge 1
        A   **G**   **D/F♯**
You can get ___ just so much ___ from a good ___ thing,
        A   **G**   **D/F♯**
You can linger too long ___ in your dreams.
        A   **G**   **D/F♯**
Say good-bye to the old - ies but good - ies,
       Em7
'Cause the good ol' days weren't always good
      A7sus
And to-morrow ain't as bad as it seems.

Verse 3

D
Learned stickball as a formal education.

Lost a lot of fights, but it taught me how to lose O.K.

G
Oh, I heard about sex, but not enough.

                                                    D
I found you could dance and still look tough any-way. Oh, yes, I did.

I found out a man ain't just bein' macho.

Ate an awful lot of late night drive-in food, drank a lot of take-home pay.

 G
I thought I was the Duke of Earl

                                                 D/A
When I made it with a red-haired girl in a Chevrolet.

   G/B   **F#m/A**
Oh, yeah, we were keeping the faith.

G   **N.C.**   **D**
Yeah, yeah, yeah, yeah, keeping the faith.

Bridge 2

     A   **G**   **D/F#**
Whoa.

     A   **G**   **D/F#**
Whoa.

     A   **G**   **D/F#**
Whoa.

            Em7
You know the good ol' days weren't always good;

     A7sus
To-morrow ain't as bad as it seems.

Verse 4

          D
I told you my reasons for the whole revival.

Now, I'm going outside to have an ice-cold beer in the shade.

          G
Oh, I'm gonna listen to my forty-fives;

                             D/A
Ain't it wonderful to be alive when the rock and roll plays.

G/B   F♯m/A
Yeah, when the memory stays.

G/B   F♯m/A
Yeah, I'm keeping the faith.

G   N.C.   D
Yeah, yeah, yeah, yeah, keeping the faith.

Outro

          D
‖:   I'm keeping the faith.   :‖ *Repeat and fade (w/Voc. ad lib.)*

Leave a Tender Moment Alone

Words and Music by
Billy Joel

Melody:

E - ven though I'm in love, _____

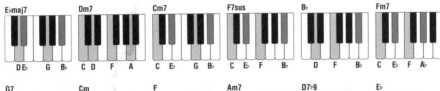

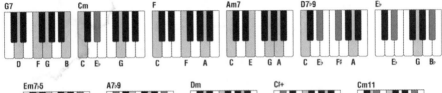

Intro

| Ebmaj7 | Dm7 | Cm7 F7sus | Bb | |
| Ebmaj7 | Dm7 | Cm7 F7sus | Bb N.C. | |

Verse 1

        Ebmaj7 Dm7
Even though I'm in love,
Cm7   **F7sus**   **Bb**
Sometimes I get so afraid.
        Ebmaj7 Dm7
I'll say something so wrong
Cm7   **F7sus**   **Bb**
Just to have something to say.
        Fm7 G7
I know the moment isn't right
   Cm   **Cm/Bb**   **Cm/Ab**
To tell the girl a comical line,
       Cm/G   **Fm7 G7**
To keep the conversation light.
       Cm   **Cm/Bb**   **F/A N.C.**
I guess I'm just frightened out of my mind.

Verse 1 (cont.)

$E\flat$maj7   Dm7
But if that's how I feel,

     Cm7   F7sus   B$\flat$
Then it's the best feeling I've ever known.

     $E\flat$maj7 Dm7
It's undeniably real;

Cm7   F7sus   B$\flat$ N.C.
Leave a tender moment alone.

Verse 2

     $E\flat$maj7 Dm7
Yes, I know I'm in love.

    Cm7   F7sus   B$\flat$
But just when I ought to relax,

      $E\flat$maj7 Dm7
I put my foot in my mouth

    Cm7   F7sus   B$\flat$
'Cause I'm just a-voiding the facts.

     Fm7   G7
If the girl gets too close,

  Cm   Cm/B$\flat$ Cm/A$\flat$
If I need some room to escape,

   Cm/G   Fm7 G7
When the moment arose

  Cm   Cm/B$\flat$ F/A N.C.
I'd tell her it's all a mistake.

     $E\flat$maj7 Dm7
But that's not how I feel.

   Cm7   F7sus   B$\flat$
No, that's not the woman I know.

     $E\flat$maj7 Dm7
She's undeniably real;

   Cm7   F7sus   B$\flat$ N.C.
So leave a tender moment alone.

Bridge

        Am7
But it's not only me

D7♭9   **E♭**   **E♭/D**
  Breaking down when the ten - sion gets high.

Cm   **Em7♭5**
  Just when I'm in a serious mood,

A7♭9   **Dm**   **C♯+ Cm11 N.C.**
  She is suddenly quiet and shy.

Interlude

| **E♭maj7** | **Dm7** | |
Cm7   **F7sus**   **B♭**
(Leave a tender moment alone.)

| **E♭maj7** | **Dm7** | |
Cm7   **F7sus**   **B♭ N.C.**
(Leave a tender moment alone.)

Verse 3

                Fm7 G7
I know the moment isn't right

  Cm   **Cm/B♭**   **Cm/A♭**
To hold my e-motions inside,

        Cm/G   **Fm7 G7**
To change the attitude to-night;

    Cm   **Cm/B♭**   **F/A N.C.**
I've run out of places to hide.

        E♭maj7 Dm7
And if that's how I feel,

      Cm7   **F7sus**   **B♭**
Then it's the best feeling I've ever known.

        E♭maj7 Dm7
It's undeniably real;

Cm7   **F7sus**   **B♭**
Leave a tender moment alone.

Outro

‖: **E♭maj7** | **Dm7** | |
  Cm7   **F7sus4**   **B♭**
(Leave a tender moment alone.)   :‖ ***Repeat and fade***
                                        (w/Lead Voc. ad lib.)

Leningrad

Words and Music by
Billy Joel

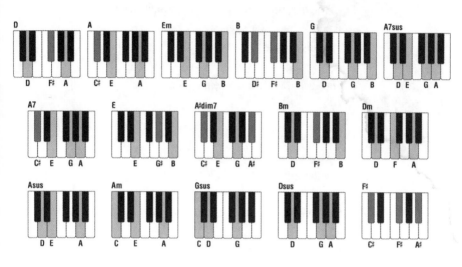

Intro

| D | A | Em | B | G | D/F# | Em | A/C# | A |

| G/B | G | A7sus | A7 | D | |

Verse 1

   D   Em/D   G/D   A/D
Victor ____ was born   in the spring of forty-four,

   D   Em/D G/D   A/D
And never saw   his father anymore.

   D/C   G/B   D/A   E/G#
A child of sacrifice,   a child of war,

   D/A   A#dim7   Bm
Another son ____ who never had

   G   A   D
A fa-ther after ____ Lenin-grad.

Verse 2

D   Em/D   G/D   A/D
Went off ___ to school   and learned to serve the state,

D   Em/D G/D   A/D
Followed the rules,   and drank his vodka straight.

D/C   G/B   D/A   E/G♯
The only way to live   was drown the hate.

D/A   A♯dim7   Bm
A Russian life _____ was very sad,

        E   A   D
And such was life in ___ Lenin-grad.

Bridge 1

Dm
I was born in forty-nine,

Asus   Am
A cold war kid in Mc-Carthy time.

Gsus   G
Stop 'em at the thirty-eighth parallel,

Asus   A
Blast those yellow Reds to hell.

Dsus   Dm
Cold war kids were hard to kill,

Asus   Am
Under their desk in an air raid drill.

Gsus   G
Haven't they heard we won the war?

Asus   A
What do they keep on fighting for?

Verse 3

D   Em/D   G/D   A/D
Victor ___ was sent   to some Red Ar - my town,

D   Em/D G/D   A/D   A/C♯
Served out his time,   became a ___ cir-cus clown.

D/C   G/B   D/A   E/G♯
The greatest happiness   he'd ever found

D/A   A♯dim7   Bm
Was making _____ Russian children glad,

        G   A   D
And chil-dren lived in Lenin - grad.

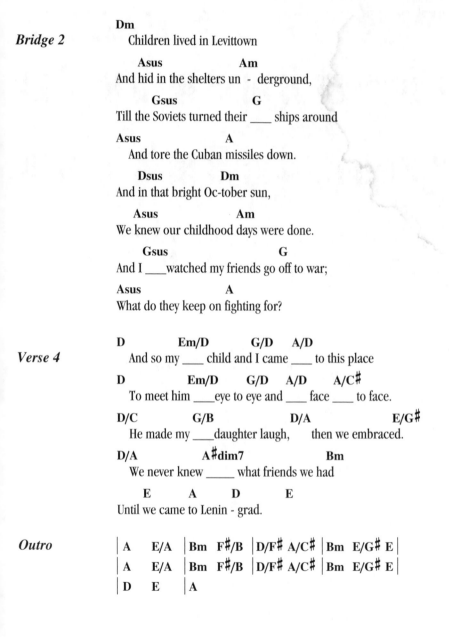

Bridge 2

Dm
Children lived in Levittown

Asus   Am
And hid in the shelters un - derground,

Gsus   G
Till the Soviets turned their ____ ships around

Asus   A
And tore the Cuban missiles down.

Dsus   Dm
And in that bright Oc-tober sun,

Asus   Am
We knew our childhood days were done.

Gsus   G
And I ____watched my friends go off to war;

Asus   A
What do they keep on fighting for?

Verse 4

D   Em/D   G/D A/D
And so my ____ child and I came ____ to this place

D   Em/D   G/D A/D   A/C♯
To meet him ____eye to eye and ____ face ____ to face.

D/C   G/B   D/A   E/G♯
He made my ____daughter laugh,   then we embraced.

D/A   A♯dim7   Bm
We never knew _____ what friends we had

E   A   D   E
Until we came to Lenin - grad.

Outro

| A   E/A | Bm F♯/B | D/F♯ A/C♯ | Bm E/G♯ E |
| A   E/A | Bm F♯/B | D/F♯ A/C♯ | Bm E/G♯ E |
| D   E | A

Light as the Breeze

Words and Music by
Leonard Cohen

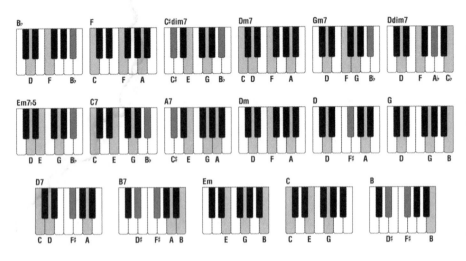

B♭	F	C♯dim7	Dm7	Gm7	Ddim7
Em7♭5	C7	A7	Dm	D	G
D7	B7	Em	C	B	

Intro |Bb | |F/C | | | |C#dim7 | |
         | | |Dm7 | | | |Gm7 F/A Bb| F/C Ddim7 Em7b5 |

F

Verse 1   She stands before you naked.

You can see it, you can taste it.

                                   C7

But she comes to you light as the breeze,

You can drink or you can nurse it.

It don't matter how you worship,

                         F

As long as you're down on your knees.

Verse 2

        F
So I knelt there at the delta,

At the alpha and the omega,

                  C7
At the cradle of the river and ____ the seas.

Like a blessing come from heaven,

For something like a second,

                F
I was healed and my heart was at ease.

Chorus 1

      A7   **Dm**
Oh, baby, I've waited so long for your kiss,

      A7
For something to happen.

B♭   **F/A B♭ F/C**   **C♯dim7**
Oh, some-thin' like ___ this.

| **Dm7** | | | **Gm7 F/A B♭**| **F/C Ddim7 Em7♭5** |

Verse 3

         F
And you're weak, and you're harmless,

And you're sleeping in your harness,

             C7
And the wind going wild in the trees.

And it's not exactly prison,

But you'll never be forgiven

                F
For whatever you've done with the keys.

Chorus 2

     A7   Dm
Oh, baby, I've waited so long for your kiss,

     A7
For something to happen.

B♭   F/A B♭   F/C   C#dim7
Oh, some-thing   like ___ this.

      Dm7   Gm7 F/A B♭ C7
Some-thing like this.

Verse 4

     F
It's dark and it's snowing.

Oh, my love, I must be going.

                 C7
The river is starting to ___ freeze.

And I'm sick of pretending,

And I'm broken from bending.

              F
I've lived too long on my knees.

Verse 5

     F
And she dances so graceful,

And you're heart's hard and hateful,

               C7
And she's naked, but that's just a tease.

And you turn in disgust

From your hatred, from your love.

             F
And she comes to you light as the breeze.

Chorus 3

A7   **Dm**
Oh, baby, I've waited so long for your kiss,

A7
For something to happen.

B♭ **F/A** **B**♭ **F/C** **C**♯**dim7**
Oh, some-thing like ____ this.

    Dm   **D**
Something ____ like this. Oh.

Verse 6

     G N.C.
Well, there's blood on ev'ry bracelet.

    G
You can see it, you can taste it.

          D7
And it's "Please, baby, please, baby, ____ please."

And she says, "Drink deeply, pilgrim,

Don't forget there's still a woman

        G
Beneath this resplendent chemise."

Verse 7

          G
So I knelt there at the delta,

At the alpha, at the omega.

                          D7
Now, I knelt there like one who be - lieves.

And like a blessing come from heaven,

For something like a second

                        G
I was cured and my heart was at ease.

Chorus 4

    B7   **Em**
Oh, baby, I've waited so long for your kiss,

    B7
For something to happen.

C   **G/B** **C** **G/D**
Oh, some-thing like ____ this.

C   **C#dim7 G/D**   **B/D#** **Em**
  Something   like ____ this.

    A7 C/D Em D/F#   **G**
Oh,   some-thing ____ like this. Yeah.

Lullabye
(Goodnight, My Angel)

Words and Music by
Billy Joel

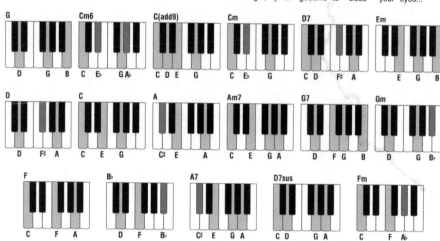

Intro   ‖: G Cm6/G G C(add9) | :‖

Verse 1

G   Cm6/G G   Cm/G G
Goodnight, my an - gel, time to close your eyes

D7   Em   D/C C
And save these ques-tions for anoth-er day.

G   Cm6/G G   Cm/G   G
I think I know   what you've been ask-ing me.

D7   Em   D/A A
I think you know what I've been try'n' to say.

Am7   G/B C   G/D D/C
I prom-ised I would never leave you,

G   G/F   C(add9) G/D   G7/D   C
And you should always know,   wherev-er you may go,

  G/B Am7 G/B   A
No mat - ter   where you are,

         C/D
I never will be far away.

Verse 2

G   Cm6/G G Cm/G G
Goodnight, my an - gel, now it's time to sleep,

D7   Em D/C C
And still so man-y things I want to say.

G   Cm6/G G Cm/G G
Remem-ber all the songs you sang for me

D7   Em D/A A
When we went sail-ing on an em -'rald bay?

Am7   G/B C G/D D/C
And like a boat out on the o - cean,

G   G/F   C(add9)
I'm rock-ing you to sleep.

G/D G7/D   C G/B Am7 G/B A
The wa-ter's dark and deep __ in-side this ancient heart.

       C/D D
You'll always be a part of me.

Interlude

Gm	F	B♭	F		Gm		Cm6	D
Gm	F	B♭	Cm6		Gm		Cm6	D
G7								
A7					C/D		D7	

Verse 3

G   Cm6/G G   Cm/G G
Goodnight, my an - gel, now it's time to dream,

D7   Em   D/C C
And dream how won-derful your life will be.

G   Cm6/G G
Someday your child may cry,

G/F C/E   G7/D A/C♯
And if you sing this lull-abye,

Cm6 G/B Cm/A G/B
Then in   your   heart

          A7   D7sus D7
There will always be a part   of

| G Cm6/G G C(add9) | | G Cm6/G G C(add9) | |
Me.

Outro

G   Cm6/G G
Someday we'll all be gone,

G/F   C/E G7/D A/C♯
But lull-abyes go on and on;

Cm6 G/B Cm/A G/B
They nev - er   die.

          A7   D7sus D7
That's how you and I   will

| G Cm6/G G G7 | Cm/G Fm/G Cm6/G D7sus | G
Be.

The Longest Time

Words and Music by
Billy Joel

Melody:

Whoa, oh, oh, oh,

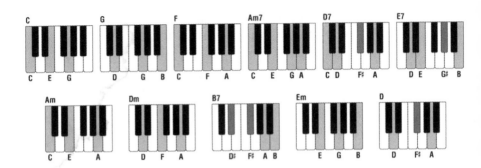

C   E   G   D   G   B   C   F   A   C   E   G A   C D   F♯ A   D E   G♯ B

C   E   A   D   F   A   D♯   F♯ A B   E   G   B   D   F♯ A

Intro

      C   G   C/E F
      Whoa, oh, oh, oh,

      G   C
      For the longest time.

      G   C/E F
      Whoa, oh, oh,

      G
      For the longest...

Verse 1

      C C/B Am7 C/G F   C
      If you   said   good-bye to me to-night,

          C/B   Am7 C/G D7   G
      There would still   be   music left to write.

      E7   Am
        What else could I do?

      G/B   C   C/E
        I'm so in-spired by you.

      F   Dm   G   C
        That hasn't happened for the longest time.

Verse 2

```
C    C/B Am7   C/G F            C
Once  I    thought  my   innocence was gone.

     C/B Am7  C/G D7            G
Now  I   know that   happiness goes on.

E7                  Am
   That's where you found me,

G/B                 C      C/E
When you put your arms a-round me.

F          Dm             G     C
   I haven't been there for the longest time.
```

Chorus

```
C     G   C/E  F
Whoa, oh,  oh,   oh,

G              C
For the longest time.

G     C/E F
Whoa, ho,  ho,

G
For the longest...
```

Verse 3

```
C  C/B Am7 C/G   F           C
I'm that  voice you're hearing in the hall.

     C/B Am7  C/G D7       G
And the  great - est   miracle of all

E7          Am
   Is how I need you

G/B              C      C/E
And how you needed me, too.

F            Dm            G     C
   That hasn't happened for the longest time.
```

Bridge 1

G   Am
Maybe this won't last very long,

  B7   C
But you feel so right and I could be wrong.

Em   Am
Maybe I've been hoping too hard,

  D
But I've gone this far

     G
And it's more than I hoped for.

Verse 4

C C/B   Am7 C/G F   C
Who knows how much further we'll go on.

     C/B Am7 C/G D7   G
May - be I'll   be sorry when you're gone.

E7   Am
  I'll take my chances,

G/B   C   C/E
I forgot how nice ro-mance is.

F   Dm   G   C
  I haven't been there for the longest time.

Bridge 2

G   Am
I had second thoughts at the start.

  B7   C
I said to myself, hold on to your heart.

Em   Am
Now I know the woman that you are.

  D
You're wonderful so far,

     G
And it's more than I hoped for.

Verse 5

C C/B Am7 C/G F   C
I don't care   what consequence it brings.

C/B Am7 C/G D7   G
I have been a   fool for lesser things.

E7   Am
  I want you so bad.

G/B   C   C/E
  I think you ought to know

    F   Dm   G   C
That I intend to hold you for the longest time.

Outro

C   G C/E F
Whoa, oh, oh, oh,

G   C
For the longest time.

  G   C/E F
‖: Whoa, ho, ho.

G   C
For the longest time.   :‖ *Repeat and fade*

A Matter of Trust

Words and Music by
Billy Joel

One, two, one, two, three, _four.

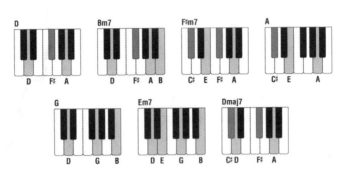

Intro

N.C.
One, two, one, two, three, four.

| D | Bm7 | D | Bm7 | |

Verse 1

D   Bm7
  Some love is just a lie of the heart,

D   Bm7   F#m7
  The cold remains of what be-gan with a passionate start.

                     A
And they may not want it to end,

                      D
But it will, it's just a question of when.

             Bm7
I've lived long e-nough to have learned

D   Bm7   F#m7
  The closer you get to the fire, the more you get burned.

                  A
But that won't happen to us,

'Cause it's always been a matter of trust.

| D | Bm7 | D | Bm7 | |

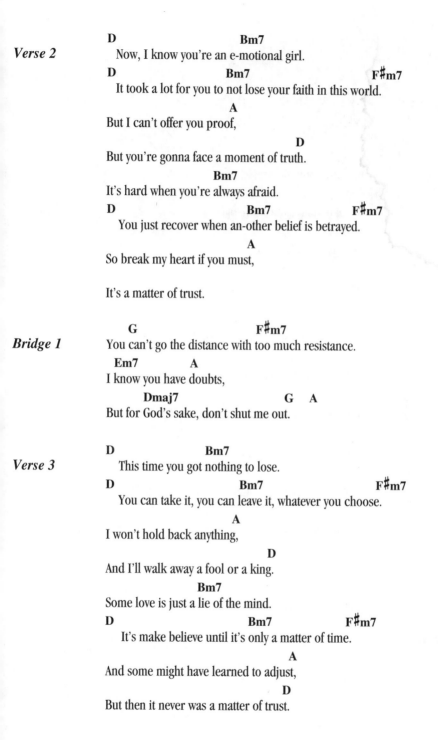

Verse 2

    D   **Bm7**
    Now, I know you're an e-motional girl.

    D   **Bm7**   **F♯m7**
    It took a lot for you to not lose your faith in this world.

                  A
    But I can't offer you proof,

                         D
    But you're gonna face a moment of truth.

                Bm7
    It's hard when you're always afraid.

    D   **Bm7**   **F♯m7**
    You just recover when an-other belief is betrayed.

                  A
    So break my heart if you must,

    It's a matter of trust.

Bridge 1

        G   **F♯m7**
    You can't go the distance with too much resistance.

    Em7   **A**
    I know you have doubts,

        Dmaj7   **G**   **A**
    But for God's sake, don't shut me out.

Verse 3

    D   **Bm7**
    This time you got nothing to lose.

    D   **Bm7**   **F♯m7**
    You can take it, you can leave it, whatever you choose.

                A
    I won't hold back anything,

                     D
    And I'll walk away a fool or a king.

              Bm7
    Some love is just a lie of the mind.

    D   **Bm7**   **F♯m7**
    It's make believe until it's only a matter of time.

                  A
    And some might have learned to adjust,

                     D
    But then it never was a matter of trust.

| *Piano Solo* | | D | | Bm7 | | D | | Bm7 | | |
| | | F#m7 | | | | A | | | | |

Bridge 2

    G
I'm sure you're aware, love,

    F#m7
We've both had our share of

    Em7   A
Be-lieving too long,

    Dmaj7   G A
When the whole situation was wrong.

Verse 4

D   Bm7
Some love is just a lie of the soul,

D   Bm7   F#m7
A constant battle for the ultimate state of control.

        A
After you've heard lie upon lie,

        D
There can hardly be a question of why.

    Bm7
Some love is just a lie of the heart,

D   Bm7   F#m7
The cold remains of what be-gan with a passionate start.

        A
But that can't happen to us,

'Cause it's always been a matter of trust.

Outro

‖: D | Bm7 | D | Bm7 :‖ *Repeat and fade*
(w/ Voc. ad lib.)

Modern Woman

Words and Music by
Billy Joel

You see her sit-ting with her cof-fee and her pa-per,

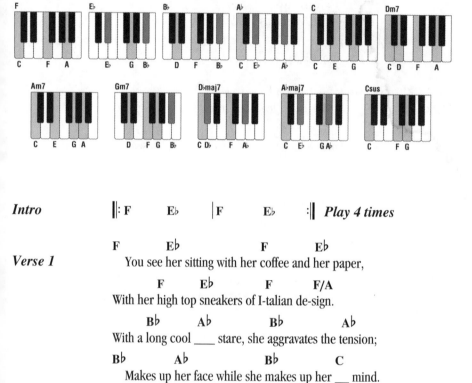

Intro

‖: F   E♭ |F   E♭   :‖ ***Play 4 times***

Verse 1

     F   E♭   F   E♭
You see her sitting with her coffee and her paper,

       F   E♭   F   F/A
With her high top sneakers of I-talian de-sign.

    B♭   A♭   B♭   A♭
With a long cool ____ stare, she aggravates the tension;

B♭   A♭   B♭   C
    Makes up her face while she makes up her __ mind.

F   E♭   F   E♭
    Now you're in trouble; maybe she's an intel-lectual.

F   E♭   F   F/A
    What if she figures out you're not very smart?

    B♭   A♭   B♭   A♭
Well, maybe she's the quiet type who's into heav-y metal.

    B♭   A♭   B♭
Boy, you got to get it settled 'cause she's breaking your heart.

Chorus 1

C   Dm7
  Don't try to put on an act,

  Am7   B♭   F/A   Gm7   B♭/F
You can't do that to a modern woman.

C/E   C   Dm7
  And you're an old-fashioned man,

  Am7 B♭   F/A   Gm7   F
She under-stands the things you're doin'.

E♭   F E♭ F E♭ F E♭ F E♭
  She's a modern wom - an.

Verse 2

F   E♭   F   E♭
  She looks sleek, she seems so pro-fessional.

    F   E♭   F   F/A
She's got a lot of confidence, it's easy to see.

  B♭   A♭   B♭   A♭
You want to make a move, but you feel so in-ferior,

  B♭   A♭   B♭   C
'Cause under that exterior is someone who's free.

F   E♭   F   E♭
  She's got style; she's got her own money.

       F   E♭   F   F/A
So she's not another honey you can quickly dis-arm.

B♭   A♭   B♭   A♭
  She's got the eyes that make you realize

  B♭   A♭   B♭
She won't be hyp-notized by your usual charm.

Chorus 2

C   Dm7
  You've got your plan of at-tack,

  Am7   B♭   F/A   Gm7   B♭/F
That won't at-tract the modern woman.

C/E   C   Dm7
  When you're an old-fashioned man,

  Am7 B♭   F/A   Gm7   F
She under-stands the things you're doin'.

E♭   F E♭ F E♭ F E♭ F E♭
  She's a modern wom - an.

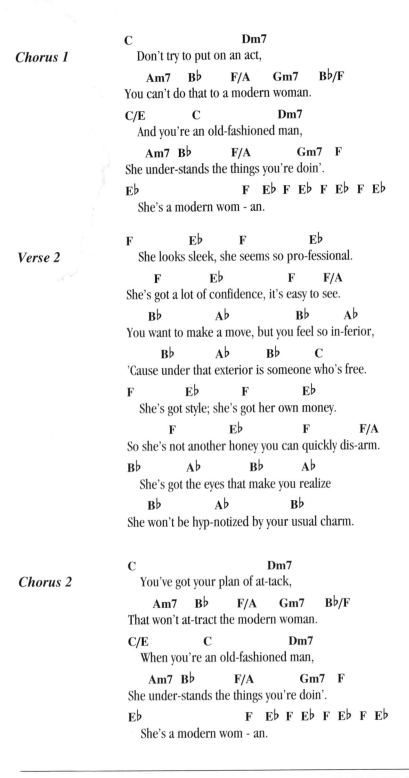

Piano Solo

| D♭maj7 | E♭ | | D♭maj7 | A♭maj7 |
| D♭maj7 | E♭ | | D♭maj7 | Csus | |

Interlude

| F   E♭ | F   E♭ | F   E♭ | F   E♭ |

Verse 3

F   E♭   F   E♭
Time goes by and you're sharing an a-partment.

F   E♭   F   F/A
    She says she loves you, but she doesn't know why.

        B♭   A♭   B♭   A♭
In the morning, she leaves you with your coffee and your paper.

        B♭   A♭   B♭   C
It's a strange sit-uation for an old-fashioned __ guy.

F   E♭   F   E♭
    But times have changed; things are not the same, baby.

F   E♭   F   F/A
    You o-vercame such a bad atti-tude.

        B♭   A♭   B♭   A♭
Rock and roll just used to be for kicks and nowadays it's politics.

        B♭   A♭   B♭
And after nine-teen-eighty-six, what else could be new?

Chorus 3

C   Dm7
    You got to learn to re-lax

        Am7   B♭   F/A   Gm7   B♭/F
And face the facts of a modern woman.

C/E   C   Dm7
    And you're an old fashioned man,

        Am7 B♭   F/A   Gm7   F
She under-stands the things you're doin'.

E♭   F   E♭ F E♭ F E♭ F E♭
    She's a modern   wo-man.

Outro

‖: F   E♭ | F   E♭   :‖   *Repeat and fade*
                                               (w/Voc. ad lib.)

Miami 2017
(Seen the Lights Go Out on Broadway)

Words and Music by
Billy Joel

Seen the lights __ go out on Broad - way; __

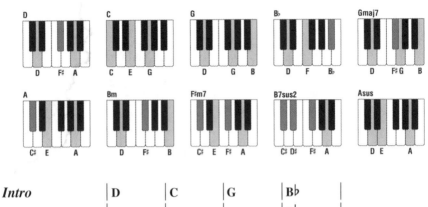

Intro

D	C	G	B♭	
D	C	G	B♭	
D/F♯	Gmaj7	D/A	G/B	
A/C♯	G/B	D	A/C♯ G/B	

Verse 1

D   G/B   D   A/C♯
Seen the lights ____ go out on Broad - way;

Bm   G   A   G
I saw the Empire State laid low.

F♯m7   Bm
And life went on beyond the Pal - isades;

B7sus2   D/A   A   G   A
They all bought ____ Cadillacs, and left there long ago.

D   G/B   D   A/C♯
They held a concert out in Brooklyn

Bm   G   A   G
To watch the island bridges blow.

D/F♯   G
They turned our power down,

D/A   G/B
And drove us un - derground,

A/C♯   G/B   D
But we went right on with the show.

Interlude 1 ‖: D | |A Asus | A :‖

Verse 2

D   G/D   D   A/C#
I've seen the lights go out on Broadway.

Bm   G   A
I saw the ruins at my feet.

F#m7   Bm   B7sus2
You know we almost didn't notice it.

          A   Asus A
We'd seen it all ___ the time

        G   A
On Forty-Second Street.

D   G/D   D   A/C#
They burned the churches up in Harlem,

Bm   G   A   Asus A
Like in that Spanish civil war.

D/F#   G   D/A   G/B
The flames were ev - 'rywhere,   but no one really cared.

A/C#   G/B   D
It always burned up there before.

Interlude 2   *Repeat Interlude 1*

D   G/D   D   A/C♯
I've seen the lights go out on Broadway.

Bm   G   A
I watched the mighty skyline fall.

F♯m7   Bm   B7sus2
The boats were waiting at the battery.

     A
The union went on strike,

     G   A
They never sailed at all.

D   G/D   D   A/C♯
They sent a carrier out from Norfolk

Bm   G   A
And picked the Yankees up for free.

D/F♯   G
They said that Queens ____ could stay;

D/A   G/B
They blew the Bronx ____ away,

A/C♯   G/B   D
And sank Man-hattan out at sea.

Piano Solo   *Repeat Interlude 1*

Verse 4

     D   G   D A/C♯
     You know those lights were bright on Broad - way,

     Bm   G   A   G
     That was so ___ many years ago,

     F♯m7   Bm   B7sus2
     Before we all lived here in Florida,

          Asus A   G   A
    Before the Mafia took over Mexico.

     D   G/B   D A/C♯
     There are not many who remem - ber.

     Bm   G   A   G
     They say a handful still survive

     D/F♯   G
     To tell the world ___ about

     D/A   G/B
     The way the lights ___ went out

     A/C♯   G/B   B♭
     And keep the mem - ory alive.

Outro   ‖: D | C | G | B♭   :‖ *Repeat and fade*

Movin' Out
(Anthony's Song)

Words and Music by
Billy Joel

Melody:

An-tho-ny works _ in the gro - cer-y store, _

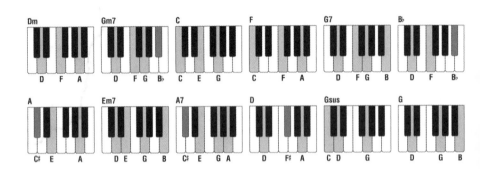

Intro | Dm | Gm7 | C C/E | F |
           | Dm | Gm7 | C C/E | F |

Verse 1

    Dm   **Gm7**
Anthony works in the grocery store,

    C   **C/E**   **F**
Savin' his pen-nies for someday.

    Dm   **Gm7**
Mama Leone left a note on the door.

        C   **C/E**   **F**
She said, "Sonny, move out ____ to the coun-try."

        Dm   **G7**
Ah, but workin' too hard can give you a heart at-tack-ack-ack-ack-ack-ack.

B♭   **C**
You oughta know by now.

Dm   **G7**
Who needs a house out in Hackensack?

    C   **C/E**   **F**
Is that all you get for your money?

```
         B♭                        C    C/B♭
And it seems such a waste of time
     A              A/C♯   Dm
If that's what it's all about.
Dm/C           B♭
Mama, if that's ____ movin' up,
              Em7    A7                 Dm
Then I'm _____ movin' out.


              Dm Gm7              C   C/E       F
```

Chorus 1
```
              Mm, I'm movin' out.        Mm, hm.
              Dm          Gm7          C   C/E  F
Oo, ____ hoo.  Ah, ha.        Mm, hm.


              Dm                 Gm7
```

Verse 2
```
Sergeant O'Leary is walkin' the beat,
     C                  C/E      F
At night, he becomes ____ a bar-tender.
                  Dm                     Gm7
He works at Mister Cacciatore's down on Sullivan Street
     C                  C/E        F
A-cross from the med  -  ical center.
                  Dm                   G7
Yeah, and he's tradin' in his Chevy for a Cadillac-ac-ac-ac-ac-ac.
B♭                      C
You oughta know by now.
     Dm                 G7
And if he can't drive with a broken back,
     C              C/E          F
At least he can pol-ish the fenders.
       B♭                      C    C/B♭
And it seems such a waste of time
     A              A/C♯   Dm
If that's what it's all about.
Dm/C           B♭
Mama, if that's ____ movin' up,
              Em7    A7                 Dm
Then I'm _____ movin' out.
```

Chorus 2   *Repeat Chorus 1*

              Dm   G7
Verse 3   You should never argue with a crazy mi-mi-mi-mi-mi-mind.
              B♭   C
              You oughta know by now.
                        Dm   G7
              You can pay ____ Uncle Sam with the overtime.
                 C   C/E   F
              Is that all you get ____ for your money?
                 B♭   C   C/B♭
              And if that's what you have in mind,
                    A   A/C♯   Dm
              Yeah, if that's what you're all about,
              Dm/C   B♭
                 Good luck ____ movin' up,
                       Em7   A7   Dm
              'Cause I'm _____ movin' out.

Chorus 3   *Repeat Chorus 1*

Outro | D | Gsus G | A | G/D D |
               | D | Gsus G | A | G/D D |
                                                    I'm movin' out.

               ‖: D | Gsus G | A | G/D D :‖ *Repeat and fade*

My Life

Words and Music by
Billy Joel

Melody:

Got a call __ from an old ___ friend.

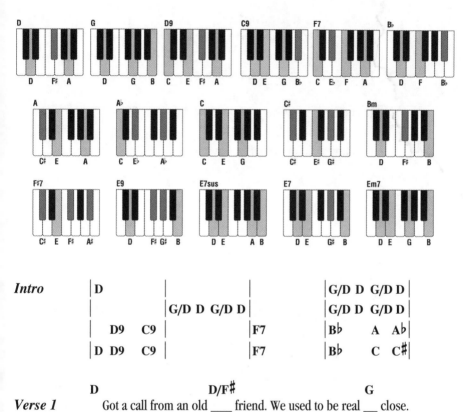

Intro

D			G/D D G/D D
	G/D D G/D D		G/D D G/D D
	D9 C9	F7	B♭ A A♭
D D9 C9	F7	B♭ C C♯

         D   D/F♯   G

Verse 1   Got a call from an old ____ friend. We used to be real __ close.

      A   D G/D

      Said he couldn't go on the American way.

      D   D/F♯   G

      Closed the shop, sold the house, __bought a ticket to the West _ Coast.

      A   D

      Now he gives them a stand-up routine in L.A.

Interlude 1

| D D9 C9 | | F7 | B♭ A A♭ |
| D D9 C9 | | F7 | B♭ C C♯ |

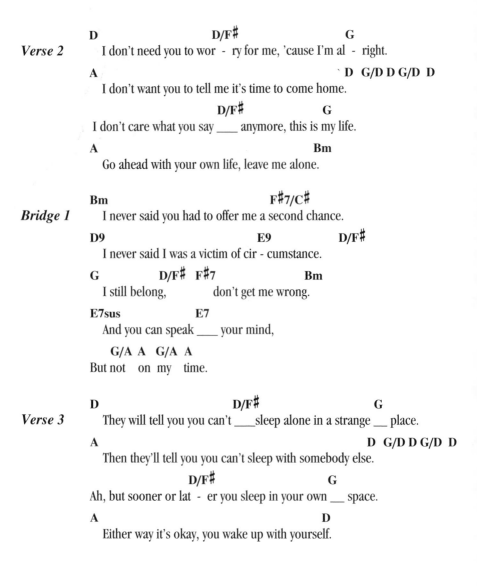

          D   **D/F♯**   **G**

Verse 2   I don't need you to wor - ry for me, 'cause I'm al - right.

         A   `` `D  G/D D G/D  D``

     I don't want you to tell me it's time to come home.

                        D/F♯   **G**

   I don't care what you say ___ anymore, this is my life.

         A   **Bm**

     Go ahead with your own life, leave me alone.

         Bm   **F♯7/C♯**

Bridge 1   I never said you had to offer me a second chance.

         D9   **E9**   **D/F♯**

     I never said I was a victim of cir - cumstance.

         G   **D/F♯** **F♯7**   **Bm**

     I still belong,   don't get me wrong.

         E7sus   **E7**

     And you can speak ___ your mind,

           G/A A G/A A

   But not   on my   time.

         D   **D/F♯**   **G**

Verse 3   They will tell you you can't ___sleep alone in a strange __ place.

         A   **D G/D D G/D D**

     Then they'll tell you you can't sleep with somebody else.

                        D/F♯   **G**

   Ah, but sooner or lat - er you sleep in your own __ space.

         A   **D**

     Either way it's okay, you wake up with yourself.

Interlude 2   *Repeat Intelude 1*

Verse 4

    D   **D/F#**   **G**
    I don't need you to wor - ry for me, 'cause I'm al - right.

    A   **D**
    I don't want you to tell me it's time to come home.

                             D/F#   **G**
    I don't care what you say ___ anymore, this is my life.

    A   **Bm**
    Go ahead with your own life, leave me alone.

Bridge 2   *Repeat Bridge 1*

Interlude 3 | **D** | **D/F#** | **G** | |
                | **A** | | **D** | **G/D D G/D D** |

Outro

    D   **D/F#**   **G**
    I don't care what you say ___ anymore, this is my life.

    A   **D D9 C9**
    Go ahead with your own life, leave me alone.

      F7   **Bb**   **A Ab**
   ‖: Keep it to yourself, it's my ___ life.
   | **D D9**   **C9** | |
   F   **Bb**   **C C#**
   Keep it to yourself, it's my ___ life.
   | **D D9**   **C9** | **:‖** *Repeat and fade*

New York State of Mind

Words and Music by
Billy Joel

Some folks like to get a-way,

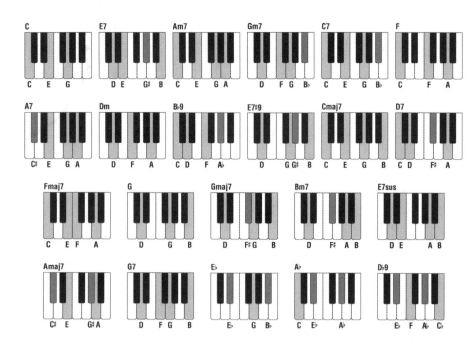

Intro

C	E7	Am7	Gm7 C7
F	A7	Dm	Bb9
C E7#9/B	Am7 Cmaj7	F C/E	D7
Fmaj7	F/G	Am7 D7	
Am7 G	F/G	

Verse 1

    C   E7♯9
Some folks like to get away,

      Am7   Gm7   C
Take a holiday from the neighborhood,

F   A7   Dm   B♭9
Hop a flight to ___ Miami Beach or to Hollywood,

C   E7♯9/B   Am7   Cmaj7/G
But I'm ____ takin' a Grey - hound

      Fmaj7 C/E   D7
On the Hudson River Line.

Fmaj7   F/G   Am7 D7 Am7 G F/G
I'm in a New York state of mind.   Mm.

Verse 2

    C   E7♯9
I've seen all the movie stars

      Am7   Gm7   C
In their fancy cars and their limousines,

F   A7   Dm   B♭9
Been high in the Rockies under the evergreens.

C   E7♯9/B   Am7   Cmaj7/G
But I know what I'm need - in',

      Fmaj7   C/E   D7
And I don't want to waste ___ more ___ time.

Fmaj7   F/G   Am7 D7 Am7 G E7♯9
I'm in a New York state of mind.

Bridge 1

    Am7   D7   Gmaj7
It was so easy living   day by day,

    Gm7   C7   Fmaj7
Out of touch   with the rhythm and ____ blues.

    Bm7   E7sus   Amaj7
Well, now I need ____ a little   give and take.

     Am7   D7   Gmaj7
The New York Times,   *The Daily News.*
| Dm | F/G G7 |

Verse 3

    C   E7#9
It comes down to re-ality,

        Am7   Gm7 C
And it's fine with me 'cause I've let it slide.

    F   A7
I don't care if it's Chinatown

        Dm   B♭9
Or on ____ Riverside.

    C E7#9/B   Am7 Cmaj7/G
I don't have any reasons.

    Fmaj7   C/E   D7
I've left them ____ all be-hind.

    Fmaj7   F/G   Am7 D7 Am7 G
I'm in a New York state of mind.   Mm.   Oh, yeah.

Piano Solo

C	E7#9	Am7	Gm7 C7
F	A7	Dm	B♭9
C E7#9	Am7 Cmaj7/G	F C/E	D7
Fmaj7	F/G	Am7 D7	
Am7 G	E7#9

Bridge 2   *Repeat Bridge 1*

Verse 4

C   E7♯9
It comes down to reality,

    Am7   Gm7   C
And it's fine with me 'cause I've let it slide.

F   A7   Dm   B♭9
I don't care if it's Chinatown or on Riverside.

C   E7♯9/B   Am7   Cmaj7/G
I don't have any rea - sons,

Fmaj7   C/E   D7
I've left them ____ all be-hind.

Fmaj7   F/G   Am7 D7 Am7 G
I'm in a New York state of mind.   Mm.

Outro

C   E7♯9/B   Am7   Cmaj7/G
I'm ____ just takin' a ___ Greyhound

     Fmaj7 C/E   D7
On the Hudson   River Line,

Fmaj7
'Cause I'm in a,

F/G
I'm in a New York state of

C   E7♯9
Mind.

Am7 B♭9 E♭ A♭ C/D D♭9 Cmaj7
Yeah, yeah.

The Night Is Still Young

Words and Music by
Billy Joel

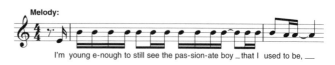

I'm young e-nough to still see the pas-sion-ate boy _ that I used to be, __

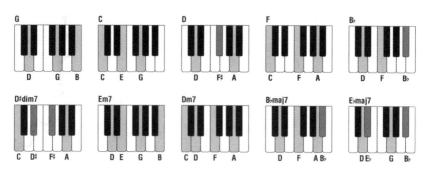

Intro | G C/G G D/G | | G C/G G D/G | |
           | F B♭/F F C/F | | D   D♯dim7 |

Verse 1

     Em7   **Dm7**
I'm young enough to still see the passionate boy that I used to be,

     B♭maj7   **E♭maj7**
But I'm old enough to say I got a good look at the other side.

     Em7   **F**
I know we got to work real hard, maybe even for the rest of our lives,

     Dm7   **C**
But right now I just want to take what I can get to-night.

Chorus 1

  G C/G G D/G
                While the night is still young,

  G C/G G D/G
                I want to keep making love to you,

    F   **B♭/F F C/F D D♯dim7**
While the night is still young.

Verse 2

Em7   Dm7

I'd like to settle down, get married and maybe have a child someday.

Bbmaj7   Ebmaj7

I can see a time coming when I'm gonna throw my suitcase out.

Em7   F

No more separations when you have to say goodnight to a telephone.

Dm7   C

Baby, I've decided that ain't what life is all a-bout.

Bridge 1

G C F Bb Dm7
Oh.

G C F Bb Dm7
Oh.

G C F Bb Dm7
Oh.

G C F Bb Dm7
Oh.

Chorus 2

G C/G G D/G

While the night is still young,

G C/G G D/G

I want to try to make the world brand new,

F   Bb/F F C/F   D D#dim7

While the night is still young.

Verse 3
     Em7   Dm7
Rock and roll music was the only thing I ever gave a damn about.

                B♭maj7   E♭maj7
There was something that was missing, but I never used to wonder why.

     Em7   F
  Now I know you're the one who's gonna make things right again.

       Dm7   C
And I may lose the battle, but you're giving me the will to try.

Bridge 2   *Repeat Bridge 1*

        G C/G G D/G
Chorus 3   Because the night is still young,

        G C/G G D/G
                    I got a lot of catching up I gotta do,

          F   B♭/F F C/F   D
But the night is still young.   Oh, the night is still young.

Interlude ‖: G | |F | |Em7 | :‖

Bridge 3   *Repeat Bridge 1*

Outro   ‖:G C/G G D/G| |G C/G G D/G| |
          |F B♭/F F C/F| |F B♭/F F C/F| :‖ *Repeat and fade*
                                                               (w/ Voc. ad lib.)

No Man's Land

Words and Music by
Billy Joel

I've seen those big mach-ines... _

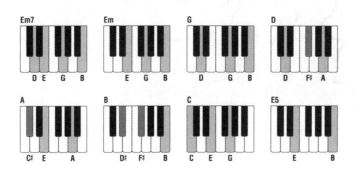

Intro   ‖: Em7 | | | :‖

Verse 1

    Em   G   D   A
I've seen those big machines come rolling through the quiet pines;

    Em   G   D   A
Blue suits and bank - ers with their Vol - vos and their val - entines.

    Em   G   D   A
Give us this day __ our daily dis - count outlet mer - chandise.

    Em   G   D   A
Raise up a mul - tiplex and we will make a sac - rifice.

Pre-Chorus 1

B   A/B
Now we're gonna get the big business,

B   A/B
Now we're gonna get the real thing.

B
Ev'rybody's all excited about it.

Chorus 1

   C   G
Who remembers when it all began

D   E5
Out here in No Man's Land?

C   G
Before they passed the master plan

D   E5
Out here in No Man's Land.

C   G
Low supply and high demand

D   N.C.   Em7
Here in No Man's Land,   in No Man's Land.

Verse 2

Em   G   D   A
There ain't much work __ out here in our consumer pow - er base.

Em   G   D   A
No major in - dustry, just miles __ and miles of park - ing space.

Em   G   D   A
This morning's pa - per says our neigh - bor's in a co - caine bust.

Em   G   D   A
Lots more to read __ about, Loli - ta and subur - ban lust.

Pre-Chorus 2

B   A/B
Now we're gonna get the whole story,

B   A/B
Now we're gonna be in prime time.

B
Ev'rybody's all excited about it.

Chorus 2

C   G
Who remembers when it all began

D   E5
Out here in No Man's Land?

C   G
We've just begun to understand

D   E5
Out here in No Man's Land.

C   G
Low supply and high demand

D   N.C.   Em7
Here in No Man's Land.   Here in No Man's Land.

Verse 3

      Em   **G**   **D**   **A**
I see these chil-dren with their bore-dom and their va-cant stares.

      Em   **G**   **D**   **A**
God help us all _ if we're to blame _ for their unan - swered prayers.

      Em   **G**   **D**   **A**
They roll the side - walks up at night, _ this place goes underground.

      Em   **G**   **D**   **A**
Thanks to the Con - do Kings, there's cable now in Zom - bie town.

Pre-Chorus 3

      B   **A/B**
Now we're gonna get the closed circuit,

      B   **A/B**
Now we're gonna get the Top Forty.

      B   **A/B**
Now we're gonna get the sports franchise,

      B
Now we're gonna get the major attractions.

Chorus 3

      C   **G**
Who remembers when it all began

      D   **E5**
Out here in No Man's Land?

      C   **G**
Before the whole world was in our hands

      D   **E5**
Out here in No Man's Land.

      C   **G**
Before the banners and the marching bands

      D   **E5**
Out here in No Man's Land.

      C   **G**
Low supply, high demand

      D **N.C.**   **Em7**
Here in No Man's Land.

Outro

                       Em7
‖: Here in No Man's Land.   :‖ *Repeat and fade*

Only the Good Die Young

Words and Music by
Billy Joel

Come out, Vir-gin-ia,   don't __ let me wait. __

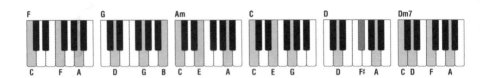

F   C   A   G   D   G   B   Am   C   E   A   C   C   E   G   D   D   F♯   A   Dm7   C   D   F   A

Verse 1

     F   G   Am
Come out, Virginia, don't __ let me wait.

        F   G   C
You Catholic girls start much __ too late.

         F   G   Am
Oh, but sooner or later it comes down to fate.

       F   G
I might as well be the one.

              F   C   Am
Well, they showed __ you a statue, and told you to pray.

       F   G   C
They built you a temple and locked you away.

       F   G   Am
Ah, but they never told you the price __ that you pay

       F   G
For things that you might have done.

Chorus 1

        C
Well, only the good die young.

F   G C
 That's what I said.

         F
Only the good die young.

      G   C
Only the good die ____ young.

          F   G   Am

Verse 2
You might have heard __ I run with a dangerous crowd.

  F   G   Am
We ain't too pretty, we ain't __ too proud.

  F   G   Am
We might be laughing a bit __ too loud,

   F   G
Ah, but that never hurt no one.

      F   G   Am
So come on, __ Virginia, show __ me a sign.

F   G   C
Send up a signal, I'll throw you a line.

  F   G   Am
The stained glass curtain you're hid - ing behind

F   G
Never lets in the sun.

         C

Chorus 2
Darling, only the good die young.

F   G
 Whoa, whoa, whoa, whoa, whoa.

C   F
 I tell ya, only the good die young.

      G   C
Only the good die young.

Bridge 1

      G N.C.   F N.C.   C
You got a nice white dress and a party on your confirma - tion.

           D   F
You got a brand __ new soul, mm, and a cross __ of gold.

      G N.C.   F N.C.   C
Well, Vir-ginia, they didn't give you quite __ enough informa - tion.

           D   F
You didn't count __ on me when you were counting on your rosary.

A F   C
Oh, whoa, whoa.

Verse 3

      Dm7   F   G   Am
And they say __ there's a heaven for those __ who will wait,

    F   G   C
And some say it's better, but I __ say it ain't.

      F   G   Am
I'd rather laugh with the sinners than cry with the saints.

      F   G
The sinners are much more fun.

Chorus 3

                           C
You know that only the good die __ young.

F   G
  Whoa, baby, babe.

C   F
  I tell ya, only the good die young.

              G   C
Only the good die ____ young.

Piano Solo

| G | N.C. | F | N.C. | C | | | |
| D | | | F | | | | |

Bridge 2
      G N.C.   **F N.C.**   **C**
      Said your mother told you all that I could give you was a reputa - tion.

                    D
      Oh, she never cared for me,

                          F
      But does she ever say a prayer for me?

      G F   **C**
      Oh, whoa, whoa.

Verse 4
      Dm7   **F**   **G**   **Am**
      Come out, __ come out, come out.   Vir-ginia, don't let ____ me wait.

      F   **G**   **C**
        You Catholic girls __ start much too late.

      F   **G**   **Am**
        But sooner or later it comes __ down to fate.

       F   **G**
      I might as well be the one.

      You know that only the good die young.

Outro   ‖: C | F | G | C |
               | C | F | G | C   :‖ *Repeat and fade*
                                                                      (w/Voc. ad lib.)

Piano Man

Words and Music by
Billy Joel

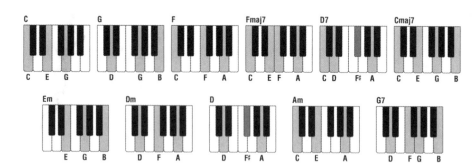

Intro

C	G/B	F/A	C/G
Fmaj7	C/E	D7	G
C	G/B	F/A	C/G
F	F/G	C	F/C
Cmaj7	F Em Dm	C	F/C
Cmaj7	F Em Dm

Verse 1

          C   G/B   F/A   C/G
It's nine o'-clock on a Saturday,

      F   C/E   D   G
   The regular crowd shuffles in.

             C   G/B   F/A
There's an old man ____ sitting next to me

C/G   F   F/G   C
   Making love to his tonic and gin.

Interlude 1

C	G/B	F/A	C/G
F	F/G	C	
F/C		

Verse 2

         C   G/B   F/A   C/G
He says, "Son, can you play ___ me a memory?

      F   C/E   D   G
I'm not really sure ___ how it goes,

        C   G/B   F/A   C/G
But it's sad and it's sweet, and I knew it complete

       F   F/G   C
When I wore a young - er man's clothes."

Bridge 1

Am   Am/G   D/F♯   F
La, la, la, ___ li, di, da.

Am   Am/G   D/F♯
 La, la, ___ li, di, da,

   G G/F C/E G7/D
Da, dum.

Chorus 1

C   G/B   F/A   C/G
Sing us a song, ___ you're the piano man.

F   C/E   D G
Sing us a song ___ tonight.

         C   G/B   F/A   C/G
Well, we're all in the mood ___ for a melody,

       F   F/G   C
And you've got us feeling al-right.

Interlude 2

C	G/B	F/A	C/G	
F	F/G	C	F/C	
Cmaj7	F Em Dm	C	F/C	
Cmaj7	F Em Dm			

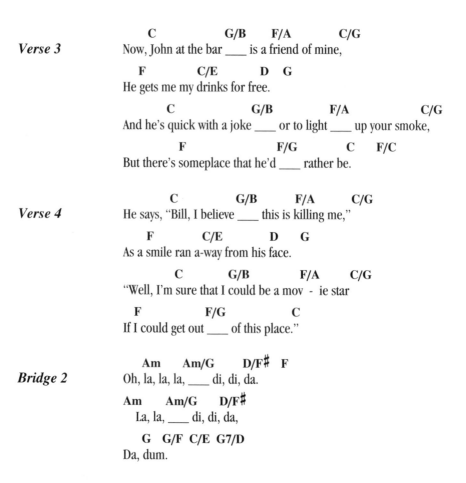

Verse 3

       C   G/B   F/A   C/G
Now, John at the bar ___ is a friend of mine,

    F   C/E   D   G
He gets me my drinks for free.

        C   G/B   F/A   C/G
And he's quick with a joke ___ or to light ___ up your smoke,

           F   F/G   C   F/C
But there's someplace that he'd ___ rather be.

Verse 4

       C   G/B   F/A   C/G
He says, "Bill, I believe ___ this is killing me,"

    F   C/E   D   G
As a smile ran a-way from his face.

        C   G/B   F/A   C/G
"Well, I'm sure that I could be a mov - ie star

    F   F/G   C
If I could get out ___ of this place."

Bridge 2

    Am   Am/G   D/F♯   F
Oh, la, la, la, ___ di, di, da.

Am   Am/G   D/F♯
 La, la, ___ di, di, da,

  G G/F C/E G7/D
Da, dum.

Verse 5

    C   G/B   F/A   C/G
Now, Paul is a real estate novelist

    F   C/E   D   G
Who never had time ___ for a wife.

       C   G/B   F/A   C/G
And he's talking with Da - vy, who's still in the Na - vy

    F   F/G   C
And probably will be for life.

Interlude 3   *Repeat Interlude 1*

Verse 6

      C   G/B   F/A   C/G
And the wait - ress is practicing politics

      F   C/E   D   G
As the bus - 'nessmen slowly get stoned.

     C   G/B   F/A   C/G
Yes, they're sharing a drink ___ they call loneliness,

    F   F/G   C
But it's better than drinkin' alone.

Piano Solo

Am	Am/G	D	F	
Am	Am/G	D	F	
Am	Am/G	D		
G	G/F	C/E	G7/D	

| **Chorus 2** | *Repeat Chorus 1* |

| **Interlude 4** | *Repeat Interlude 2* |

Verse 7

    C   G/B F/A C/G
It's a pretty good crowd ___ for a Saturday

   F   C/E   D G
And the manager gives me a smile,

      C   G/B   F/A   C/G
'Cause he knows that it's me they've been coming to see

    F   F/G   C   F/C
To for-get about life for a while.

Verse 8

    C   G/B   F/A C/G
And the piano, it sounds like a carnival,

       F   C/E   D G
And the mi - crophone smells like a beer.

      C   G/B   F/A   C/G
And they sit at the bar ___ and put bread in my jar,

      F   F/G   C
And say, "Man, what are you doin' here?"

| **Bridge 3** | *Repeat Brige 1* |

| **Chorus 3** | *Repeat Chorus 1* |

Outro

C	G/B	F/A	C/G	
F	F/G	C	F/C	
Cmaj7	F Em Dm	C	F/C	
Cmaj7	F Em Dm	C		

The River of Dreams

Words and Music by
Billy Joel

Melody:

In the mid-dle of the night... __

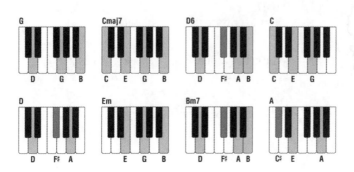

G	Cmaj7	D6	C
D G B	C E G B	D F♯ A B	C E G
D	Em	Bm7	A
D F♯ A	E G B	D F♯ A B	C♯ E A

	G	Cmaj7	D6
Intro	Oo,	ah.	

G
    (In the middle of the, I go walkin' in the,

In the middle of the, I go walkin' in the,

C
    In the middle of the, I go walkin' in the,

D
    In the middle of the...)

                 G

Verse 1   In the middle of the night I go walking in my sleep,

                   C   **D**
From the mountains of faith __ to the river so deep.

              G
I must be looking for some - thing, something sacred I lost.

        C   **D**
But the river is wide, and it's too hard to cross.

Bridge 1

      Em   G/D
Even though I know the river is wide,

        Cmaj7   Bm7
I walk down ev'ry ev'ning and stand on the shore.

Cmaj7   Bm7
  I try to cross to the opposite side,

          A   D
So I can finally find what I've been looking for.

Verse 2

                     G
In the middle of the night I go walking in my sleep,

                    C   D
Through the valley of fear __ to a river so deep.

                    G
I've been searching for some - thing, taken out of my soul.

                 C   D
Something I'd never lose, something somebody stole.

Bridge 2

      Em   G/D
  I don't know why I go walk - ing at night.

          Cmaj7   Bm7
But now I'm tired, and I don't want to walk ___ anymore.

Cmaj7   Bm7
  I hope it doesn't take the rest of my life

          A   D   N.C.
Until I find what it is I've been looking for.

Verse 3

                     G
In the middle of the night I go walking in my sleep,

                    C   D
Through the jungle of doubt to the river so deep.

                         G
I know I'm searching for some - thing, something so undefined

                    C   D
That it can only be seen by the eyes of the blind,

                     G
In the middle of the night.

Interlude		G			C		D		
		G			C		D		

Bridge 3

Em   G/D
 I'm not sure about a life after this.

     Cmaj7   Bm7
God knows, ____ I've never been a spir - itual man.

Cmaj7   Bm7
 Baptized by the fire, ____ I wade into the

A   D   N.C.
River that is runnin' through the promised land.

Verse 4

         G
In the middle of the night I go walking in my sleep,

        C   D
Through the desert of the truth to the river so deep.

       G
We all end in the o - cean, we all start in the streams.

        C   D
We're all carried along __ by the river of dreams,

In the middle of the night.

Outro

    G
‖: (I go walkin' in the, in the middle of the,

I go walkin' in the, in the middle of the,

C
 I go walkin' in the, in the middle of the,

D
 I go walkin' in the, in the middle of the...) :‖ *Repeat and fade*

Pressure

Words and Music by
Billy Joel

You have _ to learn ___ to pace _ your-self. ___

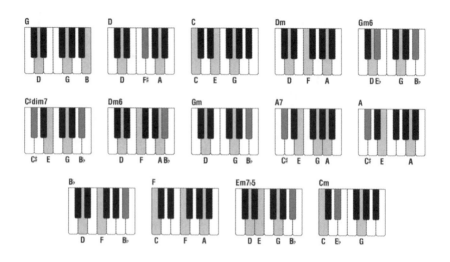

Intro

G			D	C/D D	
G			D	C/D D	
Dm Gm6/D	C#dim7/D Dm	Dm6 Gm/D	A7/D	Dm	
Dm Gm6/D	C#dim7/D Dm	Dm6 Gm/D	C#dim7/D Dm		

Verse 1

G   D   C/D D
You have to learn to pace yourself.   Pres-sure.

G   D   C/D D
You're just like ev'rybody else.   Pres-sure.

Gm   C   A/C♯   Dm A Dm Dm/C
You've only had ___ to run,   so far so good.

B♭   F/A   G
But you will come to a place

      Em7♭5   A/C♯   Dm
Where the on - ly thing ___ you feel

  Dm/C B♭   F/A
Are loaded guns in your face,

     Em7♭5   A/C♯
And you'll have to deal ___ with

|Dm Gm6/D |C♯dim7/D Dm |Dm6 Gm/D |A7/D   Dm |
Pressure.

|Dm Gm6/D |C♯dim7/D Dm |Dm6 Gm/D |C♯dim7/D Dm |

Verse 2

G   D   C/D D
You used to call me paranoid.   Pres-sure.

G   D C/D D
But even you cannot avoid   pres-sure.

Gm   C   A/C♯ Dm A Dm Dm/C
You turned the tap __ dance into   your cru-sade.

B♭   F/A   G
Now here you are ___ with your faith

    Em7♭5 A/C♯   Dm
And your Peter Pan ___ advice.

   Dm/C B♭   F/A   Em7♭5 A/C♯
You have no scars on your face, ___ and you can - not handle

|Dm Gm6/D |C♯dim7/D Dm |Dm6 Gm/D |A7/D   Dm |
Pressure.

|Dm Gm6/D |C♯dim7/D Dm |Dm6 Gm/D |C♯dim7/D Dm |

Bridge 1

G   D/F#
All grown up and no place to go.

G   D/F#
Psych One, Psych Two, what do you know?

F   C/E
All your life is Channel Thirteen,

Cm/Eb   D
Sesame Street. What does it mean?

G
   I'll tell you what it means:

D   C/D D   G
   Pres-sure.

D   C/D D
   Pres-sure.

Verse 3

G   D   C/D D
  Don't ask for help, you're all alone.   Pres-sure.

G   D   C/D D
  You'll have to answer to your own   pres-sure.

Gm   C   A/C#   Dm A   Dm Dm/C
I'm sure you'll have some cosmic ra - tionale.

Bb   F/A   G
But here you are ___ in the ninth,

          Em7b5   A/C#   Dm
Two men out ___ and three ___ men on.

Dm/C   Bb   F/A
No-where to look ___ but in-side,

         Em7b5 A/C#
Where we all ___ re-spond to

|Dm Gm6/D |C#dim7/D Dm |Dm6 Gm/D |A7/D   Dm |
 Pressure.   Mm,

|Dm Gm6/D |C#dim7/D Dm |Dm6 Gm/D |C#dim7/D Dm |
 Pressure.

Interlude 1 | G | |D/F♯ | |
         | G | |D/F♯ | |

              F   C/E
Bridge 2   All your life is *Time* magazine.

              Cm/E♭   D
              I read it, too. What does it mean?

Interlude 2 | G | |D | |
         | G | |D |N.C. |
                                           Pressure.

              Gm   C   A/C♯ Dm A   Dm Dm/C
Verse 4   I'm sure you have some cosmic ra - tion - ale,

              B♭   F/A   G
              But here you are with your faith

                  Em7♭5 A/C♯   Dm
              And your Peter Pan ___ ad-vice.

                 Dm/C B♭   F/A
              You have no scars on your face,

                  Em7♭5 A/C♯
              And you can - not handle

         | Dm Gm6/D | C♯dim7/D Dm | Dm6 Gm/D | A7/D   Dm |
           Pressure.   Mm,

         | Dm Gm6/D | C♯dim7/D Dm | Dm6 Gm/D | C♯dim7/D Dm |
           Pressure.

Outro | Dm Gm6/D | C♯dim7/D Dm | Dm6 Gm/D |
           Pressure.

         | A7/D   Dm |
           One, two, three, four, pressure.

Rosalinda's Eyes

Words and Music by
Billy Joel

I play nights in the Span - ish part of town.

Intro   ‖: G/A A/B │ D/E E/F♯ │ G/F   │   :‖ *Play 4 times*

Verse 1

G+7   C9   F+7   B♭maj7
I play nights in the Span - ish part of town.

D♭/E♭   A♭maj7   D7sus   D7#9
I've got music in my   hands.

G+7   C9   F+7   B♭maj7
The work is hard ____ to find, but that ____ don't get me down.

D♭/E♭ A♭maj7   D7sus D7#9
Rosalin - da understands.

Chorus 1

G   C   G   D
Crazy Lat - in dancing so - lo down in Her - ald Square.

G   C   G   D
Oh, Hava - na, I've been search - ing for you ev - 'rywhere.

G/B   C
Though I'll nev - er be there,

G/B   A/C#
I know what I ____ would see there.

G/D   B/D#   Em Em/D
I can always find ____ my Cuban skies

     C   D   G
In Ros - alin - da's eyes.

Interlude 1

‖: G/A A/B | D/E E/F# | G/F | :‖ *Play 4 times*

Verse 2

G+7   C9   F+7   B♭maj7
When she smiles, ____ she gives ev - erything to me.

D♭/E♭   A♭maj7   D7sus D7#9
When she's all ____ alone she cries.

G+7   C9   F+7   B♭maj7
I'd do anything to take away her tears,

D♭/E♭   A♭maj7   D7sus D7#9
Because they're Rosalinda's   eyes.

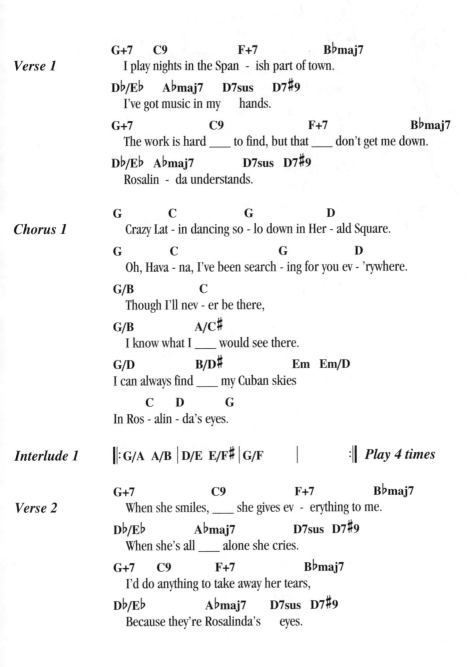

	G	C	G	D

Chorus 2   Señori - ta, don't be lone - ly, I will soon ___ be there.

G   C   G   D
Oh, Hava - na, I've been search - ing for you ev - 'rywhere.

G/B   C
And I got a chance ___ to make it.

G/B   A/C♯
It's time for me ____ to take it.

G/D   B/D♯   Em Em/D
I'll return before ____ the fire dies

          C   D   G
In Ros - alin - da's eyes.

Bridge

Ebmaj7	Dm7	Cmaj7	Bbmaj7	
Amaj7		Am7	D7b9sus	
Gmaj7	C7sus	Am Am(maj7) Am7	
	D7		

Verse 3

G+7   C9   F+7   Bbmaj7
All alone ____ in a Puer - to Rican band.

Db/Eb   Abmaj7   D7sus D7♯9
Union wag - es, wedding clothes.

G+7   C9   F+7   Bbmaj7
Hardly an - yone has seen ___ how good I am.

Db/Eb Abmaj7   D7sus D7♯9
Rosalin - da says she knows.

Chorus 3   *Repeat Chorus 1*

Interlude 2

| G/A A/B | D/E E/F♯ | G/F | | |
| G/A A/B | D/E E/F♯ | D7sus | | |

Chorus 4   *Repeat Chorus 2*

Outro   ‖: G/A A/B | D/E E/F♯ | G7/F | :‖ *Repeat and fade*

Say Goodbye to Hollywood

Words and Music by
Billy Joel

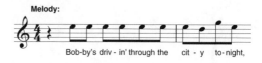

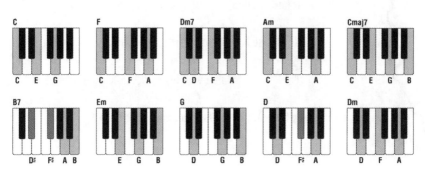

Intro	`| C	|`	

Verse 1	**C** 　　Bobby's drivin' through the city tonight,
	F Through the lights in a hot new rent - a-car.
	C 　　He joins the lovers in his heavy machine.
	F It's a scene down on Sunset Boulevard.

Chorus 1	**Dm7** 　　Say goodbye to Hollywood,
	F/G　　　　　　　**Am** 　　Say goodbye, my ba - by.
	F 　　Say goodbye to Hollywood,
	F/G　　　　　　　**C** 　　Say goodbye, my ba - by.

Verse 2

       C

     Johnny's takin' care of things for a while,

                  F

And his style is so right for trou - badours.

       C

     They got him sitting with his back to the door,

               F

Now he won't be my fast gun anymore.

Chorus 2   *Repeat Chorus 1*

Bridge 1

Cmaj7   B7   Em

   Movin' on is a chance you take anytime

             C   G   D

You try to stay __ to-gether. Oh, ho, ho.

Cmaj7   B7   Em

   Say a word out of line, you find that your friends

             C   G   Dm G

You had are gone __ for-ever, for-ev - er.

Verse 3

       C

     So many faces in and out of my life,

                    F

Some will last, some will just be now __ and then.

       C

     Life is a series of hellos and goodbyes.

              F

I'm afraid it's time for goodbye __ again.

Chorus 3   *Repeat Chorus 1*

Piano Solo

C			F	
	C			
F	Dm7		F/G	
Am	F		F/G	
C				

Bridge 2   *Repeat Bridge 1*

Verse 4   *Repeat Verse 3*

Chorus 4

Dm7
Say goodbye to Hollywood,

F/G   Am
Say goodbye, my ba - by.

F
Say goodbye to Hollywood,

F/G   N.C.
Say goodbye, my baby.

Outro

C			F	
	C			
F	Dm7		F/G	
Am	F		F/G	

Running on Ice

Words and Music by
Billy Joel

There's a lot of ten-sion in this town.

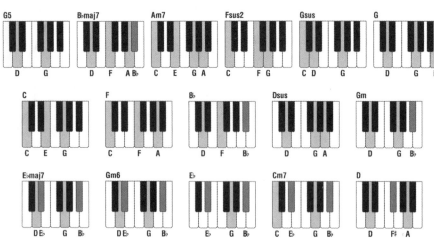

Intro   ‖: G5 B♭maj7 | Am7 Fsus2 | G5 B♭maj7 | Am7 Gsus :‖

Verse 1

G5   B♭maj7   Am7
There's a lot of tension in this town.

        Fsus2   G5   B♭maj7 Am7 Gsus
I know it's building up in-side of me.

G5   B♭maj7
I've got all the symptoms

        Am7   Fsus2   G5 B♭maj7 Am7 Gsus
And the side effects of city life an-xiety.

G5   B♭maj7   Am7
I could never under-stand why the urban attitude

Fsus2 G5   B♭maj7   Am7   Gsus
Is so su-perior.

G5   B♭maj7   Am7
In a world of high-rise ambition,

          Fsus2   G5   B♭maj7 Am7   G/B
Most people's motives are ul-terior.   Oh.

Chorus 1

C   F   C
  Sometimes I feel as though I'm running on ice,

F   C   G
Paying the price __ too long.

Am7   Bb   C
  Kind of get the feeling that I'm running on ice.

Bb   C   Dsus
Where did my life __ go wrong?

Verse 2

G5   Bbmaj7 Am7
  I'm a cosmo-politan so-phisticate

 Fsus2   G5   Bbmaj7 Am7 Gsus
Of culture and in-telligence,

G5   Bbmaj7   Am7
  The culmi-nation of tech-nology

 Fsus2   G5   Bbmaj7 Am7 Gsus
And civilized ex-perience,

G5   Bbmaj7   Am7
  But I'm carrying the weight of all the useless junk

 Fsus2   G5   Bbmaj7 Am7 Gsus
A modern man ac-cumulates.

G5   Bbmaj7 Am7
  I'm a sta-tistic in a system

  Fsus2   G5   Bbmaj7 Am7 G/B
That a civil servant dominates.   Oh.

Chorus 2

C   F   C
  And all that means is that I'm running on ice,

F   C   G
Caught in a vise __ so strong.

Am7   Bb   C
  I'm slipping and sliding 'cause I'm running on ice.

Bb   C   Dsus
Where did my life ____ go wrong?

Bridge 1

         Gm E♭maj7/G Gm6
You've got to run, run,   run, run, oh,

E♭ Cm7 F B♭
Oh.

Gm E♭maj7/G Gm6
Run, run,   run, run, oh,

E♭ Cm7 F D
Oh.

Interlude

‖: G5 B♭maj7 │Am7 Fsus2 │G5 B♭maj7 │Am7 Gsus :‖

Verse 3

G5   B♭maj7   Am7   Fsus2
  As fast as I can climb; a new disaster ev'ry time I

G5   B♭maj7 Am7 Gsus
Turn around.

G5   B♭maj7   Am7
  As soon as I get one fire put out,

         Fsus2   G5   B♭maj7 Am7 Gsus
There's an-other building burning down.

G5   B♭maj7   Am7
  They say this highway's goin' my way,

       Fsus2   G5   B♭maj7 Am7 Gsus
But I don't know where it's takin' me.

G5   B♭maj7
  It's a bad waste, a sad case,

  Am7   Fsus2   G5   B♭maj7 Am7   G/B
A rat race, it's breakin' me.   Oh.

Chorus 3
        C   F   C
And I get no traction 'cause I'm running on ice.

      F   C   G
It's taking me twice ____ as long.

Am7   B♭   C
Get a bad reaction 'cause I'm running on ice.

B♭   C   Dsus
Where did my life ___ go wrong?

Bridge 2
                Gm E♭maj7/G Gm6
You've got to run, run,   run, run, run,

E♭ Cm7 F B♭
Oh, ho.

      Gm   E♭maj7/G   Gm6
You run, you run,   you run, run, run,

E♭ Cm7 F D
Oh, ho.

Outro
‖: G5 B♭maj7 │ Am7   Fsus2   │
                        Running on ice.

│G5 B♭maj7 │Am7   Gsus   :‖ *Repeat and fade*
                      Running on ice.

Shameless

Words and Music by
Billy Joel

Melody:

Well, I'm shame-less   when it comes to   lov-ing you. —

G — D G B

D — D F# A

Em — E G B

C — C E G

Bb — D F Bb

B7 — D# F# A B

Am7 — C E G A

F — C F A

F# — C# F# A#

Gm — D G Bb

Am — C E A

Ab — C Eb Ab

Eb — Eb G Bb

Intro

| G | D | Em | C Bb/C |
| G | D | Em | C Bb/C |

Verse 1

       G   **D/F#**
Well, I'm shameless when it comes to loving you.

            Em   **C**   **Bb/C**
I'd do anything you want me to. I'd do anything at all.

      G   **D/F#**
And I'm standing here for all the world to see.

             Em   **C**   **Bb/C**
Ah, there ain't that much left of me that has very far to fall.

     D   **B7/D#**   **Em**
You know I'm not a man who's ever been inse - cure

         Am7
About the world I've been living in.

    D   **B7/D#**
I don't break easy. I have my pride.

    Em   **F**   **F#**
But if you need to be satis - fied,

G   D/F♯
I'm shameless. Baby, I don't have a prayer.

                Em   C   B♭/C
Anytime I see you standing there, I go down upon my knees.

        G   D/F♯
And I'm changing. I swore I'd never compromise,

                   Em   C   B♭/C
Ah, but you convinced me otherwise. I'll do anything you please.

        D   B7/D♯
You see in all my life I've never found

      Em   Am7
What I couldn't resist, what I couldn't turn down.

       D   B7/D♯
I could walk away from anyone I ever knew,

      Em   F   Gm   F/A
But I can't walk away from you.

      B♭   Am
I have never let anything have this much con - trol over me.

A♭   E♭   E♭/G F/A
I worked too hard to call my life my own.

      B♭   Am
Well, I made myself a world and it worked so ___ perfectly,

      A♭
But it's your world now. I can't refuse.

Am   D
I never had so much to lose. I'm

Piano Solo

| G | D/F♯ | Em | C B♭/C |

Shameless.

| G | D/F♯ | Em | C B♭/C |

| Em Em/D | C B♭/C |

Verse 3

              D   **B7/D♯**

You know it should be easy for a man who's strong

    Em   **Am7**

To say he's sorry or ad-mit when he's wrong.

    D   **B/D♯**

I've never lost anything I ever missed,

    Em   **F**

But I've never been in love like this.

N.C.

It's out of my hands.

Outro

    G   **D/F♯**

I'm shameless. I don't have the power now,

        Em   **C**   **B♭/C**

But I don't want it anyhow, so I've got to let it go.

    G   **D/F♯**

‖: I'm shameless, shameless as a man can be.

        Em

You can make a total fool of me.

      C   **B♭/C**

I just wanted you to know.   :‖   *Repeat and fade*
                                         (w/Voc. ad lib.)

She's Always a Woman

Words and Music by
Billy Joel

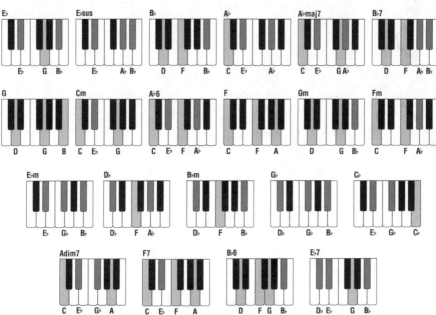

Intro |E♭ E♭sus E♭ B♭ | E♭ A♭ E♭

                    B♭   E♭
Verse 1   She can kill with a smile;

                    B♭   E♭
She can wound with her eyes.

                         A♭
She can ruin your faith

                    A♭maj7 A♭ A♭maj7
With her casual   lies.

                    B♭7   E♭
And she only re-veals

                    B♭   G
What she wants you to see.

Cm
She hides like a child,

     A♭   **B♭7**   **E♭** **E♭sus** **E♭**
But she's always a woman to me.

      B♭   **E♭**
Verse 2   She can lead you to love,

      B♭   **E♭**
She can take you or leave you.

        A♭
She can ask for the truth,

     A♭maj7 A♭6   **A♭**
But she'll never be-lieve you,

     B♭7   **E♭**
And she'll take what you give her

   B♭7   **G**
As long as it's free,

     Cm
Yeah, she steals like a thief,

    A♭6   **B♭7**   **E♭** **E♭sus** **E♭**
But she's always a woman to me.

    Cm   **F**   **B♭**
Bridge 1 Oh,_____ she takes care of her-self,

    Gm   **E♭**   **A♭**
    She can wait if she wants,

    Fm   **B♭7**   **E♭** **A♭ E♭**
    She's a-head of her time.

    E♭m   **Cm**   **A♭**   **D♭**
    Oh,_____ and she never gives out

    B♭m   **G♭**   **C♭**
    And she never gives in,

    Adim7   **F7**   **B♭**   **B♭6 B♭7**
    She just changes her mind.

                  E♭
Verse 3 And she'll promise you more

      B♭   **E♭**
Than the garden of Eden.

      E♭7   **A♭**
Then she'll carelessly cut you

    A♭maj7   **A♭6**   **A♭**
And laugh while you're bleedin'.

     B♭7   **E♭**
But she brings out the best

     B♭7   **G**
And the worst you can be,

     Cm
Blame it all on yourself

       A♭6   **B♭7**   **E♭** **E♭sus** **E♭** **B♭**
'Cause she's always a woman to me.

Interlude |**E♭ B♭ G** |**Cm**   **A♭6 B♭7** |**E♭ E♭sus E♭** |

Bridge 2   **Repeat Bridge 1**

        E♭
Verse 4   She is frequently kind

     B♭   **E♭**
And she's suddenly cruel.

     E♭7   **A♭**
She can do as she pleases,

   A♭maj7 A♭6 A♭
She's nobody's fool.

    B♭7   **E♭**
But she can't be con-victed,

    B♭7   **G**
She's earned her de-gree.

     Cm
And the most she will do

    A♭   **E♭**
Is throw shadows at you,

     Fm   **B♭7**   **E♭** **E♭sus** **E♭** **B♭**
But she's always a woman to me.

Outro |**E♭ B♭7 G** |**Cm**   **A♭6 B♭7** |**E♭ E♭sus E♭** |

She's Got a Way

Words and Music by
Billy Joel

Melody:

She's got a way   a - bout ___ her.

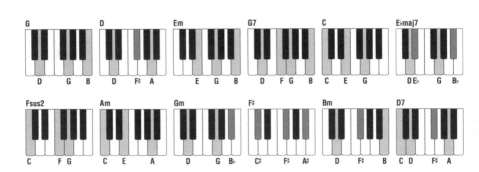

Intro | G | | |

Verse 1

G   D/F♯   Em   G7/D
She's got a way about ___ her.

C
I don't know what it is,

D   C/E   D/F♯
But I know that I ___ can't live without her.

G   D/F♯   Em   G7/D
She's got a way ___ of pleas - in'.

C
Mm, I don't know why it is,

D   C/E   D/F♯   E♭maj7 Fsus2
But there doesn't have ___ to be ___ a reason anyway.

Verse 2

     G   D/F#   Em   G7/D
    She's got a smile that heals ___ me.

     C
Mm, I don't know why it is,

     D   C/E   D/F#
But I have to laugh ___ when she reveals me.

 G   D/F#   Em   G7/D
  She's got a way of talk - in'.

     C
Mm, I don't know why it is,

     D   C/E   D/F#   E♭maj7   Fsus2 G
But it lifts me up ___ when we are walkin'   anywhere.

Bridge 1

     D   Am
She comes to me when I'm feelin' down,

    G   Gm
In-spires me with-out a sound.

    D/F#   F#/A#   Bm   D7/A
She touches me and I get turned ___ around.

Verse 3

    G   D/F#   Em G7/D
  She's got a way of show-in',

    C
Mm, how I make her feel.

    D   C/E   D/F#
And I find the strength ___ to keep ___ on goin'.

 G   D/F#   Em   G7/D
  And she's got a light around ___ her,

     C
Whoa, and ev'rywhere she goes

    D   C/E   D/F#   E♭maj7   Fsus2 G
A million dreams ___ of love ___ surround her   ev'rywhere.

                              D   Am
Bridge 2   She comes to me when I'm feelin' down,

                              G   Gm
                In-spires me with-out a sound.

                              D/F♯   F♯/A♯   Bm
                She touch - es me,   I get turned ___ around.

                D7/A G   D/F♯   Em
                  Oh, oh, oh, ___ whoa.

                              G   D/F♯   Em   G7/D
Verse 4   She's got a smile that heals me.

                              C
                Mm, I don't know why it is,

                              D   C/E   D/F♯
                But I have to laugh ___ when she reveals me.

                G   D/F♯   Em   G7/D
                  And she's got a way about ___ her.

                              C
                Mm, I don't know what it is,

                              D   C/E   D/F♯   E♭maj7   Fsus2 G
                But I know that I ___ can't live without her   anyway.

Sometimes a Fantasy

Words and Music by
Billy Joel

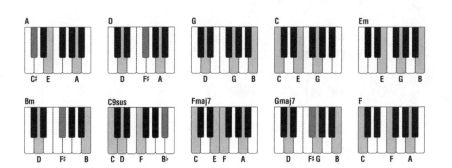

Intro	**A**	**D**	**A**	**D**	**A**

Verse 1

   D   **A**
Oh, I didn't want to do it, but I got too lonely.

   D   **A**
Mm, I had to call you up in the middle of the night.

   G   **D**
I know it's awful hard to try to make a love long distance,

   C   **Em**
But I really needed stimulation,

   G   **A**   **G/B** **A/C#**
Though it was only my imag - i - na - tion.

Chorus 1

D A   Bm
It's just a fan-tasy, (Oh.)

G A   Bm
It's not the real thing. (Oh.)

D A   Bm
It's just a fan-tasy, (Oh.)

G A   Bm
It's not the real thing. (Oh.)

D   A   Bm
Some-times a fan-tasy (Oh.)

G A   C9sus
Is all you need.

Fmaj7   C9sus   Fmaj7
Oh,   oh,   oh.

Verse 2

D   A
When am I gonna take control, get a hold of my e-motions?

D   A
Why does it only seem to hit me in the middle of the night?

G   D
You told me there's a number I can always dial for as-sistance.

C   Em
I don't want to deal with outside action;

G   A G/B A/C♯
Only you can give me sat - is - fac - tion.

Chorus 2   *Repeat Chorus 1*

Interlude | D | | Gmaj7 | |

                   | D | | C | | | |

Verse 3

    D   **A**
    Oh, sure it would be better if I had you here to hold me.

    D   **A**
    Be better, baby, but believe me it's the next best thing.

    G   **D**
    I'm sure there's many times you've wanted me to hear your secrets.

    C   **Em**
    Don't be afraid to say the words that'll move me,

    G   **A**   **G/B** **A/C♯**
    Any time you want to tell them to   me.

Chorus 3

    D A   **Bm**
    It's just a fan-tasy, (Oh.)

    G A   **Bm**
    It's not the real thing. (Oh.)

    D A   **Bm**
    It's just a fan-tasy, (Oh.)

    G A   **Bm**
    It's not the real thing. (Oh.)

    D   **A**   **Bm**
    Some-times a fan-tasy (Oh.)

    G A   **C9sus**
    Is all you need.

Outro

    C9sus
  ‖:   Just a fantasy,

    F
    It's not the real thing.

    C9sus
    It's just a fantasy,

    F
    It's not the real thing.

    D
    It's just a fantasy,

    G
    It's not the real thing.

    D
    It's just a fantasy,

    G
    It's not the real thing.   :‖   *Repeat and fade*

Stiletto

Words and Music by
Billy Joel

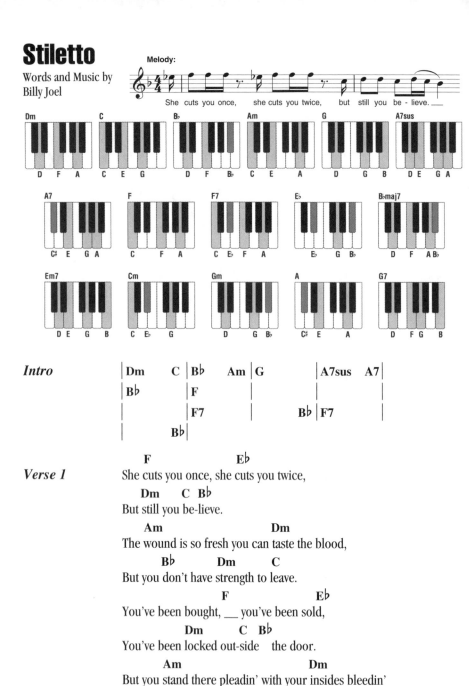

Melody:

She cuts you once, she cuts you twice, but still you be-lieve. ___

Intro

Dm C	Bb Am	G		A7sus A7
Bb	F			
	F7		Bb	F7	
	Bb				

Verse 1

    F   **Eb**
She cuts you once, she cuts you twice,
    Dm   **C Bb**
But still you be-lieve.
    Am   **Dm**
The wound is so fresh you can taste the blood,
    Bb   **Dm**   **C**
But you don't have strength to leave.
             F   **Eb**
You've been bought, ___ you've been sold,
    Dm   **C Bb**
You've been locked out-side   the door.
    Am   **Dm**
But you stand there pleadin' with your insides bleedin'
    Bb   **Dm**   **C**
'Cause you deep down want some more.

       Dm   A7/D
When she says she wants forgive - ness,
B♭maj7   Em7 E♭ A7
It's such a clever masquerade.
Dm   A7/D
She's so good with her stilet - to,
Cm   G/B
You don't even see the blade.
Gm/B♭   B♭/C
You don't see the blade.

       F   E♭

Verse 2

She cuts you hard, she cuts you deep,
   Dm   C   B♭
She's got so much skill.
   Am   Dm
She's so fascinatin' that you're still there waitin'
   B♭   Dm   C
When she comes back for the kill.
        F   E♭
You've been slashed __ in the face,
     Dm   C B♭
You've been left there to bleed.
  Am   Dm
You want to run away, but you know you're gonna stay
   B♭   Dm   C
'Cause she gives you what you need.

Dm   A7/D

Chorus 2

Then she says she needs affec - tion,
B♭maj7   Em7 E♭ A7
While she searches for the vain.
Dm   A7/D
She's so good with her stilet - to,
Cm   G/B
You don't really mind the pain.
Gm/B♭   B♭/C
You don't mind the pain.
       F   N.C.
Whoa, whoa!

Interlude

```
‖: F Bb G  C  | A Dm BbC | F Bb G  C  | A Dm BbC:‖
‖: Dm       | Bb        | G7        | Dm/A  A  :‖
 | Bb        | F         |           |           |
 |           | F7        |           | Bb | F7    |
 |           | Bb|
```

Verse 3

      F   Eb
She cuts you out, she cuts you down,

    Dm   C   Bb
She carves up your life.

      Am   Dm
But you won't do nothin' as she keeps on cuttin'

        Bb   Dm   C
'Cause you know you love the knife.

              F   Eb
You've been bought, __ you've been sold,

        Dm   C   Bb
You've been locked out-side   the door.

      Am   Dm
But you stand there pleadin' with your insides bleedin'

      Bb   Dm   C
'Cause you deep down want some more.

Chorus 3

Dm   A7/D
  Then she says she wants affec - tion,

Bbmaj7   Em7 Eb A7
  While she searches for the vein.

Dm   A7/D
  She's so good with her stilet - to,

Cm   G/B
  You don't really mind the pain.

Gm/Bb   Bb/C
  You don't mind the pain.

Outro

```
| Dm  Dm/C | Bb      Am | G        |A7sus  A7 |
| Bb       |‖: F        |          |          |    :‖
‖: F7      |         Bb :‖ Repeat and fade
```

Streetlife Serenader

Words and Music by
Billy Joel

Street-life ser - e - nad - er...

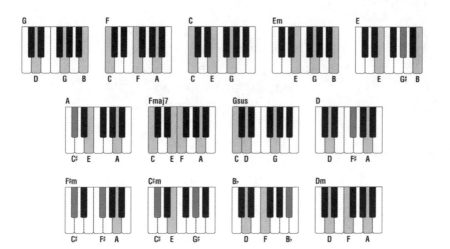

Intro

G	F	G	C	
G	F	G	Em E	
A				

Verse 1

    A   G   Fmaj7 G Gsus
Streetlife serenad - er

  G   D   C
  Never sang on stages,

  A   G   Fmaj7   G Gsus
  Needs no orchestra - tion.

  G   D   C
  The melody comes easy.

Verse 2

```
A          G         Fmaj7   G  Gsus
     Midnight masquerad  -  er,

G              D           C
  Shopping center he - roes, yeah, __ yeah.

A        G   Fmaj7   G  Gsus
  Child of Ei - sen-hower,

G              D
  New world cele-brator.
```

| G | F | G | Em E | A |

Verse 3

```
A         G    Fmaj7   G  Gsus
   Streetlife serenad  -  ers

G              D          C
  Have such under-standing;

A              G     Fmaj7   G  Gsus
  How the words __ are spoken,

G                   D
  How to make the mo - tions.
```

Interlude 1

G	F	G	C	
G G/F	A/E	A	F♯m C♯m
E A/E	E E/D	G G/D	Em G/B
D		C	A

Verse 4

```
           A         G Fmaj7      G  Gsus
           Streetlife ser  -  enaders
           G             D        C
           Have no obli-gations,
           A          G       Fmaj7   G  Gsus
           Hold no grand illu  -  sions,
           G                D        C
           Need no stimu-lation.
```

Verse 5

```
           A          G Fmaj7       G  Gsus
           Midnight mas  -  queraders,
           G                    D    C
           Workin' hard for wag - es,
           A         G Fmaj7         G  Gsus
           Need no vast     arrangements
           G                D
           To do their harmo-nizing.
```

Interlude 2 | A | G | F | B♭ Dm/A | A   G |

Piano Solo | Fmaj7 | G | D   C | A   G |
                | Fmaj7 | G | D | C |

Outro | A   A/E | F♯m C♯m | E   A/E | E   E/D |
       | G   G/D | Em G/B | D | C |
       | A

Storm Front

Words and Music by
Billy Joel

Melody:

Safe   at   har - bor,

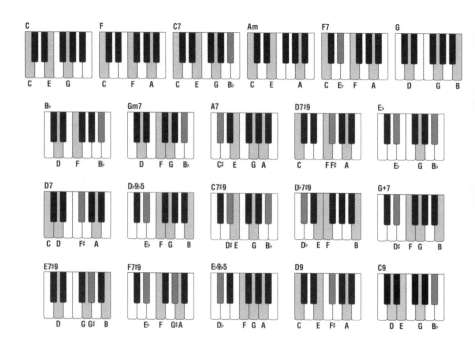

Intro   ‖: C F/C C7| |C   F/C |C7   :‖

C   F/C C7
Safe at   harbor, ev'rything is easy.

Am   F7   G N.C. G
Off to starboard, daylight comes up fast.

C   F/C C7
Now I'm restless for the open water.

Am   F7   G N.C. G Am
Red flags are flyin' from the Coast Guard mast.

B♭   C
   They told me to stay.

F   Gm7   F/A
I heard all the informa - tion.

B♭   C
   I motored away

    A7   D7♯9 N.C.
And steered straight ahead, though the weatherman said,

                    Gm7
Chorus 1   There's a storm front comin'.

E♭   D7
   (Mood indigo.)

Gm7
White water runnin',

    E♭   D7
The pressure is low.

Gm7
Storm front comin',

E♭   D7
   (Mood indigo.)

D♭9♭5   N.C.
Small craft warning on the radio.

C F/C   C7
I've been sail - in' a long time on this ocean.

Am   F7   G N.C. G
Man gets lonesome all those years at sea.

C F/C C7
I've got a woman, my life should be easy.

Am   F7   G N.C. G Am
Most men hunger for the life I lead.

B♭   C
   The morning was grey,

   F   Gm7 F/A
But I had the motiva - tion.

B♭   C
   I drifted away

   A7   D7♯9 N.C.
And ran into more heavy weather offshore.

Chorus 2   *Repeat Chorus 1*

              C7♯9
Bridge   We've got a low pressure system and a northeastern breeze,

D♭7♯9   C7♯9
We've got a falling barometer and rising seas.

D♭7♯9   C7♯9
We've got the cumulonimbus and a possible gale,

D♭7♯9   G+7   N.C.
We've got a force nine blow-in' on the Beaufort scale.

Verse 3

C F/C C7
I'm still restless for the open water,

Am   F7   G Am
Though she gives me ev'rything I need.

B♭   C
  She asked me to stay,

  F   Gm7 F/A
But I'd done my naviga - tion.

B♭   C
  I drove her away,

   A7   D7#9
But I should have known to stay tied up at home.

Chorus 3   *Repeat Chorus 1*

Piano Solo |E7#9 | F7#9|E7#9 | F7#9 |
              |E7#9 | F7#9|E7#9 E♭9♭5 |D9 D♭7#9 |

Outro

C9
‖: (Storm front comin'.)

There's a storm front comin'.

(White water runnin'.)

White water runnin'.   :‖ *Repeat and fade (w/Voc. ad lib.)*

The Stranger

Words and Music by
Billy Joel

Well, we all ___ have a face ___ that we hide a-way ___ for-ev - er.

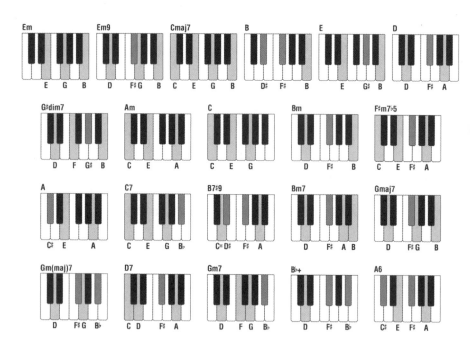

Prelude

Em Em9/D	Cmaj7	B	Cmaj7
E D/F# G#dim7	Am Em/G	D/F# C/E	Bm/D B/D#
Em Em9/D	Cmaj7	B	Cmaj7
E F#m7♭5 G#dim7	Am Em/G	D/F# C/E	
B/D# A/C#		B B/A	Em

Intro

| Em | C7 | Em | C7 | |

Verse 1

       Em
Well, we all ___ have a face

   Am   **Em**
That we hide away forev - er.

   Am   **C**
And we take them out and show ourselves

  D   **B7#9**
When ev'ryone has gone.

    Em
Some are satin, some are steel,

   Am   **Em**
Some are silk and some are leather.

    Am   **D**
They're the fac - es of a stran - ger,

   Bm7   **Em C7 Em C7**
But we love ___ to try them on.

Verse 2

    Em
Well, we all ___ fall in love,

   Am   **Em**
But we disregard the dan - ger.

   Am   **C**
Though we share so many se - crets,

  D   **B7#9**
There are some we never tell.

    Em
Why were you ___ so surprised

   Am   **Em**
That you never saw the stran - ger?

  Am   **D**
Did you ever let your lover

   Bm7   **Em**
See the stran - ger in your - self?

Bridge 1

Gmaj7   Gm(maj7)   D/F#
Don't be afraid ____ to try again.

D7   Gmaj7
Ev'ryone goes south

Gm(maj7)   D/F#   Am D
Ev'ry now and then.   Oo.

Gmaj7   Gm7   D/F#
You've done it, why can't someone else?

D/C   Bm7
You should know by now,

Bb+   A6   B7#9
You've been there your - self.

Verse 3

       Em
Once I used to believe

    Am   Em
I was such a great romanc - er,

    Am   C
Then I came home to a woman

    D   B7#9
That I could not recognize.

     Em
When I pressed her for a reason,

      Am   Em
She refused ____ to even an - swer.

       Am   D
It was then I felt the stranger

     Bm7   Em C7 Em C7
Kick me right ____ between the eyes.

Verse 4   *Repeat Verse 2*

Bridge 2   *Repeat Bridge 1*

                Em
Verse 5   You may never understand

              Am   **Em**
How the stranger is in-spired,

              Am   **C**
But he isn't always evil

            D   **B7♯9**
And he is __ not always wrong.

               Em
Though you drown in good intentions,

             Am   **Em**
You will never quench the fire.

                Am   **D**
You'll give in   to your desire

                Bm7   **Em** **C7** **Em** **C7**
When the stran - ger comes along.

Outro | Em   Em9/D | Cmaj7 | B | Cmaj7 |
              | E F♯m7♭5 G♯dim7 | Am Em/G | D/F♯C/E | B/D♯ A/C♯ |
              | B   B/A | Em Em9/D | Cmaj7 | B |
              | Cmaj7 | E D/F♯ G♯dim7 | Am Em/G | D/F♯ *Fade out*

Tell Her About It

Words and Music by
Billy Joel

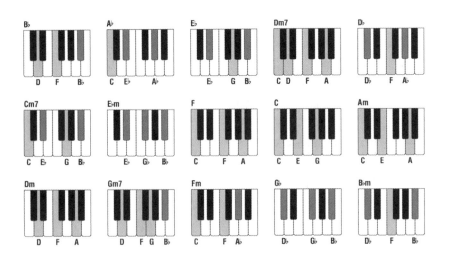

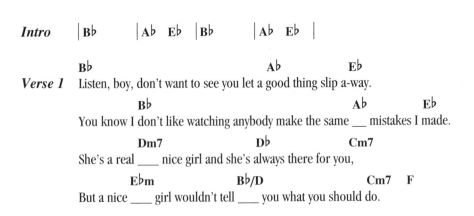

Intro | B♭ | A♭ E♭ | B♭ | A♭ E♭ |

              B♭   **A♭**   **E♭**

Verse 1   Listen, boy, don't want to see you let a good thing slip a-way.

                     B♭   **A♭**   **E♭**
           You know I don't like watching anybody make the same __ mistakes I made.

                    Dm7   **D♭**   **Cm7**
           She's a real ____ nice girl and she's always there for you,

                   E♭m   **B♭/D**   **Cm7**   **F**
           But a nice ____ girl wouldn't tell ____ you what you should do.

Verse 2

Bb   Ab   Eb
Oh, listen boy, I'm sure that you think you got it all under con-trol.

Bb   Ab   Eb
You don't want somebody telling you the way to stay in someone's soul.

Dm7   Db   Cm7
You're a big ___ boy now, and you'll never let her go,

Ebm   Bb/D   Cm7 Bb C
But that's just the kind of thing ___ she ought to know.

Chorus 1

F   Am
Tell her about it. Tell her ev - 'rything you feel.

Dm   Dm/C   Gm7   C
Give her ev'ry rea - son to ac-cept that you're for real.

F   Am
Tell her about it. Tell her all ___ your crazy dreams.

Dm   Dm/C
Let her know you need ___ her.

Gm7   C
Let her know ___ how much she means.

Interlude |Bb |Ab Eb |Bb |Ab Eb |

Verse 3

Bb   Ab   Eb
Listen, boy, it's not automatic'ly a certain guarantee.

Bb   Ab   Eb
To in-sure yourself, you've got to provide communi-cation constant-ly.

Dm7   Db   Cm7
When you love ___ someone you're always insecure,

Ebm   Dm7   Cm7 Bb C
And there's only one good way to reassure:

Chorus 2

F   Am
Tell her about it. Let her know ___ how much you care.

Dm   Dm/C   Gm7   C
When she can't be with ___ you tell her you ___ wish you were there.

F   Am
Tell her about it, ev'ry day ___ before you leave.

Dm   Dm/C   Gm7   Bb/C
Pay her some atten - tion, give her some - thing to believe.

Bridge

Ab   Fm   Gb
'Cause now and then ___ she'll get to wor - rying,

Ab   Bbm   Eb   Fm   Eb/G
Just because ___ you haven't spo - ken for so long.

Ab   Fm   Gb
And though you may ___ not have done an - ything,

Ab   Bbm   Eb   C/E   F
Will that be a consola - tion when she's ___ gone?

Verse 4

Bb   Ab   Eb
Listen, boy, it's good information from a man who's made mis-takes.

             Bb
Just a word ___ or two that she gets from you

           Ab   Eb
Could be the diff'rence that it makes.

           Dm7   Db   Cm7
She's a trust - ing soul, she's put her trust in you,

      Ebm   Bb/D   Cm7 Bb C
But a girl like that won't tell you what you should do.

Chorus 3   *Repeat Chorus 1*

Outro

   Bb   Gm7
‖: Tell her a-bout it.

Ab   Eb
Tell her how you feel ___ right now. :‖ ***Repeat and fade***
                                           (w/Voc. ad lib.)

That's Not Her Style

Words and Music by
Billy Joel

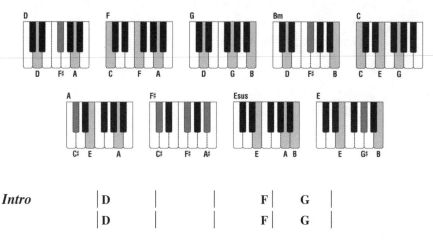

Intro

| D | | | F | G |
| D | | | F | G |

Verse 1

D   F   D
Some people think that she's one of those mink coat ladies.

                                             Bm   C
They say she wakes up at one, makes the Paparazzi run till dawn.

    D
She wines and dines with Argentines and Kuwaitis,

G   A   D
After she sips margar-itas on the White House lawn.

Chorus 1

D/F♯   G   A
That's not her style.

D/F♯ G   D
I can tell you that ain't my woman.

   D/F♯   G   A
It's just not her style.

D/F♯ G   D
I can tell you, because I'm her man.

Verse 2

D   F   D
The papers say she was seen in L.A. with a stranger.

                                  Bm   C
She found a perfect body with a Maserati right out-side.

             D
And then she _ chartered a Lear when she heard her career was in danger,

G   A   D
And gave the pilot something extra for a perfect ride.

Chorus 2

     D/F♯   G A
Well, that's not her style.

D/F♯ G   D
I can tell you that ain't my woman.

D/F♯   G A
That's not her style.

D/F♯ G   D
I can tell you, because I'm her man.

D/F♯   G A
That's not her style.

D/F♯ G   D
I can tell you that ain't my woman.

    D/F♯   G A
You know it's not her style.

D/F♯ G   D
I can tell you, 'cause I'm her man.

Bridge

G   F♯   Bm
It's not that she's nev - er done something cra - zy,

                 Esus E
Done something wild.

G   F♯
It's just that she's bet - ter

            A
At doing whatev - er suits her style.

D/F♯   G A
That's not her style.

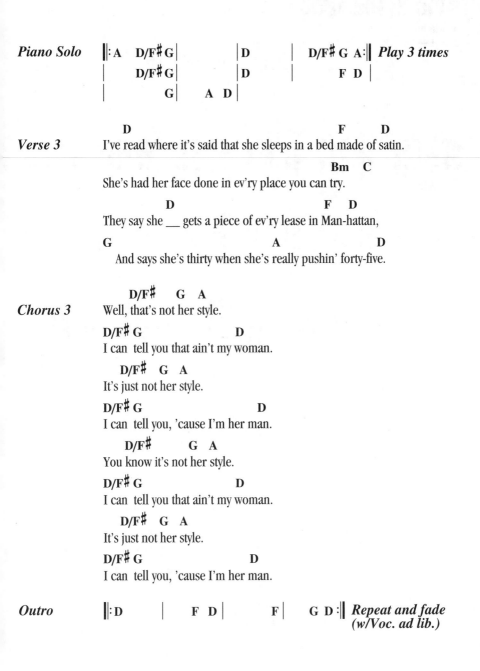

Piano Solo ‖: A D/F♯ G | | D | D/F♯ G A:‖ *Play 3 times*
            | D/F♯ G | | D | F D |
            | G | A D |

               D   F   D

Verse 3   I've read where it's said that she sleeps in a bed made of satin.

                                             Bm   C
She's had her face done in ev'ry place you can try.

          D   F   D
They say she __ gets a piece of ev'ry lease in Man-hattan,

G   A   D
And says she's thirty when she's really pushin' forty-five.

            D/F♯   G   A

Chorus 3   Well, that's not her style.

        D/F♯ G   D
I can tell you that ain't my woman.

        D/F♯   G   A
It's just not her style.

        D/F♯ G   D
I can tell you, 'cause I'm her man.

         D/F♯   G   A
You know it's not her style.

        D/F♯ G   D
I can tell you that ain't my woman.

         D/F♯   G   A
It's just not her style.

        D/F♯ G   D
I can tell you, 'cause I'm her man.

Outro   ‖: D | F D | F | G D :‖ *Repeat and fade*
                                                      (w/Voc. ad lib.)

This Is the Time

Words and Music by
Billy Joel

We walked on the beach be-side that old ho-tel.

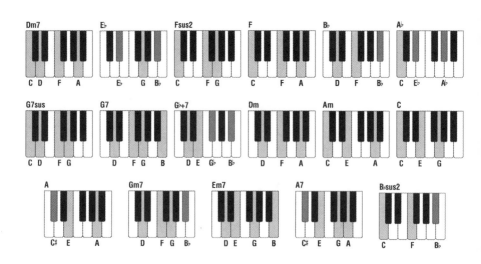

Intro

| Dm7 | E♭ | Fsus2 | | |
| Dm7 | E♭ | Fsus2 | | |

Verse 1

Dm7   **E♭**   **Fsus2**
We walked on the beach beside that old hotel.

Dm7   **E♭**   **Fsus2**
They're tearing it down now, but it's just as well.

Dm7   **E♭**   **Fsus2**
I haven't shown you ev'rything a man can do.

Dm7   **E♭**   **Fsus2**   **N.C.**
So stay with me, baby, I've got plans for you.

Chorus 1

        F/A   **B♭**
This is the time ____ to remem - ber,

      E♭   **F**
'Cause it will ____ not last forev - er.

        F/A   **B♭**
These are the days ____ to hold on ____ to,

      E♭   **F**
'Cause we won't __ although we'll want __ to.

       B♭ A♭   **G7sus G7**
This is the time,   but time is gonna change.

      G♭+7
You've given me the best of you,

      B♭/F F
And now I need the rest   of you.

Verse 2

Dm7   **E♭**   **Fsus2**
Did you know that be-fore you came in-to my life

Dm7   **E♭**   **Fsus2**
It was some kind of ____ miracle that I survived?

Dm7   **E♭**   **Fsus2**
Someday we will both look back and have to laugh.

Dm7   **E♭**   **Fsus2**   **N.C.**
We lived through a lifetime and the aftermath.

Chorus 2

        F/A   **B♭**
This is the time ____ to remem - ber,

      E♭   **F**
'Cause it will ____ not last forev - er.

        F/A   **B♭**
These are the days ____ to hold on __ to,

      E♭   **F**
'Cause we won't, __ although we'll want to.

       B♭ A♭   **G7sus G7**
This is the time,   but time is gonna change.

      G♭+7
I know we've gotta move somehow,

      B♭/F F
But I don't want to lose   you now.

	Dm Am Bb C A/C#

Bridge
Dm   Am   Bb   C A/C#
Sometimes it's so easy to let a day slip on by

Dm   Am   Bb   C
Without even seeing each other at all.

Dm   Am   Gm7 Em7 A7
But this is the time you'll turn back to and so will I,

Dm   Am   Bbsus2
And those will be days you can never re-call.

Interlude | Dm7 | Eb | Fsus2 | |
                      | Dm7 | Eb | Fsus2 | |

Verse 3
Dm7   Eb   Fsus2
And so we em-brace again be-hind the dunes;

Dm7   Eb   Fsus2
This beach is so cold on winter afternoons.

Dm7   Eb   Fsus2
Ah, but holding you close is like holding the summer sun.

Dm7   Eb   Fsus2   N.C.
I'm warm from the memory of days to come.

Chorus 3   *Repeat Chorus 1*

Outro ||: Dm7 | Eb | Fsus2 | :|| *Repeat and fade*

To Make You Feel My Love

Words and Music by
Bob Dylan

Melody:

When the rain is blow-in' in your face, __

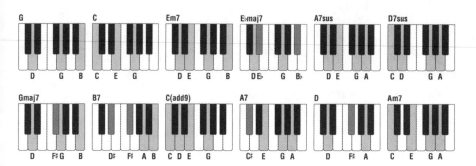

Intro | G   C/G | G   C/G |

Verse 1

  G   **G/F♯**
 When the rain is blowin' in your face,

G/F   **Em7**
 And the whole world is on your case,

E♭maj7   **G/D**
 I could offer you a warm embrace

A7sus **D7sus** **G**
 To make you feel my love.

            G/F♯
When the evenin' shadows and the stars appear,

G/F   **Em7**
 And there is no one there to dry your tears,

E♭maj7   **G/D**
 I could hold you for a million years

A7sus **D7sus** **G**
 To make you feel my love.

Bridge 1

C   Gmaj7
I know you haven't made your mind up yet,

B7   C(add9) G
But I would never do you wrong.

C   Gmaj7
I've known it from the moment that we met;

A7sus   A7   D
No doubt in my mind where you be-long.

Verse 2

G   G/F♯
I'd go hungry, I'd go black and blue.

G/F   Em7
I'd go crawlin' down the avenue.

E♭maj7   G/D
There's nothing that I ___ wouldn't do

A7   C/D G
To make you feel my love.

Piano Solo

| G | D/F♯ | G/F | C(add9)/E |
| E♭maj7 | G/D | A7sus D7sus | G |

Bridge 2

C   Gmaj7
The storms are ragin' on the rollin' sea

B7   C(add9)   G Am7 G/B
And on the high - way of regret.

C   Gmaj7
The winds of change are blowin' wild and free.

A7sus   A7   D
You ain't seen nothing like me yet.

Verse 3

G   G/F♯
I could make you happy, make your dreams come true.

G/F   Em7
There's nothing that I would not do,

E♭maj7   G/D
Go to the ends of the earth for you

A7sus   D7sus   G
To make you feel my love.

Outro

E♭maj7   G/D
There is nothin' that I wouldn't do

A7sus   D7sus   G
To make you feel my love.

Through the Long Night

Words and Music by
Billy Joel

Melody:

The cold hands, the sad eyes,

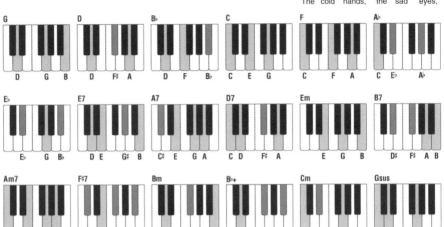

Intro |G D/F# |Bb C |G D/F# |Bb C |

Verse 1
　　　　　　G D/F#　　Bb F
The cold hands, the sad eyes,
　　　　Ab Eb Bb D
The dark Irish si - lence.
　　　G D/F#　Bb F
It's so late, but I'll wait
　　　　　　Ab E7　　A7　D7
Through the long night with you.　With
|G D/F# |Bb C |G D/F# |Bb C |
You.

Verse 2
　　　　　G D/F#　　Bb F
The warm tears, the bad dreams,
　　　　Ab Eb　　Bb　D
The soft trembling shoul-ders.
　　　G D/F#　Bb F
The old fears, but I'm here
　　　　　　Ab E7　　A7
Through the long night with you.　With

Bridge 1

Em B7 E7   Am7
You. Oh,   what has it cost you?

D   B7/D♯ Em   Am7   D B7/D♯   Em
I almost lost you a long, long time ___ ago.

B7 E7   Am7
Oh, ___ you should have told me,

       F♯7   Bm   B♭+ Am7 D
But you ___ had to bleed ___ to know.

Verse 3

         G   D/F♯ B♭   F
All your past sins are since past.

A♭ E♭   B♭   D
You should be sleep - ing.

    G D/F♯ B♭   F
It's all right, sleep tight

            A♭   E7   A7
Through the long night with me.   With

Bridge 2

Em B7 E7   Am7
Me. No, ___ I didn't start it.

D   B7/D♯ Em   Am7   D B7/D♯ Em
   You're broken hearted from a long, ___ long time ___ ago.

B7 E7   Am7
Oh, ___ the way you hold me

       F♯7   Bm   B♭+ Am7 D
Is all ___ that I need to know.

Outro

        G D/F♯ B♭ F
And it's so late but I'll wait

            A♭   E7   A7   D7
Through the long night with you.   With

Em   A7 Cm/E♭ Gsus/D G
You.

Travelin' Prayer

Words and Music by
Billy Joel

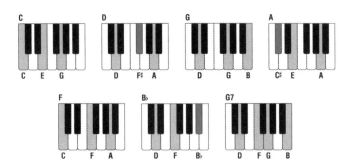

Intro   ‖: C/D | | D   N.C. | :‖ *Play 3 times*

Verse 1

          D   **G**
Hey, Lord, take a look all around tonight

                C   **D**
And find where my baby is gonna be.

                             G
Hey, Lord, would you look out for her tonight,

        C   **A**
'Cause she is far across the sea?

D   **G**   **C**
Hey, Lord, would you look out for her tonight,

        F   **B♭**
And make sure that she's gonna be all right

        A
And things are gonna be all right with

| D   G/D | D   A/D | D   G/D | D   A/D |
Me?

Verse 2

D   G
Hey, Lord, would you look out for her tonight

                                    C   D   G/D D A/D
And make sure that all __ her dreams are sweet?

D   G
Said now, would you guide her along the roads

                         C G/B   A   D/A   A
And make them soft for her ___ feet?

D   G7   C
Hey, Lord, would you look out for her tonight

                      F   Bb
And make sure that she's gonna be all right

        A
Until she's home and here with

| D   G/D | D   A/D | D   G/D | D   A/D |
Me?

Verse 3

D   G
Hey, Lord, would you look out for her tonight

                    C   D G/D   D   A/D
If she is sleepin' under the sky?

D   G
Said now, make sure the ground she's sleepin' on

C   G/B A   D/A   A
Is always warm and dry.

D   G7   C
Mm, don't you give her too much rain.

     F   Bb
Try to keep her away from pain,

       A
'Cause my baby hates to cry.

| D   G/D | D   A/D | D   G/D | D   A/D |

Verse 4

    D   G
    Hey, Lord, would you look out for her tonight,

                  C   D G/D D A/D
 'Cause it gets rough along the way?

    D
    Said now, if this song seems strange

      G   C   G/B   A D/A A
    It's just because I don't know how to pray.

    D   G   C
    Mm, won't you give her peace of mind,

              F   B♭
 And if you ever find the time,

                    A
 Won't you tell her I miss her ev'ryday?

| D | G/D | D | A/D | D | G/D | D | A/D |

Piano Solo

D		G	C	D	G/D	D	A/D
D		G	C	A	D/A	A	
D	G7	C	F	B♭	A	D	G/D
D	A/D	D	G/D	D	A/D	

Verse 5

    D   G
    Hey, Lord, take a look all around tonight

                      C   D G/D D A/D
 And find where my baby's gonna be.

    D   G
    Hey, Lord, would you look out for her tonight,

                  C   G/B   A D/A A
 'Cause she is far across ____ the sea?

    D   G7   C
    Hey, Lord, would you look out for her tonight

              F   B♭
 And make sure that she's gonna be all right

          A
 Until she's home and here with

| D | G/D | D | A/D | D | G/D | D | A/D |
 Me,   with me?

| D | G/D | D | A/D | D |

Uptown Girl

Words and Music by
Billy Joel

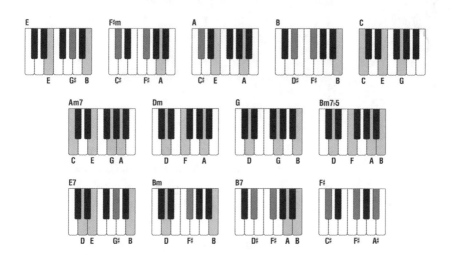

E	F#m	A	B	C
E G# B	C# F# A	C# E A	D# F# B	C E G

Am7	Dm	G	Bm7♭5
C E G A	D F A	D G B	D F A B

E7	Bm	B7	F#
D E G# B	D F# B	D# F# A B	C# F# A#

Intro | E | F#m | E/G# | A   B |
                  Oh.   Oh.

               E   F#m   E/G#
Verse 1   Uptown girl,   she's been living in her uptown world.

               A   B   E
                I bet she never had a back street guy,

               F#m   E/G#
                I bet her mama never told her why.

               A   B
                I'm gonna try for an

Verse 2

```
E        F#m                          E/G#
Uptown girl.   She's been living in her white bread world

A        B        E
  As long as anyone with hot blood can,

F#m                          E/G#
  And now she's looking for a downtown man.

A        B
  That's what I am.
```

Bridge 1

```
C            Am7          Dm          G
  And when she knows what she wants from her time,

C            Am7          Bm7b5       E7
  And when she wakes up and makes up her mind,

A            F#m
  She'll see I'm not so tough

Bm        B7
Just because I'm in love with an
```

Verse 3

```
E        F#m                          E/G#
Uptown girl.   You know I've seen her in her uptown world.

A        B        E
  She's getting tired of her high-class toys,

F#m                          E/G#
  And all the presents from her uptown boys.

A        B
  She's got a choice.
```

Interlude 1

```
|G        |A        |F#/A#    |Bm  Bm/A|
   Oh.

|G        |A        |F#/A#    |B        |
   Oh.
```

Verse 4

E   F#m   E/G#
Uptown girl.   You know I can't afford to buy her pearls,

A   B   E
But maybe someday when my ship comes in

F#m   E/G#
She'll understand what kind of guy I've been,

A   B
And then I'll win.

Bridge 2

C   Am7   Dm   G
And when she's walking, she's looking so fine.

C   Am7   Bm7♭5   E7
And when she's talking, she'll say that she's mine.

A   F#m
She'll say I'm not so tough

Bm   B7
Just because I'm in love with an

Verse 5

E   F#m   E/G#
Uptown girl.   She's been living in her white bread world

A   B   E
As long as anyone with hot blood can,

F#m   E/G#
And now she's looking for a downtown man.

A   B
That's what I am.

Interlude 2   *Repeat Interlude 1*

Outro

    E   F#m   E/G#
‖: Uptown girl,   she's my uptown girl.

A   B
You know I'm in love with an

E   F#m   E/G#
Uptown girl.   My uptown girl.

    A   B
You know I'm in love with an :‖ *Repeat and fade*
                                        (w/ Voc. ad lib.)

We Didn't Start the Fire

Words and Music by
Billy Joel

Har-ry Tru-man, Dor-is Day, Red Chi-na, John-ny Ray,

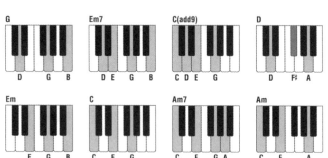

Intro

$\lVert$: G/D | | Em7 | C(add9) :$\rVert$ *Play 3 times*

| G/D | | G/B | C(add9) |

Verse 1

G   D
Harry Truman, Doris Day, Red China, Johnny Ray.

Em   C
South Pacific, Walter Winchell, Joe DiMaggio.

G   D
Joe McCarthy, Richard Nixon, Studebaker, television.

Em   C
North Korea, South Korea, Marilyn Monroe.

| G/D | | Em7 | C(add9) |

Verse 2

G   D
Rosenbergs, H-bomb, Sugar Ray, Panmunjom.

Em   C
Brando, *The King and I*, and *The Catcher in the Rye*.

G   D
Eisenhower, vaccine, England's got a new queen.

Em   C
Marciano, Liberace, Santayana goodbye.

Chorus 1

G/D
We didn't start the fire.

  Em7   C(add9)
It was always burning since the world's been turning.

G/D
We didn't start the fire.

  G/B   C(add9)
No, we didn't light it, but we tried to fight it.

Verse 3

G   D
Joseph Stalin, Malenkov, Nasser, and Prokofiev.

Em   C
Rockefeller, Campanella, Communist Block.

G   D
Roy Cohn, Juan Perón, Toscanini, Dacron.

Em   C
Dien Bien Phu falls, "Rock Around the Clock."

Verse 4

G   D
Einstein, James Dean, Brooklyn's got a winning team.

Em   C
Davy Crockett, Peter Pan, Elvis Presley, Disneyland.

G   D
Bardot, Budapest, Alabama, Khrushchev.

Em   C
Princess Grace, Peyton Place, trouble in the Suez.

Chorus 2

G/D
We didn't start the fire.

  Em7   C(add9)
It was always burning since the world's been turning.

G/D
We didn't start the fire.

  G/B   C(add9)
No, we didn't light it, but we tried to fight it.

	C Am
Bridge	Little Rock, Pasternak, Mickey Mantle, Kerouac.

Bridge

C   Am
Little Rock, Pasternak, Mickey Mantle, Kerouac.

Em   D
Sputnik, Chou En-lai, *Bridge on the River Kwai*.

C   Am
Lebanon, Charles de Gaulle, California baseball.

Em   D
Starkweather, homicide, children of thalidomide. Oh.

Verse 5

G   D
Buddy Holly, Ben Hur, space monkey, Mafia.

Em   C
Hula Hoops, Castro, Edsel is a no-go.

G   D
U2, Syngman Rhee, payola, and Kennedy.

Em   C
Chubby Checker, *Psycho*, Belgians in the Congo.

Chorus 3

Repeat Chorus 1

Verse 6

G   D
Hemingway, Eichmann, *Stranger in a Strange Land*.

Em   C
Dylan, Berlin, Bay of Pigs invasion.

G   D
Lawrence of Arabia, British Beatlemania.

Em   C
Ole Miss, John Glenn, Liston beats Patterson.

G   D
Pope Paul, Malcolm X, British polititian sex.

Em   C
J.F.K. blown away, what else do I have to say?

Chorus 4

Repeat Chorus 1

	G **D**

Verse 7

G   **D**
Birth control, Ho Chi Minh, Richard Nixon back again.

Em   **C**
Moonshot, Woodstock, Watergate, punk rock.

G   **D**
Begin, Reagan, Palestine, terror on the airline.

Em   **C**
Ayatollahs in Iran, Russians in Afghanistan.

Verse 8

G   **D**
Wheel of Fortune, Sally Ride, heavy metal, suicide.

Em   **C**
Foreign debts, homeless vets, AIDS, crack, Bernie Goetz.

G   **D**
Hypodermics on the shores, China's under martial law.

Em **N.C.**
Rock and roller cola wars, I can't take it anymore.

Chorus 5

G/D
We didn't start the fire.

       Em7   **C(add9)**
It was always burning since the world's been turning.

G/D
We didn't start the fire.

        G/B   **C(add9)**
But when we are gone, will it still burn on and on?

| **G/D** | | **Em7** | **C(add9)** |

Outro

G/D
‖: We didn't start the fire.

       Em7   **C(add9)**
It was always burning since the world's been turning.

G/D
We didn't start the fire.

       G/B   **C(add9)**
No, we didn't light it, but we tried to fight it.   :‖ *Repeat and fade*

Worse Comes to Worst

Words and Music by
Billy Joel

Melody:

To-day I'm liv - in' like a   rich man's son;

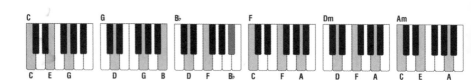

| C | G | Bb | F | Dm | Am |

C E G   D G B   D F Bb   C F A   D F A   C E A

Intro | C   G | Bb | F | C |

Verse 1

    C   G
Today I'm livin' like a rich man's son;

    Bb   F
Tomorrow mornin' I could be a bum.

    C   G
It doesn't matter which direction, though.

    Bb   F
I know a woman in New Mexico.

Chorus 1

    Dm   G
Worse comes to worst,

    Dm   G
I'll get a-long.

    Dm   G
I don't know how, but sometimes

    Dm   G
I can be strong, oh.

Verse 2

```
          C                 G
          And if I don't have a car, I'll hitch.
          Bb                      F
          I got a thumb and she's a son of a bitch.
          C                 G
          I'll do my writing on my road guitar,
          Bb                      F
          And make a living at a piano bar, oh.
```

Chorus 2

```
          Dm              G
          Worse comes to worst,
          Dm       G
          I'll get a-long.
          Dm            G
          I don't know how, but sometimes
          Dm         G       Am
          I can be strong.
```

Bridge

```
          Bb                  F
          Lightning and thunder
          C                            G
          Flashed across the roads we drove up-on.
          Bb                          F
          Oh, but it's clear skies we're un - der
          Am              G
          When I am together, when I sing my song.
```

Interlude	|C G|	B♭|	F |	C |
	| G|	B♭|	F |	|

Chorus 3   *Repeat Chorus 1*

Verse 3

    C   G
     Fun ain't easy if it ain't free.

    B♭   F
     Too many people got a hold on me,

    C   G
     But I know something that they don't know.

    B♭   F
     I know a woman in New Mexico.

Outro

    Dm   G
\|:   Worse comes to worst,

    Dm   G
     I'll get a-long.

    Dm   G
     I don't know how, but sometimes

    Dm   G
     I can be strong.   :\| *Repeat and fade*

You May Be Right

Words and Music by
Billy Joel

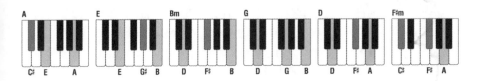

Fri - day night _ I   crashed _ your par - ty,

Intro | A | | | |
          | | | |

A

Verse 1   Friday night I crashed your party, Saturday I said I'm sorry.

                  E

Sunday came and trashed me out again.

     Bm   **G**

I was on - ly having fun, wasn't hurt - ing anyone.

       E   **A**

And we all __ enjoyed the weekend for a change.

        A

Verse 2   I was strand - ed in the combat zone, I walked through Bedford Stuy alone,

               E

Even rode my motorcycle in the rain.

      Bm   **G**

And you told ___ me not to drive, but I made __ it home alive.

       E   **A**

So you said __ that only proves that I'm in-sane.

Chorus 1

N.C.   E
You may be right,

N.C.   A
I may be cra - zy.

N.C.   E   D   F#m
Oh, but it just __ may be a lu - natic you're looking for.

A N.C.   E
   Turn out the light,

N.C.   A
Don't try to save __ me.

           D   E   A
You may be wrong, __ for all I know, __ but you may be right.

Verse 3

       A
Well, remem - ber how I found you there alone in your electric chair.

          E
I told you dirty jokes until you smiled.

     Bm   G
You were lone - ly for a man. I said, "Take __ me as I am,"

       E   A
'Cause you might __ enjoy some madness for awhile.

Verse 4

       A
Now think __ of all the years you tried to find someone to satisfy you.

       E
I might be as crazy as you say.

     Bm   G
If I'm cra - zy then it's true, that it's all __ because of you,

       E   A
And you would - n't want me any other way.

Chorus 2	N.C. **E**	

Chorus 2

N.C.   **E**
You may be right,

N.C.   **A**
I may be cra - zy.

N.C.   **E**   **D**   **F#m**
Oh, but it just __ may be a lu - natic you're looking for.

A N.C.   **E**
  It's too late to fight,

N.C.   **A**
It's too late to change __ me.

           D   **E**   **A**
You may be wrong, __ for all I know, __ but you may be right.

Piano Solo

A				
		E		
Bm		G		
E		A		

Chorus 3   *Repeat Chorus 1*

Outro   ‖:   **A** You may be wrong, but you may be right. :‖ ***Repeat and fade***

You're Only Human
(Second Wind)

Words and Music by
Billy Joel

You're hav-ing a hard time and late-ly you don't feel __ so good. __

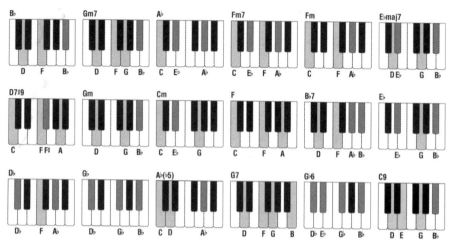

Intro ‖: B♭ Gm7 | A♭ Fm7 :‖ *Play 4 times*

Verse 1

B♭ Gm7 A♭ Fm7
You're having a hard time and lately you don't feel so good.

|B♭ Gm7 |A♭ Fm7 |

B♭ Gm7 A♭ Fm7
You're getting a bad repu-tation in your neighborhood.

|B♭ Gm7 |A♭ Fm7 |

B♭ Gm7 A♭ Fm7
It's all right, it's all right, sometimes ___ that's what it

B♭ Gm7 A♭ Fm7
Takes.

B♭ Gm7 A♭ Fm7
You're only human, you're al-lowed to make your ___ share of

B♭ Gm7 A♭
Mistakes.

```
Fm                              Ebmaj7
    You better believe there will be times in your life
            D7#9                      Gm
When you'll be feeling like a stumbling fool.
Fm                              Ebmaj7
    So take it from me, you'll learn more from your accidents
        Cm                      F
Than anything that you could ever learn at school.
```

Chorus 1

```
Bb7     Eb      Ab
Don't for-get your second wind.
|Db  Gb/Db Db|     Gb/Db Db|
Bb              Eb      Ab
Sooner or later, you'll ___ get your second wind.
|Db  Gb/Db Db|     Gb/Db Db|
```

Interlude 1

```
| Bb Gm7 |Ab  Fm7 | Bb Gm7 |Ab  Fm7 |
```

Verse 2

```
Bb              Gm7     Ab      Fm7
    It's not always easy to be living in this world of pain.
|Bb  Gm7 |Ab  Fm7 |
Bb              Gm7     Ab          Fm7
    You're gonna be crashing into stone walls a-gain and
    Bb   Gm7 Ab  Fm7
A - gain.
Bb      Gm7     Ab              Fm7
    It's all right, it's all right, though you feel your
        Bb      Gm7 Ab  Fm7
Heart ___ break.
```

B♭   **Gm7**   **A♭**   **Fm7**
  You're only human, you're gonna have to deal with

      B♭   **Gm7** **A♭**
Heart - ache.

Fm   **E♭maj7**
  Mm, just like a boxer in a title fight,

       D7♯9   **Gm**
You got to walk in that ring all a-lone.

Fm   **E♭maj7**
  You're not the only one who's made mistakes,

         Cm   **F**
But they're the only things that you can truly call your own.

Chorus 2	**B♭7** **E♭** **A♭** Don't for-get your second wind. |**D♭** **G♭/D♭** **D♭**| **G♭/D♭** **D♭**| **B♭** **E♭** **A♭** Wait in the corner un-til that breeze ____ blows in. |**D♭** **G♭/D♭** **D♭**| **G♭/D♭** **D♭**|

Bridge	**A♭(♭5)** **G7**
	  Well, you've been keeping to your-self these days
	         G♭6 **F**
	'Cause you're thinking ev'rything's gone wrong.
	E♭maj7
	  Sometimes you just want to lay down and die.
	     Gm **C9**
	That e-motion can be so strong.
	        F **N.C.**
	But hold on till that old second wind comes along.

Interlude 2	‖: **B♭** **Gm7** | **A♭** **Fm7** :‖ ***Play 4 times***

PIANO CHORD SONGBOOK

Verse 3

Bb   Gm7   Ab   Fm7
You probably don't want to hear advice from someone else.

Bb   Gm7   Ab   Fm7
   No.

Bb   Gm7   Ab   Fm7
  But I wouldn't be telling you if I hadn't been ____ there

    Bb   Gm7   Ab   Fm7
My - self.   Mm.

Bb   Gm7   Ab   Fm7
  It's all right, it's all right, sometimes that's all it

Bb   Gm7   Ab   Fm7
Takes.

Bb   Gm7   Ab   Fm7
  We're only human,   we're supposed ____ to make

Bb   Gm7   Ab
Mistakes.

Fm   Ebmaj7
  But I survived all those long, lonely days

     D7#9   Gm
When it seemed I did not have a friend.

Fm   Ebmaj7
  'Cause all I needed was a little faith

     Cm   F
So I could catch my breath and face the world again.

Chorus 3

Bb7   Eb   Ab
Don't for-get your second wind.
| Db   Gb/Db Db | Gb/Db Db |

Bb   Eb   Ab   Db
Sooner or later you'll feel that mo-mentum kick in.
| Gb/Db Db | Gb/Db Db |

Bb7   Eb   Ab
Don't for-get your second wind.
| Db   Gb/Db Db | Gb/Db Db |

Bb   Eb   Ab   Db
Sooner or later you'll feel that mo-mentum kick in.
| Gb/Db Db | Gb/Db Db |

Outro ||: Bb | Gm7 | Ab | Fm7 :|| *Repeat and fade (w/ Voc. ad lib.)*

HAL LEONARD PROUDLY PRESENTS THE

Piano Chord Songbook Series

Play and sing your favorite songs with the Piano Chord Songbook series! These collections include lyrics and piano chord diagrams for dozens of popular hit songs. At 6" x 9", these portable songbooks will come in handy just about anywhere you want to play!

Acoustic Rock
62 hits, including: Across the Universe • Catch the Wind • Me and Julio Down by the Schoolyard • Night Moves • Seven Bridges Road • Time in a Bottle • and many more.
00311813..............................$12.99

The Beatles A-I
100 of their hits starting with A-I, including: Across the Universe • All My Loving • Back in the U.S.S.R. • Dear Prudence • Good Day Sunshine • A Hard Day's Night • Here Comes the Sun • and more.
00312017 ....$16.99

The Beatles J-Y
This second volume includes 100 more songs starting with the letters J-Y: Lady Madonna • Ob-La-Di, Ob-La-Da • Paperback Writer • Revolution • Ticket to Ride • Yellow Submarine • and more.
00312018 ....$16.99

Children's Songs
80 songs kids love, including: Do-Re-Mi • The Farmer in the Dell • John Jacob Jingleheimer Schmidt • The Muffin Man • Puff the Magic Dragon • and many more.
00311961..............................$12.99

Country Standards
60 country hits, including: Always on My Mind • Crazy • Deep in the Heart of Texas • El Paso • I Walk the Line • King of the Road • Okie from Muskogee • and more.
00311812..............................$12.99

Disney
Be Our Guest • Circle of Life • Hakuna Matata • It's a Small World • Mickey Mouse March • Under the Sea • A Whole New World • Zip-A-Dee-Doo-Dah • and dozens more.
00312096..............................$14.99

Folksongs
80 folk favorites, including: Aura Lee • Camptown Races • Down by the Riverside • Good Night Ladies • Man of Constant Sorrow • Tom Dooley • Water Is Wide • and more.
00311962..............................$12.99

Glee
Bad Romance • Dancing with Myself • Don't Stop Believin' • Empire State of Mind • Firework • Proud Mary • Rolling in the Deep • Somebody to Love • True Colors • Valerie • and many more.
00312270..............................$12.99

Jazz Standards
50 songs, including: But Beautiful • Come Rain or Come Shine • Honeysuckle Rose • Misty • The Nearness of You • Stardust • What'll I Do? • and more.
00311963 ....$12.99

Elton John
60 hits from this piano icon, including: Bennie and the Jets • Goodbye Yellow Brick Road • Mona Lisas and Mad Hatters • Tiny Dancer • Your Song • and more.
00311960 ....$12.99

Pop Hits
60 songs, including: All Out of Love • Don't Know Why • Every Breath You Take • More than Words • She's Always a Woman • Time After Time • and more.
00311810..............................$12.99

Praise & Worship
80 songs, including: Above All • As the Deer • Days of Elijah • Here I Am to Worship • In Christ Alone • Mighty to Save • Revelation Song • Shout to the Lord • We Fall Down • and more.
00311976..............................$12.99

Taylor Swift
40 tunes from this talented songwriter, including: Back to December • Dear John • Fearless • Fifteen • Hey Stephen • Love Story • Mean • Our Song • Speak Now • White Horse • You Belong with Me • and more.
00312094..............................$14.99

Three Chord Songs
58 three-chord classic hits, including: Authority Song • Bad Case of Loving You • Bye Bye Love • Kansas City • La Bamba • Twist and Shout • and more.
00311814..............................$12.99

121